HE RETURNED HER GENTLE KISS

From down deep inside her there arose such a longing that Rachel cried out. She wanted to flee somewhere with this man, take him to a peaceful place where the spirits could heal his wounds, make him whole once again.

She stroked Daniel's hair and held him close.

He moved, turned his head, and spoke her name, voice blurry and soft, as if he still dwelled with his dreams and visions. "Rachel? My God, is that you? My sweet beautiful love. I dreamed you were dead."

She ran her hands over his back, let him pull her closer until she felt the urgency of his desire.

That strong passion frightened her, for she saw that what had begun as comfort had turned into something else entirely. And she pushed away, cupped his face, and whispered softly, "You must sleep now, my love."

The words were out, amazing her in their simple truth. This could never be. Never.

Trail to Forever

Elizabeth Gregg

A TOPAZ BOOK

TOPAZ
Published by the Penguin Group
Penguin Books USA Inc., 375 Hudson Street,
New York, New York 10014, U.S.A.
Penguin Books Ltd, 27 Wrights Lane,
London W8 5TZ, England
Penguin Books Australia Ltd, Ringwood,
Victoria, Australia
Penguin Books Canada Ltd, 10 Alcorn Avenue,
Toronto, Ontario, Canada M4V 3B2
Penguin Books (N.Z.) Ltd, 182–190 Wairau Road,
Auckland 10, New Zealand

Penguin Books Ltd, Registered Offices:
Harmondsworth, Middlesex, England

First published by Topaz, an imprint of Dutton Signet,
a division of Penguin Books USA Inc.

First Printing, March, 1997
10 9 8 7 6 5 4 3 2 1

Printed in the United States of America

This book is dedicated to cowboy artist and writer Ivan Denton, who, at the age of sixty-one, rode horseback the entire length of the Cherokee Trail, and wrote a book about his ride and other little known wonders of the West called *Old Brands and Lost Trails.* I will be forever grateful for his insight.

Chapter One

Early-evening shadows sent long, dark fingers across the alley at the back of Stirman's Mercantile. Rachel crouched behind a stack of wooden crates, breath catching in her throat.

If Doaks found her he would drag her back to that filthy shack to cook and clean and God knows what else. She covered her mouth, held her breath against a threatened cry. Hot tears flowed, tears of anger, sorrow, and raw fear.

He was coming, him and those drunken friends, making no effort to silence their approach.

"Come out of there, ye dirty heathen savage. Come out and maybe I'll not beat ye half to death."

The worst he'd ever done to her was fling her across the shack when she displeased him, but that whip he carried coiled at his hip frightened her into thinking he might do worse. She cringed and tried to make herself smaller.

Doaks kicked aside the crates, crashed through them with a splintering of wood, and grabbed her up by the back of her shirt like a kitten. She kicked and clawed, but he only laughed and held her out of harm's way.

"Mangy little wildcat. Spit and claw all ye want. And then settle yourself down. Paid good money for you, ain't letting you loose, so you might as well stop fighting me."

The hot stench of his sour whiskey breath washed over her and she gagged and went limp. He was a huge man and could do a lot more to her if he took a notion. There'd be other chances to get away.

She let him drag her from the alley like a gunny sack filled with feed. Even though she had quietened, he kept her at arm's length and stayed out of her reach. Recollecting her earlier escape probably made him more wary, for he carried the bloody marks of her nails along one cheek.

From out on the street, someone hollered, "Sic her, you old drunk." Another voice answered, "Ain't gonna let that skinny Injun get away, are ye?"

The crack of a distant shot cut through the crisp spring evening.

Roaring in victory, Doaks hauled his prize into the street, bellowing curses.

Grim and silent she hunkered there on hands and knees and glared at him. The men who had gathered to watch only laughed and continued their sport, stomping the packed earth and egging on the trapper in his game.

If he came too close she'd bite his dirty ear off. The chance didn't come, for he was too quick and kept her out of reach of his vital parts. And so she waited, bided her time, and glanced up and down the street drenched in early twilight.

Surrounded by the rowdy men, Rachel and her captor squared off, he almost too drunk to stand upright, but still much the stronger. He laid a hand on the whip, flicked the long leather tail out across the hard packed earth of the street. His bleary eyes gleamed. She hunched her shoulders, covered her head with both arms, and waited for the first sizzling lash of the burning whip. She would grab it and choke him to death.

"Don't you kill her now, you old fool," someone

shouted with glee. "Even red Injuns is good for something, 'specially female 'uns."

"Hear that, Injun," Doaks snarled. "They don't want me to kill ye. What do you think?"

She wanted to cry out that she was as white as she was red. White like her father. It would mean nothing to these men. To them it only took a drop of her mother's blood to make her a filthy Injun. Instead she steeled herself to take her punishment from Doaks. This time she had gone too far and he would probably beat her. But not much, she knew, because he enjoyed her waiting on him hand and foot. She would get back at him sooner or later. The chance would come, he would have to sleep. When he did she would cut off his privates and feed them to him for breakfast. Fried.

Doaks grumbled and flicked the whip so that the end popped above her. "That brother of yours is counting his money, I would 'spect, while I'm dealing with a crazy savage. Ought to have knowed myself better than to dicker with 'em. Red bastard sold me a lazy, good for nothin' runaway. Ain't even purty." He leaned down, jerked up her chin.

Choked by the sour whiskey on his breath, she gulped down bile and kept her eyes closed tightly. She loved her brother with all her heart. He had kept her alive, carried her at times till his feet were bloody during the removal. What had happened to him brought her great sorrow. One day perhaps she would understand why he had sold her to this terrible man. But she knew for sure, Eagle must have had no choice.

Doaks squeezed at her jaw until her ears rang. "You know that, gal? You ain't even purty. And what do I have to show for my trouble? Paid good honest money and what do I have? Nothin' but trouble, that's what. I git through with you, you'll damn well know how to pleasure a man."

He staggered backward on the slope of the street, feet tangling. His grip loosened. She doubled both knees into her chest, kicked out, and caught him hard in the stomach.

He let out a tremendous *whoosh* and doubled over.

She bounded away, drinking in fresh air.

She was free.

Behind her he retched, the others whooped and hollered. She chose a route that would take her up the hill onto the square and raced through the dusky dark. Rounding a sharp curve in the road, she caught a second wind and took off, only to slam broadside into the haunches of a plodding horse. With a gasp she bounced off and landed flat on her backside. Momentarily breathless, she managed to roll over and scramble to her hands and knees. In another instant she had vaulted once more to her feet.

The rider, a big man dressed in buckskins, dismounted agilely and headed for her. "Here now, what's your hurry?"

A quick glance over her shoulder told her that the drunken crowd was fast approaching.

The man's silver eyes glittered, he breathed the stench of whiskey over her. Was there nowhere to go, no escape from such men?

He had a hold on her and she jerked to get away. "Let me go, you pale-eyed snake." Switching to Cherokee she spat quick, insulting words at him, but he wouldn't turn loose.

Daniel held onto the ragged Indian girl while he eyed the passel of men charging up the hill. Didn't seem like too fair a fight, all those men against one scrawny girl, even if she did act wild as some cornered mountain cat.

The worst of the lot shouted, "She belongs to me,

mister. Grab her 'fore she run off." Wrapped in a badly cured fur skin and stinking like a skunk, the man lurched forward, knocked Daniel aside, and grabbed the girl.

Dispirited by the entire episode and not too steady on his own feet, Daniel raked his glance down past her flashing eyes to her unsightly garb, men's pants hitched up with a piece of rope and a ragged linsey shirt. He let her go, turned his back on the foray, and walked off. This sort of nonsense was exactly why he stayed away from towns, from gatherings of humans. None of his damned business what happened.

He'd drunk too much, should have stayed in the wagon, gone to sleep. Let this go on without him seeing it. Wouldn't know the difference then. He ground his teeth, shut his eyes. Girls died. Innocents died every damned day, and he couldn't do a thing about it.

The whip cracked behind him, the girl screamed, and he hunched his shoulders against the vivid images that washed over him. A dead girl's head lolling over his arm, her long black hair matted in blood hanging down into the mud. The stench of gunpowder and fear, and screams, dear God, the screams. Tearing at his gut, rendering him nearly helpless. The burning Mexican village, children running and crying, soldiers scooping up the women and riding off with them. Screaming, screaming, killing, killing.

With a roar he suppressed the memories and swung around. He yanked a long-bladed bowie from his belt and leaped on the fur-clad man before he could swing the whip again. He sank the weapon deep into the enormous dirty thigh.

The man bellowed like a raging bull, but the knife buried to the hilt in his flesh didn't slow him down much, it just turned his attention toward Daniel.

Smelling blood, the other men closed ranks. Daniel sent a quick glance toward the girl, who knelt in the dirt, a bloody slit across the back of her shirt. He damn well ought to have stayed out of this, but with the trapper lunging at him, it was way too late.

"Run, Injun, run," Daniel shouted, and took the brunt of the man's attack. The two of them went down in the dirt, the trapper's thumbs locked into Daniel's throat, his bulky, stinking weight smothering him.

Daniel gasped, grunted, freed his hands, and popped the man smartly on the ears with the heels of both palms. The thumbs buried in his gullet loosened momentarily, and Daniel grappled for the handle of the knife sticking out of the man's leg just below his hip.

Darkness closed in as he ran out of air to breathe past the choking fingers. He grabbed the bowie and yanked with all his might, twisting the blade as he did so. It was too much for the wounded trapper. He turned loose of Daniel's throat to paw at the leg and shriek.

With a final jerk Daniel freed the knife. Blood spurted from the wound, the man rolled away, eyes glazed. Daniel came to his feet, gesturing with the bloody blade.

The deadly calm of his voice caught the bleeding man's attention. "Leave her be, sir. Leave her be."

Daniel shot another quick look over his shoulder, hoping to see the Indian girl gone. She remained there in the street, both hands over her mouth, shoulders heaving.

He waved an arm at her. "Git to hell and gone, I said." But she didn't move, just blinked and stared.

One of the men in the crowd spoke up. "He ain't gonna do no more harm, mister. Not tonight, he's done for fer the time being. But was I you, I'd look to my back when he heals. Ain't no one wants to make an enemy out of Jasper Doaks, not unless he's looking to meet his maker."

"I'll keep that in mind," Daniel said, and bending over, wiped the gory knife blade on Doaks's disgusting fur wrap, reversed it, and cleaned the other side.

Doaks muttered "Bastid," and spit, but that took the remainder of his energy and his eyes rolled up in his head as he sprawled backward.

The girl remained in one spot, entranced. She had the eyes of a frightened doe who knows it should bolt but can't move.

Daniel gestured at her. "Git. Git on out. He won't come after you now. Go on, git home." He started toward his piebald mare. Up the street a ways the animal waited patiently, reins twined on the ground.

Full darkness crept lazily along the winding byways of the mountain town. Broad bands of light from the saloon pooled on the dirt street. Rachel dragged in a deep breath, studied the beaten trapper for a moment, then turned to follow after the man on the horse. She had no place to go, no bed or board. Maybe she wasn't any better off now that she was free of Doaks. At least with him she'd had a roof of sorts over her head, and game he killed and partially cooked over an open fire. What would she do now?

The man she trailed after looked like a trapper or hunter, dressed in buckskins, moccasins, and a wide-brimmed felt hat that he had resettled firmly on his shoulder-length sandy hair after the battle. But he didn't talk like a man used to living alone in the mountains. It wasn't the words so much as the way he spoke, like her friend Alice Sturdivant who attended Miss Sawyer's Seminary right here in Fayetteville. They used entire words, not just bits and pieces like most of the natives.

Up ahead the mare broke into a canter and Rachel picked up her own pace. She'd always been a good runner, and she wasn't hurt badly. The wound across her back stung like fire, but it wasn't deep and she could manage it. While living in the Nation, running had been a way to free herself of the sorry circumstances of her life. Sometimes she thought she could run all day and into the night without ever stopping. But no matter if she did, she still couldn't escape the existence forced on her people by the greed of the white man.

Darkness lay heavy as wool over the wagon yard, but she had no trouble keeping up with the man as he rode to one of the covered wagons and slid down off his horse. When he did so, he kept right on going down on his butt. He was full of whiskey, just like Doaks had been. She waited awhile to see if he stirred, but he lay where he had fallen and pulled his knees up to his chin.

The mare nosed around at him awhile, then shifted a hind leg and relaxed. The poor animal must be used to his kind of treatment, but Rachel didn't like the idea that it would have to stand there all night tightly cinched by the saddle, the bit clamping her teeth. Once she was sure the man was truly out, she crept to the horse, making soft soothing noises so as not to startle her. She loosened the cinch, slipped the saddle and blanket off and dropped them to the ground. A rope hung on the wagon, and she eased the bit from the mare's mouth, looped the rope into a loose halter, and led the animal to a corral where other horses drowsed.

After she had taken care of the man's mount, Rachel drank long and deeply from his canteen and climbed into the back of his wagon to bed down. The single slash across her back stung, but it could have been worse. The drunken fool had barely grazed her. She was grateful for the white man's interference, but had no desire to take up with yet another white man. She would just sleep there the night and steal away.

Gingerly she pulled the shirt away from the wound. Bright shards of light spiraled through her vision and off into the darkness. She sucked in air through gritted teeth and waited for the pain to ease.

Instead of falling asleep she got to thinking about going to California. From the trappers who ran with Doaks she'd heard about the Fayetteville Gold Mining Company and the new trail they planned to cut. A group of Cherokee businessmen had actually organized the trip, many of them would be going along.

That's what all these wagons were camped here for. People were gathering to join the wagon train going to California to strike gold. Was this man one of them? He had saved her from Doaks's viciousness, maybe he would take her along. She could work for him, cook, carry wood, wash and mend his clothes. It would be no better or worse than being with Doaks and she could get away from the poverty of the Indian Nation once and for all.

The western Cherokee had lived in Arkansas before the removal, and liked it here still, even though their land had been stolen by the white man just as it had been in the Great Smokies.

Imagine riding all the way to California in one of these wagons. What sights they would see. She remembered hearing the name of the man who had been chosen to head up the train. Captain Lewis Evans. The notion of gaining passage herself sent quivers of excitement through her. Maybe in California nobody would care that she was part Cherokee and part white. Her hair wasn't the raven black of the Cherokee, but rather sheened with the red of fire.

She looked out at the world through brittle blue eyes just like her father's, but her skin was too bronzed to ever be mistaken for white. She had the broad forehead and high cheekbones of generations of proud Cherokee women, but her mouth and nose were finely chiseled like the Irish ancestors of her father. What she looked like probably didn't matter. She had a hunch even money wouldn't secure her a place on the train.

Maybe the man wouldn't notice her here in the back of his wagon all burrowed down under a pile of buffalo skins, and she could just stay there until they were too far away from Fayetteville for him to throw her out. She finally fell asleep dreaming of all the wonderful possibilities of traveling west to California, even if she did have to go with a white man.

Something crawled up over Daniel's nose, rousing him from his whiskey slumber. He brushed at the intruder, snorted, and shifted on the hard ground. One eye sneaked open and stared at a chunk of sandstone. A rock poked into his butt, leaving a sore spot.

Where in the hell was he? He shivered and wrapped both arms around himself. Damnation, it was cold. Frost had formed in his hair and along the curve of his buckskins. He snorted again and got up, setting off a volley of gunfire in his skull.

With a dry-throated moan he staggered along the side of the wagon, hanging on to keep from pitching onto his face. He struggled and grunted and finally climbed over the rear tailgate and dropped inside. Iron gray light touched the sky to the east, horses snuffled, a rooster crowed. He'd slept on the damned bare ground all night. That was enough to make a man stiff for a month.

He tried to remember the previous evening, but

drew a blank. The mare Rhymer stood in the corral, hipshot and obviously sleeping. At least he'd put the poor old horse up before passing out. With an enormous effort he dragged himself into the nest of robes inside the wagon and pawed around for cover. His hand landed on a warm, soft body, and when it did, a banshee came up clawing and screaming, batting at him, kicking, scrabbling, making the most godawful noise he'd ever heard.

"Holy Hannah," he shouted and protected his head and ears with both arms. The blows continued, thunder pounding in his brain. He saw stars and his stomach lurched. Summoning the very last of his strength, he caught hold of the flailing limbs, wrapped both legs around the creature, and wrestled it into submission. Somebody had turned loose a blamed wildcat in his bed. Who would think that funny?

The animal spat and yelled at him and tried to get loose, but he had it, every inch of it, wrapped up tight. One hand clutched a firm, naked breast. Good God almighty, it was a female. But who, and what was she doing in his bed? Surely he hadn't . . . no, he wouldn't.

After he caught his breath and swallowed his indignation, he spoke. "Who in thunderation are you, and what are you doing in my wagon?" The effort drove daggers through his skull.

Immediately the wild woman he had trapped went totally limp. Well, she couldn't fool him, he wasn't about to turn her loose and let her have at him again.

"I will leave if you let me go," she said into his ear. "I am sorry, it was cold and I have no place else to go."

He tried to concentrate on the meaning of the words. The last of his whiskey thoughts boiled around in his head, then cleared, and he remembered the slight Indian girl he had rescued the night before. But what he couldn't remember was bringing her home with him.

In the time it took him to consider all the possibilities, he kept his hold tight. If this wildcat got loose she'd make mincemeat out of him.

Evidently reconsidering her earlier offer to slink away, she hissed, "Let me go or I will make a woman out of you." That sweet little voice had gone as hard-edged as the steel in his bowie.

He laughed. He couldn't help it. "You mean, after I let you go."

She thought about that awhile. "Maybe a long time after you let me go, but I will."

"Then why should I let you go?" The skin of her cheek was silky soft against the stubble of his face.

Another long silence before she replied. "Because it would not be wise for both of us to lie here like this until one or the other died of starvation."

Daniel chuckled and unlocked his legs. Just in case, he kept one arm wrapped around her torso until he knew he could get the hell away if she exploded again. This one certainly didn't talk like the ragged Indian girl he remembered from last night, but she blamed well acted like her. Perhaps this was someone else, which would indicate he'd been very busy in his nightly prowling.

"Who are you?" He released her with a great deal of care, shoving her up against the side of the wagon and scooting out of reach.

She grimaced, and edged away from the sideboards. "I am Rachel Keye. You saved me from a whipping last night, do you remember?"

He nodded, dumbstruck. "I thought you were an Injun."

"I am half Cherokee, half white. My father was a

trapper, his name was Josiah Keye." She glared at him, hunkered like a cat about to pounce.

He held up a hand. "That doesn't explain what the hell you're doing in my bed."

"Sleeping." She clammed up after the sullen reply.

"Look, if you want to stay here, do. But leave me alone. I've got to get some sleep."

"I'm not sleeping with you. I don't even know your name."

"Hell, if that's all it takes, I'm Daniel Wolfe. You're Rachel? Hello, Rachel. Now shut up and let me get some sleep."

He burrowed into the furs and let out a long sigh.

She remained on her knees, watching him while dawn sent slivers of pale gray into the darkness around them. He was not much, this rescuer. But he had a wagon and he was going to California to hunt for gold. It was decided. She would go with him, one way or another.

Lying in a tight little ball as far away from his still form as possible, she dozed off once again.

Daniel shouted himself up out of a hideous dream splashed with the gore and blood of war. Breathless he threw off the buffalo robes and scrambled outside into another day. The night terrors bled away, and he settled some, rubbed his eyes with stiff fingers, brushed back his hair, and shook himself like a great bear.

Last night's whiskey coated his tongue with a disgusting fur. He found his canteen and drank the last of the water. The barrel on the side of the wagon needed filling as well.

If he didn't get himself in hand he wouldn't make it into the Indian Nation, let alone all the way to Oregon. Damn the whiskey . . . damn the memories.

A more recent one pricked at him. The girl in his

wagon. He stood on the frame and peered in cautiously. He hadn't forgotten her temper and didn't want to get hit with a keg of crackers.

She lay on her stomach, tangled hair spread around her head, a streak of dried blood across the back of her torn shirt.

"That son of a bitch," he muttered, then went to fetch some water. When he returned she was awake.

"Brought you some water and a rag. Thought we could clean that up." He gestured toward her back.

"I am all right. Go away."

"Can't."

She shot him a dark look.

He shrugged. "My place. The way it works is, I stay here, you go."

"Inadu," she spat out.

He knelt there looking at her, silver eyes almost opaque. She thought she saw something sorrowful deep in there, but he quickly disguised it with anger.

"If that means son of a bitch, you're quite correct." He slammed the pan of water down and started to back away.

"I can't reach it," she said in a voice softer than she had used to him so far. "Snake. It means snake."

"Yea, well that too. You want me to wash . . . ?"

"Never mind, I will just leave. It will be all right, I am sure."

"Oh, hell." He moved toward her. "Turn around, take off the shirt."

Silently, slowly, she fumbled open the buttons and bared her back.

He gasped at the slash across the smooth, golden flesh. Damn that bastard to hell and back.

Pieces of shirt clung to clots of dried blood and he soaked the material with cold water. She dragged in a harsh breath but didn't say anything. Under his callused fingers her skin felt soft and downy. He pushed tangles of dirty hair out of the way. Lips pinched, he cleaned the long wound that ran from her right shoulder blade diagonally across her spine to the curve of her left hip.

It wasn't a deep cut, but it must have hurt like hell. She uttered no sound, just remained on her knees, head and shoulders drawn down.

Deep inside, the muscles of Rachel's stomach quivered with each touch of the cold, wet rag. How gentle he was for such a man, yet the fierce pain was like a flame licking at her skin.

"I have salve," he said finally, "but I'll have to find it in the grub box."

She nodded and waited, arms hugging herself to stop the shuddering.

When he turned from the wooden box in which he'd stored all the necessities of daily life on a wagon trip, he caught a glimpse of the sensual curve of her breast and halted. He'd thought he had himself a child here, for she appeared small in the ragged, loose clothing, but this was a full-grown woman. Those curves were what he had felt earlier when, half drunk, he'd wrestled her down. He had thought himself dreaming that part, for the desire to have a woman in his bed always died a quick death. He imagined the reaction when he awoke screaming and battling the demons that haunted his nightmares. Any woman would be off and running if she didn't shoot him dead first.

Closing off his yearnings, he lathered the salve over her bowed back, gave her one of his shirts to put on, and sent her on her way because he could do nothing else.

She paused at the tailgate, outlined in bright sunlight. "I do not suppose you would take me to California, would you?" The request came in a small voice.

"Wouldn't if I were going there. I'm going to Oregon."

She lifted her other leg over the gate and slid down out of sight. "Well, then. Good-bye, Daniel Wolfe."

A pang of regret hit him and he crept to the opening to watch her small figure dart away among the gathered wagons. He almost called her back, but what would he do with a scrawny Injun woman anyway? Even if she did have a set of exquisite breasts and a curvy body.

As morning broke and the camp came to life, Rachel moved stealthily from one wagon to another. Three Cherokee men, one just entering manhood and much younger than her eighteen summers, readied a large, well-equipped covered wagon for the trip. She glanced quickly into the back. Supplies nearly filled every available space. Barrels and bags, crates and crocks lined both sides and were piled four and five deep up front. Surely there was a nook or cranny in which she could hide out before the train got underway. She marked the position of the large wagon in relation to the others, then drifted away from the yard.

In town she managed to salvage some food from the back of the hotel where the café workers threw out their leftovers for the dogs. The April morning had dawned brisk, but as the day wore on the temperature warmed. By early afternoon, she picked her way down to the branch that ran off the rim of the hill to the north of town. Stripping, she sat in the cold water and washed as best she could, keeping the wound dry. After a while her flesh grew chilled and she crawled out to lie naked in the sun, soaking in the pleasant golden warmth. The filthy pants she had rinsed and spread out to dry beside her. They were still damp when she slipped into them. The man's shirt smelled like Daniel Wolfe. How odd that he would have the name of the clan of her brother and other father's people. Perhaps there was some hidden meaning there. She threw away the possibility, for she no longer believed in such nonsense. It was simply stupid Cherokee superstition.

She had no idea how long she must wait before the train pulled out. It would be best to remain close by and await an opportunity to hide away. Most of all, she had to be very careful that someone didn't spot her and tell Doaks. He did, after all, still own her, if he could catch her and keep her. With luck he would be laid up with the knife wound until the wagons pulled out.

Daniel brooded about the girl Rachel. Looking into her face brought to mind crisp mornings and winter-shorn hills. Her eyes were the color of bright, dazzling blue chicory flowers, and they were made even brighter by the bronze shade of her lovely skin. Her hair reminded him of the copper leaves of the oak just before winter struck, leaves that always managed to cling stubbornly to their branches despite the wildest north winds. She had that kind of tenacity, both fragile and durable at the same time.

He tried to forget the warmth and softness of her lush breasts, the smell of her skin, her breath mingling with his in the heat of their struggle in his bed. She would get to California without any help from him. Damn! He had to stop thinking about her. Life had been very lonely since he'd come home from the war in Mexico the previous year, but that was the way he wanted it.

That night as he lay in his own cozy bed, he found himself wondering where the girl was sleeping, what she had eaten. Aloud, he cursed himself for being foolish.

And he dreamed again of the child he couldn't save. She and her kind had been the enemy, trampled under the booted feet of the marching armies. He may not have killed her, but he felt as though he had had some part in it.

Odd how growing up he'd always admired the warrior, the mighty and the strong, and had wondered what it felt like to stand for a cause, be brave. Man was meant to do battle. But not with women and children. They should be spared, kept somewhere safe, away from the ravages of man's fierce folly.

As always the girl lay across his arms, head hanging so that her ebony hair spread in the bloody mud where he knelt. Through tear-drenched eyes he gazed into her face, clutched her to his chest and rocked. A soldier's weapon had found its mark, had killed this innocent one, and he could scarcely bear it. Abruptly her features shifted, changed into those of the Indian girl. Eyes opening to accuse him in their crystal sharpness.

And then the child's hand flashed upward, fading light caught at the steel of a blade and she plunged it into his throat.

He awoke choking, gagging, his eyes watering. Sweat poured down his body. He loosened the shirt, skinned out of it, and sat there a moment, chest heaving. Cool night air dried the sweat, chilling him. Moonlight splashed through gaps in the wagon tarp. He traced a trembling finger through a golden puddle.

Daniel had killed bear, buffalo, and on one occasion a mountain lion with his bare hands, but he had never been as frightened as he was of the memories that came to him at night. And he was ashamed because that fear made him feel less of a man. He wanted no one to ever witness that weakness, most especially a beautiful Indian girl who had enough spunk to stand up to a man with a whip.

Unable to sleep, Rachel trailed listlessly among the silent wagons, her way lit by moonlight. A terrible guttural noise caught at her senses. An animal of some sort? Or someone in pain? She stopped to listen, then moved toward the low keening sound until she found herself outside Daniel's wagon. It shook and creaked.

With an eye to a gap between the tarp and the high sideboards she peered into the darkness. Inside the tossing form wrapped in buffalo robes sat bolt upright, cried out. She jammed a fist in her mouth to keep from responding in kind.

He yanked the buckskin shirt off over his head, tousling his long hair. It tumbled like a curtain over his face and around his naked shoulders. Fingers of moonlight caressed the bare skin. Darkness cloaked his features, his breath rasped harshly.

She wanted to run, but remained frozen as he scampered like a panicked animal up and out of the wagon, springing over the tailgate and landing so that he couldn't help but see her.

Like a flash his hand clamped her arm, swung her around with a strength she couldn't overpower. Fright dried her throat and left her speechless.

"What in damnation are you doing, girl?"

He held both her wrists and pulled her in close. The smell of whiskey poured over her. She shook her head and tried to break free, a weak cry escaping her mouth. As he shifted, moonlight gleamed in tear-washed eyes. How could that be? He was a big man, a strong hunter, why would he be crying?

Would he kill her now? Or would he take her into his wagon first? She hardly knew which she feared the most. Abruptly he let her go, rubbed the back of one hand along her tingling flesh where he'd gripped her so tightly, and gazed down into her eyes as sadly as one who has lost all he holds dear.

"Get on out of here, now," he said. His voice rasped hoarsely. "And don't come hanging around me anymore. Girl, girl, what's wrong with you?"

She wondered the same thing. There was no reason for her to be here. This man was dangerous and didn't want her around. Why did she keep coming back?

Still, despite his outburst they remained facing one another. The broad muscles across his chest and shoulders rippled as he once again raised his hand toward her. She didn't flinch, but waited, holding his gaze with her own.

He cupped the side of her face tenderly, slipped his hand slowly down the length of her loose hair, and took a strand in his fingertips. His tongue ran over his lips, and unconsciously she licked her own.

Then he pulled away and turned from her. But this time when he spoke, it was with gentleness. "I'm sorry I can't help you. Go back to your people where you'll be safe. Go on now."

A smoldering coal deep in the pit of her stomach came alive and licked upward. Its fiery trail hardened her nipples until she wanted to cup them in her hands to ease their need to be touched.

"Good-bye, Daniel Wolfe," she whispered and stepped from the embrace of his terrifying, spiritual fire, then turned and ran.

Chapter Two

In the silvery hours of false dawn Rachel jerked awake. For a moment she imagined she was asleep on a pallet in the corner of Doaks's filthy shack in the woods. The comfort, the clean smell of the quilts in which she lay, allayed those fears. But where was she? Not at home, surely, with Bone Woman snoring softly nearby. When her mother died she had gone to live with her grandmother. Bone Woman was a finder of the dead who sings over the bones. She was also a witch held in great regard by the Tsalagi.

That old life had been destroyed by the misplaced intentions of Rachel's half brother. Eagle was just like his father Standing Bear, bent on destruction because he could not see that the future of the Cherokee had been written by the whites. The harder The People struggled, the more tragedy would befall them. The wise ones had become civilized many years ago.

Rachel could not go back home because there was nothing to go back to but sadness and poverty. The proud Tsalagi were no more. Eagle's father Standing Bear was long dead, killed by marshals when he refused to accompany them to stand trial for killing three cavalry officers. Her father had gone away. And none of the young men of the tribe suited her. They were either vicious or cowardly, ashamed of the fate that had fallen upon their people, who lived in despair.

With a start she sat up, clutching the quilt across her bare breasts. Was someone coming? Was that what had awakened her?

Maybe the man and woman who owned this wagon but chose to sleep at the hotel until departure time were returning early. They were Etta and James Aaron Claridge, the only husband and wife making the trip. She had slept here for three nights running, biding her time until the train would leave.

Someone said that would be another four days, and so she was prepared to exist in one way or another until that wondrous morning when they would be off to California. What a glorious day it would be too. Excitement grew within her, smothering even the pangs of hunger. Dogs had beaten her to the leftovers tossed out behind the hotel restaurant the evening before.

Always she thought of California, of leaving this place forever, forgetting the shame of her people. The blood of her white father ran in her veins. She would become one of his people and wear long sweeping skirts with threads of blue and gold, and hats with magnificent feathers. And she would stride along the streets among the laughing, beautiful women whose men dug precious metals from the ground to adorn their throats and fingers. Never again would she be Winter Dawn of the Tsalagi.

And she tried not to think of the white man Daniel Wolfe who had awakened a passion with his touch. Cherokee girls spoke of going into the bushes to be set aflame by one of the young men of the tribe, but she had only dreamed of it. None of the young men of the tribe chose her because she made it clear that she wished to live in the white world, not in some filthy hut on the barren land of Indian Territory. And she would not lie with a man she did not wish to marry. This desire for Daniel Wolfe was completely unwelcome, unexpected. He might as well be an Indian because of the life he wanted to lead on some homestead in the wilderness. Besides he had no need for her. Yet, no matter how hard she tried, she couldn't forget the image of him standing bared to the waist, sunburnt skin dappled with moonlight, silver eyes glowing with sadness, big hand gently caressing her hair.

He carried within his soul a terrible despair, an incompleteness that she understood even without knowing the cause. He wanted no man or woman to ever be close to him, and she grieved for him. Life was not meant to be a lonely journey.

She sighed and rose. Dawn lightened the sky and she had no time to waste. She could not risk getting caught here by the Claridges. They would send her back to Jasper Doaks, for to escape from slavery was a terrible sin in this world. She shrugged quickly into her clothes and crawled from the wagon, being careful that no one was around to spot her.

She was afraid to go anywhere openly in the streets of town, for fear Doaks had recovered from his wound and was searching for her. Lurking in alleyways all day became tiring, so once she had found enough scraps to still her morning hunger, she left town and sought solace in the surrounding forests. That day she chose a path that wound down off the hill west of the town square. Along its border early wildflowers unfurled petals tentatively into the spring air that smelled of sweet, moist earth. Tufts of green grass, the uncurling stems of mayapple, pale coiled fronds of fiddlehead fern carpeted the forest floor. Rachel grew careless enjoying the beauty around her and failed to hear the thud of approaching hooves until it was too late to hide. Few riders chose the forest paths but rather preferred the wider roads, and she was surprised to see this one.

Her first thought was Doaks. He had found her and she wouldn't get to go to California.

To her amazement, the approaching rider turned out to be a tall, thin white woman. She rode side-saddle on a long-legged red mare that pranced delicately.

Rachel stepped backward off the path and crouched behind a tree, even though the rider obviously had already seen her.

With a sneer of disgust the woman gazed down as she rode past. She wore a long brown coat and matching skirt and fine black riding boots. A tall hat with a veil sat on her thick, braided hair. The woman was very plain with a prim set to her thin lips and a permanent squint around her eyes. But still, Rachel thought her most beautiful. Oh, to change places with her. To sit astride that proud red animal and wear a dress of such soft and beautiful cloth and shiny boots that never had touched mud or animal dung.

"Filthy little wretch," the woman muttered as she passed.

The words stung. Why would someone so fine speak in such a way? Rachel watched in tearful awe while the woman continued on out of sight around a curve in the path. Just wait until she got to California where no one knew that she was a filthy little wretch, then she too could have fine clothes and a riding horse.

Despite her fantasy, the hateful words stayed with her and chased her as she ran on through the forest and out into the open valley.

Daniel attended the meeting Captain Lewis Evans called at the wagon yard that morning. Evans was a tall, handsome man with curly hair. He was apparently well liked by everyone. As he approached he joked and laughed in a booming voice with several of the men, until finally he had quite a contingency gathered round.

"Proud to see you all, mighty proud," he told them. At that he removed his large white hat. "Before we start there are things you need to know. This trail has been scouted by the Cherokee. With their help we have spent many months mapping it out, but still and all, no one knows for sure the difficulties we will face. I can't stress enough that any who aren't stout of body and mind with a strong need to arrive in California alive should seriously consider remaining here. There will be other trains, once we've marked the way. And plenty of gold in California to go around."

The crowd roared.

He glanced quickly at the eager faces, all men, quite a few of them Indians. Three white women, the only ones signed to go along, weren't present, leaving this business, as was customary, up to the men. One was the wife of James Aaron Claridge, the other two were grown daughters of Jacob Von Finster, whose wife had passed away several years earlier.

Daniel studied Evans and the men who had accompanied him. All well-known and respected men of the county, wealthy when compared to himself and many of the others. Considering that it cost well over two thousand dollars to properly outfit a wagon for the trip, none could be poverty-stricken. Daniel had spent a year in the mountains trapping and tanning pelts to earn enough to outfit his own wagon. At that it wasn't nearly so fine as the others, and certainly more sparsely equipped. He had lived in the wilderness with only what he could carry on his horse for months on end, he figured he could survive this six-month trip with what he carried in the wagon.

Evans was speaking again, and Daniel reined in his wandering thoughts.

"I'd like to introduce you to the men who will be in charge during the drive. I, of course, am well known to most of you, some have even spent some time as my guest, I would suppose." He chuckled and waited for others to do the same. Everyone knew that Evans had once been the sheriff of Washington County.

When the laughter died down he indicated a well-dressed gentleman standing next to him. "This is Thomas Tyner, our first lieutenant. Next to him, that big fella is our second lieutenant Peter Mankins, yonder is James Vann of the Cherokee Nation. He was once the editor of the *Cherokee Advocate* newspaper. He'll serve as secretary. And that's Martin Schrimsher, also of the Cherokee Nation. He'll handle the commissary. Our sergeant you'll meet later.

"Now, plans are to leave early on the morning of Tuesday, April 24. While I, as captain, will determine travel and camp times and am in general charge, the wagon master L. J. Wyatte will arrange the order of the march. He'll be assigning you places in the train, and you are to adhere to that plan unless you fall out for repairs or illness."

Wyatte lifted a scruffy black hat.

Evans went on. "Everyone is naturally expected to take their turn riding night guard, and any other duties we see fit. Generally, we will try to remain together, but there may be times when you'll simply have to catch up. Sergeant McCrea'll post guards at night, and will let you know when you're due up. We don't know what we'll find out there. The hostiles may be on a tear, but for the most part they'll settle for a bit of food and some doodads. Our Cherokee friends here will see to that." Some nervous laughter moved around through the crowd, but none of the Indians joined in. Evans was not deterred.

"I trust you've all laid in the necessary supplies: crackers, flour, beans, coffee, sugar, a ten-gallon barrel of water, and so on. Each man jack of you needs three blankets and . . . well, you all have the list. Twenty-five hundred pounds, not an ounce more on each wagon. And for God's sake, don't leave out the quinine, oh, and hartshorn, someone'll get snake bit once summer hits. If you're having trouble procuring any last-minute items you might have forgotten, see Schrimsher there. There is no apothecary here in town, so I do pray you've all brought your medicines.

"Now, we'll strike out west toward the Verdigris River in Indian Nation. There'll be others joining us from Fort Smith as well as the nations, then we'll head eighty miles upriver, where we'll cross and head northwest to the Arkansas River and on to Fort Mann. As you know, we plan on staying away from the traveled trails, the Overland and the South Pass. While we'll follow the Santa Fe Trace as far west as Bent's Fort, from there on we'll be cutting trail. Sticking close to the mountains ought to guarantee more water and graze for the animals. Those who come after will like as not be driving large herds of cattle. We're the trailbreakers, men. We may be headed west to dig gold, but by God we'll do our part for those who come after. Lord knows, the desert along the southern route is too barren to support cattle or folks. This is a new life we seek, and we have a lot invested. Many won't return, others won't wish to, but some of us plan to bring our riches back to this state for its good and that of the people who are settling here . . . Anyone got any questions?"

Though everyone began to chatter among themselves, no one directed anything toward Evans, and he slipped the wide-brimmed hat down on his curls. Fist held high he shouted with much vigor, "On to the gold," and strode away, followed by his minions.

When the excitement died down Daniel decided to slake his thirst at the saloon, but instead of saddling up the mare, he walked toward the square. He cut through an alleyway between Stirman's Mercantile and the blacksmith shop, and just as he emerged onto Center Street he heard the most awful commotion. A loud, high-pitched squealing mixed with gruff snorts followed by explosive laughter. Down the street a ways several head of cattle and hogs moved up the street, but the swine appeared to be in trouble. They staggered and stumbled, turned circles, and rolled on their sides. The cattle eyed their companions with disdain, stepping over some prone bodies as they went. Daniel picked his way past a couple of enormous sows lying on their sides kicking feebly and squealing. Three pigs fell all over each other, tried to get up, failed, and rolled around snorting.

"What in the hell's come over them?" Daniel asked of a couple of nearly hysterical bystanders.

The show had caught the attention of everyone on the street. Business in town came to a halt as merchants and shoppers alike enjoyed the antics of the animals. In the raw-boned settlement they were used to seeing cattle and goats and pigs and chickens wandering in the streets, but a bunch of drunken swine was something new and quite entertaining.

"Doss was making some cherry bounce," one said, then fell off into gales of laughter, unable to continue the explanation.

Daniel could figure out what had happened from there, but the jovial man's companion took up the tale, snuffling and wiping at his eyes. "He dumped the fermented cherries out back of his place, never thinking I reckon that them hogs would be partial to 'em. They're drunk. Drunker 'an the Lord. Aw, gee." The man doubled over when a sow lying at his feet, lurched upward, gave him a wide-eyed stare, staggered several feet sideways and fell to the ground with a surprised grunt.

"Some of you gentlemen could take a good lesson from this," a middle-aged woman said. "See how foolish you look when you stagger home in your cups."

Daniel grinned and shrugged as if he'd never done such a thing in his life, and the two men to whom he'd been talking broke into renewed gales of laughter. "Ain't nothin' looks like an old fat sow that can't keep her feet."

"That's just what you think, mister. Just what you think," the woman said.

"Hey, Shem, reckon if we ate us a chunk of fat back off'n that one out yonder, it'd taste like likker?"

"I don't know. We could just slice off a piece of her and see. Hell, she's so drunk she wouldn't know the difference anyway." Arms wrapped around each other, the men staggered off.

Hogs lay everywhere. In the street, up on the boardwalks of the mercantile and the hotel, some had even tumbled off down the mountain, only to roll to a halt up against a post or rock when they couldn't keep their feet.

The few head of cattle, having had enough of such shenanigans, lumbered on down Center Street and out of sight around the corner. Daniel stepped carefully over a green, steaming cowflop and vaulted up the steps to the boardwalk of the saloon.

Inside everyone had their own version of the fermented cherries. It was quite a jovial gathering. He came out an hour or so later, having managed to drink only two glasses of warm ale before calling it a night. He couldn't help but think about what the woman had said. Some of the hogs still lay in the street, others were stirring. Waking up to a new world, no doubt.

With the toe of one moccasin he touched the fat haunch of one of the passed-out hogs. Reckon the likker made that one forget all his troubles?

He moved quietly toward the wagon yard, mind still on what the woman had said about drunken men and drunken hogs. He caught sight of a figure darting between two wagons and crept quietly toward where it had disappeared. Lanterns hung on several tailgates and some of the folk were visiting around a bonfire out in the center clearing. Stepping around the front of one wagon, he was just in time to see the figure hoist itself up and into a wagon.

What in the hell?

He moved closer and peered inside. Someone was in there, he could hear them breathing. Could be the owner, but in that case why be so sneaky?

"Who is that?" he called. He felt foolish even asking, but he did know that the Claridges were staying in town and no one ought to be poking about in their wagon. Might ought to mind his own business.

From inside harsh breathing caught, stopped.

He waited, silent.

The breathing began again after a while.

"I said, who is that? I'll call someone if you don't show yourself."

"Please don't." A small voice, quavering but stern.

"Then come on out of there."

A sigh, a rustling of quilts, blankets. "It's me, Rachel Keye."

The Indian girl. Damn. He took her hand and helped her out. "And what were you doing in this wagon?"

"None of your business."

"Maybe not, but it's somebody's business, and I guess we'll have to find out whose."

"No, don't do that. I'll go, I didn't take anything, I didn't hurt anything. I just needed a place to sleep and they go up to the hotel every night."

Daniel hadn't noticed that he still held her hand until that very moment when she tried to pull away. He didn't let go.

"Why don't you go back home, girl? Why are you still hanging around here?"

"I'm going to California. If I go home my brother will just sell me again. I can't stay there anymore. My grandmother's too old to protect me. No one cares about some raggedy-assed Indian girl." Her voice grew angry and sharp-edged and she tugged hard to get free. "Let me go. What do you care, anyway?"

A painful ache grew in Daniel's chest, covering his brief amusement at her referring to herself as raggedy-assed. He had been thirteen when the Cherokee were removed from their homelands in the Carolinas and Georgia and Arkansas and sent to live in the Indian Nation. She would have been a very young girl. He remembered hearing some about it, but hadn't given it much thought. Did the Cherokee really throw away their women like this, sell them, for God's sake?

He thought of the Mexican girl who'd died in his arms after the regiment had plundered her village. He couldn't save her, but this one, well, hell. Surely he could do something.

With a heavy sigh, he gave in. "Fine, then sleep in my wagon. But just till we head out, that's all. I'll make a bedroll on the ground. I'm more comfortable there anyway. For God's sake, you can't go sleeping in some stranger's wagon. It's dangerous."

She stood very still, looking up at him so that her

eyes shined in reflected lamplight. "And is it not dangerous in your wagon?"

He fingered her gnarled dark hair. "Hell no, it's not dangerous. You got nothing I want."

She cringed from the tone. "And will you let me ride with you to California?"

He turned away. "Come on before I change my mind. I told you, I'm not going to California."

For a long while after she removed her clothing and wrapped up in the fur robes on the floor of his wagon, Rachel listened to the sounds of him bedding down on the ground beneath her. In the distance cattle lowed, night birds called hauntingly, and someone laughed. The pungent fragrance of wood smoke drifted in the air. The town quieted down at last, and she grew drowsy.

The vision came to her far into her sleep. She stood high on the rim of a mountain such as she had never seen. It was covered with snow, but she was not cold like she had been during the terrible trip from her homeland when she was just a small child.

Before her, floating in the thick mist that hung over the jagged peaks, was the beautiful wife of Chief John Ross. Long ago martyred because one dreadful icy night in the Smoky Mountains she gave up her blankets so that a sick child could live. In the vision she wore, as she had then, only a thin garment. The beautiful woman was no longer cold. Her face glowed with radiance, her bare skin kissed by a light that seemed to come from everywhere and nowhere.

She extended her supple arms as if to embrace Rachel. Wind lifted her long ebony hair that glistened with crystals of ice. She spoke, that is to say her lips moved, but no sound came to Rachel's ears. The words came from inside herself, from out of her heart and her thoughts. Whispered, sang, spoken, they clothed her in warmth and hope.

Rachel reached out to take the offered hand of this spirit from another world, but she touched only cold, dry clouds that she could not hold. From far away came the cry of a bird, a hawk, maybe an eagle, and then a great white horse galloped across the sky, breaking through the curtain of snowflakes with his magnificent head, mane and tail sparkling like the spirit's dark hair.

He took the ghost women upon his back and she rode with arms spread wide until Rachel could no longer make out anything but the flakes drifting like pale butterflies, and a mammoth shard of ice-coated rock. Wonder tinged in sadness overpowered her. The same feeling she'd experienced when Bone Woman told her of the place where her dead mother dwelled. A place Bone Woman had seen many times in her visions and promised one day Rachel would see too. "Because you are a healer. Your spirit is one with all that have gone before you and those who will come after, until our sister sun rises no more."

Those were the words Rachel sensed within herself when the spirit woman spoke in the night vision. She turned them away as she did all her Cherokee teachings, for she would be white. Restlessly, she moved in her sleep and began to dream of California and going there with Daniel Wolfe.

The next morning, while the Indian girl slept deeply, Daniel went to the mercantile and bought her a brush for her hair and a hand mirror. When he returned he pulled aside the covering and saw her sitting up rubbing at her eyes, the robes falling around her narrow waist, her firm young breasts bare. She slept naked. What a little animal she was. What a lovely, desirable little animal. He averted his eyes, ashamed of his own longings. Yet seeing her this way, he could not help the desire that leaped alive within him.

"Get dressed, I've brought you something," he said through the curtain.

She came out only seconds later, wearing his shirt and the loose pants.

She frowned and refused to meet his gaze. "I didn't ask for anything. I do not need anything."

"Oh, I know. You and I are alike in that respect. Neither of us needs anything. Come on, sit down here." He led her to a large rock and standing behind her, unwrapped the brush and mirror. The paper crackled and she turned, curious despite herself.

"No, don't look. It's a surprise. Wait, now, hold on." He lifted a long strand of her tangled hair and began to work at the knots with the bristles of the brush. "Oh, just a minute, here, hold this." He handed her the mirror and went back to work brushing her hair.

Rachel's breath caught as she lifted the silvery glass to admire it. Her reflection shone back at her and she touched first one cheek then the other and watched the movement with wonder. His fingers caught in her hair, the brush whispered through the tangled locks. In the glass she watched a tear gather in her lower lid, hang there a moment in a shimmer of sunlight, then trail down her face.

"It is a looking glass, what do you call it?" Her voice came so husky he could scarcely hear.

He glanced up. "It's a mirror."

"A mirror," she said with reverence. With one fingertip she touched her image. Then, caught up by the design on the back she studied the whorls of blue and gold. She turned it back over and held the glass so that he was reflected behind her, mouth pursed as he concentrated on untangling her hair.

How wonderful to watch him in secret when he didn't know. How beautiful he was! How finely hewn his features, even when he was scowling so.

At the corners of his heavily lashed eyes tiny lines etched the bronzed skin. Early-morning sun shone in his hair so that it appeared laced in gold. His jaw was firm, his chin strong and determined. He was clean-shaven with but a shadow of whiskers. Most white men couldn't be bothered to scrape their faces and grew heavy facial hair, but she liked the hairless look, having grown up with it. Indian men did not shave and had no beards or lip hair, what the white men called mustaches. What a majestic man this Daniel Wolfe was. How very strange that he had no woman.

Why had he given her the looking glass and hairbrush? Perhaps he thought he could buy her favors, like the white men who had offered Jasper Doaks many fancy trinkets for a turn at her after Eagle had sold her to him. How frightened she had been that he would accept from each of them, one after the other. Bone Woman often said that the white man thought he could buy anything, and if he could not then he would simply take it. Right down to the lives of The People and the land which everyone knew no man could own.

The thoughts made her angry and suspicious of this white man.

"I can't keep it, of course," she said, furious with herself for being so simple.

He ignored her and went on brushing.

"Stop that and take this looking glass." She sat very still, unsure of what she was waiting for. Why didn't she just pull away and leave him there with his stupid old brush and comb?

"I bought it for you."

"Why?" She liked his fingers twined in her hair, but the mix of emotions confused her.

He tugged a little too hard and she cried out.

"Sorry," he said and stopped what he was doing

for a moment. "If you can't keep the mirror, then give it to someone else. I don't want it back. You should learn how to accept gifts graciously."

"It is my first gift." She tried out the strange word, liked the feel of it on her tongue, but was still shy of his motives. "What do you wish in return?"

He was silent, the brush stilled for a moment. "I don't want anything in return. That is not a true gift, then. That would be a bribe. A gift asks nothing in return." He went back to brushing, vigorously now.

"I'm sorry I made you angry. It is so beautiful."

He grinned. "Say thank you, that's good enough."

"Thank you." Softly the words came.

She turned on the rock so that her knees brushed against his thigh where he squatted behind her. The warmth of her flesh inflamed him. Her mouth, so close he could feel the moist breath, was parted so that her pink tongue peeked out. He lowered his head slowly, touched his lips to hers, moved his tongue only slightly and felt hers. For that split second it was as if his heart shattered into thousands of fragments then gathered itself once again. The contact jarred him almost senseless.

He pulled away a little and stared at her in amazement.

She licked at her mouth and tilted her head, then smiled very slightly. "Thank you, Daniel Wolfe."

She leaned forward and placed her lips firmly on his once again. This time a small sound of joy came up from her throat and she threw her arms around his neck, knocking him backward from his precarious position so that they sprawled on the ground, her on top of him.

He had, after all, expected something for the gift, and even as she lay there with him, she grew angry. He had tricked her! Several men approached and she heard their chatter and was conscious of their laughter as they caught sight of them practically under the wagon bed.

Her anger faded as quickly as it had come, for no harm had been done. This way of saying thank you was enjoyable indeed, the favors more than equal on both sides. How quickly she had forgotten her fear that he wished to buy her favors. She scolded herself and tried to glower at him without much luck.

Daniel came to his senses quickly. The passion drained away in light of his earlier decision that he would not commit himself to this girl, even if she did make him feel like an animal in rut when he was around her. That was curable by a visit to a whorehouse. Messing around with a girl like this one could get a man in a lot of trouble before he even knew what hit him.

After the men passed on by, Daniel handed Rachel the hairbrush. "You can finish up yourself, I've got things to do."

Actually he had no idea what things he might have to do, but he saddled the piebald mare and got the hell out of there. It was damned scary how it had felt holding her close. She wore nothing under the coarse clothing and her firm breasts had pressed against him, the nipples taut with desire. The muscles of her supple body were tight and strong. Her legs wrapped firmly around his hips set him afire with images of the secret, warm, honey sweetness of her. The wildness of her. He could have all that and more, but then what?

He was going to the wilderness of Oregon alone and needed no complications, most especially not a woman who set his senses to reeling.

Chapter Three

Rachel hid the treasured brush and looking glass in a hollow tree where she could be sure to lay hands on them quickly. She spent a great deal of time during the next few days studying the actions of the men who had signed up to go on the trip. Of course, some were not camped at the yard because they lived in Fayetteville.

The wagon she had earlier been drawn to she learned belong to Cutter Christie and his two sons Elijah and Isaac, full-blood Cherokee, but unknown to her family. By eavesdropping she learned that the Christies had lived in Arkansas until the removal, while her people had lived in the Great Smokies. The father and sons appeared respectful and quiet, not the victims of whiskey. They wore traditional Cherokee leggings and wrapped their heads in colorful turbans just like the great Sequoyah had. Both could read and write in the Cherokee syllabary, and that impressed Rachel. They would be the ideal men with which to stow away. When they found her, and of course they eventually would, she would have nothing to fear physically from such distinguished men.

That decision having been made, all that remained was surviving until the magic day, the day they would head out for California. And surviving meant continuing to steal food scraps from behind the eating establishment in town.

Two days later Daniel caught the Indian girl going through the discarded scraps of food. He was afoot and she had not heard his approach as he cut through the back way from the yard to the square. He walked up on her silently, in the same way he moved through the forest when he trapped and hunted, coming down gently on the balls of his feet. He grabbed her as she knelt, scrambling through dried crusts of bread.

His touch sent her nearly wild with fear. She came up hissing, kicking, struggling to pull free. When she recognized him, she clamped both hands over her mouth, eyes sparkling ferociously.

"Rachel," he said in a voice that cracked. "My God, what are you doing?"

She simply shook her head back and forth and tried to fight the tears of shame that welled in her eyes. For him to have caught her stealing was almost more than she could bear.

"Dear God in heaven," he said and wrapped his big arms solidly around her so that she could scarcely breathe. "I would have fed you had you asked, girl. Don't you know that? You don't have to scrabble around like some starving animal in a pile of garbage."

He was stunned that he could have been so cruel as to not realize that she had nothing to eat, just as she had no place to sleep. Yet in his haste to be rid of her for his own selfish reasons, he hadn't let his thoughts go that far. He had kicked her out and had set about trying to forget how being around her made him feel.

"I will not beg," she said, but her voice was muffled in the warmth of his buckskin-clad chest.

"Come on back with me, I've beans on the fire, we'll make some johnnycakes or pone. I can't think of you doing this." He gestured at the scattering of scraps.

Head down, she trailed along behind him. the lure of hot food overpowering her instinct and pride. This man refused to take her to California, yet he wanted to feed her, give her gifts, put his lips to hers in very disturbing but enjoyable ways. Perhaps she could give him another of those exciting thank-yous after she ate her fill. She had to admit the idea sent chills of pleasure through her. His touch was nothing like that of Jasper Doaks, who made her want to throw up.

Daniel watched Rachel finish off a second plate of beans. He studied how she spooned up the steaming soup in quick frantic motions, and again felt ashamed. She hadn't wanted to wait for him to put together some meal cakes before she ate, and so they were just getting crisp over the fire as she cleaned up the last bite. He fingered one from the hot coals and juggled it into her open palms.

She bobbed her head forward and moved the cake back and forth, blowing on it briefly before breaking off a piece and popping it into her mouth. Small sounds of surprise and low chuckles accompanied her eating, but she still refused to look at him. Since he had given her the brush, her auburn hair was no longer tangled but hung sleek and wavy down her back, the red highlights shimmering. He wanted to brush it again for her, gather the silken tresses in his hands, and pull the bristles down their length until sparks snapped into the tips of his fingers. What a fool he was! Despite his vow to remain aloof from this sensual woman, he couldn't curb his most disturbing imagination. Rachel in his bed, that smooth hair cascading over his naked chest, the slim legs astraddle of him, his throbbing hardness deep within her.

"May I have another?" Her request brought him back to his senses, angry at himself. Tonight he would find a pretty little whore, or an ugly one even, as long as she could cure this perversity, this betrayal by his body. He had been in the deep woods much too long. The thought of such a thing immediately shriveled his erection, for he no longer desired a woman much used by others. He had an unsettling suspicion that all the women in the world would not slake his thirst for this one sitting at his campfire.

"Eat your fill." He gestured brusquely toward the remaining johnnycakes, rose, and stalked away from the smoldering coals, leaving her sitting there alone.

Damn her, anyway, why didn't she just go away? He'd thought himself well rid of her and his pesky male desires. He could not have her around. Every time he looked at her he was reminded of the child in Agua Nueva, how he'd held her in his arms until her breath stilled, the pulse in her throat fluttered, fluttered, and stopped.

There he had been in a strange country, holding in his arms a broken dream and all around him death and destruction, and he had never felt such despair. The Arkansas Volunteers had been nothing better than a bunch of wild and woolly untrained killers. The professional soldiers would have nothing to do with them. They called them incompetent and worse. Archibald Yell's regiment had finally risen above their foul reputation when the Kentucky regiment fell back under fierce attack by Santa Ana in Buena Vista. Colonel Yell had led his men to the rescue and had perished in the ensuing skirmish. Many of the hundred men in the regiment were wounded. An honorable battle fought by less than honorable men redeemed by circumstances. Daniel had met the enemy bravely, valiantly, perhaps tried to die, but even that hadn't wiped from his memory the earlier burning of the defenseless villages, the cries of the children, the girl he'd always thought he might have killed, though he'd never know for sure.

Why Rachel made him recall that day so vividly, he wasn't sure. The dead Mexican child had been no more than ten or twelve, still small for her age because she was starving, her black hair tangled down her back. That was it of course. It wasn't so much the child herself, but her circumstances, lost and alone, uncared for just like Rachel. He had to stay away from her for so many reasons. The most important one being that he wanted her so badly. If he gave in to that he feared he would go insane, for he was very near it already with the terrible nightmares that had increased in intensity since meeting her.

He came to himself within a thick stand of willow cane and was amazed to find that, totally immersed in thought, he had walked all the way to the river. A late-afternoon sun sparkled over the rushing water, tiny bright blue spring beauties carpeted the bank, a rabbit darted quickly through the brush. He sat on a fallen log, fists doubled against both temples until dusk cooled his skin and dew dampened his hair.

The year he'd spent in Yell's volunteer regiment spun out like a tale from a book. If it weren't for the bad dreams, he might almost believe it was but a story he'd read somewhere. The mounted march from Fort Smith in June of '47, through San Antonio and on to Monterey and across the Rio Grande. The skirmishes, the bragging, the yearning for an honorable death like real soldiers, when all they were was a bunch of rowdy volunteers. How foolish they'd all been, for that war brought no honor to anyone, least of all the Americans. Yell had been declared a hero only because he laid down his life, and so that worship had brushed off on his men when they had returned home to Arkansas. Everyone wanted to hear the war stories over and over again, especially Yell's charge on his great white horse and how he was cut down and made an instant hero.

Daniel wanted no part of it and so he had moved off into the mountains. Drinking and isolation were all that stilled the ghosts. After a year of trapping and hunting and living alone in the wilderness he'd found a peace of sorts. Now this young Indian woman had brought it all back, and he could not bear it, yet he wanted her with every breath in his body, with every beat of his heart.

Well, it wasn't going to happen. He would steel himself against her. If she should succeed in her plans to join the train, then he would ignore her. If need be he would head out on his own once they were well on their way. He could easily survive a singular trek to Oregon country without help from anyone, especially that strutting greenhorn Evans. The man wouldn't last five minutes on his own in mountain country.

Before darkness overtook him, Daniel rose and went back to town and directly to the saloon, where he drank until he fell asleep in the corner on the sawdust dirt floor. He awoke lying in the street, where the owners had obviously tossed him when they'd closed up.

Head throbbing, he managed to get to his knees and crawl to a horse trough, where he doused his head in the icy water and came up gasping. After a few more moments, he crawled to his feet and staggered toward the wagon yard, sobering a little in the brisk night air. At his own wagon, he paused to wash away the brackish taste from his mouth, drinking deeply from the cedar barrel lashed there. Then he climbed into the wagon and moved blindly in the dark into the mound of buffalo robes, where he lay down and curled into a shivering ball.

Rachel moved in her sleep and when she rolled over she found herself coiled around his backsides. He was cold and damp, his muscles twitching and shuddering. The stench of whiskey lay over him like an ugly blanket. Trying not to make any noise, she found another fur robe and tucked it around him, then she crawled back under and wrapped him in her arms. She mourned for this man who searched for his life in a bottle of white man's whiskey. What great sadness made him do such a thing?

Before she could find even a clue to the question, she fell asleep. Sometime in the night he wrapped both arms around her and began to moan.

"No, no, no," he babbled. "Please, no." The rest was incoherent, his movements growing wild.

She tried to hold on to him, soothe him, massage away the night terror, brought on no doubt by his own ghost spirits that would not rest.

Finally, he lurched forward to sit and doubled over, gasping for air. He didn't even know she was there until she laid a hand on his quivering shoulder, then he jerked convulsively.

"What? Who? . . . the hell?" He scrubbed at his head with stiff fingers. "Holy Hannah." Great jagged gasps erupted from his throat.

"Daniel, what is it? Are you all right?" She wanted to shake him hard, drag him back from the world that had frightened him so. A big man like him, not even afraid of Jasper Doaks and his whip, yet something as unreal as a dream could cause such terror.

"Rachel? What are you doing here? Leave me be. Get away. Go!"

She started to obey, but halted halfway to the curtained opening. "I did nothing wrong. Don't take out your anger on me. I did nothing wrong." She shouted the last repeated words. "You keep drinking that white man's poison it will kill you, Daniel Wolfe. I thought you were more of a man than that."

Covering his eyes, he lay back down. "Just leave me the hell alone. You don't know anything about me, nothing."

"No, and you will never let me know, either. You chase me away. Each time when there's a chance we could become friends, learn to know one another, you run me off. What I don't understand is why I keep coming back. You said I could sleep in your wagon, eat your food. Now you tell me I must leave. Well, this time when I leave, I won't return."

"Good. Great. That's precisely what I want." He hugged her pain to his own chest, sorry he had to hurt her but relieved that she might finally realize that hanging around him wasn't a great idea. Let someone else feel sorry for her and feed her and give her a goddamned mirror and brush her hair. Her goddamned beautiful hair. He wanted no part of it at all. She was alone and lost and too damned needful for him. So just let someone else do it, once and for all.

Tears in her eyes, but too angry to let them fall, Rachel leaped from the wagon and hit the ground running. She flew blindly between the great hulking shadows, outlined by the sheen of early morning. Rounding a large wagon, she turned into the wind and felt the bite of wet granules in the air. Snowflakes pelted her skin harder and harder as she scampered toward the edge of the forest and the tree where she had stowed her brush and mirror. Despite what Daniel had said, she was not angry enough to leave them behind. They would be the only possession she carried to her new home in California, and she had to fetch them quickly and hide herself within the Christie wagon. For this was the day they would depart.

Excitement overpowered the memories of that ugly scene with Daniel as she settled in among the crates and barrels toward the front of the heavily laden Christie wagon. Without conscious thought she brushed her hair in long, languid strokes.

Eventually the camp came awake, stirring noisily. Horses whinnied, men shouted, and chains rattled as members of the Fayetteville Gold Mining and Cherokee Company prepared to get underway.

Daniel nursed a murderous headache from drinking the night before, which he vowed served him right. On the long trek west he would take no whiskey except for medicinal purposes. It no longer drove away his demons and it left him feeling like he'd been stomped and wallered by a bear. How could he have been so drunk and stupid as to crawl into his wagon and lie down with Rachel? After he had sworn to stay away from her. Whiskey addled his brain, made him forget the things he needed to remember, but it didn't wipe away the memories, for they returned once he was asleep. Perhaps the hard work of the drive would do what nothing else had done. Cleanse his soul of its foul imaginings.

With the long-legged piebald mare tied to the back and his four horses hitched, Daniel waited patiently for his place in line, assigned two days previously by the wagon master Wyatte. He would ride near the end of the train, being of much less importance than many of the well-to-do investors and businessmen who were going along on this trail-breaking trip. He watched as each of them pulled out, following the leaders that wound around the foot of the mountain toward the Prairie Grove Road. Many didn't have the stamina this drive would take. He could almost pick those who wouldn't survive as he watched the way they handled their teams, their mode of dress, their physical actions. Soon they would be in mud up to their knees or choking on dust; some would fall to cholera or brain fever or summer complaint or just plain stupidity.

At last his turn came, and he tucked in behind the wagon belonging to the Christies. He did not know them; he had only spoken briefly with the three men around the campfire. The boys appeared well-educated but tough, the father dour, uncompromising but fair. Daniel doubted they would give much leeway to whites when push came to shove.

Each jounce of the wheels along the pocked road sent spikes of pain through his head. What a damn fool he was. He could very well be one of those who didn't make it if he didn't gather his wits about him. He raised his head and let the falling snowflakes cool his brow. Off to his left the Boston Mountains lay purple against the morning sky. Through the falling snow their peaks appeared softened, the trees feathered in early green leaves.

He might never see this place again. Never tramp along at the bottom of a deep hollow, hearing only the sound of his own passage and water tumbling from the rugged bluffs. Never walk up on a magnificent elk drinking from a still pool, his reflection shimmering in the bloody sunset painted across the surface. Never rest high on a ridge and gaze in reverence at a valley black with buffalo, lush green grass tickling their bellies.

From the side of the hill he gazed out across the valley at the wagons, winding like a crawling snake along the road west. The fertile fields showed patches of green cut by long fingers of standing water and bare soil. The wind picked up a little, sending snow down his collar, and he hunched deeper into his fur robe.

Crowds had gathered on both sides of the route out of town, people waved and shouted, children screeched, dogs barked, and good-byes echoed back from those on the train. Men left their wives and children behind, brothers left mother and father and sweetheart; Daniel left no one.

The worst thing about hiding in the Christie wagon was not being able to take part in the excitement of leave taking. The best Rachel could do was peek through gaps between the canvas and the wagon, but that gave only brief glimpses that whet her appetite. She wanted to be riding up front in Daniel's wagon, waving down at those unlucky enough to be staying behind. She wanted to cry, "Good-bye, good-bye" in a loud, happy voice. Instead she crouched in the darkness with barrels and crates jolting against her, her backsides banging up and down on the hard wooden floor.

Winter Dawn was seven years old in May of 1838 when the white soldiers came to round up her people and put them in stockades. At that time her mother Singing Bird, her mother's mother Bone Woman, and her two younger brothers lived in the home of Bone Woman. Her older brother Eagle Who Soars, son of Standing Bear, had not lived with the family since his mother married the white man Josiah Keye, who was away in the mountains trapping when the soldiers came. If her father ever returned, he never followed his family to the Indian Nation and she had never seen him again. Because her grandmother Bone Woman was a healer and a witch, the family had lived quite well.

Among the Cherokee it was forbidden to harm a witch. Rachel had learned later from her friend Alice, who attended Miss Sawyer's Seminary, that at one time white people burned their witches or stoned them, but the Cherokee were much more civilized than that.

As to the night the soldiers broke down the doors of their home while she was still Winter Dawn, she remembered terror, screaming, and the smell of the blood of those who were trampled under horses' hooves because they did not move quickly enough. She recalled very little of living in the stockades for five months, and she always thought that was best. But she had never forgotten the death march. She never wanted to. It would forever remain as a symbol of the white man's cruelty when The People had something he wanted. Eagle had protected her, sheltered her, and carried her on his back when he was too weary to do more than stumble, because their mother had to care for the younger boys. Even now she cried thinking of how Eagle had finally betrayed her.

That long-ago October morning dawned dreary and cold and a steady drizzle fell as they were taken from the stockades and loaded into the wagons, barefoot and scantily clothed. Bone Woman said there were so many wagons one could not count them in an ordinary way. Each one was crammed full of men, women, and children and it would set off only to be replaced by another, slogging up in the mud to take aboard its pathetic load.

They were like animals being carried to the slaughter. Graves lined the trail from the very first day, two of them her younger brothers, one not yet walking, and of course the lovely Christian wife of Chief John Ross. No time was taken to mark the burial plots, so that to this day the bones lay alone, separated from their loved ones forever.

An army of soldiers under the command of General Winfield Scott "escorted" the thousands of Cherokee from their Smoky Mountain home so the white man could search for his precious gold metal, and President Andrew Jackson allowed it, even turned down the pleas of Chief Junaluska, who it is said once saved Jackson's life in battle. A new home was found, a home where nothing would grow and where game grew scarce and the soil was red and thin. Probably one day something of value to the white man would be found in the Indian Nation and The People would once more be hauled to another place.

Winter Dawn learned in the eighteen summers she had lived that to survive one must be white, and since she could claim white or red, she chose white and became Rachel Keye, her father's child. So far it had not been as easy as she had thought.

When word came down the line that the Cherokee town of Tahlequah lay ahead and the wagon train would camp on its far side, Rachel crept to the back of the Christie wagon, which she had not left in several days except to see to bodily needs in the dark of night while the brothers slept in their tent. She drank and ate very little. During the long hours penned up in the gloom she had much time to think and grow homesick for one last glimpse of her beloved grandmother. She longed to tell her of her plans and bid her good-bye, for she feared she would never see Bone Woman again in this life.

As she peered cautiously around the canvas covering, she was startled to see Daniel Wolfe's wagon right behind. If she jumped out now he might see her. Perhaps she would have to wait until dark after everyone was asleep. She ducked back down.

Daniel stripped out of his shirt and cupped water from the stream, dousing his face and chest and gasping from the cold. All around others did the same, washing as best they could in the abundant water. With the evenings still chilly, no one went into the creek. Stock had been fed and corralled for the night, and he had satisfied his hunger with slices of fried saltpork and a few johnnycakes left over from breakfast. He washed the food down with bitter, boiled coffee. Arms behind his head, he lay back on the creek bank and stared up at the pale sky, awaiting the first stars. Around him the low hum of conversation and an occasional burst of laughter grew distant. Then he heard stealthy footsteps, not the noise of someone strolling openly.

He swiveled to a crouch behind a stand of oak and saw a slight figure darting into the shadows away from the Christie wagon. Curious, he followed along, keeping the figure in sight. Odd how the fellow kept away from the road, taking the more difficult route through the fields and woodlands, obviously headed for Tahlequah. He couldn't tell much about him. He appeared to wear loose britches and a long-tailed shirt. A kid maybe, but there were no kids on the train. Perhaps one had snuck out here from town to pay a visit and was returning home. If not, there was only one other person it could be. Rachel, the Indian girl he'd hoped they had left behind. Somehow she had managed to stow away in someone's wagon. He prayed she was going back to her people.

For his own peace of mind he decided to trail along and see her safely there. And if she changed her mind and started back, maybe he'd tie her to a tree so she couldn't follow the train when it pulled out.

A few minutes later she skirted several small shacks on the edge of town and tapped on the back door of yet another. Dogs barked and Daniel ducked down behind some bushes.

The door of the shack eased open, emitting pale light that outlined an Indian woman dressed in voluminous skirts and a belted shift. Rachel flew into her arms, was embraced and dragged inside. He couldn't resist getting a better look and crept to the lone window at the back. It was covered with a tanned deerskin which he was able to push aside enough to get a good view of the girl and her grandmother. They spoke, though, in Cherokee, which he couldn't understand. Yet he remained there, for he couldn't leave.

Bone Woman told Winter Dawn about her brother Eagle.

"He hides in the caves in the hills, says he will never live under the thumb of the white man, will never bow to the words of the Old Settlers' Treaty."

Winter Dawn knew the old woman loved her grandson, having lost all the others, so she didn't tell her of his treachery; she let her think she had run away to seek a life with the white man.

Bone Woman touched her granddaughter. "But you are back now from your quest. Did you find you could not be white?"

"I am white. I am white in the part that my father created."

The old woman spat. "Your father, may he die a long death if he has not already gone to his devil God."

"Grandmother!" What a witch says often comes to pass, and Rachel feared for her long-gone father. Perhaps he was dead, but that didn't put him beyond Bone Woman's powers.

Bone Woman caressed Winter Dawn's cheek. "You are hungry and weary, and dressed like a grubby white child. Let me feed you and give you some clothes. Let me put you to sleep in your own bed with a healing chant."

Rachel's throat filled and she couldn't speak for a

moment. How could she tell Bone Woman that she would soon go away and never return?

As it turned out, the telling was easy, as she should have known. Bone Woman knew all things before thoughts became words. And as a special farewell she repeated the legend of Red Bird in case her granddaughter might have forgotten.

Red Bird is the daughter of the sun, the story went, and when she became lost in Ghost country the sun grieved. She sent men to capture her daughter and bring her back. But the men were foolish and were tricked by Red Bird, who pretended to be ill so that they would open the box in which they carried her. And she flew away.

The sun grieved terribly for the loss, and also because from that time forward none of The People could ever go to Ghost country and bring anyone back. So now, whenever people died, they could not return from Ghost country.

"We must wait to see them until we go there ourselves," the old woman finished.

"Grandmother, I am not dying, I am simply going to California."

Bone Woman grew very serious. "The darkening land to the west," she murmured and fingered her charms. "It is I who will go to Ghost country, child. And I fear you will follow because of this thing you do. Follow before the spirits call. Here, I will give you these." She offered a pouch of healing potions and the small leather bag of charms.

Winter Dawn took them with trembling fingers. "I don't know what to do with them, Grandmother."

"You are of my blood, child. You too will become blessed by the spirits, but you must look for them, search and they will come to you. If you walk where I have walked, sleep and dream the dreams I have dreamed, look in the places I have been, you will find your own spirits, your own strengths. In your dream-walking look for Little Deer. He will see that you are a believer and make joy shine for you."

Tears slipped down Rachel's cheeks as they embraced and said their good-byes. Then Bone Woman presented her with bright skirts and shifts and a cinch of silver and turquoise for her waist. For her feet she produced a pair of butter-soft deerskin moccasins, and around her throat the old woman placed the golden nugget her mother had worn from childhood. Rachel slipped out of the castoff britches and shirt and into the soft clothing. She felt Cherokee again, and feared the feeling would capture her soul.

"Braid these into your hair and each time you do remember that I prepared them," Bone Woman said and handed her several thongs died deep purple with berry juice. The old woman caressed long strands of Winter Dawn's hair. "The fire of the sun, our sister," she murmured. She touched cheeks with her granddaughter once more, then turned so as not to watch her leave the room.

As an afterthought Rachel added the britches and Daniel's shirt to her bundle. She stepped quickly through the doorway and let the skin hanging there fall with a soft whisper. When at last she looked up she saw Daniel Wolfe barring her way. The gleam of lingering dusk lit his ashy eyes.

"Stay here," he whispered. "Please stay here."

She shook her head, angry that he had followed, angrier that he thought he had the right to tell her what to do. "I do what I must."

"You do what is foolish, girl. Dammit, don't you see that?"

A high whoop rose from out of the dark border of trees, the thunder of horses' hooves followed, and into the yard rode Eagle, astride his paint horse. Behind him came two more warriors, painted in the old way as if for war, a thing only the renegade Cherokee ever dared do, like those who had fled to Texas after the removal and rode with the rebellious Tatsi.

Rachel swallowed her tears and stood her ground until the pounding hooves of the paint horse hauled up within arm's reach and her brother leaped to the ground.

Daniel stepped to her side and lay his hand loosely on the butt of the bowie strapped to his hip.

"I will do this," Rachel said out of the side of her mouth, and faced her half brother without flinching.

"All the same, I think I'll just stick around," Daniel said.

He would have been amused by her bravery had not the danger appeared so great. Her small, delicate body braced in stubborn stillness, daring the warrior to strike her down. He marveled at the fierce expression as she stared up at her brother, who was almost as large as he, bare-chested, painted fearfully, but with no weapon that Daniel could see. She had a proud chin and she jutted it forward, her blue eyes snapping until he could almost hear a brittle, crackling noise.

"You have brought our grandmother sorrow, Awa'hili. I am ashamed for you and I cry for her."

He reached to touch her cheek and Daniel stiffened.

"Do not cry, sister. I did what I must, as you will."

"Selling your own sister as if she were a black white man is a terrible thing. I will never be a slave."

Eagle took a step forward. "Nor will I, my sister. Remember how it was and understand." He dropped his hand and crossed both arms across his chest in a gesture of love. "Do not judge me for what I must do."

Rachel clenched both hands at her side and felt

tears slide down her cheeks. "We will never see each other again, Eagle. I will not go back to the white man, and I am sorry if that causes you trouble."

He shrugged as if to show how little he thought of Doaks. "The white man's money is spent, the deed is done, and you are not harmed. All is well, sister."

With a dreadful shout, he leaped to the back of the blanketed pony and rode away; the other two, who had not spoken or moved during the fracas, followed him.

Daniel sheathed the bowie with some relief. He wasn't sure he could have overpowered the muscular Cherokee, and surely not all three of them.

"What will you do if he comes after you again?" he asked.

"He cannot. I am going to California," she said with a stiff smile, then turned and walked back toward the wagon train.

He stared after her until she faded into the dusk, then he lifted his shoulders and followed along at a discreet distance.

Chapter Four

With Tahlequah and the emotional parting behind her, Rachel quickened her pace to escape from Daniel. It was a mystery why he continued to follow her only to chase her away, as if she were causing the problem.

Finally, she halted and waited for him to catch up. "Stop walking in my footsteps. Do you forget you do not want me around?"

"Not hardly, but I can't get away from you, seeing as how you're hiding out in the wagon traveling just ahead of me."

"I don't mean that. I mean now. This. The other times. You tell me to go away. I go away. Then you come sneaking along behind me like some squaw."

"Not like any squaw you'll ever be." His retort was sharp, but filled with admiration.

She sighed and took a good look at his face. Perhaps she could read some message there that his words failed to convey. Could it be that she didn't understand the language as well as she thought? Darkness had captured the forest, but the sky above still shone a burnished silver, the color of his eyes. Eyes that bored into her, holding her in place so that she felt tied to the spot. It stirred something deep inside her and upset her balance.

Frustration edged her voice. "Why do you yes me, then no me, then yes me again? I have left you alone like you asked. And what do you do? Follow me around."

He laughed; he couldn't help it. Her question was one he had been asking himself. He spread both hands and gave her a quizzical look. "I don't know the answer to that myself." He lowered his glance. "I was hoping you'd remain in Tahlequah with your people, and I just wanted to see you safely there. Now . . ." He raised his shoulders.

"You are very foolish." She broke off and cleared her throat. His wish to protect her was touching. He had, after all, dragged her from under Doaks's whip. Yet his actions since were confusing. "I see only one reason for your odd behavior. You are a man, a white man. And that is enough to explain almost anything you have done."

He laughed again. "You are a very smart girl. Where did you learn so much?"

"Why are you surprised? Isn't it allowed for a raggedy-assed Indian to be smart?"

"Some raggedy-assed Indian." He looked her over and grinned despite an inclination to run like hell. "Oh, yes. It's allowed. Look around you. There are men of your race on this wagon train who earned that right just as the white men did. Businessmen, merchants, successful farmers who are intelligent and quick-witted. What I mean is, you speak as if you were white . . . almost."

"You continue to dig yourself a hole with your tongue. Perhaps it isn't allowed for an Indian woman to be smart. Of course, it isn't allowed for an Indian to be white. Many of our legends put forth being white as the ultimate goal. Doesn't that strike you as absurd? And what do you mean, 'almost'?"

"Dammit, girl. Are you bent on twisting my words? Some of the things you say are definitely from an Indian perspective, no matter how hard you try for the opposite effect."

"I do not try for anything." As soon as she said that, she knew it to be a lie, but was caught up in pondering the precise meaning of the unusual word "perspective." Actually, she did understand what he was trying to say, for he himself spoke like no mountain man. Her father had come to this country from across the broad pond and spoke with a lovely lilt to his voice that was akin to singing. She wished she remembered him better, wished she could see him again. She remembered only flaming red hair, sparkling blue eyes, and a wonderful, joyous laugh.

"What is it?" he asked.

Distracted from their conversation, she turned away and headed along the trail left by animals moving through the forest. It was best that they didn't talk anymore.

He caught up with her easily.

She moved faster. "Go away."

"Can't. This is the way back to the wagons." He had no idea himself why he was tagging along beside this woman when he'd vowed to keep his distance. Vowed to tie her to a tree, for God's sake. Surely he was entranced, and she was some woodland fairy. "I lived a long way from here. Grew up on the eastern coast, near New York. I went to school there and was going to be a lawyer."

"Don't tell me. I don't want to hear."

"I hated it. I would stand for hours at the edge of the ocean and let the tangy sea wind blow away the stench of the city. At first I dreamed of setting sail around the world. But then, the more I heard and read about this great western land, broad and open much like that ocean, the more intrigued I became."

"Intrigued?"

"Fascinated, yearned to see for myself, curious."

She nodded, totally caught up in his story, seeing him as a young boy staring out across a body of water she herself could not even imagine. Dreaming of sailing ships. To her they were mere canoes, for she had no frame of reference. But still the image came clear and crisp.

"And so you became a man who sails the waters?"

"No. But I didn't become a lawyer either. I quit before I had read the law enough to qualify, and I ran away to become like Daniel Boone. A wandering woodsman. My family will never forgive me. They don't know if I'm dead or alive, and they don't wish to know. Anyway, that's how I came to be in Arkansas just in time to join Yell's volunteers." He stopped abruptly. That ground was not what he wanted to cover.

"A soldier," she whispered, and turned to glare at him, her face a mask of fury. For she knew what soldiers did. They herded helpless women and children, old men too crippled to walk. They stood by and let them die without doing anything. They drove her people forever from their homes.

"You were a soldier?"

The hard, terrible, crackly words were aimed right at him and he flinched. "Only for a little while." Her demeanor puzzled him, but he had already said much more than he meant to say.

"Only a little while? Long enough to kill, to maim, to destroy." Pain slashed into her throat so she couldn't go on. She thought of the wife of Chief John Ross, stumbling through the icy rain, shivering in her thin, wet clothing. Finally dying one night with her head lying on the ground padded by the saddle of one of the soldiers. She could not believe that this man who had dragged her from the wicked whip of Jasper Doaks had been a soldier. And her brothers . . . the baby lying face up in the mud, rain and ice pooling around him as they hastily shoveled dirt over him. After that she scarcely remembered the death of the other; she only knew that he had died.

She clenched her fists and stared darkly at this white man.

Daniel felt awash in the venom of her hatred, and he couldn't understand why he pursued this. He had vowed to stay away from this sensual young woman. This display of sudden and unexplained hatred should only make it easier. But her scorn lanced his heart. He wanted to shout at her that he wasn't cruel, wasn't a killer, yet he didn't. For she was right in what she thought of him, of soldiers. All the same she couldn't know about the villages in Mexico, about the children. She couldn't, yet her accusations had cut too close to the truth.

"I am so sorry for you, Daniel Wolfe," she said, each syllable spitting from tight lips. "I do not want to see you or speak to you again. Do not follow me. Do not even look my way. You are dead to me. Dead."

Mouth hanging open, he watched her race through the woods and disappear into the lowering darkness. He had his wish, sure enough. There was no danger of her tempting him now.

When he returned to his wagon he found the hairbrush and mirror he had given her lying on the seat, and there was no sign of Rachel. A feeling of deep loss filled him. He crawled into the furs in the back of the wagon, but it was far into the night before he fell asleep. Twice he rose to his elbows, fetched the jug of medicinal whiskey, and took a deep swallow, until at last he slipped into an uneasy slumber.

Rachel sneaked past the tent in which the Christies slept and once again made her nest in the back of the Christie wagon. Soon she went dream-walking. There the spirit of Little Deer appeared to her. He was the immortal one of which legend spoke, the spirit her grandmother had promised would come to her. A shimmering white, and no larger than a small dog, his antlers gleamed in splashes of moonlight and he remained transfixed, enticing her with remote, dark eyes. Then he raised to his hind legs, tossed the magnificent antlers as he pawed the air with his tiny sharp hooves, and bounded away, followed by a rampaging herd that faded in his wake.

In her dream she rested for a long while, staring into the shadowy forest laced with creamy moonlight, not knowing where she was. There was a sense of waiting, of expectation, but she knew not of what. A terrible or wonderful thing was yet to happen. Little Deer had come to tell her of it, but the message was not yet clear.

How could Daniel Wolfe have been one of the soldiers? How could he not have told her? He touched her and made her want him, and then he simply said he was a soldier. Just like that. She would kill him if she could, more than that, she would like to kill every soldier in the white man's army, but she knew that would never happen.

Dragging her thoughts away from Daniel, she pondered the meaning of the visit from the sacred Little Deer. While still a child, perhaps somewhere during that winter-long, brutal trek from the Smokies into the Indian Nation, she had rejected the myths of her people. Not one of the spirits protected them from the white man's ugly and evil violence. And so she had lost her belief in her grandmother's fairy tales. The legends and myths were merely stories told to the young to frighten them, to make them go in the way they should.

Bone Woman had traveled that trail too, and despite its hardships, the deaths and suffering, had never veered from her beliefs. She had very special powers and perhaps she feared losing them if she doubted. Rachel had actually seen her summon up the spirits, had watched her drive evil from the bodies of those afflicted, had felt the power inside herself while sitting beside the old woman when she chanted over the bones of those who had passed into the darkening land to the west. Perhaps Bone Woman was right, and power was hers any time she wished to use it. Yet to do so would be to admit the myths might be true, and so she refused.

Lying there in the dark, with the visit of Little Deer still vivid in her memory, she wondered what might happen if she set the spirits on Daniel Wolfe and made him pay in some small way for what the soldiers had done to her people. The leather pouch of charms rested between her breasts next to her mother's gold nugget. Clasped in her palm, it felt hot; it pulsated with life and strength. If she used the charms to do this bad thing would she then be forever cast out? Not allowed to walk with the spirits of her people. As badly as she wanted to be white, the idea that she could never see her loved ones again, even in the land of the Ghosts, was terrifying. Her grandmother wished her father dead, could she not do the same with this soldier who had deliberately deceived her?

She opened her hands and stared at the pouch. Fool, she thought. What a fool she was. How could she believe one thing and not another? It was all lies, stupid, superstitious lies. There was no power, the bag contained only a few feathers and stones and a bone or two. Nothing magic. Tucking it back between her breasts she shifted to a more comfortable position in the small cubbyhole in which she hid. The important thing, the only thing was to remain well hidden until it was much too late to send her back to her home.

Then another thought occurred to her. What if Daniel Wolfe told? What if he went to Evans or one of the Cherokee, like James Vann, and told them that this foolish Indian girl was hiding in the Christie wagon?

The possibility rose like clouds from a noxious swamp, and she couldn't go back to sleep for the remainder of the night. Every sound became someone sneaking up to seize her and send her back to Jasper Doaks.

She still lay wide-eyed with fear when members of the train stirred awake and began to ready themselves for another day. From Tahlequah they would travel to Fort Gibson, where they would follow the Verdigris River. It would be eighty miles before they crossed over, and she thought perhaps that would be far enough. She would show herself as they were preparing to cross the river. She prayed Daniel Wolfe kept his mouth closed until then.

Once out in the open she would sit high in a wagon as the unknown plains country unfolded all around her. Smiling and waving and shouting and laughing, just like the white women. Or maybe she would walk, like the tall, thin sisters with their strange accents. One she recognized as the woman who had ridden up on her in the woods before the train left Fayetteville, the one who had sneered at her, called her a filthy little wretch. She had heard the word before and knew it was not kind.

Neither of the sisters ever rode. It was said that they vowed to walk all the way to California. What a marvelous idea. Perhaps she would do that, but the thrill of sitting high on the wagon intrigued her. Daniel's word, intrigued. It was a wonderful word, she liked the sound of it, the feel of the syllables on her tongue. Yes, that is what she would do. Ride all the way to California.

She could hardly wait.

Daniel couldn't keep his eyes off the gaping oval in the back of the Christie wagon. How could she hide in there all day without coming out for anything? Didn't she get hungry, thirsty, feel the call of nature? It had not once occurred to him to go to Captain Evans or even the Christie brothers with his knowledge of their secret stowaway. It was the girl's business entirely, and none of his.

And then, of course, there was the distraction of Zoe Von Finster, the long-legged daughter of the burly German Von Finster, whose first name he hadn't yet learned. Everyone simply called him Herr Von Finster. Zoe and her sister Minna walked all day every day. But the Von Finsters had brought along hired help so that they did not have to cook or unpack and pack the wagons every evening.

Since early this morning, Zoe, admittedly the more attractive of the sisters, though neither were raving beauties, had walked beside his wagon, glancing up now and then, nodding if he looked at her. A brazen invitation, if ever there was one. But perhaps she only wanted to be friendly. That sister of hers kept her thin lips clamped and a permanent frown creased her plain face. She kept an eye on him and Zoe as if expecting the worst. He saw nothing friendly about her at all.

When the wagons held up for water and a noontime meal, the woman Zoe approached him. He had no sooner loosened the team to graze than he saw her regarding him openly.

He spoke first to ease her obvious awkwardness. Now that she had summoned up the nerve to make the first move she didn't appear to know what to say.

He doffed his wide-brimmed hat. "Afternoon, ma'am. Daniel Wolfe."

"Zoe Von Finster." She put two syllables in her first name, so that it came out Zo-ee. Though she did not speak with the thick accent of her father, it was immediately evident that she wasn't Arkansas bred. "I thought perhaps you might like to join us for nooning, since you're alone."

The brazen invitation took him totally by surprise. He had made a point of remaining aloof from all other members of the train. "I . . . I thank you kindly. But I have some . . . some repairs to do while we're stopped, and hadn't thought to eat."

"Oh, but you must. The trip will be long, you'll need all your strength." She deliberately measured the height and breadth of him and smiled. Regally attractive with chestnut hair and brown eyes, a willowy waist, and long legs, she was most definitely flirting with him. Something stirred very deep inside his gut, not the same untamed passion he experienced around Rachel, but desire nevertheless. He recognized desire in all its guises, though he seldom gave in to it. Loneliness bred such nonsense.

His close regard caused her to blush and she tilted her head, obviously pleased.

"Perhaps tomorrow," he said. "I appreciate the invitation. Thank you." Abruptly he turned away, but not before he caught the disappointment in her expression. It wouldn't have hurt him to be kind and he wondered at his inability to do so. The war had left him curt and withdrawn, but perhaps he had always been somewhat so.

She drew a breath, then murmured, "Of course, some other time." The rustle of her skirts told him she was gone, leaving him feeling a perfect ass.

The train's arrival at the Verdigris River produced a great deal of jubilation from everyone. Remaining hidden was probably the most difficult thing Rachel had done since leaving her grandmother, but they were still in the Indian Nation. Once the train traveled the eighty-some miles up the valley where they would cross over and head northwest toward the Arkansas River and Fort Mann, she would be safe. She had to wait to show herself.

Miserably she listened to the celebration that began after supper. Someone brought out a fiddle, and in the darkness she dared hang over the tailgate to listen. Everyone must have gone to the party, and after a while she could bear it no longer and crawled out. She would creep closer to watch. No one would notice her as long as she kept away from the light of the fires. Von Finster and some of the others had lanterns that burned lard oil, putting forth a peculiar stench. The glow was unmatched by the more common star candles. She would have to be careful not to be spotted in the flickering pools of light.

Carefully she made her way around Daniel's wagon. It was silent and dark. Perhaps he was enjoying the music himself. But she didn't see him in the crowd once she had settled herself beneath the large supply wagon drawn up closest to the central fire. The two Von Finster sisters were there, and to her surprise were dancing with first one man, then another. Other men paired up together to dance, the one playing the lady wearing a bandanna around one arm. A great deal of horseplay accompanied the odd pairings. Indian men always danced together, but not in the same way. This custom of the whites to hold each other while dancing looked to be quite enjoyable, provided one was a man and the other a woman. Some customs of her father's people were strange, though it was arousing to imagine moving around in Daniel Wolfe's arms, held close to his muscular body. The thought came and went. She would never dance in the arms of such a man, a soldier, the enemy. How sad that made her, because Daniel had been so kind. And she had enjoyed being with him, his mouth on hers when she thanked him for the looking glass. How could he have done the things soldiers do and still have been so gentle and understanding with her? It was a mystery, much akin to what propelled the sun or kept stars in the sky. There would be no answer.

Then he walked past her, where she sat half under the wagon. She knew him immediately from the distinctive workmanship of the knee-high leather moccasins he wore. She had studied the needlework while staying in his wagon; at the time she had thought that he must have had a woman to do such a fine thing.

One of the sisters must have spotted him too as he stood on the fringes of the dance floor, for she waved, excused herself from those she was talking with, and came to hook her arms through one of his. The woman had lovely hair, but it was caught up on the back of her head in a tight bun. She was tall, and Rachel thought graceful as a doe, though very bony. She was the woman who had ridden sidesaddle through the woods and had spit hate-ridden words at her.

Daniel looked down at his companion a moment, his expression very serious, then shook his head. The woman laughed, turned her eyes upward, and said something else. Daniel flushed, and then she took his hands and coaxed him onto the dance floor, where a tarp had been spread to make the ground smooth.

Rachel watched as the woman placed one of Daniel's arms around the back of her waist and took his other hand in her own. They began to move in slow, deliberate circles, the woman's dress swinging out behind her. Faster and faster they danced, Daniel's long legs moving so gracefully that the woman followed as if tied to him. And she heard him laugh and wanted to cry. This white woman could make him laugh. She did not know that at night he called out in terror in his sleep. What would she think of him then? Rachel wanted to tell her, frighten her away so that she would leave him alone.

The couple didn't stop until the music faded. A burning sensation filled Rachel's breast. She didn't recognize the reaction, could not give it a name, but it was much like the way she felt when her mother would take Eagle's word over hers, or favored him with something special that should have belonged to her.

Finally she could watch no longer. Daniel had ruined it for her by paying attention to that long-legged, skinny, hateful woman. Now she was sorry she had given him back the looking glass and brush, she should have smashed them in the dirt. She crawled from under the wagon and ran blindly away from the lighted area. As she rounded the back of the wagon under which she'd hidden she ran smack into a stocky Cherokee with a pipe in his mouth.

"Whoa, girl, where do you go in such a hurry?" He stopped suddenly and regarded her with a look of confusion. "Wait, I didn't know anyone had a young girl with them. What is your name? Who are you traveling with?"

"Let me go, I didn't do anything." She struggled to break free, but his grip was harsh, his fingers cut into her arm.

"No one has said you did anything, I merely asked who you travel with."

She said the first thing that came to mind. "The Christies. I'm with Cutter and his sons."

The Cherokee snorted. "Brought along someone to

keep their loins warm, did they? Well, we shall see about this."

"No, please don't. I'll leave, please don't." She set her heels and held back as he dragged her toward the campfire. No matter how she kicked and clawed and protested, there was no getting loose. He was too strong.

"Girl, stop this nonsense. We will get this straightened out quickly." He called out in a booming voice, "Captain, Captain Evans."

The music ceased as did the dancing and merriment. All attention turned to the interruption. Rachel hung her head and didn't meet their eyes. Most especially she did not want to look at Daniel.

Captain Evans appeared in their midst. She didn't know where he'd come from, for she had been scowling down at the ground since this man had dragged her out where everyone could see what was going on.

"Who is this? Where did you find her?" Evans asked. He cupped her chin and raised her head. "Where'd you come from?"

She tightened her jaw and refused to answer.

"Where'd you find her, James?"

"Over there by the supply wagon. Says she is traveling with the Christies, but I knew they did not declare a female passenger. Thought you ought to take a look."

Daniel stepped forward. "Excuse me, sir. It's my fault. I told the girl she could ride along with me if she caused no trouble. I didn't realize I would have to declare her presence."

"Who is she, then, sir, and why does she lie about the Christies?"

"She came to me in Tahlequah, wanted to go with me. I saw no harm. After all, a fine woman is an asset, isn't she?" He grinned. "We had a little spat, that's all, and she did crawl up in the Christies' wagon. But it's my fault, sir. She's not to blame."

Rachel snapped him a fast look. He knew her name very well, yet he withheld it, and spoke as if she were warming his bed. How dare he say such a thing? Was he protecting her, or did he have other reasons? Maybe he thought saying it would make it true. He nodded at her and smiled.

She turned away and glared defiantly at the man called James.

"And did she tell you why she wanted to come with you? Perhaps she's running from something. A fugitive or something."

"Mr. Vann, you of all people should know that every Indian isn't automatically running from something."

James Vann removed the pipe from his mouth. "Young Cherokee women do not wander around alone. We are not, after all, heathens, sir. We see to our children."

"I am not a child," Rachel said crossly.

"Well, she does speak," Captain Evans said. "Now that you're in the mood, tell us what else you are or are not, child." He held up a hand and went on. "Oh, excuse me, of course you are not a child. I misspoke."

Light chuckles broke the tension of the group.

She was terrified that these people who had no objection to keeping their black white men as slaves would return her to Jasper Doaks if she told the truth. In fact, the Cherokee on this trip had brought along slaves of their own. She had seen them often enough, black white men who worked all day and were tied at night so they would not run. She saw very quickly what her options were. If she angered Daniel Wolfe, then no one would stand for her and she would be sent back to that terrible man who had bought her. So she stubbornly kept her silence.

"Well, sir . . . ?" Evans glanced up at Daniel.

"Daniel Wolfe," he supplied.

"Yes, well, Mr. Wolfe. I suppose it would be remiss of us to turn this young woman loose to fend on her own simply because you neglected to follow the rules. If you will guarantee her safety, that is, and keep her with you so that she is not forced to sneak around and steal for her survival, I see no reason why she can't remain. But you will be responsible not only for her food and care, but for keeping her out of trouble. If you take my meaning." Evans raised an eyebrow at James Vann, then at Daniel.

Vann didn't seem to take the inference that she might steal personally. He was a civilized man, as were his people.

Rachel resented it very much though, and she began to sputter. The man still had his thick fingers wrapped around her arm and she wanted loose.

Daniel stepped to her side. Vann glared at him and then released her, the message in his eyes very clear. He didn't like what had transpired and would hold Daniel responsible.

Daniel leaned down so that his hair fell across her cheek and said quietly, "Go with me and don't say another word, or by God I'll tie you up and keep you there till I can find someone to take you home. Do you understand me?"

She took a deep breath and whirled to face him.

He held up a finger and waggled it back and forth. "No, not a word. I can only do so much, and I've gone the limit. Now march. To my wagon and inside, on the double."

Fury almost blinded her, but he had kept her from being sent back, and for that she would have to be grateful. Even so she did not have to be nice to him and she certainly didn't have to make his life any easier. She wouldn't either.

"I have to pee," she hissed.

He pushed her behind a bush. "Then do it."

"Don't look."

He crossed his arms over his chest and turned from her. "I'm not looking. Just don't take all night."

"If he touches me, I'll kill him," she muttered and relieved herself quickly. How was she going to ride in the same wagon with him, knowing what she did about him? Feeling torn as she did? Day after day, week after week, even month after month, at his side.

She stomped out of the shadows. "I'm ready."

He grunted, took her hand, and dragged her back to the wagon. He lifted her up easily and set her inside. "Do I have your word you'll stay here and cause no more trouble, or do I have to tie you?"

"You tie me and I'll gnaw the ropes off, then I'll take your knife and slit your throat." She scrambled back as far as she could and waited for him to jump in and attack her. He would probably beat her for what she had done but she had been beaten before and could take that.

Panting, she touched the place between her breasts where the leather bag of charms hung. If he attacked her, she would stop him, even if she had to call on the spirits.

"All right, hellion," he muttered. "But if you don't behave, I swear I'll take you back to Tahlequah myself. Hell, the worst we were supposed to see on this trip was a few wild Indians wanting a pony or two. I didn't expect to have one riding along with me threatening to slit my throat."

He hopped inside and she scrabbled out of reach. "Oh, don't you worry, I'm not sleeping in here with you." He grabbed one of the furs and leaped out.

She held her breath, waiting for him to come back, but he didn't, and after a while she heard him bedding down underneath the wagon.

In the night he cried out, wakening her. She wrapped the fur tighter around herself and covered her ears so she wouldn't have to listen. It served him right to walk in the land of fear while he slept, after what he had done. Soldiers should have to suffer all their lives for the evil they had brought to her people. He could have only been a boy of fifteen or so when the soldiers uprooted her people and slaughtered so many, but she stubbornly clung to her judgment. A soldier was a soldier, and if she got the chance she would make him pay.

Chapter Five

Birds greeted dawn raucously. Rachel awoke, peeked out into a patch of clear sky and snuggled cozily into the robes.

She was free and she was going to California. The realization warred with her feelings about the soldier Daniel Wolfe. It would be difficult to travel with him. On the one hand was her attraction for the troubled man, on the other her bitter hate for soldiers and what they had done to her people.

Someone thumped on the sideboards, interrupting her reverie. "Get up, girl. Get moving. I need some help out here. You ride with me, you work."

Hurriedly she crawled to the tailgate and leaned out. Daniel had a fire going and was bent over making a bed in the coals for a coffeepot. He glanced at her.

"There you are. Fix us something to eat while I get the stock hitched. And when you're finished, see that everything is packed and tied down. We don't want anything working loose. Check the water barrel real close."

Without replying, she dressed and did as he asked. A cursory search in the larder turned up all she needed to make johnnycakes and some fried fatback. Molasses sweetened the steaming cakes, which Daniel bolted when he returned from fetching the team.

He gulped down a cup of coffee, then went to hitch up the animals without saying a word.

After she finished the chores he had assigned her, which included cleaning up after the meal and stowing away the foodstuffs and utensils, she climbed into the back.

In a few minutes he appeared and gazed in at her. "If you'd like, you can ride up front. No sense in you hiding back here, you can't see, and the day we bust out onto the plains will be a sight to behold, I hear." He reached up for her. "Come on, hurry."

She looked at the outstretched hand, then into his face. His eyes regarded her steadily and she sensed no animosity there.

"It's okay. I promise I don't bite, and I'm sorry if I scared you with talk of tying you up. I was just frustrated, and didn't know what else to say. Now, are you going to ride up front, or are you going to hide out here like some prairie dog in his hole?"

Her hand disappeared in the warmth of his big fist. She climbed over the tailgate. Before she could stop him he encircled her waist and swung her to the ground. Through the fabric of her clothing, the heat and hardness of his body curved to hers and her heart kicked frantically. She looked up into his face and saw that he was staring at her intently. Then his eyes flickered to dusk and he moved away.

"Get a move on, they're leaving," he said, but didn't glance in her direction when she scrambled up into the seat formed of bundles stacked on crates stored up front. She realized then that he had made a special place for her to ride. Early on she'd noticed that most of the covered wagons had no seats, not those that had been converted from farm wagons or those built as smaller versions of the gigantic Conestoga wagons which she'd seen pictured in Alice's schoolbooks. Drivers either walked or rode the left rear animal. And more often than not oxen pulled the wagons. Passengers might walk, but sometimes they found a place to ride on the cargo they carried. She tried not to be touched because he'd prepared something comfortable for her. This white soldier might do anything to worm his way into her good graces, but it wouldn't work. She would stand firm.

At last the train got underway with a cracking of whips, the bawling of cattle, the cries of horses and mules, and the shouts of men. Each wagon fell into its assigned place in line. Spare animals brought up the rear, easily herded because they had already learned that at noon they would be allowed to graze.

Daniel rode his piebald mare near the rear left flank of the team. A thin whip stood in readiness in its rack, but he didn't touch it. The four horses he'd hitched moved steadily, following exactly the wagon in front. They were well trained. Even when unhitched from the wagon, they followed Daniel to the central corral like pets.

She wanted to ask him why he chose to ride rather than walk, but that would seem too much like giving in to the peculiar situation she found herself in. Remaining outside the realm of his personal life seemed best. She also wondered why some chose to use mules, others oxen, others horses. There were many questions, but they would probably remain unanswered.

As the long line of wagons snaked up a rise and reached the top, she rose to her feet and clung to the puckered canvas to see better.

"Look out there, don't you tumble out," Daniel called. He was watching her, and it gave her an eerie feeling.

She didn't look at him, but gazed instead at the carpet of fresh green grass dotted with pink and blue and white wildflowers. How lovely they were. Overcome with delight, she leaped from the wagon and hit the ground on the run, stopping once in a while to kneel and smell the sweet blossoms and the pungent earth. For a long while she walked, keeping the wagon between her and him. Several times she glanced across the rumps of the horses to find him watching her with those shimmering eyes that reminded her of frozen woodland pools. She refused to gaze into their depths, and would look away quickly to keep from doing so.

For several days they traveled in relative silence, neither saying more than was absolutely necessary. Working together, each doing their own jobs, became second nature, and one morning she awoke to find that she was actually looking forward to spending the day beside him. She no longer feared he would come to her at night demanding favors in return for carrying her along. Yet she would not let him win her over entirely, for she couldn't forget what he had been, couldn't forget the torment of the long march that had forever robbed her people of their birthright. Most of all she couldn't forget the killings, the dark endless nights of suffering and the death of her younger brothers.

At noon of the fourth day after she began to ride in Daniel's wagon, they came to the place where the train would cross the Verdigris. They would camp for the night on the other side. It could take hours for the forty wagons to ford the river. Soon they would be out of the Indian Nation. No telling what lay ahead.

Evans, with his wagon master L. J. Wyatte and Sergeant Cletus McCrea, called everyone together to plan the crossing. She watched in silent awe as the brightly garbed Cherokee mingled with the white men on equal footing. For hadn't it been said that the idea for the drive was theirs in the first place? That they had gone to Fort Smith to present the plan, to begin what would finally become this gigantic undertaking. The Cherokee planned the journey and would follow the trail where no wagon trains had gone before. They would swing north skirting the mountains to the west, missing the dry and dangerous dessert to the southwest, bypassing the known routes where grass had been overgrazed until animals died of starvation by the hundreds. Rachel felt very proud for her people, but truly couldn't understand how they could accept the treachery of the white man.

It would be late in the evening before the last wagons moved through the river, and Daniel's was near the rear.

Rachel strolled off while the men talked. She was soon out of sight behind a wooded knoll. There she spotted a small stream of water and sat on the bank. Just as she removed her treasured moccasins and lowered her feet into the icy water, a sweaty hand clamped over her mouth. Frantically she tore at the fingers and fought against her attacker, but she couldn't escape.

"Do not cry out, sister. I only wish to talk."

She relaxed, tugged Eagle's hand away, and glared into his stern face. "I thought you would be in Texas by now." She spoke in their native tongue because he had never been comfortable with the white man's language.

"The man, Jasper Doaks?"

She waited, regarding his sharp, grim features.

"I came to warn you that he is scarcely a few days behind you."

Panic gripped her. "Does he come after me? Surely he could get another slave even better. He doesn't even think I'm pretty. Oh, Eagle, why did you do this?"

He hunkered down beside her. "I would like to tear out his heart. I would not even eat it because he is a coward. He cheats our people."

"Then why?"

Eagle shrugged and stared off toward the western horizon.

"Tell me," she begged.

He replied in a low voice, so that she had to strain to hear him. "He said he would only let you remain alive if you belonged to him. He threatened to kill Bone Woman as well."

"But that doesn't make sense."

"What white man makes sense, sister? He saw you bathing in the woods and wanted you for his own and so I took his money, but I swear I was not going to let him keep you. I brought the others to help me get you away, but before we could the white man was there."

"But he never . . . never touched me in that way."

"He is a very strange man."

"He is a wicked man. He would have taken my virginity if I had remained with him."

"You and grandmother would have been in the darkening land now if I had not sold you to him." He hesitated and touched her shoulder. "Do you believe me?"

She nodded, but didn't know if she did or not.

For a long moment Eagle stared unseeingly across the way they would go, his eyes deep pools of blackness. "The white soldiers, they beat me and kicked me and they killed our brothers, and yet you wish only to be white. You ride with a white man." He spat in the dust beside her.

"Daniel Wolfe is a kind man." She could not admit that he too had once been one of the hated soldiers.

"There are no kind white men. Beware, sister, he will turn on you. He will destroy you because you are only a dirty Indian to him. Just as I am." He grabbed her shoulders as if to pull her to her feet.

A shot thundered in the stillness. A lead ball

whined past and cut a path through the brush to the water. Shouts followed, and they turned to see Daniel on the piebald mare and another mounted man carrying a musket. The two horses charged off the top of the ridge, and Eagle leaped agilely to his feet. He had no musket, but carried a knife at his waist, a hatchet on his mount.

In the split second it took him to decide whether to flee or fight, Rachel scrambled to her feet and raced toward the men, waving her arms frantically. "Don't kill him, don't shoot. He's my brother. Please don't kill him."

When the men reined up and she turned to look, Eagle had vanished. The distant sound of horses' hooves pounded away to the southeast. More than one, she thought. Oh, run, Eagle. Fly with the wind. Go far away to Texas and never look back. One day she feared the white men would kill her brother, because he would have it no other way.

Daniel threw a leg over the saddle horn and slid to the ground beside her. He touched her shoulders and ran his hands down her arms. "Are you hurt? Did he hurt you?"

"No, no, he didn't hurt me. He would never hurt me." She swiveled her head to try to catch a glimpse of her brother, then looked back at Daniel. "He is my brother." Huge tears formed in her eyes.

"Oh, I know he's your brother. We've met before, if you recall. What was he doing here? What were you doing out here alone? " He touched the corners of her eyes with both thumbs, capturing the tears before they fell. "Don't cry. He could have killed you."

She jerked away from his touch, remembering who he was. "I go alone where I please. Eagle would never hurt me. He's very angry, very hurt. You don't know anything about him." Despite the defense of her brother, she trembled violently and hugged herself. What would she do if Doaks caught up with the train, told Evans she belonged to him, and took her away?

Daniel studied the stubborn set of her shoulders, sensed her fear, and wanted to hold her close. She looked so young, so vulnerable in the lovely clothing her grandmother had given her. Not at all like the raggedy, scruffy little thing he'd first met in Fayetteville. She'd caught her long, shiny hair up in a single braid down her back, weaving into the locks a long strand of soft purple leather. When she moved rays of the sun set the tresses on fire, played golden over her fine features. He wanted to touch her and made to do so, but pulled away. Things were best left like they were.

"Come on, you can ride with me," he said.

She shook her head and went to fetch her moccasins. "I'll walk."

He hung back, signaling the other man to go on, and rode slowly behind her all the way back to the wagon. He never stopped scanning the surrounding land for signs of that wild brother of hers.

That night the old dreams came at him with renewed ferocity, and they began with Rachel at the mercy of her brother, as she had been when he'd ridden up on them. The sight terrified him in the dream as it had in reality, for he was sure that Eagle would plunge the knife into her throat.

Jerked awake, he forced himself to lie quietly; he listened to the soft rustlings as she moved about in her sleep and was calmed. When he finally dozed off, it was to return to the village in Mexico and a dead child in his arms.

All around him fire raged, the ravening flames lighting the sky, illuminating the delicate dead face, the long silken hair, the blood on his hands, his arms, and down the front of his uniform.

"I didn't mean to kill her. God forgive me," he

cried and fell to his knees. "I will die myself. Die. God strike me dead."

The shouted words awoke Rachel and she wrapped her naked body in a blanket to creep out of the wagon. Daniel crouched on his knees beside the glowing campfire, the huge bowie he usually carried at his waist clutched in both hands, blade pointed at his chest.

Frantic to stop him, she let go of the quilt and threw herself against his shadowy form, knocking the weapon aside. It went flying and she ended up lying across him, both of them flat on the ground.

He was bare to the waist, gasping and fighting back when his hands closed around her nude hips.

"Daniel, please. What is it? It's me, Rachel."

"Get away, get away . . ." He hushed abruptly, stopped thrashing around, and gazed at her.

Then he grabbed her frantically and cradled her in his arms, rocking back and forth. "Don't die, please don't die."

He kissed her naked breasts, buried his face in her hair, and held her close, his hot tears splashing on her skin.

"Oh, Daniel, hush. Please don't suffer so."

Softly she crooned a song Bone Woman had taught her. She wound her arms around his neck and lay her head on his bare chest. She forgot that he was a white man crying for a death he had caused. Crying perhaps for the killing of Indian children like her brothers. She only knew that he was suffering terribly and it wrenched at her heart for he had been kind to her.

Slowly she began to rub the back of his neck, to thread her fingers up into his hair, to cradle his head against her own breast. Her mouth searched hungrily along his jawline, found his moist lips, and tasted of them.

He moaned and returned the gentle kiss.

From down deep inside herself there arose such a longing that she too cried out. She wanted to flee somewhere with this man, take him to a peaceful place where the spirits could heal his wounds, make him whole once again.

As his tongue trailed down her throat past the hollow and into the valley between her breasts, she imagined that lovely place where deer and lion walked together, where the spirit of all those who had passed into Ghost country gathered to ease the pain of those left to survive on this sometimes harsh mother earth.

His mouth closed around one nipple and she held his head there and offered him the sustenance of her soul.

She lay back, arched her body, and he followed to lie beside her, mouth still at her breast.

She stroked his hair and held him close.

He moved, turned his head, and spoke her name, voice blurry and soft, as if he still dwelled with his dreams and visions. "Rachel? My God, is that you? My sweet, beautiful love. I dreamed you were dead."

She didn't dare awaken him fully, for to do so could cause him to leave his soul behind. She ran her hands over his sweaty back, and let him pull her closer until she felt the fullness of his desire.

That strong, pulsing male part of him frightened her, for she saw that what had begun as comfort had turned into something else entirely.

Stricken by the size of him, she pushed away, cupped his face, and whispered softly. "You must sleep now, my love."

The words were out, amazing her in their simple truth. This could never be. Never.

His arms tightened around her until she couldn't move away. If he forced himself on her she could never stop him continuing to the end.

"Rachel?" His voice came stronger. He had emerged from the trance of dreaming and let her go. Wiping one hand down over his face, he scrambled to his feet. "My God, what . . . ?"

She stood, realized her nakedness, and ran to where the quilt hung over a wheel of the wagon. Hurriedly she wrapped it around herself, but as she started to climb back into the safety of her bed, he grabbed her from behind.

Her throat went dry. "No, no, no," she whispered huskily.

"I'm sorry. I'm so sorry. It's the damned dreams. Did I hurt you?"

"No."

"Then what did I do? How did we . . . ? Dammit, Rachel, tell me something."

"It was nothing. Nothing. Do not worry about it." She wanted him to leave it right there, not say any more, for she sensed that if she spoke much more about it she would be back in his arms. Nothing had ever affected her so much, driven her almost beyond her own power to control what her body and mind did.

"This is why . . . goddammit, this is why I didn't want you to come with me. Do you see now? I must be crazy, and I should not be around people. Especially not you."

She paused, turned, and laid a palm on his cheek. "Daniel Wolfe, you are not crazy. You simply need to return to the spirits what is theirs, and take what they will give you."

He tossed his head, puzzled. "I don't know anything about spirits, I just don't want to hurt you, ever."

In the dark she couldn't see him very well, but the tone of his voice told her of his torment. She wanted to tell him that he would never hurt her because he loved her, but she was afraid. Afraid that love was no barrier to hurt, and further afraid that the love he spoke of was only connected to whatever demons haunted him.

Besides, she herself must continue to hate this man for what he stood for, for what he was to her people. Even if she did love him. The kind of love that wished for him a release from his torment might not endure once he was freed. Compassion could indeed feel much like love, especially in women who just naturally want to care for the weak, the sick, and wounded.

So she shook off that tentative hand that lay lightly on her shoulder and climbed back in the wagon. But she didn't sleep the rest of the night, and neither did he. She knew that for she kept peeking through a gap in the canvas to see him hunched beside the fire, staring into its blistering flames, which he kept fed until breakfast.

Come dawn he would find another place for her. Daniel knew with certainty that such a move was his only choice. He could have hurt her, killed her, and he didn't even remember anything but the dream until he awoke with his arms locked around her and her trying to get loose. God, suppose he had hurt her?

An agony grew within his heart, for he would miss her company. Miss the way she skipped along beside the wagon, the cheerfulness with which she completed even the most simple of tasks, the soft rustling of her moving about above him after he bedded down for the night.

The next morning, she dressed and was gone before he could speak to her. And when he returned with the horses, his breakfast was on a warm stone in the fire. He did not know where she'd gone and didn't see her again until they were well under way.

Today they would reach the message stone. Word had been passed that anyone wishing to leave letters for folks back home should have them ready by mid-afternoon. Rachel wanted to write to her grandmother and her friend Alice, but she had no paper or pen.

The desire was so strong, especially after the emotional turmoil of the night before, that she took her courage in hand and approached the tall, regal woman she had seen Daniel dance with that night they reached the Verdigris, the same night she had been discovered and allowed to continue in Daniel's wagon. Now, he said she couldn't ride with him anymore, and she didn't quite know what to do. But first she must write her letters.

When she approached the Von Finster breakfast fire, Zoe only nodded, then turned away. The other sister, who scowled most of the time and held her lips so tightly they all but disappeared between her teeth, surprisingly spoke to Rachel with some warmth.

"It's so good to meet you at last. My name is Minna, and that is my sister Zoe." She gestured at the receding back. "And you must forgive her, she lacks proper manners."

Alice had told Rachel how much store educated whites put in proper manners, and so she bobbed her head at Minna Von Finster. "How do you do?"

Though ugly on the outside, Minna was much prettier than her sister inside, where it counted.

"I come to ask a favor. I would like to leave a letter at the message stone for my grandmother and another for my friend who attends Miss Sawyer's Seminary in Fayetteville. But I have no paper or writing instrument."

"Just wait a moment, I'll be happy to lend you a pen and ink." Minna immediately fetched the items. A smile flooded her brown eyes with genuine warmth.

"May I write them in my wagon and return these to you?"

Minna touched her hand. "Of course, dear. And again, I want to apologize for my sister's actions. Papa has allowed us to bring along our piano. Perhaps you would like to join us one evening for music."

"Oh, that would be wonderful," Rachel said. "Thank you, again." The strident objection of the other sister chased her from the Von Finsters'.

"Minna, dear, wouldn't it be wise to ask the . . . uh . . . that Indian girl to remain here to write her letters, such as they may be. She will probably just draw a few pictures, since to my knowledge she has never attended the seminary and couldn't possibly know how to write."

Embarrassment surged into Rachel's throat, burning like fire.

"Zoe, watch your manners," Minna scolded. "She'll hear you. You needn't act so superior. One would think you'd know by now that the Cherokee people are quite intelligent and civilized. Why, they have their own written language."

Rachel didn't tarry to hear more. She wanted to leap astride Zoe and pound on her, but that wouldn't go far in convincing her that what her sister said was indeed true and the Cherokees were civilized. Besides, she did so want to write her letters, and such action would certainly put an end to that.

She simply kept walking, head held high, cheeks flaming hot. When she returned to Daniel's wagon, he was stowing the utensils he'd used for breakfast. He glanced up at her and scowled.

"I thought you'd run away . . . after last night."

She'd hoped he wouldn't bring that up. As far as she was concerned it didn't need discussing. "No, I borrowed pen and paper to write to grandmother and Alice."

He was silent a moment, then just as she decided he would say no more and started to climb aboard, he spoke. "Rachel, I think it would be best if we could find someone else for you to ride with. Surely one of the Cherokees would allow you to finish up the trip to California with them. As I told you, I'm going on north to Oregon anyway and—"

"I don't wish to ride with the Cherokee. I'm half white and that part of me wants to ride with someone who is white."

"Others are white besides me."

"They wouldn't have a raggedy—"

He shook his finger at her. "Don't say it, girl." A twinkle in his eye gave him away and one corner of his mouth twitched. He hated like hell to banish her, for he truly enjoyed her company when things were going well. But last night had frightened him badly.

"Raggedy-assed Indian," she mocked, and jumped up into the wagon, carefully balancing the well of ink so as not to spill any.

"You won't be able to write in the wagon with it moving. Why don't you wait until we stop for nooning?"

She sighed with relief. At least he would not carry out his threat as yet. She would change his mind.

When the train halted at midday, Rachel located a spreading oak tree under which was a large flat boulder and sat down to write. She was partway through the second letter, this one to Alice, when Zoe Von Finster appeared, striding toward her with her skirts lifted in clenched fists and a dark scowl on her face.

"There you are, you impossible little ragamuffin. How dare you keep my sister's things half the day? When you took them, we supposed you would return them straightaway, and here you are, still lingering. Perhaps you could tell me what you wish to write and I will do it for you. That will make it much quicker, don't you think. And then I can return the pen and ink to Minerva before you damage or lose either of them."

At first, the attack so stunned Rachel that she could find no reply. By the time the words came, Zoe was actually tugging the pen from her grasp and going for the open bottle of ink. It toppled and spilled on Rachel's skirt. She watched in horror as the ugly black liquid spread over the beautiful skirt her grandmother had given her.

"Look what you've done, you little scamp. Now, who's going to replace that ink?"

Rachel came up off the ground in a fury, threw herself at Zoe and knocked her to the ground. The woman began to screech like a wounded animal. Rachel grabbed two great handfuls of the thick bun of hair, knocking Zoe to the ground. They rolled over and over, Rachel kicking and clawing while Zoe screamed.

Rough hands finally pulled them apart, Herr Von Finster holding Rachel off his daughter while L. J. Wyatte saw to Minna's bruises and lumps. Her dress was ripped off one shoulder, and the carefully coiffed hair hung in ragged disarray over her face and down her back. A few dead leaves dangled from the locks, more clung to the back of her skirt, and blood trickled from one nostril.

Wyatte glared at Rachel and raised his voice to be heard above Zoe's wailing, "Look what you've done to Miss Zoe. What do you have to say for yourself?"

Rachel shook free of Von Finster. "She started it, ask her what she has to say."

Before they could stop her she whirled and ran back to Daniel's wagon, so angry she could scarcely catch her breath.

Chapter Six

Daniel couldn't bring himself to arrange for Rachel's transfer to another wagon right away. He had only gotten as far as considering which of the travelers he might ask to carry her when she stormed into camp with a huge black stain on her skirt.

Ranting, pacing in a wide circle, she threw her arms about. He had no idea what had happened. Much of what she said was incomprehensible to him, for he didn't understand Cherokee. The gist of the story, however, that she had been involved in a physical battle with Zoe Von Finster finally emerged.

"So that's what I heard," he said when she paused for breath. "I thought someone was beating their mule, all the screaming and hollering."

"Hlesdi, uk'ten'. It is not a laughing matter." Flushed, she glared at him.

"Don't call me names, I didn't attack you, she did."

"I didn't call you names, exactly." Her mood mellowed some and she glanced up at him from under her lashes. "I only asked you to quit. And then, well . . ." She smiled crookedly despite her anger. *"Uk'ten'* is just sort of a monster, that's all."

"Sort of a monster?"

She nodded.

Sadly he picked leaves from her hair. He would miss her so much. "What sort of monster?"

"A huge snake with wings and . . . this is serious,

Daniel. She poured ink all over me. Look, see what it did to my beautiful skirt? Then she said I spilled it. Oh, Daniel, you should have seen her. How mean she is, how hateful. I should have tossed her right off the hill, rolled her all the way to the bottom, stomped out her liver. Then when she got up she wouldn't have been so quick to accuse me."

"I doubt that. You would only have made matters worse than they already are."

"I didn't cause it, Daniel. No matter what they tell you. You have to believe me." She looked all around, eyes growing wide. "Where are my letters? I forgot all about them, and now she's made me lose them."

Fury blazed over her features once again and she let out a long tirade in Cherokee. He figured it was probably a good thing he didn't understand her, for blue fire sparked from her eyes, and the incomprehensible words spewed from her mouth like lead shot from a muzzle loader. Bam, bam, bam, only faster than he knew he could ever reload.

He took her by the shoulders and was stunned by his reaction to the touch. Her heat, the passion and fury charged through his arms as if he'd been struck by bolts of lightning. He didn't let go and she began to tremble.

"Whoa up, Rachel, before you bust."

Her mouth dropped open on the next word. Occasionally someone said something in the white man's tongue that was foreign to her, and his use of "bust" brought her up short.

"Bust? I thought this was bust." She cupped under her breasts and raised them.

He glanced down at the provocative pose, thought perhaps if he just lay his head there they could put an end to all this nonsense, forget the fight and her anger.

He resisted the temptation and turned his attention back to the matter at hand. "Yes, well, it is. Actually,

I was inaccurate. The term is 'burst,' not 'bust.' I was speaking white man's slang."

She understood that, and also that he had managed to veer her off the subject once again.

Taking advantage of the lull, Daniel patted her shoulder. "That's better. Now, is Miss Von Finster injured badly?"

Jerking from his touch, she exploded again. "You did not ask if I am injured."

He laughed in spite of himself. "Look at you, girl. Do you appear to be injured? Of course you don't, or you couldn't be ranting on like you are. You're walking, you're talking."

"Well." She inspected her hands and arms and ran her fingers over her face and down her throat. "I guess not. I didn't hurt her, but next time I will."

"There won't be a next time, miss," the curt voice of Sergeant Cletus McCrea said.

He and wagon master L. J. Wyatte, along with James Vann and the tall, good-looking young second lieutenant Peter Mankins, approached. Before much could be said, Captain Lewis Evans arrived with his first lieutenant Thomas Tyner.

"Well, child, I see you've attracted plenty of attention," Evans boomed in his strong voice.

Rachel took a step forward and stuck out her chin. "I didn't hurt her. She started it."

Daniel stepped up beside her and put an arm around her waist. "Sir, I'm sure this won't happen again. It was simply a misunderstanding."

"Probably," mused Evans. "Whatever the reason, we can't allow dissension of any kind. Where law and order break down, anarchy is not far behind." His eyes flicked toward Rachel.

"Young lady, you will appear before the committee of twelve this eve after we are settled for the night.

They will hear your story and Miss Von Finster's as well, and come to a decision as to your punishment."

Rachel sputtered. "Punishment? You speak of my punishment before you even find out if I am guilty?"

Though he agreed with her in theory, Daniel tightened his hold. If she didn't shut up she would dig herself a deeper hole.

Not surprisingly, she shrugged him off. "I should have expected that your justice, white man's justice, wouldn't be fair to a Cherokee."

"Six of the committee will be Cherokee," Tyner said. "And there will be no punishment that isn't well deserved." He glanced at his superior, who nodded minutely, then the lieutenant went on. "You will be summoned this evening. Please be ready when someone comes for you."

She turned from the man's unyielding stare. "Daniel?"

"It's all right. They won't whip you." He glanced up from her worried gaze. "Will you, gentlemen?"

Evans replied, "We, sir, are more civilized than the likes of that. The young lady is not a slave, after all. Is she?"

Rachel gasped and covered her mouth. If they learned she was Jasper Doaks's property, then would they whip her? Suppose they found out she belonged to him. She knew the meaning of "slave," all right. Even rich Cherokee had black white men as slaves. These men would whip her and return her to Doaks. She tried to run, but Daniel held her tight.

"She'll be there, Captain," he said curtly, then turned her forcibly around and marched her to the wagon. In her ear he said, "Get in and stay there. I don't want you out of my sight until we stop tonight. If you run, I'll come after you myself."

Gritting her teeth, she flounced from his grasp and scrambled into the wagon, crawling as far back in the corner as she could manage. In there with the kegs of vinegar and molasses and a barrel of crackers.

He had betrayed her. Would serve her up to these whites like scraps to a mongrel dog. And they would tie her to a tree and lash her until her back ran rivers of blood. Then they would throw dirt in her wounds and toss her in the next river. After that they would drag her out and tie her on the end of a rope and haul her back to Doaks behind a pony. In a loud voice so he could hear, she called Daniel everything she could think of in Cherokee, from son of a dog, to coyote who eats dung, but he didn't understand a word she said. She was sorry the language didn't furnish curse words and so tried out a few in the white man's tongue. She had learned well from the likes of Jasper Doaks.

Standing outside the wagon, contemplating his next move, Daniel heard and understood the last of the outburst and smiled grimly.

Poor little mite. Probably scared right out of her britches about now. Imagining all sorts of things. She might run too, and so he'd have to watch her. He hadn't taken her in only to see her perish in the wilderness all alone. What in the hell had that snooty Zoe done to get Rachel's dander up so bad? Accidentally spilling ink all over her skirt couldn't have caused such an uproar. There was certainly more to this little episode than met the eye. It was worth pondering because it took his mind off his actions of the night before, and what he was going to ultimately have to do about the situation between himself and the fiery Cherokee girl.

Daniel decided to call on Zoe before the committee met that evening to try to soften her up a bit. Would such a visit be ethical, considering that she'd been quite amenable to his attentions the night they'd danced together? He didn't know, but would do it anyway, for Rachel's sake.

At first Zoe refused to come out of her wagon when her father beckoned her. Herr Von Finster was a tall, angular man with pale, thin hair and blue eyes, the kind that usually sparkle. His didn't. It was clear that he thought a lot of his two daughters. Three brothers also hovered nearby, as if they might be needed to protect their sister from this rugged mountain man. Inwardly Daniel was amused. His looks were often deceiving and certainly concealed his past quite well, especially when he was decked out in buckskins with the bowie hanging on his hip. Life on the frontier could be tough, and he'd quickly learned to be tougher, or at least to appear so.

Zoe finally emerged when Von Finster told her that her visitor was Daniel Wolfe. She carried a delicate white kerchief which she held under one eye. It appeared quite black and swollen.

Daniel cringed, bowed slightly, and removed his hat. "Miss Von Finster, are you recovering?"

"I will, when that dreadful heathen gets her just rewards."

This didn't look too promising. He plowed on. "I wanted to express my regrets about the incident. I'm sure that Rachel misunderstood your ministrations. You are too kind a woman, I would wager, to actually be rude to a young, innocent girl."

"Innocent, sir?" Zoe's eyes flashed. "She bloodied my nose, blacked my eye, and ruined my dress, not to mention that she literally tried to scalp me."

One of her brothers gasped. Minna stepped down from the wagon about then. "Zoe, I seriously doubt that. Cherokee people don't scalp their enemies."

"Well, just look at me. She pulled my hair quite viciously. I suppose you want to tell me they don't fight either?"

Minna chuckled. She obviously was not nearly as bothered by the occurrence as the rest of her family. It appeared that Zoe was the spoiled and pampered one, while Minna the no-nonsense tough one who didn't mind seeing Zoe get her comeuppance once in a while.

"This is not a laughing matter, my dear sister. I've taught those little vagabonds long enough to know they will resort to just about anything to come out on top. Despite their hair bows and dresses they are ornery little scrappers, those girls that attend the seminary."

"Zoe, you should be ashamed. Indian children are as well behaved as any I've seen. They dress in fine clothing, they are neat and clean and well-mannered. Why are you saying these things?"

"What do you know?" Zoe spat. "You only have them one at a time to teach their stubby little awkward fingers to chop away at piano keys, as if they could ever learn Mozart or Bach. You've never had to deal with them in groups."

Minna put her hands on her hips and pinned her sister with a harsh stare. "Oh, I beg your pardon. I didn't realize Rachel came at you in a group."

One of the brothers snickered.

Zoe whirled from Minna and gazed up at Daniel, voice softening pathetically. "I want to thank you for your concern. I know you must feel somewhat responsible, seeing as how you agreed to keep her. I'm sure this behavior will cause you to change your mind."

The look she gave him spoke volumes on what she thought of his keeping a young woman in his wagon. Daniel didn't care to get into it.

Instead he twisted the brim of his hat through both hands for a moment before replying. "Miss Von Finster, I would ask that you request they not punish the girl too harshly. I would consider it a great favor to me. She's frightened and alone. She has endured a lot in her short life, and we should try to make up to her and her people what we put them through."

Zoe straightened her shoulders and lifted her head. "I put her through nothing, sir. Is it my fault that the Indian doesn't have enough sense about him to know the value of gold, the value of his land? So that it takes the white man with all his education and superior intelligence to develop that land? That, sir, is none of my doing. I didn't herd her people off the valuable land and put them here." She swung her arm around to indicate the surrounding countryside. "You are to be commended for your concern for the savages, however, Mr. Wolfe."

"Daniel," he murmured.

"And you may call me Zoe," she returned demurely, and once again patted the bruised eye with the delicate handkerchief.

The turnaround gave him little hope. The woman's judgments were harsh, and even as she flirted with him, he knew she would give Rachel Keye no quarter. He nodded, screwed the hat down on his head with a great deal of frustration, and hurried back to his wagon. He'd already been gone longer than he planned and hoped to hell Rachel was still there. He wasn't in the mood to saddle up and go after a runway.

When he arrived Second Lieutenant Peter Mankins stood between the wagon and the fire, hands clasped at his back in a loose at ease. He was a formidable man, standing six and a half feet tall with thick shoulders and thighs. Daniel decided he wouldn't want to go up against the man, though he was pleasant enough. Rachel was nowhere in sight.

"Where is she, sir?" Mankins asked sharply, coming to attention.

"Isn't she in the wagon?"

"I called and got no reply. I do not intrude into a lady's quarters."

"I'll get her, then," Daniel said, and prayed he would. She'd better be there.

He bounded onto the tailgate, which he'd lowered earlier, and peered inside. She was there all right, all dressed in fresh clothes, her hair brushed to a shine.

She touched it self-consciously. "I thought it would be all right if I used the brush. It was right there."

He held out a hand. "You look fine. Come on now, let's get this over with."

"Daniel, what will they do to me? I didn't mean to really hurt her, and she is such a terrible woman."

Nodding, he took her hand and felt it tremble in his. "Oh, Rachel. It's going to be okay. I won't let them hurt you." He pulled her close and held her, her head resting on his chest. For a brief moment he closed his eyes and imagined her as his woman, the one he would protect and love and cherish for all time. It was a fleeting fantasy, and he shoved it away to repeat his last words. "I promise I won't let them hurt you. Now, come on and take your medicine."

The twelve members of the committee were seated on camp stools, six abreast in two rows near the large central campfire. A pot of coffee bubbled in hot coals, the steam putting off a pungent aroma. The cozy fragrance did little to calm Rachel. She tried to shut out visions of what these men might do to her, and stood proud and straight, boldly meeting the eyes of those who would judge her.

Zoe Von Finster strode into the clearing after everyone else had settled. It seemed to Rachel that every member of the train, Cherokee and white man alike, had gathered to watch. Even the woman Etta Claridge, wife of James Aaron Claridge, stood on the fringes. It was the first time Rachel had seen the woman many spoke of quite fondly. She was the only wife to accompany her husband on this trek.

Evans officiated at the trial. Daniel insisted on standing beside Rachel, as Herr Von Finster was allowed to remain with his daughter.

"Miss Von Finster has accused you of attacking her without provocation," Evans said to Rachel. "Do you understand what that means?"

Lips tight, Rachel glared first at Zoe then at Evans.

Daniel nudged her.

She favored him with the same look.

He gestured and mouthed some words.

"Let her speak for herself, Mr. Wolfe," Evans said. "Well, miss, we are waiting."

"Keye," Rachel said.

"Beg pardon?"

"Miss Keye. She's Miss Von Finster, he's Mr. Wolfe, I'm Miss Keye."

A corner of Evans's mouth quirked, but the amused expression didn't reach his blue eyes. "Miss Keye," he said formally.

"Thank you."

Everyone waited, looking at her.

"Would you answer the question, Miss Keye?"

"What question?"

"Rachel," Daniel growled, and the nudge was more forceful.

"I asked if you understood what Miss Von Finster has accused you of?"

"Yes, but I do not understand why because she is the one who struck first."

"What?" Zoe asked. "I did no such thing. She flew at me like a wild animal before I had a chance to defend myself. She almost pulled every hair out of my head."

"That will be enough." Evans's voice boomed, quieting the murmurs and the muffled laughter.

Daniel gripped Rachel's upper arm.

She jerked free.

Evans finally elicited the responses he required and each woman told her version of the fight that by this time had been told and retold around every supper fire so that no one actually had any idea of what had really happened.

The committee strolled away a few paces, huddled for a few minutes, heads shaking back and forth, up and down, then they returned.

"Have you reached a decision, gentlemen?" Evans asked.

"Yes, sir," the Cherokee Martin Schrimsher said. "We have decided that Miss Von Finster must replace Miss Keye's ruined skirt with a suitable garment, and Miss Keye must serve on the wood-gathering detail for a period of two weeks."

Rachel turned to Daniel. "Is that all?" she whispered.

"All? That's tough detail, gathering wood. And sometimes it'll be buffalo chips if there's no wood."

"I thought they would make me go back . . . go back to that terrible man. I truly did."

She looked up at him with eyes brimming over, and he saw how terrified she had been. Wood detail appeared mild to a woman who might well have imagined the cruelest of treatment at the hands of a monster.

She began to shake and take deep breaths. "I can gather wood, it is easy. I can do that. And then will they let me come back to your wagon?"

He put an arm around her waist and felt her go limp against him. God, the poor child.

Right there in front of everyone, he lifted her into his arms and carried her away from the judgment. She cried great jagged sobs and buried her face in his shirt till it was soaked with her tears. She nestled against him, the buckskin of his shirt fisted in both hands.

He lay her inside the wagon on the bed he had made within the supplies for her to sleep on, but she wouldn't let go of his shirt, and so he settled beside her. He tried to ignore her hot breath against his chest, the tickle of hair on his chin, and the ragged sobs that faded slowly.

Sometime in the night she awoke and removed her skirt and shift, then curled back up within the sleeping man's embrace.

When he awoke to the blare of the trumpet that sounded wake up each day, he found her lying naked in his arms. There would never be any explaining how he felt at that moment. How her being there like that, open and trusting, gave him a special pride within himself. Not a pride of what he was exactly, but a realization that she must see something good within him, noble even, that she would put herself at such risk. She had seen him at his worst of times and yet could fall asleep in his arms.

He took her small hand in his and held it to his mouth, then kissed the palm and the inside of her wrist. The steady thrum of her heartbeat caressed his lips. Eyes closed, he could imagine their hearts beating in rhythm, one only existing because of the other. Gently, fleetingly, he stroked his fingertips down into the hollow between her breasts.

She stirred and moved into his touch. Her hand found his and placed it over one breast, then she sighed and lifted a leg so that it rested across his thigh.

Sleeping with her in his arms had kept the monsters of his dreams at bay. But morning had come, bringing reality with it. He put her aside gently and climbed out to greet another day.

She soon arose, and as she emerged, Lieutenant

Mankins showed up leading a mule. He grinned broadly at Rachel. "This is hers."

"What is that for?" she asked, entranced by the animal who looked at her with soft brown eyes, big lop ears perked forward. He had a white chin with a fuzz of whiskers and stood no taller than eight or nine hands.

"To gather wood. Sometimes you have to cross the river. They will show you. You must come soon." Mankins glanced at Daniel, obviously embarrassed. "She will not ride with you until her sentence is up."

"Wait, where will I sleep?"

"Under the supply wagon, ma'am, with the others."

"Whoa," Daniel said. "Just hold on there. You can't mean you'd put this young girl under there with men to sleep?"

Mankins glanced quickly at Daniel's wagon, then blushed. "Sir, the slaves help gather wood."

Rachel swallowed painfully. They knew after all, they had just been teasing.

"Slaves?" Daniel took a step toward Mankins and hoped like hell he would not have to fight with the giant of a young man.

Mankins didn't budge, his hands continued to hang loosely at his sides. He feared nothing, that was clear. "Some of the Cherokee brought their slaves."

"And you expect her to work and sleep with black men? I think we'd better have a talk with your captain."

"As you wish, sir."

Daniel grabbed her hand and dragged her along, following Mankins past each and every wagon, one snugged up against the other to form a tight circle, tongues lying to the outside. At Evans's wagon, which traveled at the head of the procession, Mankins signaled them to wait. As did many others

Evans had a tent pitched within the circle, and he was sitting inside eating his breakfast from a tin plate.

Almost everyone else was still eating as well. A few men though already led teams from the corral toward their wagons in preparation for getting underway.

Mankins spoke through the partially opened flap. "Sir, Mr. Wolfe wishes to see you."

"Ah, yes. Well, it can wait until I finish. What's it about?"

"The girl, sir. He doesn't—"

Daniel, still hanging on to Rachel, went to join Mankins, but the man filled the entire tent opening so he couldn't see past him. "I don't wish her sleeping with men, sir," he said in a loud voice.

Rachel jerked her hand free. "Let me speak."

Mankins moved aside for her and gazed down in rapt attention when she spoke. She had obviously enchanted this man too.

Anger flooded her, she knotted her fists and took a deep breath. "I will gather your wood, I will work hard and carry out the punishment, but I do not see why I cannot sleep where I have been sleeping. I too do not wish to sleep with men, and it does not matter if they are black white men or slaves or Cherokee like me. I have never lain with a man. You cannot make me do so."

Evans came out of the tent, eyes blazing. "Girl, no one has ever caused as much trouble as you. For as little as you are, you sure do cut a wide swath. It is my understanding that you have been sleeping with this man since you stowed away on this wagon train, however, we do not wish to make a whore out of you. Henry Rattlingourd has offered the safety of his wagon, which travels just behind the supply wagon.

He is an honorable man of your race, and will not sleep in the wagon with you.

"Is that satisfactory to the both of you?" The words were sharper than the edge of Daniel's bowie.

But Rachel swelled beside him. "You are a captain, so I would guess that makes you a soldier. So it is no wonder that you are so rude and stupid."

Daniel shook her arm.

She jerked free, as mad at him as at the rest of them. "Leave me be, all of you. I will say what I will do and won't do. I will say what I have done. I have not lain with this man in the way you mean. You would not accuse Miss Von Finster of such action, so why do you accuse me?"

"Miss Von Finster has not been sleeping in Mr. Wolfe's wagon," Evans shot back.

The two went at it toe to toe, and Rachel's fury overpowered her fear of the evening before. "My father was a white man, and I am half as white as she."

"This has nothing to do with your color, ma'am," Mankins said soothingly.

"Stay out of this, Lieutenant." Evans swung on Rachel. "You will serve your time gathering wood, and you will sleep in Rattlingourd's wagon and you will not open your mouth to me once more, or by God I'll have you trussed and hauled back to Tahlequah if I have to send a regiment to get it done. Is that clear?"

The threat did her in. She whirled, grabbed the reins on the mule, and headed away from Evans.

The mule had other ideas and stood his ground, so that when she reached the end of the reins, she was yanked to a stop. She remained there for a moment, trying to think what she could do without turning around so they could see her face.

"Come on, Dagasi. Can you not move?" Since she didn't look at the mule when she spoke, how could he know she called him a terrapin? He only regarded her with a stubborn patience. He understood her no more than she understood these white men, Daniel included.

Fury spent, she turned to deal with this little animal that would probably be her companion for the rest of the trip, for she couldn't imagine that she would be able to curb her temper well enough to escape wood-gathering duty forever. The captain was a soldier, and she was lucky he hadn't beaten her to the ground, then stomped on her. Even with Daniel standing right there, for he appeared to have lost his voice in light of the captain's orders.

Ignoring the men who hadn't moved since the incident, she bent toward the stubborn mule and breathed into first one flaring nostril then the other. He fluttered rubbery lips at her.

With a small chuckle she tickled under his chin. "Now, you know me and I know you. We will show these white men who know nothing about us, won't we, little Dagasi?"

She moved away. The mule followed her, his nose practically touching her backside.

Daniel turned back to Evans. "Anything happens to her, there'll be hell to pay."

"I should imagine there will," the captain said, his tone no longer cutting. "Keep an eye on her, Mankins."

"Yes, I will, sir."

Though Mankins sounded a little too eager, Daniel felt better. He had no choice but to let the matter stand, and so he went to fetch his team and hitch them. He had a notion he was going to miss Rachel, but the separation might be just what they needed to break the bond forming between them. A bond that could bring both of them nothing but heartache.

Chapter Seven

To Rachel the black white-men slaves appeared very strange. They walked with their heads down and did exactly as they were told, yet they wore no shackles. None would speak to her. There were as many as she had fingers on one hand, but not all of them gathered wood at all times. They served their Cherokee masters as well.

Henry Rattlingourd, whom she had never met, greeted her in the tribe's custom as if she were of a respected family, which her mother and grandmother were. Before long she returned his greetings in the Cherokee language and stopped speaking the white man's tongue. She ate at his campfire, but wasn't expected to do any work for him. He spoke to her of many things, but asked no personal questions at first. It frightened her that she had so easily returned to her old ways.

Henry liked to talk of what he would do when he struck gold, but she could tell by his supplies and the other goods in his wagon that he was already quite wealthy according to the standards of her family.

Gathering wood was usually not difficult. As they headed northwest toward the open prairie, woodlands skirted their trail. It meant that she and Dagasi must walk in the timber, her fetching limbs and bundling them on the mule's back. The most difficult, of course, was when she and Dagasi had to ford the river in order to find their share of wood. She took to wearing the old clothing she had worn before her grandmother had given her the dresses.

All day every day, she carried one load after the next to the wood supply wagon. Around noon she would eat a biscuit filled with whatever had been left from breakfast, and then continue her task. She seldom caught sight of Daniel, and found herself missing him.

On the fourth night while she cleaned her own plate at Henry Rattlingourd's fire, he spoke to her for the first time of personal things.

"Why do you wish to dishonor your people, Winter Dawn?" He used a Cherokee derivative of her name, surprising her with its intimacy.

"I don't." She scrubbed the plate in hot water and sat it near the fire to dry. "Why do you say that?" Settling a respectable distance from him, she stared into the flames.

The evening was warm, a breeze from off the prairie touched her hair and kissed her cheek. With it came the vague but certain odor of buffalo.

Henry talked on. "You leave them to go west. You wish to be white like your father?"

Avoiding the question, she said, "You go west as well."

"Ah, but for a far different reason. I want to take back gold to our people, help them rise from the poverty the white man has imposed. You wish to run away and never return."

The accusation stirred resentment. How did he know what she wanted? Because he was right, the indignation cut deeper. "I am running for a different reason, one I cannot tell you."

"Ah, your brother Eagle."

Surprise washed through her. "You know?"

"I know he is not your white father's son. His father Standing Bear is of the Ani-Waya Clan as is Eagle. He wants the Cherokee to go back to the old ways. Scalping and warring with other tribes, like it was before we knew the white man existed. We were indeed a fearsome warrior people." He smiled at her, an ironic smile. Henry had a true sense of irony. "We learned that to get along with the white man meant becoming like him, so we are civilized now. I fear Eagle will learn many tricks with that wild bunch down in Texas."

"I can only pray he is in Texas." Perhaps he was, perhaps after Daniel and the other man had caught her and Awa'hili together her brother had run away.

She eyed Henry, waiting for him to answer the question about the whereabouts of her brother, but he only moved his shoulders slightly. His skin was much darker than hers, his jaw square and his features blocky. He was only a head or so taller, but broad and strong. He had a gravelly voice that made him sound terse, but she knew he was not.

Three nights later, sitting at the night fire, he said quite unexpectedly, "My wife is in Ghost country."

Rachel had a bite of bread in her mouth at the time and she stopped chewing, jaw bulging as she stared at him. He eyed her with chocolate brown eyes, sorrowful, questioning. Whatever he wanted her to say, she couldn't. After a while, she went on chewing.

The conversation continued as if the important pause hadn't occurred. "Two years now. A disease of the white man. They kill us with more than their guns. Many of us died that year, if you remember."

"My mother."

"I know. It was the same time." He drew in the dirt and glanced up. "I am of the Blue People."

He had given her the reasons she could consider marrying him, and perhaps she should. The idea came wholly unexpected, unbidden by any other considerations such as love, admiration, respect, or desire.

Actually, it would be much easier on her if she married Henry than if she married Daniel. And of course Henry was the only one who had asked. All Daniel had ever done was stir her passions then turn away. Such strange notions flowed through her head lately. And the desires of her body had quickened since meeting Daniel. Henry evoked none. But it was time she chose a man, she was growing much too old to be without one. This would be her nineteenth summer. Henry appeared to have made a choice, the rest was up to her. Together they could go to California. What she had always wanted, but then of course, married to Henry Rattlingourd, she could never pass for white. Worse, she could never be transported to such heights of ecstasy as Daniel had already awakened in her.

She slept that night within wildly rampaging rivers of dreams. In them, the silver-eyed white man with gold in his hair beckoned and pushed aside the Cherokee memories as if they were nothing. Her grandmother pleaded with her to look to her Cherokee heritage, but all she could do was vow to go to the white man. She wanted him so that her body ached with it. The vow to go to him the next evening when she finished gathering wood came in the dream, but she did not forget it when the vision vanished and she awoke.

Zoe Von Finster hadn't left Daniel alone for a moment since Rachel had been sentenced to wood gathering. Anytime he looked up she was there, walking beside him, or perhaps on the other side of the team so that she could keep an eye on him.

The second evening after Rachel left, Zoe brought

him some zingers, slick little dumplings swimming in ivory slices of apples seasoned with a dash of cinnamon. How could a man turn down such a toothsome offering? She didn't stay, but ducked away from the firelight and disappeared almost while he was thanking her in a tongue-tied way. He'd felt like a fool.

The next time she showed up she brought a sourdough biscuit and a slice of pink cured ham.

"I noticed you were eating fatback and thought you might enjoy a treat. My father smoked these last winter, then salted them down to carry along."

Daniel took the napkin-wrapped offering. "I've eaten, but I do thank you." He didn't know what else to say, his mother had raised her three boys to be polite even when at a loss for words.

"For breakfast then," she said, and glanced pointedly at his bedroll beneath the wagon. Fanning herself with a white handkerchief, she lingered. "My, isn't it a warm evening for so early in the year?"

He thought of telling her she was standing too near the fire, but didn't.

Her pale, freckled complexion flushed and she spread one hand over her heart. "My goodness, my heart is simply pounding. Might I sit for just a moment?"

Allowing that, he thought, was a mistake, for from then on every night she either asked him to join them for supper, or after supper, or to go for a walk to protect her from whatever might lurk out there in the dark.

And after a while he kissed her. It was inevitable, though only a brief touching, his hands chastely on her upper arms, their bodies not making contact. He couldn't help comparing it to being with Rachel. He experienced a vivid picture of the girl's lithe, naked body glowing in the firelight, pressed up against him.

Zoe's kiss didn't come off even a distant second, and he was immediately sorry for her and the man she might eventually marry.

Eyes wide, she leaned back and gazed up at him. Obviously, her reaction was far different from his.

"I suppose we ought to tell Papa."

"Papa?" He felt dumbstruck, cornered.

Zoe leaned her head against his shoulder, playfully running her fingers up his chest and under his chin. She tilted her head and with a strong grip guided his mouth down to hers once again.

They had strolled up from the train a ways, up a slight rise. Around them the sky glowed pink and purple and gold.

Finding Daniel's camp deserted, Rachel ducked down and scampered beneath the high wheels of the wagon to the outside of the circle. As she stood up, she saw the couple outlined against the sunset colors. At first she didn't recognize the man and woman, but soon saw that the tall figure whose sandy hair caught the dying light in a halo had to be Daniel, and he was kissing . . . kissing that awful Zoe Von Finster.

Disappointment and anger rooted her to the spot. She wanted to rip the woman's hair out, an action surely to get her further punishment. The captain might not settle for wood gathering the next time. The slaves spoke of when there would be no wood on the plains. Then they would gather buffalo chips most of the day and that evening dig a fire pit in which to burn them. She prayed daily that her time would be finished before that happened. If she attacked Zoe again, it would never be finished. No matter how she felt about the woman fawning over the man she desired, she had to control her instinct to fight for him.

How could he hold that stick of a woman in his

arms? She had skin like flour spotted with weevils, her hair was pulled back so tightly her eyes were slanted, and she always looked as if she had eaten a persimmon not yet ripened by frost. Worst of all her skimpy lips remained pulled into a permanent grimace. And she was old, at least twenty-five, maybe more.

Pleading with all the spirits that neither Daniel nor Zoe would see her and demean her even more, Rachel backed silently away. As soon as she felt safe, she turned and ran as fast as she had run the night Jasper Doaks had chased her through the streets of Fayetteville right to the feet of Daniel Wolfe.

But instead of Daniel she ran smack into the tall, broad, and slightly embarrassed Peter Mankins.

He held on to her arms for a moment until she stopped tottering, then took a step backward and doffed his hat. "Beg pardon, ma'am. Are you all right?"

Rachel liked the bashful second lieutenant. He always treated her with respect. But she was so upset over seeing Daniel and Zoe in each other's arms that she darted around him and ran on. She could hear him following along and stopped.

"Why are you following me? Do you want something?"

"No, ma'am. Well, that is, er . . . no, ma'am. But you see, I'm supposed to keep watch over you."

"Keep watch over me? Who said?"

"Captain Evans, ma'am."

"Why?"

Mankins looked down at the ground and didn't answer.

"Why, Lieutenant? Does Evans think I will somehow get out of my punishment?"

"I'm sorry. It wasn't my idea, and believe me, while I don't mind in the least keeping an eye on you, pretty as you are, I don't think you're a shirker. You work as hard as any of those blacks, far as I can see. But, ma'am, don't you think it best I keep doing it just in case any of them get the wrong idea? Pretty as you are, that is."

Rachel regarded the tall, handsome young man for a moment, then touched his arm. "That's very nice of you, Lieutenant. Thank you."

He lifted her hand from his arm and raised it to his lips. "You're welcome, Miss Keye. I'll wish you a good night, now."

He followed her when she continued toward Henry's wagon. Inside, Rachel reverently lifted Bone Woman's leather bag from around her neck and opened it. Henry let her burn one of the star candles inside if she was very careful, and she had melted a little wax to hold it firmly on top of a barrel of crackers. The flickering wick cast an eerie glow inside the domed canvas.

One by one she fingered through the mysterious contents of her grandmother's bag: the bones of a small snake, a leathery patch of the skin of something she hoped wasn't human, two smooth black stones through which she could see the candle flame, a tooth that appeared to be canine, maybe that of a wolf, a gallstone from a deer, and downy feathers drawn together in a puffy ball.

She picked up the smooth stone, squeezed it in one hand and closed her eyes, concentrating very hard. Nothing happened. She expected at the least to experience a brief vision. After all, Little Deer had come to her in the night. That proved she had her grandmother's exceptional gift. At this moment, she wanted to be a witch more than anything else in the world. She wanted to do something very clever and discomforting to that Zoe Von Finster without being blamed for it.

But no matter how she arranged the charms, how she held them, and she tried everything from clasping them to her heart, eyes, and breasts to chanting over them, she felt nothing but remorse for Daniel's betrayal. Maybe it would take a while. Perhaps Zoe would fall in the next river they crossed and be floated off to some distant village, or break out in some devilishly itchy and ugly rash. Finally, Rachel gave up and placed all the objects back in the bag and hung it around her neck once more. She was very careful to blow out the candle and pinch the wick cool before stowing it away and lying down to sleep. She had marked off the white man's measuring of days and knew that only three remained before she could return to Daniel's wagon. If he preferred Zoe, though, she could not go back to him. She had to come up with something by then.

It was during her last night of punishment that Eagle returned. Early that morning she rose before dawn, dressed, and slipped out to the corral to fetch Dagasi. The mule whickered and came to meet her. She hated telling this new friend good-bye, and repeated her promise that she would visit on a regular basis. As was her habit, she rode the small creature from the encampment to the edge of the woods. A guard noticed her, waved, and watched her out of sight.

They were currently traveling along the Cottonwood Creek and there was plenty of wood. Soon the rolling hills would give way to a flat, unending prairie. Some of the men who had ridden this way before spoke of it with awe, and she listened in wonderment and anticipation.

Like an ocean, they said. Stretching in all directions, nothing to bar the view, not a tree in sight. In the fall, they said, the golden grasses grew as high as a man's shoulder and danced in the wind, swaying in a strange tempo of dramatic swirls; a majestic and breathtaking sight. Each day she searched the horizon to be the first to spot this legendary prairie.

Cottonwood is a brittle tree that doesn't live too long. The gentlest of winds cracks limbs from its trunk even as it causes the leaves to sing like rain falling. She rode Dagasi into the dark fringe of whispering trees along the bank of the creek. Unexpectedly, the mule held back, snorted, and tossed his head.

She glanced around and didn't see Peter Mankins anywhere, which she thought odd, since he had continued his watch of her pretty much out in the open. Perhaps Evens had sent him on an errand. It was, after all, her last day. There was little danger of her escaping punishment when it was all but finished.

She addressed the little mule. "Don't want to work this morning, lazy one? Hey, ha." She nudged his ribs, and when he refused to move, slid from his back and tugged at the reins. Clearly, he didn't want to go into the woods. After much cajoling he followed along, eyes rolling.

She spotted a tangle of dead limbs caught up in a growth of sand plum bushes frosted in white blossoms. Turning the reins loose she inched into the thick brush and leaned forward to grab at the smaller limbs.

An arm snaked around her waist, a sweaty hand clamped over her mouth. Behind her Dagasi screamed and ran away, crashing through the trees, leaving behind only the sounds of her struggle, the muted grunts of her aggressor.

Tight against her ear so that his moving lips left her flesh wet, he said, "Hold, little sister. Do not be afraid. You must listen. Be still and listen."

She went slack. He bent forward, supporting all her weight, and she kicked backward hard, her heels connecting with his shins. He grunted, crouched before her. She panted and watched him for a moment in silence, then caught her breath.

"What are you doing here? Someone will see you."

"I come to take you home to Grandmother. I cannot let you do this thing. Besides, Doaks will find you if you do not leave this white man's train. Go home with me now. Go back to your people, my sister. Winter Dawn." He spoke the Cherokee words in a weary voice.

Across his cheek an ugly wound, scarcely healed, pulled the corner of his left eye down.

She went to him. "You're hurt. What happened? Who did this?"

He turned his head from her to hide the wound. "Never mind. It is of no importance."

"What is, then, my brother? You betray your people, yet you expect me to return to the poverty, to live a life that you yourself refuse to live."

He raised his eyes to the lightening sky. "I am a warrior, I will fight in the only way left to me. You must survive as a daughter of the Cherokee."

"I am not a daughter of the Cherokee. I am white." She whirled and tried to run away, but he grabbed her.

"If you will not go then I have no choice but to tie you and drag you back. It is my duty as the eldest man of our family. You will not lie with this white man while I have breath in my body."

Before she could cry out for help, he clamped his hand once more over her mouth. "I will not hurt you, but you will go home with me, little one. I did not carry you to our new home in the Nation to have you do this terrible thing."

In his tone, the strain of his burdens rang clear. She understood, and yet she hated what he was trying to do to her.

He gagged her, trussed both hands behind her back, and stood her on her feet. "Now you will come with me. Or do I have to carry you once again?"

She shook her head miserably and stumbled along beside him.

Dagasi would go back to camp, Daniel and the others would come searching for her. But did she really want that? The idea that Eagle and Daniel might one day face each other in combat terrified her, for no matter the outcome, she would not rejoice.

Where were Eagle's friends who had ridden with him earlier? Had they deserted him? And why did he continue to talk of Jasper Doaks as if he were coming after her?

They crossed the creek, which was swollen from spring rains. Rocks along the bottom were slick and twice she stumbled, almost fell. She could do nothing trussed up this way. Nothing except exactly what he told her. Across the creek, and back the way the train had come, they reached his camp. And she had been right, he was alone. His painted pony waited. He led her to it and bent to boost her onto the animal's back. Then he changed his mind and untied her hands first so she could mount on her own. The pony's reins in hand, he started off back down the trail toward the Indian Nation.

For many miles they moved away from Daniel and the train to California. She searched her mind trying to think of a way to convince Eagle that he must let her search for her new life away from the dirt and despair of her old life in Tahlequah.

Occasionally he spoke of something he saw, or of their life together as children, but with the gag over her mouth, she could not reply. They had ridden several hours when Eagle trotted quickly off the trail, urging the pony behind a heavy growth of trees and outcropping of rocks. He cupped a hand over the animal's soft muzzle and she heard the sound of several riders passing by.

After they had passed, she tried to speak, only able to make grunting sounds.

"That was your friend Doaks, my sister. You see how close he is to catching up with the train. He goes to California now himself for his share of the gold metal. Do you not think he would take you back if he saw you?" Eagle regarded her thoughtfully, then said, "Lean down and I will remove the cloth from your mouth. I trust you do not want Doaks to hear, so you will not scream."

She shook her head back and forth vigorously. Her mouth and tongue were dry from lack of water and she could scarcely swallow. As soon as the rag came off she asked for a drink and was surprised at the ragged sound of her own voice.

They were soon on their way again, but he didn't tie the gag back on.

"How do you know about Doaks?" she asked after a long silence.

"I listened to them talking one night. I wanted to see if he would come after me or you. The son of a coyote caught me and we fought."

"He cut your face."

Eagle refused to answer, but she knew it was true. "I thought you were going on to Texas. Why didn't you go, Eagle? Away from Doaks and me and—"

"Your white man?"

"I'm afraid he might kill you."

"Ha! It is I you are afraid will kill him."

"Either way would be terrible."

He made a rude noise in his throat and didn't speak of the matter anymore.

They traveled through midday and almost until dark before Eagle settled on a place to spend a few hours before moving on. He led the pony down a steep trail into a deep gully, the banks of red dirt towering above them ten or twelve feet.

He tied her with a length of rope to the sturdy roots of a scrub oak that protruded from the bank about head high.

"So you will be here when I return. I will find us something to eat."

"Untie me and I'll build us a cook fire. It will be ready when you return."

He snorted and tugged at her hair like he used to do when she was little. "I cannot trust you that far, sister. You would surely be gone and this would all be to do over again."

Eagle returned after dark, a rabbit tied to his belt. He paid her no attention, but built a small fire and began to skin his prize. She looked at the blood on the knife blade and shuddered with a feeling of dread. How soon would that be the blood of his enemies, the white men?

Turning away, she gazed toward the west and the twilight land through which spirits pass on their way to Ghost country. Breathing slowly, she let her mind settle as her grandmother had taught her. She must accept the coming of the spirits, let them tell her what she must do, for she no longer could think straight. She could not return to Tahlequah and that old life. Somehow she had to convince Eagle of that. Barring that, she would have to escape.

A light flickered and grew brightly within her mind. The song of Red Bird, daughter of the sun, came to her. She had escaped her captivity and flown away. Winter Dawn could do the same.

And then she was riding above the tiny campfire, her brother kneeling beside it with the rabbit speared out over the flames. She floated as if on a great cloud and found herself looking down upon the wagons. They were far away from where she had left them, circled up for the night. She moved toward Daniel's, hovered there a moment and then drifted down to touch her lips to his.

He moved and made a sound down in his throat. She breathed into his mouth, said his name, and stepped into his dream.

Cloaked in sudden horror, she waded through dark crimson rivers. In their midst, a young soldier covered in blood and dirt, held the body of a child. He knelt with his head down against the young girl's still face, his tears wetting her dead flesh.

"Come away from this," Winter Dawn whispered. "Come to me, come with me. I will heal your wounds."

Daniel raised his head, his silver eyes sparkling. "Winter Dawn, is that you?"

That he had called her by her Cherokee name was not at all surprising, for this was her dream walk.

"It is me, my love," she said. "I've come to take you home. Away from this. It is enough, you have paid enough." She held out her arms. "Give me the child, she is too heavy for you. Let me take her into the twilight place where she will be happy. You don't need to carry her any longer, my love."

He raised his tear-streaked face, gave her the child, and smiled. Rachel offered the beautiful little girl to the western wind and the tiny soul slipped from her arms and faded into a pale mist.

Taking Daniel to her breast, Rachel whispered. "Now, you must save me. You must come to me. I will show you the place."

He kissed her tenderly and she held him for a moment, then moved from his arms. "Come, Daniel. See where I am and come to me." She gave to his mind a picture of the red rocks, the trees, the gully where she lay so that he would know it well.

* * *

Daniel drifted from the dream, gazed around expecting to see Rachel. "Where are you?" he whispered. "Where are you?"

He crawled out from under the wagon, pulled on his boots, and rose to his feet. It was early yet, true night hadn't really begun. How had he fallen asleep so deeply?

Frantic, he raced to Henry Rattlingourd's wagon. The man still sat beside his fire, puffing at a pipe. The aromatic smoke mingled with the smell of burning wood.

"She is gone. She has not returned, has run away," Henry said sadly.

"She didn't run away. She didn't come back tonight because she's in trouble," Daniel babbled. "Bad trouble. We've got to search for her, go after her."

Did he dare tell the man of his dream, let him think he had gone totally insane? There was no time to waste.

"How do you know?" Henry said, rising.

"I'll tell you as we go. Get your horse, we've got to help her."

"Where is she?"

"I don't know. I'll know when we get there." He turned, looked behind them. "Back that way. Are you coming?"

Henry studied Daniel, then tapped the tobacco from his pipe. "Yes, yes, I'm coming. Go on, I'm right behind you."

Henry brought along two muskets, one a short-barreled Hawkens that he handed to Daniel along with a powder horn and possible bag.

"You might need this. Know how to use it?"

Daniel wanted to turn down the offer, having sworn never to shoot at a living man again, but he took the weapon. "Yes, I can use it."

Together the two saddled their mounts and rode

out, not stopping to explain to the guards what was going on. There just wasn't time. An urgency such as he'd never known spurred Daniel on. Not once did he stop to think that it had all been a dream. He only knew that he had to reach her and quickly, or she would die. And at the same time he felt as if a great burden had been lifted from his heart. How he could feel both ways at once, he had no idea, but it was there and there wasn't time to puzzle it out.

A great half moon rose late, casting a light so bright the riders threw shadows out behind them as they traveled. They came across the gully and followed along for a time without talking much. The moon moved across the sky and the deep cut swung back toward the east.

"We're close, see that outcropping? I recognized it because we rode by here the day before yesterday. We'd better dismount, move down in there," Daniel said.

"She came to you in a dream?" Henry asked for the third time.

"I told you all I know. It sounds crazy, I know."

"Not really. Rachel's grandmother is a witch and a healer. It is said that the power is passed on. I've known stranger things to be true."

Daniel led the mare into the cut, their passage sending pebbles rattling noisily to the bottom. Henry had surprised him by not balking at the strange story he'd finally related, leaving out the part about the dead girl who had haunted his dreams for more than a year. Her ghost had been banished, and speaking of her would gain him nothing. He hadn't told Rachel, had he? He thought not. How she had appeared in his dream he would never know, but he could no more doubt it than he could doubt the moon hanging in the sky. Simply not being able to explain a thing did not make it impossible.

Up ahead a horse whinnied. Rhymer stomped and Daniel cupped her nose. Henry quieted his own mount.

"Let's tie them here," Daniel whispered, and they looped the reins over a massive root in the bank.

Henry loaded the musket, stuck a couple of spare balls in his mouth, and signaled with his hands that he would climb out and circle around to come up on the opposite side.

"Just don't shoot me," Daniel mouthed, and moved on as Henry disappeared. The man crept like a cat in the night and could blend with every shadow.

After a few more cautious steps, Daniel saw the outline of a horse, the white spots on its butt shining in the moonlight. Someone was careless, must think he hadn't been followed.

Daniel grinned wryly. He hadn't been. Not exactly.

A lone figure lay on the ground, back in the shadow cast by the high bank. Alone? It wasn't possible. Rachel must be here. Had the dream lied?

Where was she? My God, had she already been killed, her body done away with? The possibility squeezed at his heart. Had he come all this way only to lose her?

Chapter Eight

Rachel's arms wrapped around Daniel's neck and she held on tightly, coming up out of sleep not knowing if she were still dream-walking or was awake.

With relief he spoke against her soft hair. "I thought you were dead. Are you hurt? What did he do to you?"

Behind Daniel, Henry kept the muzzle of his long musket pressed against Eagle's chest. Her brother lay sprawled where they had surprised him, sleeping near the fire.

Rachel grew agitated. "Henry, stop pointing that gun at him. Daniel, make him let Eagle go. What are you doing?"

Hands that had been clasped around his neck began to shove and push at his chest. "Let me go."

He did and stepped backward, confused. He glanced quickly from the Indian on the ground to the one struggling to get past him. "What the hell is going on here? We thought he kidnapped you."

"He did but . . . I mean, he didn't."

"You came with him on your own?" Daniel's voice revealed his amazement.

"Not exactly, but . . . well, that is, he didn't hurt me."

"But he took you against your will?"

Henry hadn't removed the gun barrel from Eagle's chest and her brother's anger appeared ready to explode from his tensed body. Eagle shouted at her in Cherokee.

"Make this man take the gun away or I will gut him."

"Oh shut up, Eagle," she replied in Cherokee, then switched to English. "Daniel, if you two will just calm down and stop acting like little boys playing a game, I'll explain things to you. And, Henry, if you don't quit pointing that gun at my brother, he says he'll gut you."

Henry let out a nervous laugh.

Daniel's was genuine. "Like brother, like sister." At last he saw that Rachel was tied by one wrist to a tree root. He took out his bowie and cut the rope. "If he didn't kidnap you why the hell does he have you tied up?"

"Maybe for the same reason you once threatened to do the same thing?" The words were meant to lighten the situation, but it didn't work.

Daniel's retort was instantaneous and dry. "If you'll recall I never did so. Henry, do what she says, but watch him. If he makes a wrong move, lob him over the head with the butt of that mean gun of yours."

Henry obviously didn't care for the suggestion of letting Eagle out of the sights of his weapon, but he did so anyway.

Rachel rose to her feet and swayed, reached out, and Daniel grabbed her arm.

"Hey, easy. Stood up too fast?"

"I don't know, my stomach feels . . . feels, oh, I'm going to be sick." And she promptly was.

Daniel held her head and when she was finished gave her a drink of water. "You're hot as a pistol. What'd he do to you?"

"Nothing. He didn't do anything. Must have been the rabbit."

Daniel glowered at Eagle, who watched now as if trying to decide whether to run or stay. "He eat any?"

Eagle nodded and took a step toward his sister, but Daniel held out a hand. "Keep your distance. I'm not real sure I want you touching her just yet. Henry, there's something wrong with her."

Rachel clung to him weakly. "I'll be all right. Daniel?"

He leaned close to listen.

"Don't hurt Eagle. He was trying to protect me from . . . Doaks . . . from . . . Let him go. Send him away, but please don't hurt him. Promise me." She moaned and clutched at her stomach. "Promise?"

Gazing into her feverish eyes, he could do nothing but make the promise, though he hated like hell to do so. And what was she talking about—Doaks? Obviously she was out of her head.

Both men remained there with her, holding her, talking to her, feeding her sips of water until dawn. By then she was incoherent, babbling in words that made little sense to Daniel.

Henry translated for him, disjointed references to charms and secrets and ghosts, the darkening land and dream-walking.

"We need to get her back to the train, get a doctor to look at her," Henry said.

Daniel agreed, afraid that she had contracted something dreadful. What if she died? He realized that he would not be able to face that happening to her.

"You go for help, I'll stay with her." He stroked her hair, leaned forward, and kissed her forehead.

"No, she is to be my wife, I'll remain. I should be with her if . . . should she . . ." Henry shrugged and gazed down at her face.

The word "wife" hit Daniel with the ferocity of lead shot. He could scarcely repeat it aloud. "Your wife?"

How had this happened? And when? Why had the

man let him hold her, kiss her, if he was to marry her? He wanted to shout fervently that she had entered his dreams, not Henry's. It was Daniel, not Henry that she had sent for, that she loved. Daniel whose pain she had eased by lifting his heavy burden. He didn't pretend to know how she had performed such a miracle, but it had happened. Between him and her, not Henry. The fool hadn't made any attempt to find her until Daniel had insisted.

Miserably, he watched as Winter Dawn reached for Henry's hand, saw how he cupped it in both of his and leaned down and spoke gently in the rhythmic Cherokee language.

It was plain to see that he had been a damned fool and had lost her to this man, and there was nothing he could do about it. He prayed only that she would live. He'd give her up to this man if only she lived. God, suppose she had cholera or something even worse? She had to live, at any cost to himself.

He would go off into the wilderness alone, like he'd always wanted. That was no life for a woman anyway, living with a man who only found happiness in solitude. A man who awoke in the night with blood on his hands and murder in his heart.

After a while Henry rose and fetched a blanket from Eagle's bedroll. Surprisingly enough, though neither of them would let him touch her, the Indian continued to hover near his sister, a look of concern on his harsh features. Someone had cut him across the cheek recently and that only added to his frightening appearance.

Wordlessly, Daniel helped Henry ease Rachel onto the blanket, so she was no longer lying on the bare ground. He stripped off his dusty shirt and covered her with it. Soon her eyes drifted closed.

Henry glanced up at Daniel. "One of us should go

fetch a wagon for her. What about him?" He indicated Eagle.

Daniel nodded. "I'll go. Nothing about him. I promised her we wouldn't harm him, so leave him be."

Rachel whimpered weakly.

"She is to be my wife, I should have final say. And I say take him out there and stake him out for the bears to eat."

"Wife or no, she has final say," Daniel retorted, his voice as harsh as a whip cracking. "You'll let him be."

Their eyes met, the dour Indian and the huge white man. Daniel thought for a moment he would have to fight the man, and that he would do too, for her. For Rachel. But Henry broke the eye contact to glance down at her once again. He looked back at Daniel and shook his head up and down once, briskly.

Daniel looked at Eagle. "For some reason she wants us to spare your life, but I'm telling you now, you get and you stay gone. You come near her again, and it won't matter what she says. Nothing will protect you if you so much as harm an inch of her. You got that?"

Eagle stared, mouth twisted, then he spat at Daniel's feet and moved off to where his pony waited. No one moved or spoke. They watched until horse and rider passed out of sight around a bend, leaving a thin trail of dust that whipped away in the wind.

Henry muttered in Daniel's ear. "This is a big mistake. Let me follow him out of hearing and shoot him."

"No. Try and I'll stop you. It's what she wants. I won't see her hurt anymore."

A knot formed in his throat, for he knew that if Winter Dawn married Henry it would break his heart. Yet, at the same time, he knew it was the best thing for her and himself, for he was capable of hurting her more than anyone else.

Daniel knelt beside her once more and touched

each cheek with a kiss, then rose. "I'll ride back and get my wagon. It's lighter than yours and I can move faster. Take care of her. He comes back, shoot the son of a bitch."

Henry nodded grimly. In silence Daniel saddled up the mare. He stuck the Hawkens Henry had given him in the scabbard without thinking. It seemed a natural thing to do.

After a few days recovering in Henry's wagon, Rachel began to grow stronger and was glad when Minna Von Finster came to visit. She spoke to Henry outside his wagon, then climbed inside. Henry carried so many supplies that Rachel's bed was actually made on top of the stacked crates, in among the things necessary to everyday life on the trail. The mousy woman settled herself as best she could and smiled, transforming her plain features.

"It's good to see you healing," she said. "Henry says you will soon be on your feet."

"I would already, but he won't hear of it. I'm pleased you came."

Minna held a towel-wrapped bundle. "I brought you something, a treat. I'm sure Henry has been feeding you his plain cooking."

They both laughed. Minna unwrapped a bowl of fluffy dumplings swimming in apples.

Rachel clapped her hands. "Wherever did you find apples?"

"We took them from our trees last summer and dried them for the trip. It seemed as if we peeled and sliced thousands. The boys hated helping. Father spread sheets on the south slope of the roof and we laid them out in the sun. Thank goodness we had a dry spell." She offered the bowl to Rachel, then held out a spoon. "Can you manage?"

Rachel squirmed and made a face but managed to

sit up, leaning back against some crates. She took the bowl and began to eat. "These are delicious. Oh, thank you so much." She cleaned the bowl without speaking again, and when she was finished, she licked the spoon thoroughly.

Minna chuckled. "I could go get some more."

"Oh, no, but do bring me more sometime soon."

After Rachel set the bowl aside Minna took her hands. "I am so sorry about what happened with the letters. My sister is often harsh in her judgments. I never got the chance to tell you, but I found them and posted them at the stone marker. I would imagine they have been delivered by some thoughtful traveler by now."

"Oh, thank you. That was very nice."

"It was only right, after what my sister did. You know, she is seeing Daniel Wolfe, has told Father that they are walking out. I expect they will marry soon. Father does not approve, but he will set them up, I'm sure."

Pain shot through Rachel's chest. She clutched at her throat and tears filled her eyes.

"What is it, dear? Should I call Henry? Oh, my, you're so flushed. I'll call Henry."

"No . . . no, please." She hung on to Minna's long, bony fingers. "I'm all right. I didn't know . . . I mean, I thought he . . ."

Minna studied her thoughtfully, then gently pushed hair from the feverish cheeks. "You love him, don't you?"

"Oh, Minna. I tried not to. He was a soldier and I cannot forget what they did to our people. But he is so kind, and he has suffered more than enough for what he did in the war. I had hoped . . . when he forgot, healed, he would come to me. But I guess . . . oh, Minna, what shall I do?" She dissolved in tears.

Minna gathered her into her arms. "There, child.

No man is worth such suffering. Henry loves you and you are here with him. We all thought . . . I mean, when Daniel brought you back in his wagon, and immediately Henry moved you to his, we supposed that the two of you had grown close. He is your kind, Daniel is not."

Rachel shoved at Minna's chest. "My kind? What do you mean, my kind?"

"Why, Cherokee, of course, child. What did you think I meant?"

"I am also white. You are all alike no matter how kind. You think if we are only a little Indian then we are all Indian. I am as white as I am Cherokee."

"But, child. I didn't mean anything. It's just that you are all so proud of your heritage, I only thought . . ."

"Well, you thought wrong. I am white like my father, and that is what I want to be, that is my heritage as well. And when I get to California where they don't know what a Cherokee is, I will prove it. I can wear fine dresses and roll my hair and you will never know.

"Besides if the Cherokee are so proud of their heritage why did they take up the white man's ways? They dress and live like the white man, and have for many years. In the Smokies we lived in two-story homes, owned plantations, had slaves, just like the white man. Yet you looked at our skin and wanted our land and ran us off like all the other Indians in this country. You look at our skin and choose where we will live, and who we may marry."

Henry leaned into the wagon. "What's going on in here? Are you okay, Winter Dawn?"

She glared at Henry, then back at Minna. "No, I am tired now and want to rest."

"I was just leaving," Minna murmured, gathered up the bowl and towel, and left.

Henry came in to sit with her until she fell asleep, but she refused to talk to him. The doctor said she had a bad case of summer complaint, and she had been very ill. Now that her body was on the mend, she knew her aching heart would never heal.

Occasionally she thought of her brother with sadness, but the love she had for him and her memories of their youth together would not ever dim, and she gathered that to her soul. Despite Eagle's warning that Doaks and his cronies planned to catch up with the wagon train and head for California, there was no sign of them. After a while she stopped being so jumpy about the possibility that he might leap out of the brush around the next bend and grab her up. Henry was, after all, a fierce defender and scarcely let her out of his sight.

Soon she recovered enough from her illness to walk alongside the wagon for a short while in the warmth of the afternoon sun each day. In a few days they would reach Fort Mann and there would be a celebration. Henry told her that if she felt well enough she might attend. She hadn't seen Daniel during her recovery, for his wagon no longer traveled behind Henry's. With so many in the train, it was hard to spot his, though she searched in vain each time she rode up front in the padded seat Henry had fashioned for her.

Ever since Minna's announcement about Daniel and Zoe she thought of nothing but coming face-to-face with him. She must hear from his own lips that he would marry that stick of an old maid who was too mean to deserve a man like him. Before the celebration she would put on the finest dress her grandmother had given her, the one she had sewn with tiny stitches from the white man's softest fabric, a blue brighter than her own eyes. She would brush her hair till it shined and color her lips so that he would only notice her and no one else. She was well enough to dance, and once in his arms she knew she could convince him of her love.

As soon as the wagons were unhitched and circled, everyone ate their evening meal, and even before darkness fell began to gather for the dance. A large tarp was spread on a smooth, grassy patch, and two men brought out fiddles and began to play.

Henry claimed Rachel for the first dance, and she saw Minna twirling around with Lieutenant Tyner. Mrs. Claridge danced with her husband James, and Zoe stepped into the arms of Captain Evans.

Brow furrowed in concentration, Henry held her so that their bodies did not touch. "You sure you can do this?"

He might wish she would say no and release him, for he stomped his feet as if he were moving around a campfire for a ritual dance. Slowly they circled the improvised floor. With each turn she searched the groups of men gathered along the fringes. Nowhere did she see the tall, broad figure of the man in whose arms she yearned to be. Disappointment filled her. Was he not coming?

The song ended and another began. Grudgingly Henry gave her to Peter Mankins. He had come to see Henry to apologize for having been otherwise occupied when Eagle had kidnapped winter Dawn, but this was the first time he had spoken directly to her.

"I see you are as pretty as ever, ma'am," he said, smiling in his winning way. "I am relieved to see you up and about, as I took it personally when you were stolen."

"No need, sir," Rachel told him. The man was even larger than Daniel, and she had heard that he had once killed a bear without even a knife, twisting its neck until it broke. He was a good dancer, though, and she relaxed. Still, she continued to search for some sign of Daniel.

As the evening grew dark, lanterns were lit and hung on surrounding wagons. Their glow softened the harsh features of some of the men who had known hard work most all of their lives.

Henry had claimed her once again when she finally spotted Daniel. He moved from the shadows into the light, and her heart lurched. She trod on Henry's toe and took a false step.

Concern crossed his features. "Do you want to stop? Are you tired?"

"Yes, if you don't mind," she said, uncomfortable that she was lying to Henry.

"Shall I take you back?"

"No, I'll just sit a moment. I'm fine. Go enjoy yourself. Have a drink with the others. Please, Henry, don't treat me like a child."

The tone of her voice produced a puzzled frown, but he escorted her off the floor and left her sitting on a log with some men who obviously preferred to be spectators.

As soon as Henry's broad back blended with a group of men gathered near the Schrimsher wagon, Rachel searched out Daniel once again.

Instead of woolsey pants and worn shirt, his customary work clothes, he wore buckskins the color of rich butter. Without a hat his well-brushed hair gleamed golden in the lamplight. Out of the corner of her eye she spotted Zoe heading his way. Rachel slipped quickly through the crowd and, coming up behind him took his hand before the other woman had a chance.

Daniel blinked in surprise, but let her pull him onto the dance floor. They stood facing each other for an instant, gazes locked, then she moved close to him and eased her left hand along the back of his neck.

So startled was Daniel that he lost his normal grace and stumbled through the first few steps of the dance. Then his arm locked around her waist and the other hand took hers. No one else danced so close.

His breath feathered her hair, the supple buckskin caressed her cheek that rested on his chest, their hips and legs moved in perfect unison.

She was afraid to speak for fear she would break the spell, and he had only sighed from deep below his heart as he settled close and guided her round and round.

In his arms, she knew once and for all that this was the man she needed, and she would not give him up to Zoe. Somehow there had to be a way they could be together.

When the music drew to a close, with still not a word spoken except the silent language of their bodies, she deftly whirled them into the shadows, took his hand, and ran from the pools of golden light, out of hearing of the merriment.

There, under the spill of a crescent moon, she moved into his embrace, murmuring only his name. Arms locked around his neck, she pulled his mouth down to hers.

Tentatively, he tasted, then drank hungrily from her lips.

They sank into the green, lush grass, so that she lay on her back and he knelt beside her.

Her breasts ached for his touch, his kiss; her fingers itched to caress every inch of him, her mouth yearned for the heat of his skin. She breathed deeply of him, of leather and sun-drenched skin, of wild winds and green grasses. It made her eager to lie naked with him.

She pulled the sleeves of her dress down her arms,

slipped the bodice away from her bare breasts, all while he kissed her mouth, her eyes, her chin, and throat. As the faint stubble of his chin tickled her flesh he cupped a nipple and moaned before taking it into his mouth.

She felt his hardness against her leg and she rested her hand gently there, with only the soft deerskin between his flesh and hers.

"Ah, God," he moaned, and for an instant he held very still while she caressed him.

She imagined his hands tanning the leather, moving over it stroke after stroke until the animal's hide turned soft as silk. Silk that glided like sweet, warm water along his hardened muscles, between his legs, down his thighs. Touching him in all the places she yearned to caress. She traced the vision with her hands, slowly, sensually, not missing any part of him. He shifted across her, his body swaying in some savage rhythm that caught her up like the pounding of a thousand drums that wouldn't stop.

His hands lifted her skirts, bunched the fabric until he could touch her flesh. His broad warm hand spread over the mound of her sex.

He took his mouth from her breast and lay a cheek against her stomach, held her like that for a long time without moving. "Enough, it has to be enough," he said, choking on the words.

"I will have you, Daniel," she said into his ear. "I will not let her. I will do what I must to have you. Don't stop."

"Her? I don't understand." He kissed her, trailed his hand away, and shifted so he lay beside her. He kissed her again, gently, longingly. Moist, warm, sweet, his tongue lapped gently. "Oh, girl. Sweet girl. You don't know what you're doing."

He took away his lips, his hands, his body, and sat up.

"Marry Henry, be happy. This . . . well, this is just our wildness coming out. We can't ruin your life because of it."

She felt deserted, betrayed. "I am wild. Wild with love for you. When we choose who we will marry, we lie with them. We go to the stars with them. I want to feel that. We were going to the stars. Don't ruin that, Daniel. That is what we must have. I do not have it with Henry. You don't have it with that skinny frump of a woman."

"Skinny . . . ? Who are you talking about, what are you saying?"

She sat up, straightened her skirt, shuddered with the leftover emotions that would not leave her alone and that kept her breasts tingling and her secret place of love hot and wet. Daniel smoothed the blue fabric over her breasts and she gasped at his touch, leaning into it.

"No, girl. Now stop. You'll drive me crazy, maybe you already have."

"Then why would you think of marrying Zoe Von Finster?"

"I wouldn't. Who told you that?"

"It is all over camp. Her sister Minna told me. Herr Von Finster has been informed. Even Henry knows all about it."

Daniel laughed dryly. "Well, then someone should have informed me. I have no intention of marrying anyone, and certainly not Zoe Von Finster. She's cruel and insensitive and overbearing."

"Have you told her that, or do you lead her on?" Rachel felt a relief so vast it almost drowned her anger at Daniel for not giving her what she wanted.

"Over and over. The woman doesn't take no for an answer, but no matter what, she can't drag me before a preacher." He regarded her for a moment. "And just why do you care? Henry says you are to be his wife. Are you out here betraying the man you will wed?

"He what?" Rachel leaped to her feet, straightened her sleeves, and covered the swell of her breasts. "I have not told Henry I would marry him. It seems we both have the same problem." She moved toward him once again. "It is something we can solve easily. You tell her no, I'll tell Henry no, and we'll have no more problems."

He had not risen with her and still knelt on the ground. She moved forward until his face was close to her stomach.

"Love me, Daniel. I will make you a good wife, I promise I will."

He remembered the dream and her taking the girl from his arms, the way she had appeared like an angel of mercy. And he thought of all the peaceful nights since then. She had saved him from something dreadful. Dare he trust that the guilt and shame were gone forever? That she had truly taken on the burden herself? She had strange powers, no doubt about that. But did he believe all that mumbo jumbo, or was it just coincidence that the dreams had gone after she had appeared to him?

He stood, took her hands, but remained at arm's length. "Ah, Winter Dawn, I know you would make me a wonderful wife. It is I who would make a dreadful husband. I don't wish to marry. I want to live alone, away from civilization. That's no life for a woman, especially one like you. Go on to California and fulfill your dreams, and leave me to mine."

Saying the words split his heart open, and before he could give in and take them back he turned and hurried away.

Chapter Nine

The next day Rachel told Henry that she wanted to walk and be alone. She couldn't bear to speak to him about his telling everyone they would marry. He was a kind man, but he had no right to do that. Her anger was only overpowered by an enormous sadness that Daniel didn't want her. She couldn't deal with both, so she chose not to deal with either.

Instead she went in search of Dagasi. The little long-eared horse could offer just what she needed. Silent understanding and acceptance. When she found him, he twitched his hairy ears and nuzzled her with his soft nose, then together they wandered a little ways off from the train. While picking an armful of deer eye, the lovely black-eyed Susans, she carried on a conversation with him as if he were human. He regarded her occasionally between bites of early spring grasses and tolerated petting and complaining with patience.

The open prairie was a marvel. Born in the Smokies and raised in the rolling green hills of the Indian Nation, she was not used to a view of such enormity. Holding a handful of the golden blossoms, she began to whirl round and round. The brilliant endless sky was like a giant bowl turned upside down over her. She wondered how fast and how far she would have to run to reach the edge of the world and tumble off. And where would she be if she did? Indian legends spoke of twilight land far to the west through which the spirits of the dead passed to reach Ghost country. But one didn't go there in this life.

She grew dizzy with the whirling and closed her eyes. The world tilted beneath her, rocked and swayed, and she staggered forward and opened her eyes. There before her stood an immense and quite magnificent Osage brave.

Unafraid, she greeted him with sign.

From behind her arose the frantic shout, "Indians, Indians," and other voices joined in a clamor of panic.

The Osage glanced over her shoulder, then back into her eyes, an expression of extreme anguish immediately wiped away by fierce pride. He signed that there were some fifty men with him and they were hungry. It was only a hunting party in search of a buffalo herd said to be nearby, but they had been on the trail many days and needed food.

Mixing Cherokee and sign language, she told him to wait, she would return.

She ran all the way back to the train, Dagasi trotting along behind her like a pup. Wagons had drawn to a halt while people raced around in some kind of frenzy she didn't understand. Even some of the Cherokee were upset.

She searched out Henry. "Make them stop yelling. What do they think one large Indian is going to do, scalp them all?"

Henry eyed the handful of wilting flowers. "What were you doing out there? What does he want?"

"Food. There's a hunting party and they haven't eaten in a while. I said I would ask."

Henry lifted his shoulders. "Well, let's talk to Captain Evans. Come on."

It took a while to wade through all the curious, because each wanted to know what was going on and Henry had to stop and explain. Rachel was afraid one of them would shoot at the Osage, maybe even kill him, the way they were acting.

They found Evans, Sergeant McCrea, and L. J. Wyatte in excited conversation. Rachel saw why immediately, for a large band of Indians had seemingly appeared out of nowhere to join the lone Osage. The flat plains could be deceptive, Rachel decided, for she had seen nothing and then there they were, riding their ponies as if erupting from a depression in the earth.

"Captain Evans, sir," Henry said.

Lieutenants Tyner and Mankins appeared, adding their opinions.

Rachel fidgeted and glanced once again at the hunting party.

"Not now, Rattlingourd. We're trying to decide what to do about that war party."

"But, sir, that's what I'm here about. Rachel here says that it's a hunting party and they only want something to eat."

Evans regarded her closely. "Are you sure she knows what she's talking about?"

"Yes, sir," Henry said.

"I do," Rachel added. "He told me." She swung an arm toward the Osage.

"Ah. Well." Evans addressed Mankins. "Get James Vann over here. He knows his Indians."

Exasperated, Rachel said, "They only want something to eat."

"Perhaps," said Evans. "Then, on the other hand, they might want to get close enough to do us harm. We'll wait and see what Mr. Vann says."

Mankins paused a moment, looking from Rachel to Evans and back again. "Sir, perhaps—"

"Fetch Mr. Vann, Lieutenant."

Mankins made a face and shrugged in her direction, then hurried off.

Rachel tugged on Henry's sleeve. "It would be better if we just gave them some food."

"Probably, but let's wait a minute."

Vann strode up a few minutes later. The mounted hunting party of Indians waited patiently, but those in the wagon train were growing extremely nervous. Someone could panic and fire a shot at any minute. Then it was no telling what would happen. The possibilities chilled her.

Evans explained the situation. Vann glanced at Rachel. "You the girl who caused all the trouble? Cherokee, aren't you?"

"And white," she said curtly.

"Ah, yes. Of course. Aren't we all? What are they, Osage?"

She was flattered that he asked her. "Yes, sir. He explained that they are after buffalo but haven't come upon the herd yet, and they are hungry."

Vann turned to Evans. "I'd suggest we invite them over and give them something. They aren't painted for war, and they certainly could have ridden right over us the way they appeared like that."

"You sure it's safe?"

"No, sir, I'm not," Vann snapped. "But then neither is driving these beasts along unbroken trails to California. There are much worse things than a bunch of scraggly Osage. My God, sir."

Evans held up a hand, obviously accustomed to Vann's forthright manner. "Sergeant, you take a couple of men and go down the line. Collect some hardtack and sugar from each wagon and bring it back here." He looked at Rachel. "Girl, you go tell them to dismount their ponies and come on in, but they better mind their manners, you tell them that. And tell them we are heavily armed."

Rachel nodded solemnly. She would tell them what she pleased, but she was glad they had chosen her to carry the message.

Henry insisted on going with her, and that took some of the excitement away from the important task. He was adamant, though, and so she ran out ahead, laughing because he couldn't keep up, and neither could Dagasi, who was so excited he did more kicking and braying than running.

Her heart beat fast and hard as she approached the mounted men. The one to whom she had spoken earlier sat astride a beautiful paint pony with splashes of white so brilliant it hurt her eyes. A colorful blanket lay across its back. She walked right up to the pony, rubbed the velvety nose, and spoke to the man.

With signs she indicated the fear of those in the wagon train, then beckoned them all to follow. Each brave dismounted and led their ponies across the wide expanse.

Once inside the perimeter of the wagons, the stoic Osage formed a shoulder-to-shoulder line.

McCrea and two other men passed in front of them, handing each a thick slab of bread and sprinkling it liberally with sugar. Rachel watched in amazement as each Indian dropped to his knees and ate. They made not a sound, and when they were finished they rose, took up their mounts' reins, and walked away. The Osage to whom she had spoken was the last to be served. When he finished he paused in front of her and touched a fist to the center of his chest.

Sadness chased her earlier gaiety. Written across the brave's features was the sorrow of a proud man driven to such extremes as begging from the people who rode across his land without so much as a word of gratitude.

Someday they will take it all, she thought. Someday we will be no more.

It was the first time since leaving her grandmother that she had truly allowed herself to think like an Indian. It surprised her. The blood of her father hadn't erased her heritage despite all her talk about being white.

To get along, some of her people often said, we must become white or we will die. Even legends spoke of the peacefulness of being white. Right up until that moment, when she watched the band of Osage ride away, she had thought that acceptable. Now she wasn't so sure.

Henry took her arm. "You look sad, what is it?"

She could think of no way to explain how she felt. Not to Henry. Daniel would understand, for his heart and soul had been stripped bare. He had been forced to look upon the worst of himself in order to discover the best. While he had not yet found inner peace, he understood the need to do so. Henry did not even see the necessity of such a thing.

In all the excitement she had forgotten about Dagasi, and so she went in search of him. She finally found him drinking at a pond in the company of several of the other animals from the remuda. Attracted by the smell of water, they had broken away from the several hundred head of stock animals that brought up the tail end of the train. The coming of the Osage had captured everyone's attention temporarily, allowing some of the beasts to wander.

Kneeling, Rachel cupped up some water, but only took a tiny sip. It tasted brackish, something like a bitter salt mixed with chalk. She spat and rubbed her lips and tongue dry.

McCrea rode up, shouting and chasing the animals. "Git, you stubborn critters. Git away from that poison. It's alkali water, not fit to drink."

Dagasi bolted a few feet away and halted, feet spread, long ears skinned back, lips bared to show yellow teeth. Rachel waved her arms and ran at him, shooing him off, and finally he trotted back to join the herd.

They traveled far past the pond before stopping for their noontime break, so that no more animals would stray to the poisonous water.

By midafternoon two horses were down and had to be shot. By dusk and circle-up, three more animals grew sick and were destroyed. Rachel listened with dread to the thunderous booms that faded into the distance across the endless plains. In the mountains a shot could be heard over and over as its echo bounced from one peak to another, in and out of one holler and then the next. But out here in this vast open space, sound just went on until it died and fell to the ground.

She walked back from Henry's wagon to check on Dagasi.

"He's not doin' good, that one ain't," one of the men told her. "But he's still on his feet. Don't 'spect he'll last much longer."

She searched out the little animal and put her arms around his neck. He breathed noisily and his normally perky ears flopped dejectedly. She whispered in his ear and rubbed at the stubbly chin. In his great brown eyes the specter of death lurked.

A painful knot formed in her chest. The stubborn little mule had been good company and she hated to see him suffer. She had spent many days with only him to talk to, and even after her wood-gathering duty was finished they had walked miles of trail together. She had told him of her heartache when she lost Daniel and had spoken her innermost secrets in his ear. Yet, she knew his spirit would walk free when he no longer could.

Cutter Christie approached. "Ma'am? We can't wait any longer, he's suffering. You run on, and I'll see to him."

She nodded mutely and arms stiff at her sides walked away. Behind her the shot cracked and she closed her eyes. Tears poured over her cheeks and she began to sob, running blindly past one wagon after another. Her breath came in huge gulps, but still she couldn't stop, as if something pursued her. At last she could not take another step and stumbled to her knees.

Someone touched her shoulder, put an arm around her. "Here, here. Where're you going?"

Daniel knelt beside her, lifted her chin, and wiped the tears away. "What is it? What's happened?"

"Dagasi died," she sobbed and threw herself into his arms.

Daniel lifted her gently and carried her to his wagon, where he placed her inside, then climbed in himself.

For a long while he sat beside her, one hand on her head while she cried. It grew dark around them, activity within the train slowed, and at last all was quiet except for the muted plodding of a few horses carrying guards around the perimeter.

He thought she had fallen asleep until she turned over and spoke in a small voice. "I should go back."

He swallowed harshly and could no more stop the words that came than he could have stopped breathing. "I don't want you to."

She didn't answer for a minute and he held his breath. "Daniel?" she finally said.

He didn't reply; he just waited. His mouth turned as dry as a summer wind and his heart beat so fast he could scarcely breathe. He had to be sure this time, of himself and of her. He mustn't hurt her again. Holding her in his arms had broken down the barriers he'd so carefully erected. It seemed they only worked when she was out of sight, and then not very well, for they hadn't stopped the yearning he had to be with her.

Without touching him, she spoke barely above a whisper. "Ask me to remain here with you and I will. But I cannot have you turn from me again. I couldn't bear it. I love you, but if I must be without you, I have to know it now."

He leaned toward her in the dark, feeling a joy so immense he could hardly contain it. Her breath came sweet upon his mouth and when their lips touched, something inside him unfurled like petals to the sun.

When at last the kiss ended she curled into his arms and nestled there.

"What about California?" he asked softly.

"What about Oregon?" she returned.

"What about Henry?"

"And Zoe?"

They both laughed.

"Will you ride with me?" he asked.

A slight hesitation, a long breath. "Yes. Daniel?"

"Mmm?" He rubbed her back with the flat of his hand.

"Will we marry?"

He pulled her close and hugged her until she grunted. "As soon as we can find a preacher. I suppose Captain Evans could marry us, I don't know."

"We could marry now, right here, Daniel. We will ask the spirits to bless us and they will."

"Show me how."

"Outside, we must go outside."

He nodded and together they crawled from the wagon. Taking his hand she led him away from the wagons into an open field. Above them stars blazed. She took his hands and faced him. Over his shoulder, a sliver of moon cradled a brilliant pinpoint of light.

In the gentle wind his hair stirred, and she cupped a hand at the side of his face.

"I give you my spirit so that we shall be blessed," she said.

Dim light caught at the moisture in his eyes and gleamed a moment. "And I give you my spirit so that we may have peace," he said in a choked voice.

As they lifted their eyes heavenward, a star streaked across the sky, leaving a sparkling trail beneath the moon.

"Loving you, Daniel, will be like riding among the stars. Out there."

He gathered her into his arms, thinking that if he was never any happier than at that very moment, it would be enough. Then he lifted her up and carried her back to the wagon.

Before he undressed her, before they made love, there was something he had to know. And so he asked it gently, with his arms around her and her warm body pressed against his.

"Do you remember when your brother kidnapped you?"

She stiffened against his chest. "He did not—"

"Okay, took you against your will. Do you remember what happened . . . I mean, coming to me . . . I don't understand . . ."

"You mean the dream?"

He took a deep breath, not daring to believe. "Yes, the dream. Do you remember it?"

"I took the child into the land of the spirits, Daniel, so she would not weigh on you any longer. Her spirit forgave you because you were so sad. Do you forgive yourself now?"

"My God, Rachel. Things like that don't happen. You can't go into someone else's dream."

"Oh, but you see, it wasn't really a dream. It was a journey you continued to make because you needed to cleanse your soul. I went on that journey with you because I needed you to save me as well. And because I loved you."

"I'm sorry, I just can't believe—"

"Have you gone on that journey since? Has the memory of the child haunted you?"

"No, but . . ."

"Daniel, because you cannot believe doesn't change anything. What happened happened, and you were there. Your heart knows it is true, it is just your mind that cannot believe, but one day it will. It is enough for now that your heart knows. How did you find me?"

"I'm not sure."

"Yes, you are."

"Winter Dawn, are you a witch?"

She laughed. "Probably, but don't worry, it isn't so bad. Our people revere witches. It is forbidden to kill a witch."

"Really? Somehow I have trouble thinking of you in that way. You are a temptress, but a witch? No."

"Temptress? I do not know the word."

He trailed a finger down her throat into the cleft between her breasts. "Did you say we are married, my little temptress?"

"Yes. Yes, we are." She whispered the words, backing out of his embrace to unfasten her skirt.

He listened to the rustle of fabric, felt her shift once, then twice. She touched him, felt for his hands, and guided them to her bare breasts.

The skin settled soft and warm against his palms, the nipples hardening.

"Oh, Rachel. Oh, my love." He scarcely breathed as he thought of her kneeling before him naked.

"Let me take off your shirt." She rolled it up over his head. He didn't want to take his hands away from her to slip it off his arms.

She eased the fabric between her breasts and his palms, dropped the shirt and settled against his bare chest.

He moaned and wrapped his arms around her. There they knelt facing each other, thigh to thigh, stomach to stomach, flesh upon flesh.

Tangling her hands in his hair she nibbled at his neck, behind his ear, down onto his shoulder. Muscles rippled under her lips and she took bigger bites, moving down to his nipples, where she tasted first one then the other. A fine line of hair ran downward to his belly button and she trailed through it with her tongue.

"Now, let's take off these," she said, and began to unfasten the buckskin leggings. The belt holding the knife and sheath fell away under her expert fingers and soon she had popped the buttons down the front of his pants.

She ran both hands around back to cup his bare buttocks, and had a little trouble slipping the pants down past his erection.

"I think I will call him Agili," she said with a chuckle.

"What does that mean?"

"He is rising," she said.

"Ah, yes," he said. "Indeed he is."

They sank onto the quilts and she pulled off his boots and skinned down the pants. Kneeling between his legs, she slowly ran her hands upward toward his hips, moving forward and resting astraddle his thighs. She leaned over so that one breast grazed his cheek. He turned, took the nipple into his mouth, and at the same time guided himself into her warm sweetness.

She took all of him with an explosive cry of delight. And she had been right when she said that loving each other would be like riding among the stars.

She was a noisy and wild lover, matching his unbridled desires as they rolled and tumbled and nipped at each other's flesh, exploding together time after time.

He feared waking the entire train, but couldn't contain the exuberance of coupling with this beautiful creature.

After a long while, as they lay resting, each panting and slick with perspiration, they talked.

"Everything they said is true," she told him. "Loving is a little like dying, and a lot like being born."

"You have never done this before?"

"No."

"But it was so . . . I mean, I thought it would hurt you, being the first time and all." He was ashamed to admit that he presumed she had had other men, being a savage.

"Ah, no. We ride very young astride ponies that race with the wind. Most of us have no barrier by the time we marry. Some tribes cut their women there."

"Yes, I've heard that." He shivered at the thought of someone taking a knife to her silken smoothness. Hurting her in that way.

"Daniel?"

He laid a hand on her moist belly and the flesh tightened under his touch.

"Again?"

"He is not rising," he joked.

"He will," she said and threw one leg across his thighs.

She was right.

Early the next morning while Daniel worked hitching the horses and Rachel cleared away their breakfast things, Henry Rattlingourd approached.

Catching sight of Rachel evidently told him all he'd come to find out.

"I worried when you didn't return. I looked for you into the night." A scowl darkened his face, his jaw clenched over the words so that they were curt and harsh.

Daniel paused in the harnessing, the jingle of chains on the singletrees faded, but he didn't interrupt this thing between Winter Dawn and Henry. It was hers to do, and he would stay out of it unless Henry grew violent. He did touch the shank of his bowie to make sure it was where it belonged and he could get to it if need be. Then he went on with his work, keeping an eye on the couple.

Rattlingourd wore his traditional Cherokee garb, a feathered turban, leggings, and a tight-fitting shirt. Many had abandoned the dress and wore clothing much like Daniel and other white men of the area.

Somehow he looked more suited to Rachel than did Daniel. Despite her spoken desire to be white, she wore the clothing her grandmother had given her. It was all she had.

Rachel felt ashamed for the way she had treated Henry, yet she was so filled with happiness she couldn't express that shame. Instead, she hid behind her newfound joy and pretended she owed him nothing.

"I am married to Daniel," she told Henry boldly.

"How can that be?" Henry clenched his fists but held them down at his side.

"I love him, Henry."

"Because he is white."

She wiped the inside of the coffeepot with a cloth and set it aside, keeping her eyes down. "Think what you will."

"What I think is that you are afraid to be who you

really are, like so many of our people. We will one day be sorry."

"Josiah Keye married my mother Singing Bird. She was never sorry."

Henry sent her a sharp gaze. "Was she sorry that the white men killed her two young sons? How can you do this?"

"Oh, Henry," Rachel said. "You don't care about all that. It is in the past and there's nothing we can change about it. We must go on. What you do care about is that a white man took me away from you. It has injured your pride."

He regarded her sadly. "I loved you, Winter Dawn. We should have married and erased the streak of white in your blood with sons. Now you will wipe out the Cherokee with sons from this white man's loins."

She grabbed up the coffeepot and a frying pan, whirled from Henry. "I hope I do, Henry. I hope we have many sons with blue eyes and pale skin and hair the color of gold just like his. Then perhaps they will be able to go about their business without the pain and anguish of being Indian. He is beautiful and I love him. Go away, Henry. Go away and leave us alone."

Without waiting to see if he obeyed, she stowed the cooking utensils inside the wagon and went to join Daniel. When she climbed into the wagon a while later there was no sign of Henry.

It seemed to Rachel that the prairie would go on forever. She would tire of riding and walk, then tire of walking and climb back up in the high seat. She wished for a pony to ride to break the monotony.

When she told Daniel, he said, "Ride one of the horses pulling the wagon. Or ride Rhymer and I'll ride one of them."

She noticed that some of the drivers actually did ride the left rear animal of their team, whether that animal was mule, horse, or oxen.

"I would need britches or a blanket," she said, but wasn't very enthusiastic. It wouldn't be the same as having her very own animal to ride.

About an hour after their noontime stop, the shouted word came back to hold up. Since Daniel's wagon was near the rear of the long train, they could see nothing.

"I'm going to see what's up," he said and rode off.

She climbed down to wait for his return. Others were doing the same. After what seemed like a very long wait, Daniel came riding back. He reined up beside her and reached down an arm.

"Come on, get up here. You've got to see this."

She vaulted up behind him, clasped her arms around his waist, and off they went.

"What is it, Daniel?"

"You'll see."

She couldn't coax him to tell her what they would see and couldn't guess.

Finally, they reached the front of the train, on a rise that looked down and out across a prairie black with buffalo as far as the eye could see.

The huge animals browsed in the spring grass, paying no attention at all to those who gazed at them in awe.

"Aren't they something?"

Rachel nodded. She had never seen such a sight, though she had heard tales. There were plenty of buffalo in the Indian Nation and even over in Arkansas Territory, but nothing like this.

"This must be the herd those Osage hunters were tracking, but I never thought there would be this many."

"Can we ride out among them?" she asked.

"No, I wouldn't. They might stampede. Can you imagine what that would be like? The earth would shudder and shake and they might run right over the train. No, we'd best be careful."

"But how will we get around them?"

"I'm happy to say I don't have to figure that out," Daniel said. "I reckon the captain will come up with something. Meanwhile, since we're stopped, why don't we ride on back and see if we can't find something to do?"

She lay her cheek against his back and hugged him tightly. "I am sure that will not be too difficult."

He laughed and the deep sound vibrated inside her head. She had never felt so happy.

Chapter Ten

When the signal came back to move out, Rachel remained in the wagon. After several consultations, the decision had been reached to ride slowly through the tremendous herd of buffalo, and she didn't want to be on foot. As a precaution Daniel rode Rhymer, explaining that he wanted to be able to move fast should the animals get rambunctious. For three days they rode alongside the huge, shaggy beasts. Occasionally a bull would challenge one of their own animals, but for the most part they simply moved languidly out of the way and regarded the trespassers with big brown eyes. Even when Evans ordered one of the buffalo shot for fresh meat, the herd of huge animals offered no resistance.

The biggest trouble came from domesticated stock. Spare horses, oxen, and mules took it into their heads to wander off with these strange creatures, sometimes as far as fifteen miles from the train. There didn't seem to be enough mounted men to prevent it. That meant riding off after the straying beasts regularly.

Several times Daniel rode with the men who went to round up the wanderers and bring them back. On the morning of the fourth day of traveling through the buffalo herd, Daniel left with three others to hunt down a dozen or more horses that had run off with a group of rowdy buffalo cows. Minna soon joined

Rachel, who walked along beside Daniel's team, carrying his whip.

After greeting each other, the two strolled side by side in silence. Rachel did not know how to begin a conversation with this intelligent and well-educated white woman. It was an unspoken agreement that Minna would always speak first.

True to that agreement, Minna broke the friendly silence. "I haven't ridden a single mile yet," she said. "I vowed to walk all the way to California, and I'm determined to make it." She glanced out from under her lashes and said what she obviously had really come to say. "You are not with Henry any longer?"

"Daniel and I are married."

Minna blushed. "You mean you are living together. There is no preacher on this train to marry you."

"Well, we are married just the same. We spoke our vows and asked the spirits' blessing."

"But that doesn't count in the white world, Rachel. You must know that. It's a sin for the two of you to live together without a preacher saying words, asking God's blessing. Everyone is talking."

"It is no one's business."

"Of course it is. If you are going to be white you have to learn there are conventions that must be obeyed. Now, I have heard of folks in an emergency who agreed to consummate their marriage and then when the traveling preacher arrived they would say their vows. In some small remote settlements that is acceptable. If you were to go to Captain Evans and tell him that is your intent, then people would stop gossiping."

Some of the words confused Rachel, but she didn't want to admit that she didn't understand them. "I'll ask Daniel what he wants to do," she told her friend.

"Thank you for telling me. Is your sister one of those talking?"

Minna was quiet for a moment, then she nodded. "I'm afraid so. She's telling everyone that you bewitched Daniel and took him from her."

Rachel laughed. "That's true, Minna. But how would she know?"

Minna gaped. "True? What do you mean, true?"

"I went to him in a dream." Rachel glanced at Minna, saw the expression of disbelief, and decided not to say any more. "We believe differently, that is all," she said and closed the subject.

Yet she was determined to talk to Daniel that evening about going to Captain Evans. She didn't want everyone talking about them living in sin, even though she didn't know what "consummate" meant and wasn't sure she and Daniel were doing such a thing. Actually it bothered her more that Zoe was telling lies about Daniel's intentions. He had explained about the kiss Rachel had witnessed and had told her the entire episode had been Zoe's idea. Zoe made it sound like Rachel had stolen the man she was going to marry.

For some time Rachel wanted to ask Minna when she could come and listen to her play the piano, but clearly that would have to wait. Minna seemed put out with her, and she didn't quite understand why. If only her friend Alice were here, she could explain a few of the rules of living in this white world. It was going to be much more difficult being white than she had imagined. The only time she felt completely comfortable was when she was with Daniel.

She would speak to him of these things that night when he returned.

By nightfall Daniel and the other men still hadn't shown up, and Captain Evans sent Cutter Christie to help Rachel bed the wagon and horses down for the night. Isaac and Elijah could handle the Christie camp alone.

Cutter was not happy. He muttered all the while he unhitched the horses and jockeyed the wagon into position. Rachel tended to her own chores of unloading, building a campfire and preparing a meal, and tried not to listen to the Cherokee's grumbling. She couldn't help but overhear as his fuming grew more pronounced.

"This is why we didn't want to bring any blamed women along in the first place. Can't pull their own weight. Got no place on the trail." Chains jingled as he unhooked the lead horses from the doubletree and moved them aside. The team, unused to Cutter, pranced and showed off. He smacked one smartly between the eyes with a doubled-up fist.

Rachel glared at him. A Cherokee ought to know more about how to treat horses than that. She started to say something, but the look he gave her changed her mind. He managed to unhitch the other pair and let the tongue drop where he stood. It would have to be laid to the outside of the circle as the wagons were drawn together for the night.

While Cutter took the horses to the corral, Rachel decided to move the ungainly wagon tongue to its proper place. She rose from the fire where water sizzled and tossed a couple of handfuls of Arbuckle coffee into the pot. A low, distant rumble shook the ground underfoot, and she forgot all about the misplaced wagon tongue. Hair rippled across her arms, and her hair, loose from its braid, crackled and stood out about her head.

It wasn't quite dark yet, and without warning the wind suddenly stopped blowing, just like that. Heavy, hot air hung about her and it was hard to breathe, as if some hidden creature had sucked the air from her lungs. Her skin grew slick with sweat. She gasped and hugged herself.

Where was Daniel? Why didn't he come back?

Lifting her face toward the western sky, she sniffed and caught the fresh smell of rain. A beast waited out there, ready to pounce. The tang of its wildness lay on her tongue.

The buffalo milled, bawling plaintively deep down in their throats. Toward the southwest a black wall of clouds boiled up from the horizon, its underbelly spewing jags of lightning.

The beast had a name. Cyclone!

As if summoned by the dreaded thought, a vicious gust of wind slammed into her, tangled strands of hair about her head, and whipped the long skirt around her slender form, then abruptly headed back in the direction from which it had come.

The ominous cloud rose, enveloped the burnt yellow sky; long, dark plumes spilled from its bottom, some touching the ground, others swaying, rising, dipping, and rising again. Her ears popped, her skin crawled, and as the wall of rain hit she lit out for cover.

A gully or even a low spot on the flat plain would be better than remaining out in the open. A few hundred yards away, the ground sloped gently to the northeast and she threw herself face down in the wet grass, already drenched to the skin. The storm roared overhead, the ground shook and rumbled under her, animals screamed in panic and fear, men shouted.

Cautiously she raised her head. Rain fell so hard she could barely see the outline of wagons. And racing alongside, between her shelter and the wagon train, a long, thick twister filled with debris. Trails of torn canvas slapped in the wind, broke away, and sailed into the churning maelstrom. Wooden crates flew up into the vortex as if they were mere feathers.

She watched a cedar butter churn lift and whirl, the dash wobbling madly as if some crazy hand worked it. Before she could blink, the long arm of the cyclone lifted, carrying its stolen cargo.

Abruptly the storm passed. The cloud moved on, dragging with it the rotating tails of destruction that bounced across the empty prairie. Sheets of rain swept along in its wake like a huge curtain.

She rose to her knees, wrung out the soaked skirt, and staggered to her feet. To the west bright rays of setting sun burst through a hole in the clouds. For a few moments there was no sound at all. The air turned to ice, her breath fogged around her face, goose bumps tickled her arms. She took several steps and halted and moved in a slow circle. The prairie was empty; the buffalo gone. There was no sign of even one of the shaggy beasts, as if they had all been snatched up by one of the whirling dervishes. In their fear of the storm, they must have stampeded, the fearful noise of their galloping hooves swallowed by the fierce roar of the cyclone.

Wading through several inches of water, she returned to the camp.

Miraculously none of the wagons had sustained more than minor damage. Some had lost their canvas coverings, a few supplies had gone off with the departing winds, and the Claridges' milk cow had disappeared as if into thin air. Talk was someone saw it actually carried away by the cyclone. Others said they doubted that and accused the storyteller of having been at the medicinal whiskey.

Rachel couldn't find the coffeepot she'd left simmering on the fire, and of course all campfires were soggy, sooty messes. Cutter Christie didn't return, so she assumed he had gone to help his sons clean up their own camp.

After recovering a few things—one of their blankets had been picked out of the wagon and deposited on the covering of the Schrimsher wagon—she gave in to her concern about Daniel and went to hunt up Captain Evans.

She had not even formed a question of the harried man when Second Lieutenant Peter Mankins rushed up.

"They're gone, sir. Ever' damn one of 'em."

"What, Mankins?"

When the man continued to sputter, Evans barked, "Settle down, Mr. Mankins, and make your report."

The young man took a deep breath, whirled, and pointed out across the prairie. "The buffalo, sir. That blamed storm done blowed ever' last one of 'em to kingdom come. I'll swear it did."

"Nonsense," Evans said. "They've run off, that's all. I hear those critters stampede at the drop of a hat."

"But, sir—"

"Enough, Mankins. No storm blows away thousands of head of buffalo. It just isn't possible."

"Well, then, how did they stampede without touching so much as one wagon? Tell me that, sir. I mean, excuse me, sir, but . . . well, sir, you have to admit it's queer."

Evans dismissed the excited lieutenant and turned to Rachel. "How did you fare, young lady?"

"Fine, just fine, sir. Captain, what about the men who . . . what about Daniel Wolfe? Has anyone heard from the men he left with?"

"I'll swear, that is a puzzlement. They haven't returned?"

"Not that I know of, and since all the buffalo are gone, what about the stock they went to round up?"

Evans shrugged. "I'm sure they'll turn up by dark. We've got a lot of assessment to do around here. Some of our own stock ran off with those shaggy beasts. Frankly, young lady, you ought to get down on your knees and thank God for your life, and all of ours too. You go on back to your camp and get things cleaned up. I'm sure they'll be back before long. If not, well, then we'll send someone out to look for them."

Disappointed, Rachel watched Evans walk away and said to his back, "I'll not wait around till someone drags in his dead body."

She whirled and ran to the corral, spied a likely-looking bay horse and hampered somewhat by her wet clothing, struggled onto its back without bothering with bridle or saddle. Unerringly she rode off in the direction in which Daniel had gone earlier in the day.

If she didn't locate the men before the sun set, it was likely she wouldn't. There was very little time to spare. The prairie was big and deceiving in its distances. Sitting astraddle of the horse, she concentrated completely on Daniel. She searched for his spirit, letting her body and mind drift into the place of visions and sink into a cloud of silent mist so that the Yunwi Tsunsdi' could lead her in the correct way. The little people spirits were kindhearted and would help, if only she allowed it.

The rocking motion of the horse, the fresh cool breeze, and flickers of last light from the setting sun, faded. Only one thing occupied her mind. Finding Daniel.

On and on she rode, darkness chasing at her heels like a soundless predator. Though she made no noise, her soul called out and prodded the silence for sign of the man she loved. A calmness closed over her, and in the distance she saw ripples in the settling dusk, small, indistinct creatures beckoning her onward.

Off to her right something flickered. Pale stars

pierced the ashy sky, glimmering brighter as their velvet bed darkened. When she first noticed the faint flame she thought it only a low-lying star or dying traces of the setting sun. With both fists she tugged at the horse's mane and swung his head around. The light flared, her heart leaped, and she headed in that direction, kicking her soaked moccasins into the animal's flanks. For a long while the light appeared to remain the same distance away, but she had learned that out here on the plains that was the way things were. She continued moving toward it. A few times she lost sight of the fire burning and knew that she had ridden into a depression, but she kept moving.

At last the dim glow began to grow in her vision, and she cupped both hands around her mouth to call out. She shouted his name once, twice, three times, then waited for an answer. None came. Fear smothered the hope she carried. She repeated the action again and continued to ride and listen for even the faintest of replies. None came.

Who had built the fire, then, if no one was out there? Surely not lightning, for the drenching rain would have put it out. There were no forests here to burn, only grasses, a few of the brittle cottonwood and the iron-hard bois d'arc that they called Osage orange in many places.

She tried calling out again and waited. The horse plodded on, his own mission defined by the fingers curled through his mane, the knees pressed to his ribs, the stubborn passenger who would not let him slow.

Finally, when it looked as if the fire would go out, her name came through the night on whispering feet. The vague sound wavered across the plains, nearly indistinguishable. She kicked the animal into a run and shouted Daniel's name over and over, almost overrunning the flames before sliding from the horse's back.

A faint, nearly indistinct voice repeated her name as if it would be for the very last time.

In the starlight she made out his form sprawled beside a small pitiful pile of wet wood. There was no fire there, never had been. Dropping to her knees beside him, she touched his wet, trembling shoulder.

"Daniel, it is me, Winter Dawn. Are you hurt?"

"Caught . . . caught in a stampede," he said, grabbing at her hand. "The others, I don't know where they are, but I think they're dead. How did you find me? I tried to build a fire, but all the wood was wet. Couldn't get anything to burn. I think I broke some ribs, it's hard to breathe. Hurts like hell. Thought I'd wait till morning to light out to find the train. Did you see anyone else? How did you find me?"

His babbling frightened Rachel, and she touched a hand to his cheek. He was burning up with fever. She turned once more to gaze at the few sticks of wet wood and wondered about the fire she'd followed through the darkness, then dismissed it. She had to get him back to safety, and she was as sure that she could do that as she had been that she would find him.

"Daniel, I have a horse. You're going to have to help me get you mounted. I'm taking you back."

"No, can't. Don't you see them out there? All around us. They'll shoot if we move."

"Sshh, Daniel. No one is out there. I'll help you. Come on, put your arm around my neck. I can't do this alone."

"Winter Dawn?" Her name spoken in Cherokee came out of the darkness like a spirit. Yet it was no spirit who spoke to her, and she managed to ask in a quavering voice, "Who is that?"

"Your brother, Awa'hili."

She had known, of course. Almost the instant he spoke her name, but had not trusted that knowing. So much had happened, so much time had passed. Surely this was a dream walk, and she lay asleep in the wagon at Daniel's side. True to what her grandmother Bone Woman had taught, though, she must open herself to such a happening, embrace it, and learn its meaning.

"What do you want? Surely you know you must leave us alone."

"I followed you. I saw what happened. It was the Yunwi Tsunsdi' who helped you find him." His voice held a sort of awe as he spoke of the little people spirits who help those who are lost. "I've brought his horse, let me help. I promise I won't try to take you back. I only want to help."

"You are afraid. Why are you so frightened?" Winter Dawn asked him.

"I am not afraid. I am only very sad. Surely, my sister, you can understand that sadness."

A lump grew in her throat. Did this mean that her brother was no longer of the living? That his spirit had left his body and only stopped here for a moment before moving on? Or perhaps this was not her brother, but might instead be Tsistu, the trickster and malicious deceiver who sometimes appeared in the form of a rabbit. Many spirits were able to take human form too.

"Get away from me. I can do this."

He said nothing and watched her motionlessly.

She knelt and wrapped Daniel's arm around her neck, then planted her feet firmly and tried to raise him.

"Help me, Daniel. Please try."

A low moan came from his lips.

She sobbed and tried again, straining until dancing lights flashed in her vision.

Eagle appeared beside her, bent, and lifted Daniel in his arms as if he were a child.

"Go to the other side, balance him so he does not fall when I put him over its back."

As he shoved Daniel headfirst onto the piebald mare, she helped turn him so that he straddled the saddle but lay facedown. A guttural moan escaped his lips while he clamped both arms around the animal's neck and rested his head in the shaggy mane, his breath jagged.

Winter Dawn turned to thank her brother, but he was not there. She had not heard him ride away, he was simply gone. She raised her face and lifted her arms in a moment of reverence, then took Rhymer's reins, mounted her bay, and led the animal and its burden back in the direction from which she had come.

Puzzling things had happened this night. Her grandmother Bone Woman would have explanations for it all. In the years to come the story would become a part of the family legend; the family she and Daniel would one day have.

Had Eagle really been there, or had the part of his spirit from that small lost boy who lived within his tortured soul come to help the sister he once loved? Or worse, had his spirit truly left his body? She might never know.

Because they had to move so slowly, stopping once in a while to dismount and reposition Daniel before he slipped to the ground, the trip back took much longer than her search. By the time they reached the circled wagon train, everyone was in bed except the guards. In the light of the central fire she could see that much of the damage from the cyclone had been repaired or cleared away.

She explained only a little of what had happened to the guard who came to meet her and told him to inform Evans about the lost men, then took Daniel to his wagon. By walking the horse right up against the tailgate, she was able to tug Daniel off its back and inside. There she stripped his wet clothing off, took off her own, and bundled up with him in a cocoon of blankets.

He groaned and encircled her in his arms, the heat from his feverish skin warming her like a fire. The next morning she would bind his ribs tightly so that they would heal. She could only pray that he had no injuries they could not see or feel. Then he would surely die. If that happened she would join him, for she could no longer imagine life without him. Before falling asleep she thanked Little Deer, the spirit people, and Awa'hili for rescuing her and the man she loved.

Sometime before dawn Daniel roused enough to realize that he was not dead and that Winter Dawn lay curled beside him in a nice, warm bed. The rampaging storm and resulting buffalo stampede were too real in his memory to have been a dream. He moved and pain shot through him. What he remembered had indeed happened, but he had no idea how he had come to this place.

He remembered the storm approaching, the smell and taste, the roar that had blended with the thundering of thousands of hooves, the scream of his own mount. Men shouting, riding in all directions, going down under the cataclysm of snorting, pawing beasts. And later, awakening with the fire in his chest. Crawling, fighting the agony that clutched at his lungs and stole his breath. Trying to build a fire with matches from his tin box. Unable to find the others, though he crawled in ever-widening circles until the pain felled him like a massive tree crushing his chest. All these things he recalled, but nothing more.

She had come to him then, as in the other dream, and he had thought himself dead. How was it he lay here now in her arms? He would think himself dead except for the pain. And he was pretty sure there wasn't supposed to be pain in heaven. Since his chest hurt damnably, he figured there was no doubt about it. He was alive and lying with Winter Dawn. After a while, he shut off the confused jumble in his brain and drifted once more to sleep. Safe in her arms. If this was heaven, if this was eternity, then he was right where he belonged.

The banging went on and on. The wagon rocked with the force. Rachel stirred first, but Daniel began to move as well.

"What? What is it?" Her voice was muffled by the quilts and she skinned them down to her shoulders. "Who is that?"

"Need to talk to Wolfe. Now!"

She touched his shoulder.

"I heard," he said and started to sit up, but discovered he couldn't. He hugged himself, but that only made matters worse. "Ah, hell. Who is it, what do you want?"

"Evans. We want to send out a party to search for the two men who were with you. We need you to go with us and show us the way."

"He's not going, he's hurt," Rachel shouted. She scrambled around for some dry clothing and went through several things folded neatly on a trunk before slipping into a skirt and shift. As she crawled over the tailgate she flipped her long hair from beneath the blouse.

"Wait, Winter Dawn. Tell them I'll dress and go."

She scowled at the way he held himself as he tried to put on his buckskins, still wet from the night before. "You'll not go. Those are wet. Get back under the blankets and stay there. I'll be right back."

He gazed at her in amazement.

"I'll tend to you when I return," she added and left.

Daniel stared at the opening. What had come over her? His memory of the night before returned full-blown. The woman was truly very unusual; she had senses he could only guess at. How had she found him out there on that wide open prairie? And how had she managed to get him on a horse and back here? And now, ordering him about as if he were her child. She had never spoken like that in his presence before.

He heard her voice raised outside and listened.

"I found him, I can lead you there. As for the others, he said they went down under the hooves of the buffalo when the storm hit and they stampeded. They are dead, I think. I found no one else. He has broken ribs, maybe much worse. He must not ride, it could kill him."

A man answered her. It sounded like Evans. "Well, ma'am, I can appreciate what you're saying, but we can't leave them men out there. We'll lay over a day and send out a search party. No use your bothering. What direction did you say?"

There were some murmurings he couldn't make out, then she climbed back inside.

"Now for you," she said. She began tearing wide strips from feed sacking. "I told them where I found you."

"How?"

She raised her brows but didn't answer; she just kept ripping those cotton sacks like she had nothing better to do. Daniel lay flat on his back and crossed his arms over his chest. It eased the pain a little, especially if he didn't breathe. Watching her, the way she tilted her head and nibbled at her lip, the long smooth line of her arms, the graceful way she had of performing even the simplest task, filled him with wonder.

"How did you find me?"

She moved nearer, spread her fingers over his mouth. "Hush, now. Be still. You're going to have to sit up. I'll help you."

He grunted with the effort, sweat popping out on his face, but together they got him into a position where she could tightly wrap the cloth round and round his upper body.

Long strands of her hair lay across his lap as she bent in concentration. He wanted to kiss the golden skin along the back of her neck when she leaned forward, wanted to hold her. All he could do was sit there with his arms stuck out and bite at his lip so she wouldn't think him a baby for taking on. It was worse than the time he'd wrestled around with that damned bear, but he could take it.

She finally finished, but instead of moving away trailed her hands along his sides to rest at his waist. He was extremely conscious of being naked under the blanket that lay across his hips.

"Lie down gently," she whispered.

Cradling his shoulders, she eased him back until he lay flat. Her tongue lapped past his ear and down the side of his neck.

He shivered, trying to breathe shallowly to keep the pain away.

She moved to the hollow in his throat, being careful not to put any weight on him. As she did so, she tugged her skirt down over her hips. For an instant, she was gone and he opened his eyes to watch her skin out of her clothing. She wore nothing underneath.

"Don't worry, I'll be gentle."

He laughed, then wished he hadn't. "Oh, God. God, that hurts."

"I won't hurt you though. Just lie very still and I'll do everything. You don't even have to move. Look at that, would you? Agili."

"Winter Dawn?"

"Sshh, hush, my darling. I am going to heal you."

She pulled the blanket aside and circled her long, warm fingers around Agili. They were slick with some kind of salve.

"See, He Who Rises knows what to do. He is very silent and prepared." She leaned forward and kissed an ugly bruise on his thigh. Her firm bare breast brushed his skin.

Daniel moaned.

"Do you hurt?"

"No. No, not at all. Keep going."

She laughed. "You lie so well, Daniel Wolfe. But this is very serious. All necessary in order to heal you."

"Yes, of course. I agree. Could you move just a little, a little more? Ah, yes. Your power is coming through . . . right there. Yes. Now. Yes. Ahhh."

After a while she moved both hands upward to rest on his hipbones and shifted so that her knees straddled his thighs. Her hair lay in pools over his skin.

With gentle fingers she began to massage his shoulders, working down one arm into the hand and then shifting to the other arm. Occasionally she applied more of the mysterious salve to her palms before going back to her task. He couldn't see what it was, but it grew warm as she rubbed it into his flesh, being very careful not to hurt him.

The insides of her bare legs whispered against his outer thighs as she moved backward on her knees. Moist fingers splayed along either side of his waist, she began to knead with both thumbs. Each time she found a bruise or scrape she kissed it before rubbing the salve there.

"Relax, please," she murmured and circled the heels of both hands tenderly along his upper thighs.

A long drawn-out sigh escaped his lips.

Desire swelled through him, but no matter how hard he tried he couldn't budge. Passion sizzled through his brain, he moved his arms, longing to hold her and kiss first one breast then the other.

"No, lie still. I have not finished." Down one leg, fingers and slick palms rubbing, soothing, right to the bottoms of his feet and back up the other leg.

One moment he wanted to make love to her, the next he wanted only to drift off into the relaxing darkness. Finally the darkness won, and he was scarcely conscious of her pulling the blanket over him right up to his chin, her warm lips moist against his for a brief moment. He opened his mouth to her and drifted away, her taste vivid on his tongue.

Chapter Eleven

The days stretched before and behind the travelers in a seemingly unending chain, one hard day running into the next. Being young, they all took to it well and shrugged away dire predictions of hardships to come. Spring warmed toward summer. If there were any problems, they were shortages of water and firewood, but they made do with few complaints. They met no hostile Indians, suffered from no diseases. Breakdowns and repairs were minor and to be expected. Grass was abundant, and if long stretches without water sometimes grew tiring, there was always the next stream or lake or spring. Optimistic talk of gold in California dominated nearly every conversation.

A break in the normal routine came when they reached the Santa Fe Trace a few days after the tragedy of losing two men to the buffalo stampede and storm. Both were hard workers and would be missed, though they had tended to keep to themselves.

When the wagons came to a halt much before noon, word was passed that it might be a while before they could swing west on the trace. It was said to be crowded with wagons and they would have to wait their turn.

When the messenger rode on, Rachel settled the team and went to find Daniel, who was taking a turn at riding herd on the four hundred animals accompanying the train.

She found him on Rhymer, moving through the choking dust with a bandanna tied over his nose and mouth, his big hat tilted down over his eyes. He kicked a foot out of the stirrup so she could mount up behind him to tell him the news.

The animals milled to a halt, the dust blew off to the northeast, and they began to crop grass. He maneuvered his mount to keep an eye on the restless animals and pulled the bandanna down.

"Everything okay?" he asked.

"Just fine. I've missed you." She tightened her arms around his waist and laid her head against his back. The smell of leather and dust tickled at her nose.

"Me too," he said and pressed her fingers with a gloved hand. "Good thing you're along with me. They almost didn't let me sign up for this drive 'cause I had no one to spell me on the wagon so I could do my share." He grinned and she thought he looked almost boyish. Deep lines of fatigue from restless nights no longer carved through the flesh around his eyes and mouth. "Must be 'cause I'm such a big fellow that they let me come along."

She patted the bulging muscles along his arm. "I like that about you myself, and I like driving the team. It's better than picking up buffalo chips or just walking along with nothing to do."

He spread her hand over his mouth for a kiss and at the same time deftly swung Rhymer in a circle and cut off a couple of oxen that had determinedly headed across the prairie. "Ho, cows. You ain't goin' home yet, skeedaddle."

Rachel hung on and tightened her knees to keep from slipping off the sweating horse. "Will we see the mountains soon? I can hardly wait."

"A few days, if we ever get to moving again. They

say at Bent's Fort you can sit on the walls and see the snow-covered peaks. I don't know. It's just what I heard. Reckon what's taking so long?"

"I'm not sure. Seems like we're wasting a lot of time just sitting here. If I could have that bay I'd ride up and see what's going on."

Daniel thought about that a minute. He could see no harm in it and so he stepped Rhymer into the herd to drop a rope over the bay's neck. Rachel scrambled agilely from the piebald's back onto the gentle little horse she'd ridden the night she rescued Daniel.

He watched with admiration when she rode off without benefit of bridle or saddle, signaling the bay using knees and heels. From what she'd said, she had been riding since before she could walk. While he felt right at home on horseback, he'd never be the rider she was. He wished he could buy her that horse so she wouldn't have to walk so much, but what cash he'd had left after outfitting his wagon had gone to Evans to pay his way west.

Rachel slowed when she saw her friend Minna walking. "Going to see the trace?"

Minna turned her head to gaze from under her bonnet. "And find out what's holding us up."

"I'll ride you."

Minna eyed the saddleless bay. "I've never ridden clothespin style."

Rachel laughed. "It does chafe some, but if you wear bloomers it's not so bad."

Minna blushed. "I hear tell some of the women are wearing bloomers with a short skirt over top. Say it keeps the burrs and stickers out of their skirts, but I'd not expose myself like that. You go on, I'll walk. Meet you there."

Rachel nodded and prodded the bay into a gallop, swinging wide of the wagons. The wind lifted her hair and dried the perspiration on her face. She didn't understand how Minna and Zoe and Mrs. Claridge could wear those slatted bonnets all day. They could see nothing without turning their heads, and they must be very hot. The sun and wind kissed her skin and she glowed under the touch and felt the healing powers.

She rounded the great curve of wagons and gasped with surprise. As far as she could see to the east and the west wagons rolled in a steady line. It was an amazing sight, and one she could never have imagined. Gentling the bay to a walk, she rode to meet them, studying the families and their wagons.

Youngsters and women walked for the most part while the men handled the oxen. Moving two abreast were large farm wagons being pulled by six oxen, smaller wagons pulled by four horses, and even some smaller carriages with two horse teams and genteel ladies riding beside a driver. It was evident that all kinds of people from the rich to the poor were headed west to the gold strike, or to homestead land. There were men and women with large families as well as young couples who had no children at all.

One young man, no more than a boy, walked beside a team of oxen and carried a long whip. He greeted her and she turned to ride alongside him for a while.

"Where did you come from?" she asked.

"I'm with my folks. We lived up in Iowa, but times got real hard, and my dad, he's always had the yen to be somewheres else. We're going to strike it rich in California. They's ten of us, and so we outfitted two wagons. Worst was crossing the Missouri. We had to take the wheels off the wagons and carry the bodies onto the flatboats. Sometimes they could take two or three small wagons at a time."

Rachel was fascinated by the tale. "How did they keep the boats from just floating away down the river?" she asked.

"Oh, they was attached by a pulley to a rope stretched across the river. Even at that, with the men rowing hard as we could, we fetched up far down the opposite shore and had to be towed back upstream to the landing. It took our group over a week just to get across the river. 'Course there's a hundred and twenty wagons struck out with us. Some have turned back."

"Turned back?" Rachel was aghast. "After so much work why would they do that?"

The boy shrugged as if he didn't understand either.

No member of the Evans train had even discussed turning back, so far as she knew, but she supposed that was different, since they hadn't started out with entire families. She could see where women and babies might be put under more of a strain. Men and unencumbered women fared better on the trail, for though they were all responsible for each other to an extent, each had only themselves to look out after.

"Where'd you'all come from?" the boy asked.

She saw that they were approaching the long line of waiting wagons from the Evans train, but she wanted to talk to the boy some more, so she kept riding right on past, with Minna hollering yoo hoo at her in a high voice.

She told the boy something about the Evans train, and he was amazed that it contained "wild savages."

"We worry about Indians," he said, his eyes bright and wide. "Captain has even had us drill what to do should we be attacked. Ain't you afraid?"

Rachel couldn't resist her reply. "I can't be afraid, I'm part Indian myself." Immediately she wished she could recall the words. It was important that she learn not to tell folks what they had no need to know, especially if she were to pass for white.

The boy pulled up in his tracks and the oxen he was herding kept right on plodding along. "You sure don't look it," he finally said, then turned and ran to catch up.

Rachel watched the boy a moment longer, absorbing what he had said. She didn't look like an Indian. Did that mean no one would guess her secret out West? She reined the bay around and rode back to join Minna.

When a gap finally appeared behind the long line, Evans sent a rider off to the east to inform the next train that they needed to halt while he moved his forty wagons onto the Santa Fe Trace. Excitement hammered in Rachel's chest as the lead wagon moved out. At last they were actually going west and soon would see the mountains. She rode back as fast as the bay would gallop to tell Daniel and keep their place in the line. If she fell out, she'd have to bring up the tail end and they would eat dust.

The Arkansas River, which they had followed up out of the Nation, swung west at the trace and went with them. The Cherokee Trail would share the route for only a while, splitting off to the north before they reached the Rockies. They would cross the mountains at what was supposed to be a much easier pass up north beyond the Laramie Plains. Many insisted that the hardest part of the trip was yet to come.

Rachel continued to drive the team while Daniel put in time with other duties. Though he still had some pain from the broken ribs he could tolerate it well enough. At the outset of the trip every man had agreed to serve a certain amount of hours at other duties, such as driving the tremendous herd of stock, and serving as an outrider, a forward scout, and a night guard. Each took an occasional turn at wood gathering as well.

The second day on the trace, Daniel slept all morning because he had been on guard duty all night. He awoke when the train stopped for nooning, and ate with Rachel. There was so little time to enjoy each other's company that even the thirty minutes or so between unhitching the animals for their rest and rehitching to be on their way were precious. Most of the time they ate leftovers from breakfast, a scrap of bread or cold slapjacks, maybe some buffalo jerky or the like. They had long ago eaten the last of the fresh buffalo meat killed while they rode through the herd. Occasionally someone would kill a few rabbits and there would be rabbit stew for the entire train.

Rachel had not mentioned Minna's suggestion that she and Daniel were living in sin. Everything that had happened had driven it right out of her mind.

One night Henry Rattlingourd appeared at their supper fire, dressed in his traditional garb and looking very serious. Grim, Rachel thought. She dreaded what he had come to say.

Daniel politely asked him to sit and have a cup of coffee. Henry accepted, sank cross-legged across the fire to stare at Daniel. He never once let his gaze settle on her, but studied first the flames, then the steaming liquid in his cup.

Finally he spoke. "I was pleased to see that your injuries were not too severe."

Daniel inclined his head, sipped, and waited. Rachel started to get up and leave. Men's business was none of hers. Daniel touched her arm and shook his head. He was uncomfortable in the company of this man Rachel had once ridden with. Henry might wish to say something Daniel would rather not hear, especially without Rachel present.

"She will stay," he told Henry.

The expression in Daniel's gray eyes was enough to make her sit back down beside him, though she had no idea why he wanted her to remain.

Henry nodded. "Some of us are going to split off,

scout an alternate route in a while. A more southerly route might be much less dangerous. I am here to advise you of the dangers awaiting the train as it heads north and see if you can be persuaded to accompany us. You and Winter Dawn. I am frightened of what will happen to her if you remain with Evans."

"Is Evans not to be trusted?" Daniel threw a stick into the fire.

Henry shrugged. "That has nothing to do with it. All along it was known that some of the Cherokee would track in different directions searching for better water and grass, easier passage." He shrugged. "It is normal. At any rate, about sixteen or so of us plan on heading south after we reach the Laramie Plains. That'll take us below the Snowy Mountains. We would like to know if we can count on you to go with us." He gazed, not at Daniel, but at Rachel.

"Everyone's had confidence in Evans all along. Even the Cherokee who first proposed this trip settled for him as their leader. I don't think it's wise to separate. This is a foolish move. We'll do better staying together.

"The original agreement was that at least one hundred of the men on this trip would carry rifles and plenty of ammunition. The reason for that seems plain. Protection of the entire train. If you go your way, how many of those will go with you, leaving the main body unprotected?"

"Only a few. Like I said, it is arranged. But I'm not concerned with anyone except Winter Dawn."

"Well, you should be," Daniel said. "If we fail as a group, then she is in danger as well. Besides, I don't think she wants to go with you."

Henry rose and tossed the dregs of his coffee into the fire. It hissed and sent up a cloud of smoke. "Damn fool," he muttered. "You could make her go with me where she'll be safe."

Daniel came to his feet as well. "That's nonsense. No one is safe in this country. If you wanted her safe, you should have stopped her coming, or taken her home while you still could."

"Wolfe, you'll get her killed, and for no good reason. The way Evans chooses is treacherous. She will drown in some river, or some wild Indian will carry her off, or she will fall from a cliff. If you won't follow our route, then let me take her with us."

Rachel spoke, startling both men into silence. "I will not go with you. My place is here, with my husband."

Henry flinched. "Your husband. You lie with this man. He is not your husband and you are no better than a squaw. What would Bone Woman say? What would your dear mother Singing Bird say?"

Rachel scrambled to her feet, and before Daniel could prevent it pulled the bowie from its sheath at his waist and held it out in front of her, the point wavering in Henry's direction.

"*Kanegwàti,*" she spat. "*Suli.* You dare speak the name of the dead. Leave, do not ever come to us again or I will cut out your heart." She repeated the Cherokee words for the vicious moccasin snake and buzzard, adding the English as well. They tasted bitter on her tongue and made her throat ache with the venom of her hate.

Daniel watched in awe. The power of her emotions emanated like heat off the fire. For just an instant he'd thought she would launch herself at Rattlingourd and he'd have to pull them apart, but she held herself in check. In any battle, he'd take her on his side and be glad of it.

"Rachel, give me the knife," he said softly. "Come on, darlin', you're scaring the man."

She whirled, eyes flashing shards of ice. "Don't

mock me, Daniel Wolfe, or I'll put you on the same side of the fire with this . . . this . . ."

He held up a hand and grinned, because he couldn't help himself. "Snake, buzzard. I like the Cherokee better. You'll have to teach me more." Without taking his eyes from the wavering knife point, he said, "Rattlingourd, I'd appreciate it if you left now. You can see this could easily get out of hand, and I don't believe I could stop her if she takes a notion to cut out your heart."

"No one could," she spat, whirled, and threw the knife with such precision it stuck in the ground between Henry's feet. The dull thud of blade biting deep in the soil was the only sound between them for a split second, then Henry muttered something neither of them could understand and strode away.

After a moment Daniel said, "Now that you're not armed, would it be safe to give you a hug?"

She turned, the ice melting from her blue eyes. "I love you, Daniel Wolfe, but don't think I won't fight for what I believe, because I will. That man insulted me and my family, and I had every right to do what I did without your trying to scoff at me or tease me out of it. The next time, you throw the knife at him, because if you don't I'll bury it in his evil heart."

"Aw, Rachel. He's not evil. Ill-advised, perhaps, but no one who loves you could be all evil. He is frightened for you."

"Love. Ha! He wants me in his bed, and that is all. He would never be half as good to me as you are, and don't you forget it!"

"Don't worry, I won't." Daniel took one giant step and swept her into a bear hug. "And you are the best thing in my life."

He could feel her still trembling with rage, but she returned his hug and lay her head against his chest. The fury that had arisen within her chest frightened her. How could she be white if she could not control that wild part of her from her Cherokee ancestors?

"From now on, Daniel, I will try to behave like a white lady, I promise."

He wanted to beg her not to go getting too civilized on him, he liked that wild streak, it lent excitement not only to their lovemaking but to their day-to-day life. But he knew now wasn't the time to say so, so he kept his silence and kissed her ear through the fall of hair. With gentle fingers he swept the locks aside and growled playfully against her throat.

"I think it is time we went to bed," she said, and took his hand and led him toward the wagon.

He paused long enough to light a stick in the campfire, and inside carefully lit and placed a candle so he could watch Rachel prepare for bed. He liked to watch her dress and undress. As always on readying herself to sleep, she turned away from him to slip out of her clothing, revealing the supple curve of her back, the single dimple above each hip, the shapely line of her legs. Candlelight gleamed on her bare flesh and set the red highlights in her hair afire.

With anticipation he awaited her next move, one he knew quite well. She would turn to him slowly, chin high so she could look him in the eye. Then she would shyly offer herself to him, running her graceful fingers over the swell of her breasts, down across the tiny mound of her stomach into the nest of dark hair below, at last reaching out for his hand to guide it slowly into place.

As she performed the ritual he removed his shirt, unlaced his knee boots and kicked out of them and the buckskin leggings, never once taking his eyes from her graceful movements. By the time she reached for him, he was more than ready.

Her hand, though, clasped his then paused. Concern clouded her features, she squeezed until his fingers hurt.

"Have you heard talk about us?"

"Talk?"

"About what Henry said. Living in sin. Minna said the same thing. Said everyone is talking. I want to know if this is true."

"That's nonsense. I don't listen to the foolish things people say."

"Then it's true?"

"No, of course not. Besides, what do we care?"

"I care, Daniel." She almost whispered the words and lowered her head.

"Why? We owe these people no explanation for the way we live. It is our way, not theirs."

"But in the white world it is frowned upon for a man and woman to live together without . . . without being married."

He stepped forward and touched her shoulder. "I thought you said we were married . . . when we said the vows."

"That is in my world. But—"

"But what, my darling?" He cupped the side of her face with both hands and raised her head so that she was looking at him. Her pale blue eyes shimmered with unshed tears.

She blinked and one tear overflowed to trail down her cheek.

His tough little Cherokee had her soft side as well. Rattlingourd's visit had brought this on, he was sure. Yet she had obviously given it a lot of thought for a long while.

He inched closer so that their naked flesh brushed evocatively, then leaned down to kiss the tear away, lowered his hands to her shoulders, and buried his face in the warmth of her neck.

"I love you, Winter Dawn . . . Rachel. With all my

heart, with all my soul. You are my life, my very being. Without you, my spirit would return to the depths of hell where you found it. You made me whole and I won't lose you. Tell me what you want, and I will do it, but don't tell me we have to part. Please don't tell me that, for I won't survive."

As he finished, he encircled her in his arms, pulling her so close she could scarcely breathe. His ragged desperate words drove out every thought but the love she felt for him. The doubts she'd voiced, her desire to live in the white world, her fear of the poverty which she had escaped, all paled in the light of his adoration.

"Oh, Daniel, I'll never leave you. Never."

She succumbed to his desire and her own, as together they sank to the nest of quilts. They made love with a tender reverence akin to worship, each endearment murmured as if in prayer. Where stormy abandonment usually ruled, there grew instead a gentle persuasion, a coaxing of the most delicate of emotions. Nips turned into languid tastings. Each moved slowly, swaying with the other as if in leisurely dance, and when he brought her to the edge, they lingered there a long time among the shooting stars while the heat smoldered between them, within them. The ride lasted so long that each lost their consciousness of time or place, aware only that they were together in some wonderful, bright and beautiful place known only to them. A place where angels and spirits dwelled together, where love was all and pain unknown.

She slept even as he withdrew himself, and he lay on his back, head resting on one crooked arm. It had been a long time since he had feared sleeping, feared the horrible dreams, for Winter Dawn had taken the child to a peaceful resting place where she no longer haunted him with her death. Yet this night he could not sleep, nor could he stir, but it was for a totally different reason. Contentment. It must be savored, explored, enjoyed, for he had never experienced such a feeling before in his lifetime. He lay as if unconscious, every bone and muscle relaxed, unmoving. Beside him she breathed softly, he imagined he could hear her heartbeat. What would he do if he lost her? Why had Henry come to remind him of the tenuous existence of their lives? He finally dozed off, and when he awoke before dawn his body was curved around hers as if he could in that way keep her safe and with him always.

Daniel and Rachel went to speak to Captain Evans the next morning and found him eating breakfast. He offered coffee, Daniel accepted and poured himself a cup. Rachel waited in silence.

Daniel finally broached the subject. "I hear some of the folks want to ride south."

Evans chewed a bite of salt pork. "Thought they might, reckon they'll wait a spell till we're closer to the mountains."

"Any problems?"

"Nah. A few men want to check out some alternate routes, that's all. We'll join back up later. We've always considered the possibility of scouting different routes as we move west."

"Any danger that the Plains Indians will give us trouble?"

"We'll go north of both the Arapahoe and the Cheyenne stomping grounds. The Cherokee are friendly with the other tribes, we shouldn't have trouble. Hardest thing we'll see is the actual trip. Swollen rivers, muddy trails, bad water. It's gonna get real rough once we leave the plains no matter what route we take."

"I thought the agreement was that at least a hundred of the men would be well armed with plenty of ammunition. Seems to me they ought to stick together, protect the train."

Evans squinted at Daniel. "You armed, Mr. Wolfe?"

He thought of the Hawkens that he had returned to Henry and wished now he had it. "No, sir. Just this." He patted the bowie strapped to his waist. "Always been a trapper, not a hunter."

"Be wise if you armed yourself." Evans stuffed the last of a biscuit in his mouth and washed it down with coffee before speaking again. And when he did he rose to his feet.

"Time we moved out, we may see mountains today if we're lucky. These plains can get to a fella real fast if he's used to mountains. Nothin' much to see."

When Daniel continued to stand there, Evans said, "Something else I can do for you, young fella?"

"Yes, sir. As a matter of fact, there is. I was wondering . . . that is, we were wondering, Rachel and I . . ." He broke off, cleared his throat. "We want to get married, sir."

Evans grinned. "Today?"

"Well . . ."

Evans glanced at Rachel and pulled Daniel out of her hearing. "Son, just what's the point? I mean, she's already under the blanket with you. Isn't it a little late? Besides, she's a . . . well, she's an Indian. Don't you think you ought to mull this over a while?"

"No, I don't. Can you marry us or not?"

"Hell, boy. I can say you some words, if that's all you need. It'll be a while before we come somewhere where there's a real preacher . . . in the eyes of God, and such. But, hell, boy, words I can say. Bring her on over tonight when we stop, I'll mutter a few things. Make everyone happy, huh?" Once more that crooked smile appeared.

Daniel ground his teeth and glanced at Rachel. "I don't think that will be necessary. We'll wait for a preacher." Fuming, he captured her arm and marched with her back to their wagon.

"Condescending son of a bitch," he muttered.

At their wagon Rachel jerked her arm from his grasp. "Don't drag me around like some dog, Daniel Wolfe. Tell me what he said."

"The man's a fool."

"Fools aren't put in positions of such importance. Perhaps he didn't understand."

"Oh, he understood all right. He understood just like Zoe and Minna and the rest of them understand. It's people like these that make me happy to live in the wilderness. Winter Dawn, we are married in your eyes and in mine, and that's all that matters. Forget all the rest of them. When we get to the next town we'll find us a preacher, until then I'll sleep under the wagon if you like."

She wanted to chide him for calling her by her Cherokee name, but perhaps it was a sign. It seemed she could not move into his white world so easily. She put her arms around his neck and raised on tiptoe to kiss his clenched jaw. Tight muscles rippled under her lips. She had never seen him so angry. What had the captain said when they had had their heads together? She decided she probably didn't want to know.

"You will not lie on the hard ground while I sleep in our bed alone. Not for one night. You are my husband, my love forever. No one can change that. Words won't change that. I'm sorry I caused trouble by asking."

He relaxed, curved his arms around her waist, and held her tightly for a moment. "You didn't cause the trouble, they did. Now let's get loaded up or they'll leave us behind."

He gazed off into the distance. Tomorrow he would approach Henry Rattlingourd and offer him some prime pelts for the Hawkens he'd let him use when they went after Rachel. For he couldn't still that small voice whispering in his head, urging him to light out across the prairie, just him and this woman he loved, before something dreadful happened.

Chapter Twelve

The next day they saw the dead corpses lined up alongside the trail. Two wagons had pulled off the trail and a man and woman were busy digging graves.

The Evans train didn't slow, but Rachel lagged behind, unable to take her eyes from the sight. Two children hung from the back of the wagon, eyes wide, faces white. They were still as death.

She asked what had killed the dead ones, two women, a man, and a young boy.

The lank, dirty man spat in the dust and kept on digging, as if she hadn't spoken. The woman, perhaps remembering a few social graces in the face of such tragedy, peered up from under her slatted bonnet, tossed a shovelful of dirt out of the shallow hole on which she toiled, and said, "My boy, my man, this 'un's woman. Cholera."

She went back to digging. There were tear trails in the dust that coated her cheeks, but she was no longer crying.

"Will you go on?"

The two dug awhile and Rachel decided she would not get an answer.

The man stopped and gazed a moment at his dead wife lying wrapped beside the grave. Then he squinted up into the sun. "There's gold in California.

Nothing back yonder." He swung an arm toward the east and jammed the shovel deep in the soil.

Rachel thought of other graves and choices she and her people had never been allowed to make. She should feel vindicated that the whites were suffering so, but somehow she didn't. This was different and had nothing to do with what had happened during the removal.

"Well, I wish you well," she said.

She ran as if being pursued, passing by Daniel and the wagon, not slowing until she caught up with Minna.

"No sense in stopping, child. Nothing any of us can do." Minna kept watching the trail, the bonnet shading her eyes. "What was it killed them?"

"Cholera."

Minna shuddered. "Lord God, let's hope we don't get infested with that. It's a killer, sure enough. I've heard stories of hundreds dying on the Oregon Trail from it. You didn't touch them or anything, did you?"

"No. Is that how you get it, touching?"

"No one really knows. But it spreads like wildfire sometimes. Perhaps it's in the very air we breathe, yet some can be in proximity and never come down."

Rachel arched her brows. "Proximity?"

Minna studied her. "Where did you learn to speak English?"

"My father when I was small, and my friend Alice attends Miss Sawyer's Seminary for Girls. She helped me, but there are so many words I do not yet know."

Minna took her hand and swung it between them. "Proximity means being very close together. I have an idea. Every day I will teach you a new word you do not know. It will be like a game that will help pass the time."

Rachel was very touched by the offer, but feared

it would be similar to the invitation to come and hear the piano played. That had never happened either.

Before Minna could continue, a great clamor arose ahead. Men shouted, a woman screamed, a baby cried, and the wagon train came to a grinding halt.

It had been so long since she'd heard the sound of a baby crying that Rachel darted between two wagons to get a better look. A pair of gaunt oxen strained to pull a huge wagon along the trail toward her. The high-wheeled vehicle was much too large for the team and they could scarcely move it. A woman stumbled along beside the two weary beasts, a baby on one hip. The unhappy faces of three dirty children peered from the opening with expressions much like those Rachel had seen at the burial. The woman appeared not to register those she moved past. Her eyes were glazed over and she stared at something in the middistance, ignoring the crying child.

Elijah Christie approached the woman, took her arm, and spoke to her. She jerked free and took another two or three steps, then collapsed. Rachel reached her side in time to grab the baby as the woman fell. The pitiful woman, who seemed not to miss the child at all, began to crawl, shreds of her skirt catching first under one knee then the other.

Over and over she repeated one word. It sounded like "hard." Just "hard, hard," cried over and over. Even when she finally went to her stomach in the grass she didn't stop the crawling motion.

Rachel hugged the child against her breasts. "Please, somebody help her."

Minna shoved between the two or three men who had gathered around, sank to her knees, and put her arms around the woman. The baby in Rachel's arms turned a hungry mouth against her blouse, wetting the fabric in a feeble search for a breast to nurse. A sting of tears at the back of her throat, Rachel kissed the feverish forehead and crooned.

She turned to Elijah. "Go to Etta Claridge, get some milk. She'll have some and it'll be warm. This child is starving. Hurry, and bring a spoon or something to feed it with."

Elijah nodded and raced off, evidently relieved to have something to do.

"Hard, hard," the woman screamed and tore at her face with ragged nails. If she had worn a bonnet she'd lost it somewhere; her skin was parched from the sun and lack of care. Her brown hair had come loose from a bun, remnants of which bobbled between her shoulder blades.

Rachel leaned closer and asked Minna, "What is that she keeps saying?"

"I think it's a name, she keeps crying something else I can barely understand. It might be 'Don't leave me, don't go.' "

About that time Sergeant Cletus McCrea and Second Lieutenant Peter Mankins rode up.

Mankins dismounted and stood with the others, speaking to no one in particular. "Evans says we got to move on before we get run down."

"We can't leave this poor woman like this," one of the men objected.

"Evans says if someone wants to drop out and see to her, that'll be fine. Otherwise, we got to pick her up and take her along. Says we lost some time getting on the trace, ain't got any more to waste. Says unload her wagon of what supplies it's got, turn her animals in with the stock and someone load her and them kids up. We'll sort it out tonight."

By then a crowd of a dozen or so had gathered. Daniel stood beside Rachel, who continued to soothe the child. Elijah arrived with a cup of milk and a spoon.

"Daniel, I'm taking the baby in our wagon to feed it. Would you bring her?"

He watched her for a moment, then nodded and turned to do as she bid.

"I'll see if the Claridges will take the children. They have the milk cow and we'll supply some food," Minna said.

As Daniel stooped to pick up the woman from the ground, the three scared white faces opened their mouths in unison and started bawling. They fought so wildly that it took two strong men to lift them down and cart them off, following Minna Von Finster.

Mankins organized some men to unhitch and unload the wagon. The Christie brothers were assigned to the task and told to distribute all foodstuffs between the Claridges and Daniel, seeing as how they were taking in the indigents, and to see that the woman got her personal belongings.

Cutter leaped into the back, then called out. "I swear, would you look at this? They's nothing here, she's been gutted."

"Aw, surely to goodness not," Elijah said, and went to see for himself. "Yep, he's right. Empty as can be."

"What I said," Cutter told his older brother disdainfully.

Elijah ignored the tone. "Reckon what happened?"

"Nothing's wrong with this wagon. Maybe we ought to bring up some spare oxen and yoke 'em up, take it along."

Mankins shook his head. "What for? Leave it, pull it off the trail out of the way, and let's get moving before Evans ups and runs off and leaves the lot of you standing here gaping at each other."

Cletus McCrea, who had helped unyoke the two bony beasts, said, "These cows ain't worth nothing but for food, and they're awful skinny even at that. Been run plumb to death, be my guess. Reckon if they can keep up till nightfall, we'll have us some beef to eat. Beats letting them fall down dead on the trail and getting nothing out of it."

Daniel absorbed the conversation as he carefully loaded the thin woman into the back of his wagon. It was like toting a bag of sticks. Inside Rachel was already spooning the rich milk into the child's mouth. It sucked at the spoon hungrily, tiny fists clenched against each side of the round, flushed face. He watched as the child fell asleep, unable to take his eyes away from the sight of Rachel tending a child. Something grabbed at his heart and squeezed it so tightly he almost lost his breath.

Rachel placed the baby on the bedding and stripped off the wet, soiled clothing. A little boy. She touched the sleeping child's cheeks with the tips of her fingers, then looked up at Daniel with a sadness in her eyes he'd never seen there before.

The scene so touched him he could barely speak. "What is it, what's wrong?"

"Why do children have to suffer for what we do? Isn't the mother suffering enough, without this little one . . . ?" Her voice cracked, she leaned forward, sobbing so hard her shoulders heaved.

Daniel moved to take her in his arms. He could think of nothing to say, had no idea how to comfort her, because he wasn't sure what had set her off, so he cradled her and spoke of the sleeping child.

"He'll be fine. Look at him. He's sleeping and fed. Tonight we'll clean him up. Please don't cry, darlin'." He rocked her gently, remembering how she had taken the girl from his arms in his haunted dream, how she had healed him. Now he felt helpless that he couldn't seem to do the same for her. "What is it? Tell me. I can't stand to see you so upset."

Before she could reply someone hammered on the

outside of the wagon. "Git moving or we'll leave you behind." The shouts went on down the line.

Daniel's stare cut away, then settled back on her. He couldn't bear to leave her like this.

"Go, I'm all right. Just leave me here and go." Rachel wiped at her face with shaking fingertips and tried to smile at him. How foolish of her to be so weak at a time when her strength was needed.

This tiny babe was not her brother. He was dead and buried along the trail somewhere in the Smokies. Crying for him here did no good. She took a deep breath and left the child to tend to the mother, who had gone silent as a stone, bloodshot eyes gazing at nothing.

Daniel spared Rachel another long glance, then jumped to the ground and urged the team forward to keep his place in the winding train.

Rachel took the woman's limp hand and began to stroke it, speaking gently.

"You are safe. Your baby is fed, your children are being taken care of."

The woman suddenly tightened her fingers. "Hard? Have you seen Hard?"

"It is a name," Rachel murmured and shook her head no at the woman. "Who is this Hard?"

"No. No. No. He's gone."

"What happened to all your belongings?"

The woman's eyebrows went up. "Belongings?" A foreign, strange-sounding word coming from her dry lips.

Rachel tried to pull her hand away so she could get out and fetch some water, but the woman wouldn't let go. She held on with an amazing strength.

"No, don't leave me too. Children. Where are they?"

"They are safe. The baby is here. Let me get you some water to drink. Water." Rachel felt silly signing to the woman, but it seemed to work and she was able to climb out and fill a dipper from the barrel strapped to the outside of the wagon.

She allowed the woman a few slow swallows, then held the dipper away from her until she was sure the liquid wasn't going to come back up.

"Are you hungry?"

The woman shook her head no and reached again for the water.

"Slow, please go slowly. What is your name?"

"Em . . . Emma . . . Emmaline Hardesty. Hard is my . . . was my husband." The brown eyes filled with tears that she wiped away with an angry gesture. "Everyone called him Hard, everyone called him that, and he was. But not hard enough, I reckon. Damn him, he had no right . . . to die, to desert us . . . I didn't want to go to Calif . . . California, but I did. A woman goes with her man. Gold is only a dream. And then he . . . he—"

"Hush," Rachel said, but the woman interrupted, eager now to tell her story.

"I was . . . I knew the child was on the way. It didn't matter. It never matters to men what is in a woman's heart. All they know . . . all they care about is what they want. He wanted gold. Strike it rich. And look at us . . . look what it got him."

"It is okay if you do not talk about it."

But nothing could have stopped Emmaline short of a gag, and so Rachel sat patiently while her story poured out, in stammered bursts at first, then with more clarity.

"It was the gold fever. His family had some money so he outfitted too big a wagon so I could take all my things. And it was too heavy to go over the mountains. We threw out the piano, my mother's rocker, the cupboard, and dishes. Everything but what we had to have to survive. He said . . . he said we'd buy 'em all back and then some when he hit pay dirt.

"It didn't help, it was horrible. Times we had to practically carry the wagon. And the rivers . . . they looked a mile wide. Me and the children almost drowned more than once. I got to where I couldn't stand to wake up another day. Then he took sick with the mountain fever, and I was afraid the children would get it, but more afraid he would die and leave me there all alone. And that's what he did. Damn, damn, damn him." Fury rose around her like smoke from a fire, her face grew red, her brow furrowed.

"He died." The last, a whisper of disbelief. "One would have thought it would have been me or one of the children. The weaker ones, especially the baby, being born out on the plains in a driving rainstorm. Surprised he even lived. Or I could have died borning him and left Hard with the three girls. He scarcely could boil water for his own coffee. God knows what he would have done."

She laughed harshly. "I didn't do much better without him, did I? The other four oxen died . . . I don't remember when."

"What happened to your food and clothing?"

Her eyes narrowed. "I threw them out. Threw them all around his grave, covered him up in them. I didn't want them. I didn't want to do this. Please take me home." Abruptly, her eyes closed and she was asleep, as if she had spewed forth every last word left in her, every ounce of strength.

The baby whimpered but didn't awaken. Rachel sat silently for a long while between the woman and her child. The wagon bumped along, its cargo rattled, chains on the singletrees jingled, dust trickled out from under the wheels. The afternoon sun moved ahead of them like a beacon lighting the way west. For several moments she studied the golden ball through the oval opening in the canvas at the front of the wagon and thought of that seven-year-old child she had once been, uprooted from her home by the white soldiers and dragged to a place she was never intended to be. Thought of her poor mother and the hardships she had endured. Women were forever made to pay for the folly of men.

She herself had agreed to follow the man she loved to some faraway wilderness where she would have no one to talk to except the bear and the wildcat. Love might endure, but would it be enough? Would the two of them survive, their love intact when life got so terribly hard? She found herself suddenly very frightened of what lay ahead. Not so much a fear of the hardships as a dread that the love she and Daniel enjoyed would be lost forever in those mountains ahead, where it would be a struggle just to survive. She had lived through worse and so had he, but perhaps they couldn't do it yet again.

The creaking of the wooden wheels as they turned endlessly around the hubs had become a familiar rhythm to which Daniel could regulate his steps. He moved beside the team and guided them without conscious thought. But he was worried about Rachel. He should have noticed that she wasn't happy. That something was wrong, but he hadn't. It might have been a mistake to finally agree to her continuing this trip. It would only get more difficult when they reached high country. The rivers they had crossed thus far had presented only mild problems, but the rougher the terrain the harder the crossings as rivers grew wilder on their journeys down out of the Rockies toward the plains. It wouldn't be much longer until they saw those magnificent mountains, but he dreaded reaching them because of his concern for Rachel's welfare.

By all calculations of the wagon master, the train had covered around six hundred miles since leaving Fayetteville. Not even halfway. The routines of each day were settled into Daniel's system, he lived and breathed, ate and slept around them. He'd always needed routine, even when all alone in the mountains. When something happened to break that schedule, he almost felt resentful. Happiest away from the rest of the men, he relished the long days of solitude, but had become dependent on having Rachel along. She was the one person he always looked forward to seeing.

How odd it was that he didn't miss his family, who had shut him out because of his wanderlust, his refusals to become what his brothers were. He had come along late in his mother's life, and she and his father had just assumed he would be like the other boys. But he wasn't, never could be, and finally had given up trying.

The scene in the parlor of their home when he announced his intentions to stop reading the law and head west was best forgotten, but it had led to him being disinherited. His father never wanted to see his face again. He shouted, ranted, raved until his cheeks and nose flushed purple.

His poor mother fanned herself, gasping within the confines of her tightly laced corset until she finally had to have smelling salts. Both brothers, Lucas and Zekial, who had resented his late arrival after it seemed they were to be the only heirs, smirked at the goings-on, in a hurry to be set free of this burdensome and troublemaking younger brother. He was glad to be gone, they happy to be rid of him.

After the year in Mexico fighting that dreadful war he had been so angry that he had not ever wanted a companion. Even now he had no one but Rachel, and he desired no one else. Though he had not sought her out, she had been thrust into his unhappy life as if it were meant for him to have something more. Hell, he hadn't even known he was unhappy until he met her and saw his existence for what it was. A lonely, furious, wild, drunken brawl kind of affair in which he continually tempted fate in the hopes he could end it all.

Tramping along through clumps of buffalo grass, he felt bits of gravel working up into his boots. One of the soles had worn clean through. He would have to repair it after supper. Then he would crawl into the lonely singular bed under the wagon, for with the woman and child inside he could not hope to sleep with his wife. There wouldn't be room or privacy for what he knew he must do if he lay beside her. There was no keeping to himself once she stretched her lithesome body out beside him.

Just thinking about her sent chills of pleasure straight to his loins. How he had ever lived without her by his side, he would never know. When he thought of that untamed Cherokee girl he'd literally snatched from certain tragedy he had to laugh, for now she had become the most loving and exquisite partner a man could ever want. If he lost her, he wasn't sure what he would do.

Long after dark that night, after the woman and babe settled into a deep slumber, Rachel gathered a blanket around herself and slipped out into the warm night. The moon hadn't yet risen, and when it did it would be only a half slice. She had always kept track of the phases of the moon, almost as if her mind automatically knew where it would be each night, and how much of its golden beauty it would reveal.

The central fire glowed, a few flames licked at the darkness, casting long wavering shadows on the canvas of the circled wagons. In the corral a horse snorted and stomped the earth, then quieted.

Rachel stepped carefully in her bare feet and knelt beside the large spoked wheel. Daniel slept on his back, head turned away from her and his hair spread over one shoulder. His left arm was flung upward beside his face, the other lay across his bare stomach. A blanket covered him to the waist, but one leg was crooked so that his knee poked out. He had removed his buckskin leggings and wore only thin underdrawers.

She crawled over beside him and dropping the blanket away from her naked body, spread it on the ground. Then she lifted his covering quickly and crawled in with him.

He squirmed a little, made a sound down in his throat, then his breathing smoothed out again.

She smiled, eased the arm from across his belly and tucked it under her head. He smelled warm and sunshiny. She licked at his nipple with the tip of her tongue. He turned his head and sighed.

The long, hard days were exhausting for him, she knew, and so he slept deeply. Unlike when she had first met him and he was haunted by the nightmares, drinking himself insensible in order to get a little rest.

Thinking of his suffering, her heart went out to him. She smoothed one hand over the front of the pants, felt his strength, his gentleness through the thin fabric. A muscle twitched under her palm.

How she did love this man, how she wanted him. Now.

Moving against him she eased one leg over his hips and lay there just a moment, satisfied to feel him grow under her touch. It was exciting to have that happen while he still slept, as if even in the land of dreams he wanted her and reacted to her presence.

The arm that had been flung up beside his head

shifted, fingers trailed over her ankle and moved up the long curve to the underside of her thigh. Still he slept.

Silently, she sat across his lap so that he entered her smoothly, slowly. Because of the wagon above them, she could not sit up, and so stretched her legs down along his, keeping him snug within her.

He awakened in slow, heated beats, saying her name so that it flowed like warm honey over her lips when they met his. At first his mouth remained soft and she tasted of him languidly, finally getting a response. His fingers tangled in her long hair, and his kiss became insistent. He tried to move about under her, pushing upward in rhythmic thrusts accompanied by throaty cries.

She rocked with him, getting the beat as if their hearts were entwined to nourish the same body.

At last, when the drumbeat reached its peak, he rolled her over once, twice, and they lay out in the open outside the circle, grass tickling her backsides. He cradled her into his arms, and rising to his knees, her legs wrapped around his waist, answered the ancient pounding rhythm that lay within their souls, poised and waiting to be awakened.

She could not make love without crying out, her voice rising like the mournful cry of the wolf or coyote, and so she arched backward bending over his arms. The night embraced her song, kissed the tips of her lovely breasts with dew, and the first light of the half moon sneaked out to bathe the prairie.

Daniel fell into the grass beside her, pulled her close, and began to rub at her back with the fingers of one hand.

He spoke to her quietly, reverently. "I love you, and no matter what you say, you are my Cherokee Winter Dawn when we make love. Don't ever change that, as you become white. Oh, and you can wake me up like this anytime you please." The last, a teasing tone that made her laugh.

"I did not think you would mind. Do not white women howl when they make love?"

"White women don't even take off all their clothes with a man," he said and tweaked her bare breast.

"Oh? And how would you know that, my singular mountain man?" She proudly used the new word Minna had taught her only that morning.

"Never mind. It's true. Don't ask me how I know."

"It does not matter," she said and kissed him. "Now, if we don't wish the white men to see what you have and become angry—"

"Envious," he supplied.

She went on without missing a beat. "Envious of your good fortune, we had better get back in our beds."

"Beds? You could—"

She put fingers over his lips. "No, because if I did we would only do the same thing again."

"Nothing wrong with that."

"Nothing at all," she agreed, scrambled to her feet, and ran nimbly back to the wagon, where she climbed up and disappeared into the darkness.

Daniel enjoyed the pleasure of watching her prowl through the moonlight like some lithe and muscular feline, moonlight flashing along her curves and hollows. Quickly, lest someone see him standing with his drawers down around his ankles out on the prairie, he slipped back under the wagon, fetched her blanket and tossed it inside, then moved back into his own lonely bed. He was asleep almost immediately, holding close the memory of her.

Early one afternoon a lone rider approached fast, shouting without slowing down as his horse galloped the length of the train.

Rachel's heart leaped, and she clutched at her

friend Minna's hand. Was there trouble? Wild Indians, perhaps?

"Mountains, it's the mountains, ma'am. Yonder." The man rode on toward the end of the long line of wagons.

Like children Minna and Rachel took off running, the older woman holding up her skirts to keep them out of the scrub brush and tall grass.

Rachel halted and studied what looked like a distant storm cloud along the horizon. "Oh, is that all?"

"It's them, it must be," Minna said, breathless as they paused to gaze at the sight. "I thought they'd be bigger."

Rachel felt a vague disappointment as well. "They are nothing. The Great Smokies are much more beautiful."

She told Daniel of her disappointment that evening.

He was amused. "In two nights we will camp at Bent's Fort. They say from there you can see the snow on the highest peaks. Then you will realize how formidable these mountains are. We will head north to miss the most treacherous passes, but it will still be hard."

"And how far are we then, from California?"

Daniel scraped the last of the beans from his plate. "Still a long way." He looked up, his eyes wary. "But we aren't going to California, are we?"

She glanced at the ground. "No, no, of course not. I just wondered. Oregon, how far will Oregon then be?"

"Well, we'll leave the Santa Fe Trace and head into Utah Territory through the mountains. We'll veer north for the Oregon Trail just short of the Great Salt Lake. I'd like to see it though. There the Mormons have built them a city. There'll be others going our way as well. Perhaps we'll spend time there before we go on to Oregon, if you'd like."

"Daniel, what are Mormons?"

"Just some people who traveled all over the country looking for a home. No one wanted them, but their leader Brigham Young finally settled his people on the banks of the Great Salt Lake."

"Are they a white tribe?"

"White? Oh, yes, they're white. They have a different belief than other whites though, and so they were ostracized, uh, banished."

"What kind of belief?"

"Well, it's . . . I mean, they sort of . . . well, the men take more than one wife is the main problem."

She chuckled. "I suppose I don't understand the meaning of the word 'belief.' I thought it had something to do with gods and spirits, the way people worship. But having more than one wife is quite common among some Indians. It really has nothing to do with the way one worships. It is a personal thing, and not something others can say yes or no about."

He laughed uproariously. "You certainly cut to the heart of the matter. And what would you think if I wanted to take another wife besides you?"

"It's not what I would think that needs to worry you, Daniel Wolfe, it is how sharp the knife is I would use to cut off all her hair." She tugged at his long locks. "Maybe yours too."

"Is that all? Just cut off her hair? You wouldn't scalp her, too, would you?"

"You know we Cherokee are quite civilized. This isn't something you are thinking about, taking another wife, is it?"

He hooked an arm around her neck and wrestled her backward to the ground, their tin plates clanging off their laps. "Not even for an instant. How would I handle more than one anyway? You wear me out, girl. All by yourself. What would I do with another woman? Agili would have to change his name. What is the Cherokee word for lies down exhausted?"

She laughed again and buried her face in his chest, hugging him tightly. She missed their togetherness. With Emmaline and the baby boy riding along, they didn't have the privacy of their wagon. But Emmaline would leave them at Bent's Fort. There she would get a ride back to her people in Iowa.

The moon rose over the plains, bathing the circled train in a silver light. Around them, men settled in for the night. Fires died down, long tendrils of smoke snaked off with the prairie wind. Daniel thought how lucky he was to have this woman with him, while most of the men had left their loved ones behind.

"Come on," he said abruptly, pulling her to her feet. "We'd better go to bed."

She rose and brushed dirt and twigs from her clothing. The shift in his mood made her nervous and brought unwelcome thoughts of Eagle and his lust for revenge. She glanced around quickly. "What is it, Daniel? What's wrong?"

He led her to the wagon. "Nothing, I guess. I just had a strange feeling, that's all. Don't pay me any mind."

He kissed her and boosted her up into the wagon, but the feeling of dread didn't go away and he was a long time falling asleep. He was glad he had dealt with Henry for the Hawkens, which he had taken to keeping beside him when he slept. If Rachel's brother was right. Doaks might be out there somewhere near. Many lone men traveled by horseback to the goldfields. They preferred it to the encumbrances of a wagon. Such men often lived off what they could steal or beg from those well supplied. They tailed along behind trains waiting for someone to fall behind because of illness or breakdowns. From what he'd seen of Doaks, the man wouldn't hesitate to prey on such unfortunates.

Let the bastard come near Rachel and he would never see California.

Chapter Thirteen

At Bent's Fort, they would leave the trace and strike out to the north, totally on their own. Scarcely one hundred fifty souls once more alone, at the mercy of the elements and chance, reaching out for their dreams. As the day wore on excitement rippled through the train, everyone straining to catch a first glimpse of the fort.

Minna had come back to walk beside Rachel to keep her company while Daniel helped with stock.

The older woman chatted amiably, glancing at her companion occasionally from the shadow of her bonnet slats. "I've seen paintings and drawings of Bent's Fort rendered by a young lieutenant who was out here with Fremont's expedition a few years ago. I am most anxious to see the real thing. It is said to be a marvel for this country."

"Daniel says that you can see the snow on the mountains from the walls. They must be very high."

Minna chuckled. "Two stories and then some. There are turrets at the corners, and it appears almost like a castle."

"Look, look there." Rachel pointed at the purpling shadows along the horizon that looked more like storm clouds approaching than the legendary Rocky Mountains. "They don't look so formidable." She used the word Minna had taught her the previous day.

"You are a very quick study, Rachel. Why didn't you attend Miss Sawyer's with your friend?"

"When Alice went away, my mother was very ill. I decided to stay with her, and then when she died it was so horrible. Nothing has ever hurt me like that, Minna. Nothing could ever be worse, unless it would be losing a child. My mother, Minna. My dear, sweet mother, who loved me like no one else, and she was gone in the snap of a finger. I could not leave. And then the longer I waited, the less it mattered.

"Why would an Indian girl get an education anyway? So she could marry some poor Cherokee and live in that scrubby oak country? Or if she was lucky, marry one with some money who had sold out to the white man?"

"So instead you simply decided to do nothing? That was not very wise, Rachel."

"And are you happier than me, Minna?"

Minna walked along in silence, watching her feet. After a long while she said softly, "I don't know, Rachel. I suppose I'm not. Better off, perhaps. But happier. No. I've never had a man love me like your Daniel Wolfe loves you. If I did, then I would be happier."

"Or perhaps just as happy," Rachel teased. "No one could be happier."

"Except?"

"What, I don't understand."

"In your voice, no one could be happier if only. That's what I heard."

"Oh, it's nothing. I've always dreamed of going to California and living in a big house and being white. I am white, as white as I am Cherokee. But Daniel will only be happy living in the wilderness. It is my one great sadness."

"Have you told him?"

"Once. I have said no more, and I suppose he assumes I have forgotten, or changed my mind."

"Why don't you tell him, strike a compromise?"

"Because it would make him unhappy."

"Ah, better a woman be unhappy than her man."

They laughed together, held hands, and swung their arms high and wide.

"I can hardly wait until we see this wonderful castle fort," Rachel finally said. What she didn't say was that she would be glad to see Emmaline Hardesty safely deposited there so that she and Daniel could have the privacy of their wagon once again. Fall asleep in each other's arms.

Bent's Fort came into view later that afternoon, standing in the forks of the Arkansas and Purgatorie River, a mammoth structure alone on the flat plain. In its center a high watchtower displayed an American flag. A few trees grew around the riverbanks, lush prairie grasses waved in the wind. Indians had set up a village outside the walls. Bent's was the largest fort they had seen since leaving Arkansas, and Minna said the largest west of the Mississippi River. She spoke of warehouses, wagon sheds, offices, meeting halls, staff apartments, guestrooms, and an inner court.

"It garrisons two hundred men and three hundred animals and the walls are four feet thick," she said as she and Rachel walked.

Minna loved her history, and sometimes she could get boring with her recitations of details, but Rachel so loved hearing the wonderful words flow that she never tired of listening.

A message came back that the train would circle up within sight of the fort and would remain there for repairs and resupplying. For a long while after they halted, Rachel shaded her eyes and gazed at the large structure and beyond toward the mountains.

Then she turned and looked back the way they had come, trying to see some sign of her past, some shadow of the Smokies or the Ozarks, but there was nothing there but endless plain, going on into forever.

By the time Daniel came to unhitch the horses she had climbed inside the wagon to help Emmaline get ready to depart. The woman had done nothing to help herself. Listless, she slumped on a crate regarding the baby lying on a quilt kicking and gurgling.

Rachel tried to keep the annoyance from her voice. "Are you about ready?"

Emmaline glanced up but didn't answer.

"Etta is bringing the girls over as soon as they are cleaned up, and then Lieutenant Tyner will escort you."

Emmaline grimaced. "I wish we didn't have to think of that long horrid trip back home. I wish I could just close my eyes and we'd be back there. Oh, how I wish we'd never left."

"But wishes aren't horses," Rachel said, trying to keep her tone light. The woman was addled, purely addled, and ought to be ashamed. She had four lovely children and a family to return to. "I'm sorry, Emmaline, you must get ready, and I need to air the bedding."

The woman sighed, stirred, and finally climbed over the tailgate, leaving the baby for Rachel to manage.

Her whiny voice stabbed at Rachel. "Just look at this dress. It drags the ground. I'm a sight. Dear me."

Minna had given Emmaline one of her dresses, and while it was too long, the woman had made no effort to take it up, nor to thank the German woman for her generosity. She would be glad to be rid of the selfish Emma, who would do well to think more of her children and less of herself.

Handing the baby over to its mother, she tried to make up for her unkind thoughts. "He's a beautiful child. You are so lucky to have such wonderful children."

"Lucky! Ha. And me alone to raise them. How is that lucky?"

"My mother lost two children and two husbands. You'd be wise to count yourself lucky." Rachel wished she could call back the retort, but it was said, and she was glad to see Etta Claridge approaching with Emmaline's three daughters.

During the days on the trail that wonderful woman had somehow managed to fashion each of the girls a simple frock from feed sacks, and their faces were scrubbed shiny, their hair combed and braided.

"Here's your mama, girls," Etta said and bobbed her head toward Rachel and Emmaline. The Claridge woman, like most of the other folks on the train, would not look directly into Rachel's eyes. They preferred to think of her as not existing. In a strange way, she understood, but she resented them for it nevertheless.

All the same, she smiled at Etta. "It's so kind of you to care for the children so Emmaline could recover."

Etta cut a glance at the ungrateful mother, who did not add to Rachel's praise.

Lieutenant Tyner arrived driving a carriage he'd borrowed at the fort.

Emmaline sighed. "Come on, girls, we'd better get started. Lord knows we've got a terrible ordeal yet ahead of us."

Without further word either to Rachel or Etta, Emmaline Hardesty loaded her girls, handed up the baby, and climbed into the carriage, shaking off the gallant Tyner's efforts to assist her.

For a moment Rachel watched the woman's departure, then turned to say something to Etta Claridge, but found she was alone. Etta had left without a word.

Daniel had taken the horses to stake them out in the green grass. Rachel decided to wash some clothes while there was an abundant water supply. Perhaps Minna would like to go with her.

When she had everything bundled, she changed quickly into the old ragged britches and one of Daniel's work shirts so she could wash what she'd been wearing. When she returned she would do her evening chores and then maybe Daniel would take her to the fort, where they could climb the wall to look at the mountains.

With her mind on the enjoyable outing and being alone in the wagon with Daniel tonight, she jumped down and picked up the bundle of dirty clothing. Toting it on one hip she set out. As she approached the Von Finster wagons she found herself gazing at the mountains in the distance, not paying much attention to the route. That's how she stumbled onto Zoe and a man she had seen on several occasions but didn't know. The two were at the far corner of one of the wagons, out of general sight. Zoe had a hand on his arm, was speaking earnestly, quietly, looking up into his eyes. It reminded Rachel of when the skinny white woman had danced with Daniel and had looked at him in the same silly way.

Zoe turned a harsh stare on Rachel. "Who are you looking for?"

The man leaned insolently against the side of the wagon, crossed his arms over his chest, and brazenly gazed at Rachel until she felt naked.

For a moment she had trouble replying to Zoe.

When she did, she stammered. "Minna . . . I . . . your sister. I thought she might like to go with me."

Zoe glanced at the soiled clothing and lifted her lip in a sneer. "I doubt that very much. She's busy, isn't she, Tate?" She rubbed the man's arm with the back of a hand.

Something had been going on between the two, that was obvious. The woman was probably just angry at Rachel for interrupting. She heard the tinkle of piano music drifting from the nearby wagon. Minna was playing.

Rachel glared at Zoe. "I'll just ask her myself."

She made to move away, but the man stepped into her path and caught at the bundle. "I'll go with you, little lady. Looks like you could use some help with this." His tight smile revealed large, well cared-for teeth.

"No, I couldn't," Rachel said and jerked away. The bundle of clothing fell to the ground.

Before Rachel could stoop to retrieve it Zoe stepped close, breath hot on Rachel's neck as she whispered viciously, "Keep your savage promises away from this man, street urchin."

The man smiled at Zoe as if he had done nothing, as if he thought she was the sweetest thing he'd ever seen. He reminded Rachel of a feral dog. Obviously Zoe felt differently, for she captured his arm and rubbed against him, sending Rachel yet another harsh glare.

Chafing at the unfairness of Zoe's accusation, Rachel searched out Daniel's tall, muscular frame in the distance. He stood out among the others, with his broad shoulders and golden hair. In the heat of late afternoon he had removed his hat and shirt, his arms and back glistened with sweat. Seeing him like that, Rachel could almost forget Zoe's hatefulness.

The other woman wasn't content to let it be,

though. It was as if she couldn't resist making cutting remarks, and she raised her voice once again. "Your man is otherwise occupied. Ladies should not go unaccompanied in this country, though judging from your attire, one could not refer to you as a lady. But be careful, nevertheless. One never knows when some wild savage will come along, does one?"

Rachel wrestled the awkward bundle of laundry up into her arms. It was the only way she could keep from busting Zoe Von Finster in the jaw. "You are a very rude woman, Zoe. If I recall you owe me a dress, or had you forgotten? Perhaps I ought to take the one you are wearing."

Before Zoe could react, anger overpowered Rachel's better judgment and she dropped her bundle and made a lunge for the simpering female. She grabbed at the front of the brown dress, got a fistful of fabric.

Zoe howled with outrage. "You little savage. Tate, do something."

Tate grabbed Rachel from behind, encircling her waist and lifting her from the ground easily. Rachel kicked out at Zoe with both feet, but only connected with air as the woman staggered backward.

"Tate, stop her. Do something."

Minna shouted from inside the wagon, "What's all the ruckus, Zoe?"

The awful man tightened his hold until she could scarcely breathe and skinned one hand up under the loose-tailed shirt she wore. His touch burned across her flesh and made it crawl.

Just as Cletus McCrea appeared, Minna came from the wagon and stepped between Zoe and Tate, who still struggled with Rachel.

"She attacked me, Sergeant. Mr. Tate was trying to hold her back." Zoe pushed at her hair and wiped her flushed face.

"Is that true, little lady?" McCrea asked Rachel.

"Make him let me go." She glared at the sergeant.

"You the one that attacked Miss Zoe once before, ain't you?"

Rachel clamped her lips shut. Belatedly, Tate let her slip from his grasp.

"Git on out of here, gal," McCrea said. "Count yourself lucky I don't report you to Evans. Can't you stay away from honest folk, or do we have to chase you and your man plumb off this train?"

"That isn't necessary, Sergeant," Minna said. "Rachel, are you all right?"

"Leave me alone, you and your sister just leave me alone. I don't need either one of you." Rachel whirled on the sergeant. "And you just try to kick us off this train. I didn't do anything. It's her that's causing all the trouble."

She grabbed up the bundle and hurried away. Zoe's laughter and Minna calling her name in a forlorn voice chased her all the way to the riverbank.

Kneeling there in the soft mud she beat each garment quite thoroughly on a flat rock beneath the surface of the river. By the time she finished washing the small pile of clothing most of her anger was exhausted. Her fury was replaced by the realization that she had lost Minna's friendship.

After she spread the clothes, she glanced back toward the wagons, but discovered she could scarcely see them through the thick foliage. Quickly she skinned from the shirt and britches and slipped into the brown water.

She would have to be fast, but it felt so good to immerse her body completely instead of just washing from a pan, that she couldn't resist. White people didn't seem to be quite as taken with river-bathing as were the Cherokee, who believed in doing so with regularity, especially in such fine weather. Actually it was one of the formulas for curing disease, and she wondered that she had not been taken ill from a lack of it.

The water embraced her, absorbed the ache of tired muscles, the flush of her earlier battle. Her nipples puckered and she imagined Daniel's mouth there. For a moment, as she splashed her shoulders and face, she was transported into his arms, lost to the world around her. Coming back to herself, she took a deep breath and ducked under.

When she came up, she thought she glimpsed movement on the far bank of the river. Clearing streaming water from her eyes, she stared into the distance for a long while. Nothing moved.

Quietly she paddled farther out into the river to get a better look, but the sun was shining on the water and the glare blinded her. Keeping an eye on the spot where she'd thought she had seen the figure of a rather large man, she back-paddled toward the shore and her clothes. She felt mud under her feet and stood, turning at the same time. Someone stood there.

She covered herself, looked around frantically for a way to escape, before realizing who it was.

"Daniel, you scared me half to death."

"What are you doing out here alone?" The harsh tone surprised her, and following so close on the heels of the clash with Zoe and Tate, brought quick tears to her eyes.

Daniel gathered her clothes and reached out for her. The fire in his eyes cleared as their hands touched. "Hey, you okay?"

She nodded, not trusting her voice to speak. Spotting the man on the other bank had frightened her more than she realized. Was it Doaks? Had he found her at last?

Instead she took her blouse and skirt and slipped

quickly into them. Her hands trembled as she took the moccasins Daniel held out.

"What's going on here?" he asked softly.

"I don't know. I thought I saw . . . over there . . . I don't know. Zoe and I had a fight and I was upset. Then I wanted a bath because I didn't feel clean after that. And when I was in the water I saw this man over there." She pointed.

Daniel looked. "No one there now." He put his arm around her shoulder. "Just don't go away from the train alone after this. Eagle just might be right about that Doaks and his friends. If they are tagging the train it wouldn't do for him to spot you, especially not alone."

"You were busy. Daniel, I can't hide in the wagon all the time. There are things I have to do, just like you have things you have to do."

"I know. Come on, I'll walk back with you. Next time, see if you can't get someone to come along."

She clamped her lips together. She had tried to do that and look what it had gotten her. She didn't say so though, she just nodded.

When they drew near the men still at work, she said, "I'm sorry if I frightened you. Now, go on back to your work and I will start our meal. You must be hungry."

"Rachel, if anything happened to you—"

She nodded and kissed him lightly on the mouth. "Nothing will happen to me. I had hoped that before it gets dark we could go to the fort and climb the wall and see the snow on the mountains."

He looked at her for another long moment, then nodded. "I'll be back soon and we'll do that."

She could tell he was not satisfied, but he did finally go back to his work and she returned to the wagon, where she began unpacking supplies and setting up their camp. Daniel returned as she was stacking wood for the supper fire.

"Want to ride or walk?" he asked and splashed water over his hands and face from the washpan.

"Let's go get the clothes. I want to wear my good dress for the first time I see the mountains."

"Think they'll be dry?"

"In this wind? Yes, if they haven't blown all the way back to Indian Territory."

They laughed together. It had been difficult to get used to the prairie winds after living in the Ozarks. Many a tale said that it literally could blow the hair off your head. And that would appear to be nearly the truth. And on and on it blew, day and night, snapping the canvas on the wagons, popping women's skirts out behind them, whipping at men's hats. Everything had to be tied down including plates of food.

After fetching the dried clothes they returned to the wagon to change, Daniel joining her mood and putting on his best buckskins. Hand in hand they set out walking toward the shadowing hulk in the distance.

A piece of moon trailed the sun across the vividly blue sky. In the distance the purple mountains cut huge jags into the sun's bed. Pink-and-lavender clouds streaked through the brilliant sunset. From somewhere across the prairie a quail whistled, another took up the call, a few more answered.

"Listen to the bobwhites," Daniel said. "I wonder what kind of birds there'll be in Oregon. I hear there are wild mountain cats near big as mules and deer twice the size of our little white tails. And beaver and grizzly bears and—"

"Daniel?"

He squeezed her hand, glanced down at her, and

thought he had never felt so filled with glory and contentment. "What is it?"

"Will there be people?"

"Some I reckon. You saw the wagons headed west. Plenty, I'd wager, are going to Oregon to homestead land, not being foolish enough to go after the dream of gold."

"What will we do, I mean, you. What will you do?"

"Do?"

Before she could explain what she meant, the gates of the fort ahead swung open and four soldiers rode out. Daniel and Rachel moved aside and watched them pass, then Daniel hailed the gatekeeper.

"Ho, can we come in?"

The soldier, who had started to swing the gates closed, regarded them a moment, then waited until they had slipped through the gap before pulling the huge double doors shut.

Rachel shivered at the gathering of soldiers within the great walls, but she saw Indians and whites as well. Above her head a walkway ran completely around the inside of the thick walls. The place was buzzing with activity.

Daniel felt her tense and pulled her hand and arm up under his so that they walked with thighs and hips touching.

He led her to a staircase where people walked both up and down and they were forced to walk single file, her in front. At the top she was disappointed to see that another story filled with rooms greeted them. How would they see the mountains?

Then Daniel approached one of the soldiers. She didn't want to go with him, to stand so near the hated white soldier, but had no choice, for he had a good hold on her.

"Sir, would it be all right if I took my wife up in the turret? She wants to see the mountains."

"I'll escort you there, sir," the polite young man replied.

Rachel watched the soldier's stiff back as he led them around the walkway past all the rooms and along another wall dotted with peepholes until they finally reached a ladder that led to the top of the large round room at one corner, obviously what Daniel had called a turret.

She was scarcely aware of the questions Daniel asked the soldier, but heard the young man tell him the Indians were Cheyenne and they were celebrating a victory over their enemy the Pawnee. She knew very little about the tribes of which they spoke, and so she let her attention wander to the dress and actions of the people. Obviously Indians were mixing with whites all over the country, and not just in the Nation. She thought that might be just as well, though it made her feel a strange melancholy that she couldn't explain.

At the top of the ladder, she didn't look out or speak until the young man left them. This experience should be shared only with Daniel. When she raised her face a dry warm wind kissed her cheeks, and the foreboding wall of mountains leaped into view. The setting sun splashed vivid reds and purples on the snow that lay along the sharp ridges and deep in the hollows. Here and there a flash of bright light slanted briefly off ice as the burning orb eased behind the peaks. Above them the bit of moon glowed white.

Daniel put his arm around her shoulder and pulled her close so that his heat warmed her.

"My God, isn't it beautiful?"

"Oh, yes." There were no words she could think of to express how she felt looking upon such awesome grandeur. No word her father or Minna had taught her, nothing from the Cherokee she'd spoken all her life expressed what she felt. This is where the spirits lived, this was most surely the Twilight Land. She felt their caress, the whisper of a thousand voices.

Looking upon the mountains was frightening but soothing, breathtaking but wildly exciting, and a dreadful expectant silence closed over her until she felt as if she had passed into another world. One of visions and myths.

"Oh, Winter Dawn, we're going to be so happy in Oregon. I promise. I'm going to build us a home in that wilderness such as you've never seen. With rooms big and bright and huge fireplaces to keep us warm. I hear it rains there but seldom snows and everything is so green it takes your breath away."

Tears spilled from her eyes, poured down her cheeks, but she made not a sound.

He tilted her head and cupped her cheeks. "What is it? Tell me what's wrong?"

"Nothing. Nothing. I just love you so much and I'm so afraid." She didn't tell him what she was afraid of, and he didn't ask.

He wrapped her in a bear hug that completely enveloped her against his chest. "Don't be afraid. You don't ever have to be afraid again. Nobody is ever going to hurt you as long as I'm around. And I'm always going to be around. If we hunt we'll hunt together, we'll trap together, we'll plant seeds and watch them grow, and fell giant trees to build our home."

She sobbed loudly into his chest, her shoulders heaving, and he felt totally at a loss.

"What is it?" he asked. "Tell me what to do, what to say. I can't stand you being so sad."

Did she dare tell him what she feared? That someone would take all this away from her, and it would be so much worse than the day her brother had sold her, or the day her mother had died, or the babies. When she had nothing, she could bear things getting worse, she could stand up to anything. But she had to stop crying, for she could sense in Daniel a fear she wanted him never to have to experience.

He rocked her, murmured soothing words, called her darlin' in that gentle way he had, and she pushed away all the terror that chased at her heels. Perhaps everything would be all right. Something would happen and Doaks would not come for her and Eagle would truly be in Texas, where he was supposed to be.

"It's all right," she finally managed to murmur into his chest. "It was just all the soldiers and . . . and seeing the mountains. Oh, Daniel. How will we ever get our wagons over such a barrier? It's not possible."

He drew in a ragged breath of relief. "Well, if that's all that's worrying you, forget it. I know for a fact that folks just keep moving across those mountains. It'll be hard work, but we're up to that, you and I. Nothing is going to stop us, Winter Dawn. Nothing.

"And you know, when we get settled in our place, there in Oregon, why we'll take a trip to California so you can see how all those unlucky folk are doing, scrabbling around in the dirt for a hunk of gold. And I'll take you to San Francisco and we'll attend the opera and I'll buy you dresses as pretty as any those women out there wear. Believe me you'll soon be glad that we settled in the wilds."

He was only trying to cheer her up, she was sure, and he hadn't had much experience doing that, so she forgave him talking to her as if she were a child. Perhaps she was acting a bit like one and deserved it.

She turned to get another look at the mountains and saw sitting on the wall a large clay pot with the most wonderful plant growing in it. It had long round fingers covered with spikes and at the top of each bloomed deep red flowers that looked like the finest of silk.

With the tip of a finger she touched one of the spikes.

"It's a cactus. Be careful, the needles are sharp."

"But so beautiful."

"Exquisite."

She repeated the word. "What a wonderful word. It's perfect."

He looked down into her sparkling eyes, bright in the evening light. "Yes, perfect. Just like you. Exquisite, but with sharp needles."

"Oh, is that right? And if I'm a cactus, what are you Daniel?"

He laughed, happy that her mood had changed. "I give up, what am I?"

She looked all around and pointed. "Over there, see that tree?" In the near darkness, he strained to see the gnarly, supple trunk of a huge tree standing alone away from all the others. Against the silvery sky long sharp thorns protruded from its skeletal fingers, larger than those on the cactus, more deadly.

"See how beautiful, how strong, how dangerous it is? See how alone it is, its arms are empty." The last she said rather sadly.

He took her shoulders and turned her from the sight of the mountains and the prickly tree and the sprawling plains so that she was looking once again at him. "Ah, my darlin', but I am no longer alone, am I? I think you clipped my thorns."

She lifted her face for his kiss, so sweet, so deep, so caring that she forgot all about her fears. If he held her like this always, no person or place would ever frighten her again.

They remained in each other's arms for a long

while. From across the prairie came the sound of violin music and laughter, the tang of wood smoke.

He ruffled her hair and lifted her chin. "Want to go to a dance? We're all dressed up for it."

She nodded. "As long as we don't stay too late. Maybe one or two dances, and just you and I together, no one else. Then," she said softly, "I have something very special I want to show you."

She ran the tips of her fingers down the front of his pants, just barely touching him. He grabbed her hand and held it there for a moment.

"I have something to show you too," he finally said when he could speak.

"Agili?" she asked in a whisper.

"How did you know?"

They laughed and he led her carefully down the ladder.

Chapter Fourteen

Rachel stood on the bank, eyed the swirling brown water of the South Platte River and thought how much it looked like moving sand. Earlier word had come down the line that the river could be forded, though not easily. Scouts had found it only two to three feet deep, but very swift. It would take the better part of the day, perhaps longer. If they were lucky they would all camp on the other side this night, if not, some would remain to cross the following day. All but eight wagons had now made it across safely. Two were still in the river ahead of them. It was their turn.

Daniel sat astride Rhymer, ready to prod the team into the water, and called up to her. "Want to ride across?"

Ahead the wagons moved slowly but steadily forward with no mishap. She nodded. It would be better than getting her dress soaked by wading. Her inclination on her own would have been to strip naked, plunge into the water, and come out on the other side, none the worse for wear.

She imagined the expression on that old prune Zoe's face. Even Minna might draw her prim lips together and frown in holy disapproval. Not to mention what the others would do. Daniel might not find such a thing amusing, but she found it fun to contemplate as he urged the team down the gentle bank.

With an unexpected lurch the wagon tilted far to the right and she grabbed hold of the bowed framework; Daniel's mount lunged into the water, taking him almost even with the lead pair pulling the wagon. As he did, all his attention was concentrated on the team. Without warning, the left front wheel dropped into a hole, twisting the wagon viciously so that she lost her hold and went flying, landing with a splash. She came up gasping, fighting the swift current but with her feet finding the sandy bottom and the water swirling around her waist.

Daniel dismounted beside her and took her arm. "You okay?"

Nodding, she shoved the heavy wet hair off her face.

He spanned the wheel with both arms, braced himself, shouted at the team, and heaved, once, twice. Muscles bunched along his back and down both arms, but the wagon didn't budge.

"She's stuck. Take my whip and when I shout, use it on the team. Just pop it over their rumps, don't beat them. They'll pull."

She nodded and plowed awkwardly through the water, wishing once again she weren't bound by the burdensome clothing.

"Ready?" he shouted. "Now."

He bent his knees and gave the wheel a mighty shove.

She cracked the whip above the horses and yelled at the team. They strained forward, bellies down in the water as they pulled with all their might to dislodge the mired wagon.

Behind them Henry Rattlingourd came down off his own horse and added his muscle.

Daniel glanced up and saw that Rachel had stepped between the left rear animal and the wagon wheel and cried out a warning, but everything happened much too fast for him to do anything but watch in horror. The wheel came up and out of the hole and knocked her down under the doubletree, where she disappeared from sight beneath the rolling wagon.

Mouth open in a scream, she gagged on the thick water just as the axle struck her a vicious blow to the head.

Daniel lunged into the murky depths, and on hands and knees moved back and forth raking through the rolling water without success. He could see nothing though several times he stuck his head under and looked around. Henry joined him, and he was the one who finally came up with her bedraggled body. She looked dead, with her head hanging backward over Henry's arm and water streaming from her hair and clothes.

Henry stumbled bank up the bank and dropped to his knees with her still form clutched against his chest. Daniel fell down beside him and fingered the wet hair off her face.

"Is she alive?" He felt disconnected, stunned, and somehow thrown back in time to that Mexican Village. The dead girl he'd mourned became his beloved Winter Dawn and he wanted to tear at his hair and eyes. His heart beat so hard and fast he thought it would burst from his chest.

She gagged, coughed up a stream of water.

"Lay her down, lay her down on her face. My God, Rachel. My God, she's alive."

Daniel practically tore her from Henry's arms, rolling her over and pounding on her back. She spit up another stream of water and began to whimper. He gathered her close, fists clenched into her wet shift, and buried his face in the hollow of her throat.

For a long time he knelt there cradling her gently, crooning against her skin.

He was conscious of Henry rising, standing over them, and then moving away, but still he couldn't let her go. Her breath in his hair was too precious a sign to move away from. He'd almost lost his only reason for living.

Rachel struggled against him, coughed, and gasped.

Henry shook his shoulder and said roughly, "Better see to your wagon, Wolfe, or you'll lose it. I'll take care of her."

"Never mind the goddamned wagon," Daniel said. He propped her against a rock, grabbed her hand, and began to chafe it.

"You lose the wagon, you've got nothing. Don't be a fool. I said I'd see to her."

Ignoring Henry, Daniel turned her head and cupped one cheek. "Rachel, are you hurt?"

She tried to shake her head, tried to speak, but could do neither. She looked at him with glazed eyes.

From across the river rose a great deal of shouting, and Daniel glanced up to see his team halted midstream and the wagon drifting away in the current.

He touched Rachel's shoulder, staggered to his feet and out into the river. He turned and pointed at Henry. "You see to her, you hear me. Take care of her, or by God—"

"I love her as much as you do, Wolfe," Henry said. He then knelt to talk to her.

Daniel hesitated an instant longer, then took off for his floundering wagon. In it was everything he owned in the world, what would give them their start in Oregon. With one more glance back he made a desperate attempt to catch the now-floating wagon. The team had lost their footing and were being pulled along in the swift current. For a time the wagon floated, and he leaped into the water and began to swim. Then it tumbled onto its side, horses screaming as they were yanked along. A box floated from the back, then some blankets and a keg or two.

By that time several riders had plunged into the river from the other side. One attempted to lasso one of the horses, but had no luck. At last Daniel gave up. He grabbed hold of the bobbling box, wrapped the other arm around a keg and headed back for the bank, his heart as heavy as it had ever been. To add even further to his despair, when at last he came out of the river, Henry's wagon was already halfway across the Platte and there was no sign of Winter Dawn. He'd taken her with him.

Rhymer had plunged on across the river as well. Another wagon started across and he tossed his pitiful salvage into the back and lent a hand guiding the six oxen that pulled it.

Fear that Rachel was badly injured tormented him, he felt like a great hole had opened up inside him. Even the loss of all their possessions couldn't compare to that kind of dread.

It took some time to coax the oxen up the other bank, and all the while Daniel kept looking around for Henry's wagon.

Finally he addressed the man he'd been helping. "You handle it okay now?"

"Sure, thanks," the man said. "Sorry about your outfit. I reckon you can move along with me, if you're a mind."

Daniel nodded morosely. "I'll just leave my stuff in the back for now, then. It ain't much, and I expect whatever's in there is soaking wet, but . . ." He lifted his shoulders.

"Sure am sorry. Maybe they'll fetch up downriver and you can salvage something."

"Yeah, maybe." Daniel lost concentration on that hope and headed toward the Rattlingourd wagon. Henry had taken his place in the ragged circle forming in a meadow up a ways from the banks of the river. He was removing the yokes from his oxen. By the time Daniel reached him, Rhymer was tagging along behind. One thing he'd never lose was that mare. She beat all.

He shouted at Henry, "Where is she?"

The man kept working. "Lying in the back. She's bruised and dirty, there's a goose egg on her head, but I don't think anything's broken."

"I'll just fetch her."

"Don't be a fool. Leave her be. What're you going to do with her? You got no outfit anymore, and she sure can't sit a horse for a while. Besides you could hurt her worse if you move her before we know anything."

A thick anger built in Daniel's throat. It had more to do with his fear than any feelings he might have for Henry's opinion, yet he was immediately overcome with a need to pound the man silly. Of course Henry was right, though he hated like hell to admit it.

Daniel settled for going to the back of the rig and vaulting over the tailboard to Winter Dawn's side.

His heart nearly stopped in his throat when he saw her. She lay on her back, heard turned to one side, and she was so pale it frightened him. Her hair was matted with blood just above the ear. Her chest moved with her breathing, though, and when he felt her throat with trembling fingers, a steady pulse throbbed under the cold skin.

Minna Von Finster's voice came from outside. "Let me in there. I'll get her out of those clothes and see to her."

"Wolfe," Henry shouted. "Miss Von Finster wants—"

"I heard. I can take care of her." He smoothed her

muddy face with the back of one hand. "Rachel, my love, you've got to be okay."

"Mr. Wolfe, please let me in there to see to her."

"I said, I can take care of her. I am her husband."

Rachel twitched when he shouted, but neither opened her eyes nor moved further.

"Sir, you are no such thing," Minna announced. "It isn't fitting for you to be doing this. Now, do I have to get someone to move you out of there? This is Mr. Rattlingourd's wagon, and he wants you down, sir, immediately."

"Bastard," Daniel muttered, and laid a hand on the hilt of his bowie.

He came out of the wagon with a roar, landing right in the middle of the unsuspecting Cherokee. They rolled around in the dirt for a while, until Daniel finally got his knife out.

"Drop that instantly, Wolfe," a gruff voice ordered. "Drop it, sir, or I'll drop you."

Daniel came up from a crouch to face Cletus McCrea and the man meant business. He held a sidearm and the hammer was back.

"My wife is in that wagon," Daniel said, but he dropped the knife in the dirt. He cursed himself over and over. Why hadn't he listened and married her proper to the white man's thinking?

"She is not his wife," Henry panted, coming up off the ground. "She's hurt and can't be moved, but she is most certainly not this man's wife. Miss Von Finster has agreed to see to her, but this man wouldn't let her."

McCrea glared at Daniel, who was clearly the outcast in this battle. No one knew much about him, and so judged him as being less than savory. He thought they might be right, but by God he wasn't leaving Rachel in the care of the very man who had tried to win her away from him. And they were married. In the eyes of her people, by God, in the eyes of Rattlingourd's very own people, they were married. What did a damn piece of paper signed by some white man matter? He damned himself for being so stubborn.

About that time L. J. Wyatte, who had been bossing the wagon crossings, approached. "What the thunder is going on?"

McCrea filled him in quickly. "Reckon we need to get Captain Evans to settle this?"

"Man's busy. So's everyone else, so am I for that matter. Wolfe, you let this here lady take care of the woman. You and Rattlingourd cross back over yonder, we could use your help moving the stock." The sergeant walked away, grumbling to himself. "Nothing like fighting over a pretty woman to get a man's dander up. Foolishness, plumb plain foolishness. Knew it when I first laid eyes on that pretty little squaw. Women ain't nothing but trouble, never have been, never will be." He moved out of hearing, still carrying on.

Daniel glared at Henry, fetched his hat out of the dirt, and slapped it on his thigh. Henry brushed at his wet pants, and both did as they were told, leaving Minna to care for Rachel.

It was nearly dark before the last wagon forded the river and the men brought the stock across.

Rachel came to herself slowly and peered into the plain face hovering over her. At first nothing registered.

The woman wiped at her forehead with a wet cloth.

"Rest easy, don't move about. You've had a terrible blow to the head."

Incomprehensible words rolled off her tongue, as strange as the situation in which she found herself.

She touched her lips with shaking fingertips. Tried once again to say something she could understand. She didn't recognize the woman who offered her a tin cup of water, and when she moved pain slashed through her head so that she wanted to cradle it and moan.

"Easy, child, you've had a bad fall. You certainly did frighten us," the woman said as Rachel sipped the cool water.

"What happened? What is this place?" Rachel asked, wiping her mouth with shaking fingertips.

Minna frowned. "Goodness, I can't understand that Indian talk, but I'd guess you would like to know about the accident. You fell under the wagon, right beneath its wheels, right into the river. It ran right over you, gave you a good knock in the head. You'll be fine in a few days."

Rachel moved one leg, realized she had no clothes on, and frowned. No memory of the accident the woman spoke of came to her. "What are we doing here?" She asked the question in English and was amazed.

The woman's face lit up. "That's much better. Well, this is Mr. Rattlingourd's wagon. He's the one who helped Mr. Wolfe drag you out, he brought you across the river and we decided it would be best if you weren't moved."

"No, no, no." Frustration filled her. "Please tell Bone Woman where I am and she will come and care for me." She then began to speak in Cherokee, which obviously puzzled the plain white woman.

"You just lay right still, I'll get someone who can understand you." Minna hopped from the wagon and fetched Henry. "I'm worried about her, she's not herself. I believe her brain's addled."

Henry climbed inside. "Winter Dawn, how do you feel?"

She spoke to him in Cherokee. "My head hurts and it's hard to breathe. Are you Mr. Rattlingourd?"

Henry took her hand. "Dear child, you've had quite a blow. I don't want you to worry yourself. I'm sure you'll be fine in a few days. Don't worry now, we'll take good care of you."

Rachel sighed tremulously and closed her eyes. She wanted only to sleep because all the questions rolling around in her head only made it throb. The Cherokee had a kind face, and so she wasn't frightened by him, but she wished they would tell her why they were traveling in this wagon and where they were going.

It rained during the night, and the noise of the storm awoke her. She had been dreaming about the soldiers who had killed her brothers, and the face of a man that seemed at once familiar and hateful had intruded on those dreams.

With each flash of lightning, another memory emerged, pieces of her past that crackled from her brain. Someone was after her, but all she could think was beware of the white wolf. Someone from the wolf clan? Or a white man, perhaps, a soldier? The same man's face kept coming to her each time she closed her eyes. A soldier, a white man. A man who had killed children and now went in disguise.

She finally dropped off to sleep to the sound of a gentle rain that followed the storm's passing, and in the morning when Minna brought her breakfast, she felt much better. Before she had finished eating, though, there was a great deal of noise outside.

"I will see her, and you can't stop me. Rachel, Rachel." The voice was familiar, yet it sent dread through her. What did she have to fear from this man who shouted her name?

He bounded into the wagon, Minna hastily following.

Winter Dawn took one look at his face and

screamed. Terrified, she back-kicked herself as far into the wagon as she could go to get away from him. This was the soldier, he had the face of the one in her dreams, the one who had killed her brothers. She would never forget that face. Why had he come here for her?

Daniel reached out. "Rachel, Winter Dawn, it's me. What's wrong with you?" He turned to Minna, who was trying to shove past him in the crowded wagon. "Why is she screaming, my God, what have you done to her?"

Minna placed herself firmly between the man and her charge. She had never trusted this one, not since he had betrayed Zoe with his lies and then took the Indian girl to his bed. How could you have any faith in a man who would do such a thing?

"You leave. You're upsetting her. Leave now, or I'll call someone to make you go."

Rachel, who had been shouting in Cherokee, switched to English. "He kills children," she cried and pointed at Daniel. "He is a soldier."

Daniel felt as if she had punched him. He staggered and could not utter the denial that lay on his tongue. "Oh, Winter Dawn," he finally whispered. "My darling Winter Dawn, what has happened to you?"

She clutched the blanket under her chin. "Get him out of here. Make him leave now."

Minna glanced at Daniel over her shoulder. "If you care about her at all, you'll do as she asks. She is very ill and you are only upsetting her more."

He knew the woman was right, but he might as well take the bowie off his hip and cut out his own heart as leave her like this. How could he bear to do such a thing?

The uproar had attracted the attention of several men in the party, among them Captain Evans, who stuck his head in the opening. "You, get down here and stop annoying that girl. Down, sir, or so help me I'll have you dragged out."

Daniel took one more look at the woman he loved, terrified out of her mind because of him, and bounded from the wagon. Shaking loose from those who tried to lay hands on him, he found his horse, mounted and rode away. The fresh wind brought tears to his eyes, his heart ached so badly he could scarcely breathe. He rode blindly, not knowing or caring in which direction he went.

The train pulled out the next morning without Daniel Wolfe. Mankins left the waterlogged crate and keg he'd salvaged from his lost wagon under a tree. He had not returned during the day spent drying and repacking supplies and performing some badly needed repairs, nor during the long night. They did not even consider waiting for him. Henry said it was good riddance, others agreed.

As the days passed, Rachel recovered physically, but great gaps remained in her memory. Huge blank places that were as black as caves. She recalled some terrible things and some wonderful things. And she grew to depend upon Henry Rattlingourd more than she had thought she might. She did not wonder where the frightful man had gone to, but she began to have some disturbing dreams about him, dreams that aroused in her a fierce passion she didn't quite understand.

One night when they were camped on the Laramie Plains, Henry spoke to her of his plans. Prior to then, they had talked only of inconsequential things, happenings along the trail, whether it would rain or not.

"Some of us," Henry said, lighting his pipe with a burning stick, "are going to take a route south of the mountains yonder." He gestured vaguely.

"Separate from the Evans train?"

"Yes, we want to scout an alternate route. Many herds will follow us in the years to come. We must make sure they have the very best of everything, feed and water, the easiest of the trail."

"I thought you only journeyed to California in search of gold."

Henry chuckled. "We do. But we are also preparing this trail. It will carry our name, we must do the honorable thing."

"Name? Your name?"

He puffed. "Ah, no. They will call it the Cherokee Trail."

She wrapped her arms around both knees and rocked. Her headaches were rare and she felt much better, despite the lapses of memory that plagued her. "Henry? Why am I going on this trip?"

Pipe poised halfway to his mouth, Henry gazed at her. "Why? I suppose . . . well, I guess I really don't know."

"My father was a white man, that I know, and I feel as if I am torn between your people and his, but no matter how hard I try I do not know why I have come on this trip. There are few women, it is a man's undertaking, that is for sure. And I worry about something I can't quite remember. Someone is after me, yet I don't know who or why. I believe it is the man who left and hasn't returned, but I am not sure."

It bothered her greatly that Henry didn't respond; he simply continued enjoying his tobacco for a while, then knocked the pipe against a rock and rose.

"Come on, it is time you were in bed. You still need to rest to make sure you don't relapse."

She nodded and stood, allowing him to hold her arm all the way to his wagon. As she started to climb up, she turned. "Henry, who was that man?"

He didn't look at her. "What man?"

"The one who ran away after he tried to . . . after he came after me in there." She nodded toward the shadowy opening.

Henry still wouldn't look at her, but he did answer her question. "His name is Daniel Wolfe, but I don't think we'll be seeing him again. Now, go to bed. Call me if you need anything. Tomorrow we head south."

The name slammed into her like a vicious wind off the prairie. Daniel Wolfe. The white wolf she had been warned of while dream-walking. So that explained it.

That night in her dream she rode in his arms on a silvery winged horse while crystals of ice danced around them. And when he put his lips over hers, her breasts ached and her loins pulsed. She felt as if he sucked at her very life, and yet she desired only to give him what he wanted. She awoke crying, a great feeling of loss swelling within her.

How could she feel this way about such a man? She wanted to pound on her head and make the memories return, but she only lay there wide awake waiting for dawn.

The next morning she watched the other wagons out of sight, then turned to gaze at the great Rocky Mountains that were like walls of enormous granite sprouting from the earth. How would they ever cross them?

Daniel followed the trail of the Evan's train. The silence that surrounded him made him feel so lonely he could hardly bear it. He yearned for Rachel's laughter, her touch, the love in her eyes. He longed to lie with her under the stars, to kiss her, to make love with the abandon they had once shared. Yet the thought of being alone brought a wry chuckle from his throat. Hadn't that been what he'd always wanted? To be completely alone? But that was before he'd met Winter Dawn, before he'd lain with her, before she'd worked her magic and freed him of his demons. When he'd ridden away from her and left her in Rattlingourd's care, he'd fully expected the nightmares to return, but they hadn't. She had done a good job cleansing his soul of guilt, and he missed her all the more terribly because of it.

By the end of the third day on the trail the wagon tracks parted, one set heading on northwest, the others cutting back to the south. Long ago Rattlingourd had spoken of this and had urged Daniel to let Rachel go with him because she would be safer. Had he now taken her that way, or had she remained with the main party under the watchful eye of Minna Von Finster?

He spent the night where the trails parted, battling with himself. Should he follow her obvious route, or should he head on northwest, where he would finally hit the trail to Oregon? He could not stand being rejected once again, but suppose she had come to her senses and remembered their love? The questions without answers bedeviled him all through the night, and because he couldn't sleep, he saw someone passing by that he would otherwise not have seen. He didn't know whether to count that as a good sign or a bad one, but it did help him make up his mind which way to go.

The moon hung low in the western sky and his fire had burned down to embers when the riders passed by. Men moving at night were to be looked upon with suspicion, and these three were no exception.

From where he lay in the lee of an outcropping that hid him and Rhymer, he had a good view of the riders. Three white men riding heavily packed. Traveling cross-country. In the bright moonlight

Daniel knew the big, burly one immediately. He was the bearded trapper Jasper Doaks. The other two he wasn't sure of, but thought they'd been with Doaks the night he'd first laid eyes on Winter Dawn out in the street of Fayetteville, trying to defend herself from them. All had muskets on their saddles and knives on their hips.

"I'm sleepy and hungry," the burly man complained in a voice that told Daniel he had no fear anyone was near.

"Long as the moon shines, we had best ride," Doaks said. "We can't always be stopping to fill your big belly and still keep up."

The third man chuckled.

Daniel contemplated confronting the men, but the Hawkens was not loaded and they would be out of range before he could measure out the black powder and ram a ball home. He couldn't put up much of a fight against all three with only the bowie.

He waited to see what they did.

The men drew up for a time, studying the tracks in the tall grass. In the moonlight, he might have missed the tracks going off to the southwest, where Rattlingourd and his bunch had gone in search of an alternate route, or he might simply have thought them insignificant. Whatever the reason, Daniel knew he had to go in the same direction as the three men, for if Winter Dawn had remained with the main train she was in great danger from these three. If she had remained in Henry's wagon she would be safe and out of sight of these three for the time being.

He didn't wait for dawn, but as soon as the riders were well out of sight, he saddled Rhymer and started on his way.

Great stone formations pierced the night sky, throwing long shadows across the pale washed meadows. Spring was later coming to this country.

Back home in Arkansas the air would be warm and balmy. Wildflowers would carpet the forests, and deer and elk would run in herds, the does dropping fawns in thick lush woodland grasses, and the bucks sporting magnificent antlers.

An odd feeling of homesickness rose within him. He had never once missed his real home, but had found supreme satisfaction in the lovely but rugged Ozarks. Would he now ever find a place to call home again? Perhaps he was destined to wander from place to place, alone for the rest of his life.

The idea pursued him like a wild thing, drove him on in search of the woman who could keep that from happening.

Chapter Fifteen

Crossing the Laramie Plains Daniel rode in grass knee-high on the mare, and as green as any he'd seen. A river cut through the valley like a ribbon of dark blue ice shining in the sun. He remembered that the Laramie River Valley lay at about ten thousand feet above sea level.

Since leaving the Santa Fe Trace the trail had climbed steadily. Sometimes it was hard to tell they were climbing until he would notice Rhymer sweating a bit more heavily, his breath coming thicker. At that elevation the air was thin and bright-tasting with a clean, crisp smell. At first he had trouble breathing, but soon he grew used to the altitude. A brisk wind blew across the high plains, steady and certain, as if it were a forever thing. He didn't doubt that. Gusts whipped around him as he rode, Rhymer's mane and tail danced wildly. Off to the southwest the great Rockies cut jags into a brilliant blue sky; the snowy range of the Medicine Bow Mountains blocked the way west like gigantic walls of ice. The maps had only been able to indicate that they were there. No amount of lines on paper could have prepared him for their majesty. The sight literally took his breath away. By no stretch of the imagination could he see driving wagons across them. Plans were, he knew, to go north of the Snowy Range and cross the Sierra Madres south of Bridger Pass. The crossing had been scouted. The Overland or Oregon Trail crossed north of Elk Mountain, but the Cherokees would remain south of that in order to avoid the Arapahoe and Cheyenne, the Plains Indians. Their thinking also was that if they remained close to the mountains on this virgin route, they would find pure and abundant water as well as plenty of timber and game.

Henry had taken his group to scout a way south of the snowy peaks, but would eventually join back up with the main train. Daniel had to be there when they did, for whether Rachel wanted him or not, he would not let her fall into the hands of Doaks. No telling what the man would do.

Sitting astride his mare and gazing at the breathtaking view, he had to restrain himself from galloping Rhymer through the sea of waving grass across the bowl of the river valley, shouting Winter Dawn's name. Surrounded by such beauty, he knew finally and surely that she was all it would take to make his life complete. Not some lonely cabin in the woods or a homestead in Oregon, but Winter Dawn. Together, they would make a life that would suit them both, if only he could get her back.

The trail of the train cut double tracks through the grass as far as he could see. He spotted, so far away they appeared like ants, three riders following those tracks north, keeping to the skirts of the Medicine Bow Range. He wondered where Rattlingourd and the others were and how Winter Dawn was getting along. He yearned for the warmth of her voice, the blue-eyed twinkle of her lovely eyes, the touch of her gentle hands.

Before he loved her he had nothing, and really didn't mind. But now that he loved her, he could no longer abide having nothing. He would find her and get her back, that he vowed.

He urged the mare into a trot and headed down the slope and across the vast, lush plain.

Rachel sat on the bank of an icy stream, squinting into the sun sparkles flashing off the water. The seven wagons had left the main body two days earlier and were camped for the night circled in a small meadow. Around them wildflowers blossomed like a colorful patchwork quilt. Henry would not yet allow her to work, but being idle made her restless, so she took a long walk and picked a large bouquet. The yellow-eyed white daisies and golden-petaled deer eye filled her arms. She had stopped at the stream to pluck a few blood red spires, but couldn't resist taking off her moccasins and dangling her feet. The delicious aroma of food cooking reached her there and reminded her of how hungry she was, but the sun on her back felt so wonderful, the fragrance of the flowers and the water and the damp soil so soothed her that she remained yet a while longer.

She didn't hear Henry approach and when he spoke it so startled her that she dropped some of the blossoms. He lay a warm hand on her shoulder.

"Sorry. I didn't want to bother you, you seemed so relaxed. So content." Crossing his legs, he sank onto the ground beside her and picked up one of the long-stemmed flowers. He held it under her chin and dusted some pollen there.

She didn't bother with a reply, but kicked at the water so that droplets flew into the sunlight and sent out rainbow flecks of color.

"You look wonderful today," he said and brushed stray locks of hair from her cheek. "Winter Dawn?"

She waited, looking straight at him. His eyes were the color of the chocolate centers of the deer eye blooms. The questions there made her uneasy, though, and she turned away.

"Have you thought more about what I asked? About you and me. I would take very good care of you. Give you anything you want. Take you to California. Once we get a gold strike, we can do anything, go anywhere."

She touched the coppery brown skin of his arm and held her own against it. "We are alike, you and I, aren't we?"

"Tsalagi. We are of The People."

"I know. The spirits have returned to me, spoken of the things Bone Woman taught me. Still I remember nothing of why I am here with you. I know only the Nation and its ways, and it's frightening to be traveling every day and not knowing why I have come. It is as if I were a little girl yesterday and woke up to find I am a woman, with the needs of a woman."

He cupped the side of her face. "I can teach you how to fulfill those needs, Winter Dawn. Let me teach you." He leaned forward and touched her sun-warmed mouth with his.

She moved into the kiss and felt desire bloom within her like the rising of the sun.

He moaned against her lips, pressed her backward into the grass and knelt over her. The flowers lay scattered across her like a fancy dress. He raised the hem of her shift until her bare skin was exposed.

She felt the cold water on her feet, the heat in her loins, the green grass crushed beneath her arms, his mouth moist along her belly.

"Daniel," she cried. "Daniel, I love you."

The words cut through the mist of passion like heat lightning, stilling the movement of his hands and mouth, drenching her desire.

He jerked away as if she were afire and he would be burned. She opened her eyes, feeling a great loss within herself, a hole that might never be filled. What had they done? What had she lost? Somewhere back along the way, a thing she couldn't yet quite touch had been stolen.

"Him again," Henry said angrily, stiffly, looking at her as if she were crazy.

The tang of blossoms crushed between them filled her nostrils. She sat up, straightened her shift, and did not look at Henry.

"You won't see him again, you know. He is gone and good riddance. Before the mountains are behind us you will learn to love me, wait and see." The words were brittle and crisp and in the language of the Cherokee, for he expressed himself much better that way, she knew.

Without answering, she scrambled to her feet and ran back to his wagon. She climbed inside and settled into the deep shadows there. For a long while she sat in silence, thinking about what Henry had said and what she had said.

Daniel's face appeared as if he were sitting beside her, and the memories came flooding back just as quickly. How angry Henry would be to know that his caresses had brought back her memory of the man she really loved, had opened the last closed door in her mind. Eagerly she stepped through it.

She saw herself in Daniel's arms, experienced the joy of lying with him, praire grasses crushed fragrantly beneath them, the sky a brilliant blue bowl under which they made love. She remembered the dream-walking and banishing Daniel's demons. And she remembered love. A love so sweet, so passionate that her nipples puckered and her loins tingled. Her heart twisted with the agony of loss because she recalled sending him away and the look on his face. How that must have hurt him, when all he wanted was to hold her.

Memories of him were so real he might have been

there. A phantom breath feathered across her skin, long locks of hair brushed her breasts, gentle hands caressed the places he knew that drove her wild. Their tender sweet love enveloped her completely, so that she hugged herself in remorse and cried forlornly.

How could this have happened? How could she have forgotten such a love? She had to be with him. But where was he? He had ridden off and not come back after that terrible day on the Platte when she had forsaken him. Surely he would have come to his senses and returned. Henry said later that Daniel's wagon and team had been swept away by the current of the river. What would he do? Left with nothing but his horse, where would he go? Back to Arkansas? Or perhaps on to Oregon. That was all he had ever spoken of, homesteading land in Oregon, and how beautiful it was there.

In this vast land how would she ever find him again? The idea that she wouldn't tore at her heart.

Somehow she had to return to Daniel Wolfe. She did not belong here with Henry Rattlingourd, yet he had let her believe that she had loved him and that made her very angry.

That night when he returned to his wagon, she challenged him. "Why have you been lying to me?"

"I have not lied to you. You are just upset because of your ordeal."

"Ordeal? What a strange word to use. I am not talking about my ordeal. I am talking about Daniel Wolfe. You let me believe he was bad, that I did not care for him."

Henry turned his back on her and pretended to inspect a wagon wheel. She could barely hear his reply. "Only because I love you."

"You don't deny your deceit?"

He shrugged. "Of course not. You are safer with me. He is not respectable."

She practically snarled. "Oh, you mean like yourself?"

"I am respectable."

"So respectable that you told spiteful lies. You took advantage of what happened to me. Daniel and I were married and living together."

Henry snorted. "Only in the eyes of our heathen gods."

"Our heathen gods? How dare you speak that way? You are Tsalagi, even more so than I."

"No one is more or less. We either are or we aren't. You wished to turn your back on our people, become white like your father. How did you dare ask our gods to marry you to a white man who would desert you just as your father did? I only tried to protect you from being hurt."

"I loved Daniel Wolfe, and now he is gone. Left to a terrible fate because of your lies. I will never forgive you for this. I am going to find him if I can."

Henry whirled and grabbed her arm. "No, I won't let you do that."

She gritted her teeth and glanced down at his hand squeezing her arm until the flesh throbbed. "Will you beat me, tie me up, force me? Will you do that?"

"If I have to tie you to keep you here, I will, but I will not beat you or force you to do anything you do not want to do."

"Except remain here." Her voice grew dull, listless.

"It is best. I know what is best for you."

"Only I know what is best for me," she shouted into his face, then remembered Daniel Wolfe saying the same thing once a long time ago.

Daniel was the man she loved, and she would go to him. Henry couldn't watch her all the time. Sooner or later Henry would turn his back, and when he did, she would be gone, and for that she would prepare. First she would need a horse.

The next few days while Henry continued to keep an eye on her as if he were a hawk and she prey, she studied the surrounding landscape closely. To bypass the snow-covered mountains the other wagons had headed north where they would cross. As she saw it, she could either backtrack to where they had parted and then follow the other trail, or she could cut across, riding through the jagged escarpments and perhaps intercept the Evans train before it started through the pass. That route would be shorter and faster, but much more dangerous. Nothing guaranteed that Daniel would be with the train, but it was the way for her to get to Oregon and it was all she knew to do.

Ideally, she could use a map, but the Christies had the only map she had seen since leaving the main train. Even a good look at it would help. Perhaps she could sketch quickly some of the landmarks that would guide her way. For that she needed pen and paper. It seemed hopeless, but she would not give up.

As it turned out, the Christies had all she needed, and it was made available to her the very next evening when the brothers went hunting in the hopes of bagging an elk. They had spotted a few small herds throughout the day, all out of range of their muzzle loaders.

Because she had made no further mention of Daniel for several days, Henry had relaxed a little. He quit accompanying her when she sought privacy for her bodily needs, though he still kept a close eye on her meanderings.

"I'm going into the woods before I go to bed," she announced after a supper of beans and hardtack washed down with coffee.

"It's almost dark, don't go too far."

"I'll be careful."

She looked back once just before stepping into the shadow of trees, but Henry was sitting by the fire filling his pipe. She moved quietly through the woods until she came even with the Christies' wagon, then being careful to see that no one was watching, she darted quickly to it and climbed up through the front so as to be away from Henry should he come looking. She dug out the maps and papers kept at hand just inside. They were wrapped in waterproof canvas and she found a candle, moved deep into the recesses of stacked supplies, and lit the waxy stub with a match she'd secreted in her apron pocket.

Two pencils lay in the wooden box that held the maps, and she was able to make notations on a piece of brown paper. The men obviously saved the wrappings that mercantiles used to wrap their purchases. It made ideal writing paper. They wouldn't miss one piece.

She noted the warning against riding north as far as the Red Desert, drew a squiggly line for the Laramie River, and marked a few more significant landmarks, but mostly she decided if she kept her eye on the Medicine Bow Mountains she couldn't go too far wrong. A route in that direction must bring her to a crossing with the Evans train before it headed over the high peaks and west toward Fort Bridger.

As she quickly folded the map and replaced everything the same way she had found it, she tried not to think what she would do if Daniel had not rejoined the train. The idea that she might never see him again was something she didn't want to even consider.

When she crept back to rejoin Henry, coming out

of the woods as near to the place she'd gone in as possible, he spotted her immediately.

Relief was evident in his voice when he spoke. "I was just about to come looking. Figured you might have fallen in a hole."

She didn't bother to reply. Soon he could come looking all he wanted, she would be far, far away. She felt a little sorry for Henry; he wasn't a cruel man and her going would hurt him. But he shouldn't try to keep her when she didn't want to stay.

On the afternoon of the second day discarded furniture and a few dead animals, some partially butchered out, littered both sides of the trail that Daniel rode. Obviously, the travelers were lightening their loads as the way became more treacherous. One of the many reasons most westward-bound pioneers used oxen to pull their wagons was so that they could eat those that perished, which explained the butchered animals. All along he had thought the allowable twenty-five-hundred-pound load was too much. Now he was being proved right. The men carried fewer personal possessions than would entire families, so some were discarding large amounts of flour, sugar, and the like they'd taken along for trading purposes.

By traveling late into the night under the light of the moon and resting a few hours and moving on, he managed to catch up with the Evans train on the afternoon of the third day. They had spent the better part of that day ferrying their belongings across a vicious little stream swollen by mountain rains. In order to cross, lines had to be rigged, wheels removed from wagons, everything unpacked, and each one horsed across by sheer muscle power.

Daniel arrived in time to lend a hand with the last few wagons. It was far into the night before wheels were back on and everything was repacked. Exhausted, the weary travelers bedded down for the night.

Daniel couldn't rest. In spite of tired muscles and a sleep-deprived body, he continued to scan the camp for some sight of Winter Dawn. Nowhere did he see her. It was a relief that he also didn't find Doaks and his cronies. Daniel dared not inquire of Captain Evans, for the man would certainly not be well disposed toward him since his forced departure out on the plains. He was sure they hadn't forgotten the episode, and it would take little to rile everyone up against him once more. It would do to keep a low profile.

In the morning he would speak to Minna Von Finster, who, being a lady, might be a little more inclined to discuss the matter with him without violence. He scarcely slept the night for worrying about Winter Dawn.

Rachel was ready. She had hidden a pack in the woods fashioned from a blanket, taking supplies to it a little at a time so that Henry wouldn't notice. In it was a linsey shirt and leggings belonging to Henry—all her clothes save what she had been wearing had been lost when she fell in the Platte and Daniel lost the wagon—a length of rope, some food and water, and a small knife from Henry's larder. He always kept the bowie close by and so she couldn't dare take it. She had chosen a tough, shaggy brown mare from the spare stock and would go this night, as soon as everyone was asleep.

She heard the vague noise of stealthy footsteps as she lay waiting for time to leave.

Who was out there? Someone still unable to sleep? A guard? She thought he had passed by only a few moments before, not making any attempt to silence the noise of his horse's hooves. No, this was someone on foot, trying very hard not to make any noise. Henry slept beneath the wagon, she inside. She knew now that she and Daniel had the same arrangement before they had their union blessed by the Tsalagi spirits, and that made her all the more homesick for him.

She listened closely to what sounded like Henry tossing about in his sleep. Odd, he usually slept soundly and scarcely made a noise. Someone grunted once, twice. What was going on?

She slipped to the back opening just as a face loomed there. A face she knew only too well, even in the black of night because he smelled just like he had the night he had chased her through the streets of Fayetteville. Sour whiskey breath with that peculiar odor of dead animals, because he scarcely cooked his meat.

She screamed, a high-pitched sound so ear-piercing that Doaks himself hesitated, giving her a chance to leap out of his reach and hit the ground running.

Shouts abounded throughout the camp as she ran and headed unerringly for the horses and escape. All she could think of was getting away, far far away. Doaks had done something terrible to Henry, she knew, or he would have been up when she had screamed. Someone was running behind her, stumbling around falling over obstacles that she cleared without thought. One thing she could always do was run, in the daylight or the dark.

Someone fired some shots, the deep, booming sound of the black powder guns making her ears pop. Reaching the horses that milled about and whinnied, she moved into the herd and stopped running. They'd never find her there, and not until she ran again would they know what had happened to her. She had some time.

The camp was fully awake now; a few men had lit lanterns and were scurrying about. She moved gently from the side of one horse to another, searching for the shaggy brown mare she'd made friends with. She was the best of the lot and used to carrying her bareback. The mare whickered in recognition and nosed at her. Rachel fisted up a handful of mane and waited.

"Someone's killed Rattlingourd," a male voice shouted. "Buried a knife in his chest up to the hilt. Where's that girl? Get her out here. Let's see if she heard anything."

It was a long time before she could make out any more conversation, though there was a lot of chattering and confusion.

"No sign of her anywhere. Reckon she run soon as she done it."

Winter Dawn shuddered. They thought she'd killed Henry. She dared not stay. Stealthily she moved alongside the mare until they had separated themselves from the herd and had moved off into the shelter of some trees to the north of the encampment. The back of her neck twitched with every step. She imagined someone spotting her, sending up a shout and riding to fetch her back. Or walking up on those who had killed Henry. Poor Henry. There wasn't even time to cry for him, but she was sorry. He had been very kind to her. Somehow she had to get away. Away from the men in the train and the men who had come to get her. They must have been watching her for a long time to know right where to find her.

Moving quietly, she led the little mare to where she had stashed her pack, took out the rope and fashioned a quick halter, tied the pack to her back and mounted up. She was miles away from camp before she put her heels into the mare's sides and let her gallop.

She rode all the next day, only stopping for water and a little food for her and grass for the horse. By dark the next evening she figured she had put only half as much distance between herself and those hunting her as she needed, and so when the moon rose, she mounted up after taking a brief supper and pressed on, choosing not to stop for the night. The mountains rose in grotesque purple shapes across the moonlit sky; somewhere a wolf howled forlornly and a bobcat screamed. The smell of snow and pine sap tinged the air.

After a while the nervous mare pricked her ears and danced sideways, her muscles twitching. Rachel hugged the warm, hairy belly firmly with both knees and spoke soothing nonsensical words to the skittish animal. Horses feared the scent of the wildcat and the wolf, but Rachel welcomed the song of the wolf. It was perfect accompaniment for this frantic flight. Wolves did not attack humans, and rarely horses for that matter. Perhaps these were watching over her.

"Wa' ya, wa' ya," she crooned. The wolf was a hunter and a watchdog and the Cherokee never killed one. The wily animal repaid that kindness many times in legend.

Her brother and his father were of the wolf clan, and the man she went to find was called Wolfe in the white man's tongue. Perhaps the sleek gray predators accompanying her were a sign, but whether of good or evil she couldn't guess.

Before morning a pack ran with her, their golden eyes gleaming, and she called out their Cherokee name, *"Wa' ya,"* like a chant. The mare threw her head, eyes showing the whites, but Winter Dawn kept her running like the wind so the creature could not give thought to dislodging her.

The beautiful beasts led her unerringly through a rocky promontory, down a steep decline, and safely in and out of a wildly churning creek. Pawing her way onto the bank, the sure footed little horse kicked aside rocks that tumbled loose, rattling loudly in the night. The moon set, but dawn already silvered the sky. The pack barked a farewell and veered off into the shadows. She bade them good-bye and kept on, stopping only to sip from the canteen and rest the horse occasionally.

By the middle of the next day, the sun burned hot and bright, and the mare was giving out. She had to stop or else she would kill her, and so she found a cluster of great smooth boulders that cast enormous cool shadows across the earth, and she and the mare rested until the sun dropped behind the mountains. For a long while she remained there, staring out across the rugged countryside. She thought of Henry and how she could not love him, of Daniel and how she must find him, no matter what. And she thought of what would happen to her when they caught her. Everyone thought she had killed Henry. It would not be so easy as the day she had spoken before the committee after that silly fight with Zoe Von Finster.

Daniel headed south along the skirts of the Medicine Bow Mountains. He would follow the route Minna had pointed out the previous evening.

Doaks and his friends, it seems, had ridden along with the train for a full day. He and his companions had asked a lot of questions about an Indian girl, who they claimed was a runaway, wanted by the law of the Nations. Their description fit Rachel Keye, known also as Winter Dawn.

The white man claimed to be a lawman of some sort, up out of Fort Smith in Arkansas. He said he had hired the other two to guide him and help him bring back the girl. Minna had been suspicious.

"He thinks he owns Rachel," Daniel told Minna. "Her brother Eagle sold her to the white man, who is a vicious bastard."

Minna blinked at the word, but he plowed on, not giving her a chance to say no. "You have to tell me where she is so I can find her before they do."

Even after he had talked Minna into imparting the information, she appeared distrustful of his motives. He thought he would never wring it out of her, and had it not been for her distrust of the other three, she probably wouldn't have said a word.

Daniel could tell she didn't completely trust him, even after she finally agreed to speak to him in private. He pleaded shamelessly. "Miss Von Finster, you were her friend. What did she tell you about me?"

Minna dropped her chin for a moment, then faced him. "At first or later?" The words were definitely a challenge.

"Before she got hurt."

"That . . . that she loved you, that the two of you were married. But I knew that to be untrue."

"Only in the eyes of the whites. As far as she was concerned, and myself too, we were married. We said our vows in the way of her people. That should count for something."

"But they are savages."

Daniel ground his teeth. He was getting nowhere. "Now you sound like your sister. I thought you were more open-minded than that. Beliefs are beliefs, no matter who has them. She is a beautiful woman, with a clear idea of right and wrong. Her way is joy and happiness and she has never hurt another living thing. She was . . . she is my life, Minna. Why won't you tell me where she is? Where those men have gone in search of her? They will hurt her, and you don't want that, I'm sure. I only wish to save her. I love her more than my own life, and I will give it to save her. I promise you that."

She regarded him primly for a very long time.

He sighed and made to rise from where they sat beside her father's fire. There was no more he could say.

That's when she finally relented and told him Rachel had gone with Henry and a group of Cherokees who were exploring an alternate route to the south of the Snowy Range of the Medicine Bow Mountains.

He thanked her, but before he could walk away she spoke his name. "I hope you find her before they do. I'm sorry . . . and I'm ashamed. Tell her that for me, will you? If you find her."

"Yes, I'll do that," he said and jammed his hat down tightly on his head.

Within the hour he rode out. He had a general idea where the Rattlingourd expedition planned to go and where they would rendezvous with the main train. He would find Rachel and she would know him. Nothing would happen to her. He would not allow such a thing.

Chapter Sixteen

Fear drove Winter Dawn onward for many miles before she dared stop again. Though she never spotted anyone, she was sure she was being followed. There was a sense of eyes watching her, a feel of danger she couldn't shake. While the mare drank, she chewed on a tough strand of elk jerky and gazed into the distance, her thoughts reaching out for Daniel Wolfe.

Out there somewhere the Evans train made its lumbering way west, and with luck she would find it and the man she loved. They would go to Oregon together and no one would ever be able to punish her for what they thought she had done to Henry Rattlingourd.

Around midafternoon she rode up a long rise that gave her a wide view across the rocky terrain. Far ahead a lone rider moved into view, so distant that she couldn't make out anything about him except that he rode a long-legged piebald horse and wore a big black hat.

Her heart played games in her chest. Her mind told her this could not be Daniel Wolfe, it was impossible that they would simply ride up on each other in this vast land. And yet, she had led him to her once before and found her way to him another time. Who could say it wouldn't happen again?

Though the mare danced impatiently, she held there a moment longer until she was sure. It was

Daniel, of that she finally had no doubt. In spite of her desire to spur the horse on and race into his arms, she cast one last glance back over her shoulder. Someone was back there, of that she was sure. Either Henry's killers or men from the train coming to take her back for punishment.

As if in reply to her fearful expectations, three riders emerged from out of a depression, as far behind as Daniel was ahead, and her caught in the middle. Halfway between salvation and destruction. She felt her stomach sicken.

Fisting up thick strands of the mare's mane, she dug in her heels and clung tightly with both knees when the animal exploded in a mass of newborn energy. It would be close, but maybe she could reach Daniel before those chasing her caught them both. No matter what happened, they had to be together.

Daniel silently blessed Henry for supplying the Hawkens. He had managed to salvage it because it had been on Rhymer's back when the wagon had floated away down the Platte River. In the instant after he spotted the distant rider heading hell-bent for him, he slowed, whipped the short-barreled musket from the scabbard, and measured black powder into the barrel. He hadn't fired a weapon since the Mexican War, not even for hunting. What game he needed, he snared. He probably couldn't hit a moving target if he had to, and figured he'd be just as well off throwing the bowie.

He took two lead balls from his pouch, popped one in his mouth and dropped the other in the barrel, hitting the stock smartly on the pommel to seat it. In the process he had scarcely, slowed the horse and kept his eyes on the approaching rider even as he bit down on the copper cap and slipped it on the nipple of the weapon. The damn fool was moving way too fast for the rough, rocky ground, hugged down on his mount's back to keep from being a target. Someone must be after him, but though Daniel raked a quick gaze over the distant terrain, he could see no one. Then what he had figured would happen did. The horse skidded sideways and went down. No one sat the animal when it scrambled back to its feet a few moments later. As he urged his piebald forward, three riders topped a rise off to his left.

What the hell was going on? Out here in the middle of nowhere and he was meeting up with a damned crowd. They were way off any established trail. All that ought to be out here were rabbits and lizards, and damn few of them.

Momentarily he lost sight of the fallen rider, but when he emerged from around a promontory of boulders and scrub, he spotted him climbing to his feet, long hair whipping in the wind. The slight figure might be a woman or a young kid, he couldn't tell. One thing was for sure, he had no business out here alone.

Amazingly, the kid started waving his arms and running toward Daniel. The horse, made skittish by the fall, ran off into a stand of tall pines. The runner reached a creek and plowed right through it, falling and getting up several times. It was then Daniel saw clearly that it was a woman. She wore men's britches sure enough, but there was no mistaking the shape hugged by the wet clothing. Strands of long, loose hair flamed red in the blazing sun, and his heart thudded hard in his ears. As unrealistic as it might seem, that was Winter Dawn, and she was in trouble.

He spared another quick glance at the three men pursuing her and urged Rhymer forward. If she hadn't fallen they might have made it to each other before those three caught up, now he wasn't sure. It would be close. If the men had a musket . . . well, he didn't want to think of that, and so he kept moving, wishing somehow he could just leap through the air pluck her up and spirit them both away.

She shouted something, but the wind whipped away the words. No matter, she knew him and was coming to him. But would she make it? The three riders moved faster, definitely after her.

Even though she would never hear him, he called out her name, first Winter Dawn then Rachel. Rhymer chuffed; hooves scrabbling and rattling. He dared not run her faster or she'd go down too. Winter Dawn stumbled toward him. It seemed as if they would never reach each other. The men rode hard, closing the gap, and he could hear the heavy snorts of their mounts, the thunder of their hoofbeats. If he did the right thing he might reach her first and snatch her out from under them.

Without slowing Rhymer, he slammed the Hawkens in the scabbard, reached down, grabbed Winter Dawn's uplifted hand and swung her up behind him. He reined the tall horse's head sharply to the right before she was even settled. Clinging to him, she slid sideways.

"Hang on," he shouted, and rode, not back the way he had come, but off into the shelter of tall pines.

Her arms tightened, nearly cutting off his breath. She hugged up so tight against him they might as well have been one. Before Rhymer came to a halt within the shadows of the huge trees, he reached back and grabbed her.

"Off, get off quick," he said.

She hesitated only a moment, then let him drop her to the ground. Stumbling a bit, she righted herself and gazed up into his eyes.

"Don't go, don't leave me. Please."

"Hide and don't move." He wanted to say something more to reassure her. There just wasn't time. He was gone before she could reply, for he had seen where he needed to be.

Past the stand of pines, the way led upward toward a huge outcropping of gray boulders. They offered the ideal point from which to shoot. If he could take out one or two of the men he and Winter Dawn might stand a chance.

Hawkens in one hand, he kicked free of the stirrups and hit the ground running, scurrying through the loose rock that tumbled into a small avalanche behind him. Once situated on the backward slant of a smooth, gray boulder, he raised the musket, found his target, and nodded with satisfaction. He drew a bead downward and tried to allow for the natural drop of the lead ball at that distance, then he tightened his finger on the trigger. The Hawkens could kill a bear two hundred yards, but you had to hit him first. And besides, Daniel wasn't interested in killing, just in stopping. That's all he and Winter Dawn needed. To stop these men.

The one in his sights spotted him about then, but it was too late, the deadly fifty-caliber lead ball was on its way, the puff of smoke warning the riders before the deep-throated boom echoed in their ears and shook the ground beneath their feet. Daniel had taken no chances and had aimed dead center of the man's body. He would be surprised if he cut rock fifty yards from any of them, the shot was so long, his ability so doubtful. The one next to the huge man he'd aimed at jerked upward off his horse as if lassoed.

For a miss it was the luckiest damned shot he'd ever made, but he didn't take time to congratulate himself. He hurried to reload, tonguing the second ball out of his cheek. With a bit more luck, he might get another one before they disappeared out of sight in the trees where Winter Dawn hid.

One man only gets so much luck though, and he could see he wasn't going to make it. Without finishing the reload he skidded back down to where Rhymer waited and mounted up. Once beneath the canopy of trees, he might get another chance, but he needed to be closer to Winter Dawn so he could keep that bastard Doaks from laying hands on her.

The two men floundered around like noisy bear cubs, and Daniel slid silently from the mare's back, hunkered down, and disappeared behind a growth of Juniper. There he lay the gun aside and drew the wicked bowie from its sheath.

"Come on, get closer," he muttered under his breath.

Doaks appeared first, hunched over and scooting along as if he thought by doing so his huge body would not be a target. The bowie sliced the air with a hissing sound and buried itself in the big man's upper arm.

Doaks screamed and fell like a tree.

"I'd think you'd learn," Daniel muttered, picked up the Hawkens, and quickly crimped a cap into shape. Musket to his shoulder, he waited.

The other man didn't appear. Probably smarter than his fallen companion. Daniel waited in silence, sights trained on Jasper Doaks. The trapper screamed curses and thrashed around for a while, then lay panting. Still no one came.

Daniel cocked his head, checked carefully all around in case Doaks's companion might be sneaking up on him. The woods were absolutely silent, except for the ragged breathing of Doaks and the thumping of Daniel's own heart. His ears throbbed with it, but still he waited, praying that Winter Dawn wouldn't reveal herself quite yet.

After a while he thought he heard a horse walking, gravel rattling underfoot, then the drum of hoofbeats fading. The other man had pulled out, but he wouldn't go far. He would wait to gain the advantage and dog their tracks to hell and back. Of that he was sure.

Finally he went in search of Winter Dawn, calling her name softly and ignoring the trapper, who had renewed his cursing.

He found her horse first, a stocky little mare with only a blanket tossed over its back and a quickly fashioned halter. He talked it into standing while he gathered the dangling rope. Behind him he heard a rustling and turned in time to catch the full force of her hurtling into his arms. He let out a grunt and staggered backward a few steps, arms hugging her so tightly that she gasped. The mare danced away once again, but Daniel had no more time to worry about that. Winter Dawn entwined her arms around his neck, buried her face in his chest, then into the hollow of his throat. Her breath came hot and wet against his skin.

While she planted kisses up his neck and ear, along his jaw and chin, he kept his eyes shut for fear he would open them and she would not be there. So often he had dreamed of her in his arms only to awaken and find her gone. He was afraid to believe they were together at last. When her lips found his, he drew sustenance from them like a thirsty man at a spring. He'd thought never to see her again, and the hot stone of pain that had settled in his chest burst into bright joy. He almost choked on the sensation of pure love that flooded over him.

"I'll never let you go again, never, never," he said into her mouth.

At last he lowered her to the ground, for Doaks had begun to make so much noise he feared he might gain his feet and come at them. Holding her hand because he couldn't bear to break the connection between them, he peered at the trapper, who had managed to sit up.

"Git this danged pig sticker out of my arm, you bloody savage," he shouted.

"Who's a bloody savage?" Daniel glared at him.

"Hurts like hell."

"And well it should. You'd a done it to her if I hadn't been quicker." Daniel stepped a little closer and eyed the wound. "Looks like you'll have another scar from my blade. Want to try for three, just move an inch or two and I'll oblige you."

Daniel placed the flat of one moccasin against Doaks's arm, grabbed hold of the shaft, and jerked the blade free.

Doaks bellowed, grabbed the arm, and rolled around on the ground some more.

Daniel watched with no pity. "I guess that hurts like hell."

"Bastid," the man spat. He dragged in several breaths. "What're you gonna do with me?"

Daniel glanced at Winter Dawn. She had covered her mouth with one hand and her eyes were wide with fear.

"Can you ride?" Daniel asked Doaks. Like the first time, he bent to wipe the blood off his blade on the man's own clothing.

"Damn right, if Rake didn't take my horse."

"If he did, you're just out of luck." Daniel saw Rhymer sauntering across the bed of pine needles as if she were out for a stroll. The little horse Winter Dawn had ridden in on, moved to join the larger mare. "I just see two mounts, one for her, one for me. Guess you'll have to walk."

"Hey, wait a minute, where you going?" Doaks

watched in dismay as Daniel offered a boost to Winter Dawn, then climbed on his own horse.

"Oregon," Daniel said bluntly, and touched heels to Rhymer's flanks.

"You can't just leave me here."

"I'll tell you what you do, Doaks. You call some of your friends, maybe those fellas you rode in with. 'Cause I've got to tell you, we don't feel any real goodwill toward you right at the moment. Can you think of a reason we should?"

"She's mine not yours, you bastid, and you know it. I bought her, fair and square."

Daniel gazed down at the pitiful creature. "She isn't anybody's, mister. She's not mine, and she sure as hell isn't yours."

Winter Dawn rode beside Daniel in silence all that afternoon. She could not bring herself to tell him about Henry and how everyone thought she had killed him. What would he do or say? Would he believe her, or think that perhaps she had buried a knife in Henry's chest? He had made her stand before the committee after that fight with Zoe Von Finster. He was an honorable man, his life ruled by strong beliefs. What should she do? Her mind in a turmoil, she finally spoke.

"Where are we going?"

"Oregon." He hesitated, as if he regretted the bluntness of his tone, but didn't know how to say so. Then, "Or you can stay with the train. I'm sure the Von Finsters would give you a ride to California. I want you to do what you want, Winter Dawn, not what I think you should want."

"I remember, you know. Everything."

He glanced over at her and smiled till he thought his cheeks would split. "Figured you did."

"Where did you go . . . after . . . ? I was afraid maybe you—"

"Would make an ass out of myself again? No. I wanted to, hell, might have too if there'd been a saloon within a thousand miles. Or maybe one of them Arkansas stills." He grinned and shrugged. "Instead I just rode this old horse till she begged me to stop."

"You lost the wagon, everything?"

"Yup, I lost the wagon, but not everything."

"Oh?"

He reined in Rhymer and she stopped too. He reached for her hand and she gave it. "Turns out I didn't lose you, though I thought for a while I had."

A lump swelled in her throat and tears burned her eyes, but she didn't shed them. Instead she blinked and smiled brightly. "Then I guess we'll go to Oregon with what we've got. You and me."

"Let's get to it, then." He nudged the mare and they rode along still holding hands.

They camped that night above the rolling banks of a creek. The country was full of such waterways that drained the melting snows out of high country. Daniel built a fire and then disappeared for a while. When he returned he had a rabbit, which he skinned and gutted and threaded onto a stick that he balanced over a bed of glowing coals.

Every time he looked up she was watching him, a strange look in her blue eyes. Desire for her overpowered all his other instincts. It had been so long since they had held each other close and he could wait no longer.

The sun had set behind the mountains, the sky glowed in shades of violet and pink and gold. Remnants of sunlight slid across the dancing water, fingered at her hair, and dueled with the firelight reflected in her eyes. He moved to touch her, fingers trembling with anticipation.

Without a word she rolled the buckskin shirt up over his head. She slipped it down his arms, then loosened the leggings at his waist. Desire turned his gray eyes the color of smoldering ashes and with trembling fingers he lightly touched her breast through the fabric of the rough linsey shirt.

"Oh, dear God, Winter Dawn, I've missed you. I thought I'd lost you." He moved so that they were touching, his bare skin to her clothed body.

Shivering in delight, she ran her hands slowly over his taut stomach, past the laddering of his rib cage and to the hollow of his throat where his heartbeat fluttered.

He began to unfasten her shirt. It was much too big for her and fell down over her shoulders before he finished with the buttons. Her full, firm breasts gleamed in the dancing firelight, the small dark nipples rising even before he caressed each one in turn with a brush of his fingertips.

"Oh, my love," he whispered and bent to kiss them tenderly without touching her with his hands.

She tilted her head back and gazed into the darkening sky. Forgetting Henry, forgetting those who would come for her, punish her for his death.

An early star flickered. Off, on, off, on. A breeze caressed the dampness where his lips had touched, cooled the moist flesh and sent goose bumps skittering across her skin. His hair tickled her when he bent to undo the pants she'd cinched up with an old belt of Henry's. They fell down around her ankles and she stepped free without taking her eyes from the stars.

That's where they would go, a familiar place for lovers, where stars dwelt.

"Winter Dawn," he gasped hoarsely, then threaded his fingers into her loose hair.

She looked into his silver eyes, moved her own

hands to the back of his neck, and pressed against the long leanness of him. His hardness throbbed against her. She opened herself to his desire and enclosed it into the sweet darkness with a gasp of pleasure.

Groaning, he spread his hands across her buttocks and lifted her so that they fit together. A joining that sent waves of noisy passion out into the night. Far off, a hoot owl answered their cries of pleasure.

He held her that way for a long while, content just to be one with her, until the backs of his legs began to ache. There grew within him such a need that he tumbled her into the thick grass and fell awkwardly on his knees between her legs. She laughed throatily and played with his nakedness with feathery touches. Hands propped on either side of her, he leaned forward, body glistening in the moonlight.

He could scarcely bear the desire, yet he held on to it for another moment. Wanting her and knowing she was within reach filled him with a raging passion, but one that would soon be fulfilled. What sweet agony it was to deny himself, to think of the pleasure within reach and yet wait to take it.

He kissed her breasts languidly, trailed his tongue through the soft down in the center of her belly, moved to explore the very depths of her being.

Lights burst across the night sky, waves of green and gold that quivered and flowed up from the horizon. She thought she would explode with the hot, sweet joy that filled her, that swept through her being, taking away her breath, glazing her sight, squeezing her heart.

Slipping his hands beneath her buttocks, he rolled her over so that she was on top of him, and lay there sprawled in the grass, laughing, crying, hugging, kissing, and throbbing inside her like some great volcano that didn't seem to know when to staunch the flow of glowing hot lava.

The northern lights faded and sent out a few more futile rays, then went out.

He laughed again. "My God, did you see that? Did you see what we did? We lit up the sky."

"Of course we did, my love. Why are you surprised?"

She wiggled, felt him stir once again to life and remained astraddle him, reluctant to let go. If she could keep him inside her forever, then they would never again be parted. She laughed at the idea. It would be difficult to get through the day, to do ordinary things. Somehow she had no need for the ordinary just now, and that would be fine with her.

With the tip of a finger, she traced the fine bone above his eyes, down around the temple and to the lips, slack with passion. He took her fingers into his mouth.

"Mmm, tastes sweet."

Leaning forward, she licked at his lips. "Yes, sweet as honey." He grew inside her once more, and she smiled against his mouth. They had been too long apart. It would take a long while to slake the thirst of this giant of a man.

For an instant she stiffened. Had she heard someone walking? Did her hunters lurk out there in the dark, waiting, waiting?

Daniel's lips moved from her mouth to her breast and she sighed, pushing away the images until they sank into waves of passion.

Sometime later the aroma of meat cooking dragged Daniel up with a low moan. "Ah, God, I can't move. You've worn me out, I'm ruined."

She laughed gently. "I don't think so."

"If I weren't starving, I'd just lay here and die a happy man."

He rose with exaggerated weariness and went to turn the rabbit. He raked more glowing coals out over which it could cook, then he joined her in the icy water of the creek.

"Yeow, that's cold." He shouted and leaped about while she laughed in delight. He thought he'd never heard a more joyous sound and grabbed her up in his arms.

White rapids churned around them, taking away their breath. They hugged each other, bobbing up and down, their teeth chattering.

"Which one says when it's time to get out?" he finally asked.

She laughed. "You first."

"I'm fine. He is rising isn't exactly rising, though."

Puzzled, she frowned, then remembered the pet Cherokee name they'd given his most private part. "Then we must get out. I don't want Agili damaged in any way, though he appears to rise very well and often."

"Oh, yeah." He growled and pulled her close. "Feel that? Nothing. Absolutely nothing."

With a glint in her eye, she reached down into the water. "I think I can fix that right away."

"Time to get out," he shouted and pranced out of the water with her right on his heels, chasing him through the rocks back onto the grass near their campfire.

They hugged each other and shivered beside the fire until finally she fetched the blanket which she'd bundled around her clothes when she left Henry's wagon.

Henry, poor Henry. She shuddered until her teeth rattled and hoped Daniel would think she was only cold. He mustn't know, he mustn't know.

She settled in his lap, wrapped the blanket around his shoulders, and drew it closed over herself. After a while they ate wolfishly of the meat until their fingers and mouths gleamed with grease. They fell asleep with limbs entwined and awoke before dawn.

As they were packing their few belongings, Daniel squatted on the creek bank to rinse his hands and spotted the coiled bones of a tiny snake, lying undisturbed just as the creature had probably died. All the meat was gone, the bones bleached ivory white by the sun. He called Winter Dawn and pointed it out to her.

She knelt beside him and touched the minute pale bones with a trembling finger. Then she tore a square from the bottom of Henry's shirt, gently tied the skeleton into a pouch and stuffed it into the pocket of her britches.

He didn't comment, and she didn't offer an explanation. It was just another of the things that separated their cultures, but affected in no way at all the love they had for each other.

She didn't think any more of Henry during that first glorious night they spent together, but he came to haunt her on the following nights after they had exhausted themselves in lovemaking and had fallen asleep.

Finally, when she had taken all she could of the visions, she went dream-walking in search of Bone Woman. From her grandmother she learned what she must do to rid herself of the visitations. She didn't know how to tell Daniel, but the next morning she would try.

He listened with disbelief, and when she had finished he stared at her. "You have to what?"

"Because I have not told the truth, because they think I killed Henry I must go into the mountains and fast until Little Deer comes to tell me what I will do. It is a coward's way to flee and let them think I killed Henry. I might never walk through the darkening land and join my ancestors."

"Dammit, I won't let you do this."

She shook her head sadly. Only last night she had hoped that would be what he would say. But now she knew that it was she who must insist that they not run away. At least not until she consulted Little Deer and the spirits.

"It is my way," she said softly.

"Suppose I tie you to your horse and force you to go with me? Then it is out of your reach."

Slowly she shook her head and gazed at him as if he understood nothing. He wanted to shout at her, but the sad expression on her lovely face tore at his heart. She was suffering, no matter how illogical it might seem to him. And he wanted her to be happy.

"I will go with you," he said. If she said no he would just sneak along behind to make sure she was safe.

"You would not like it, what I will have to do. You might try to stop me."

"Why, what do you have to do? You're right if you think I will stop you hurting yourself in any way."

"It is a private thing, not something anyone can help me with."

"Goddammit, I'm not 'anyone.' I'm the man who loves you."

He felt the situation getting quickly out of hand. He could handle a lot of things, but Winter Dawn's strange sense of logic defeated him. "I will not lose you again, I don't care what you say." He bellowed the words, then whirled away so as not to see the flash of fear in her eyes. He did not want to frighten her, but dammit, he couldn't let her go off alone, no matter the reason.

"Winter Dawn, please don't punish yourself or us for what some evil white men did. It isn't right."

"I cannot sleep without Henry's spirit coming to me. He must be avenged. It is all I can do. You must understand and trust me. I love you more than I do myself. I cannot be the woman you need as long as this thing haunts me.

"Daniel, do you remember how it was for you before? The dream-walking and the dead child? What happened to you because you could not rid yourself of the feelings of rage and guilt you felt?"

He clenched both fists against his thighs and beat them there until his flesh ached. This couldn't be happening. Not now, not when they had finally come back together again. Not when he loved her more than life itself. He thought that if she loved him it should be enough, but he knew it would not be. He knew she was right in what she said.

He shook his head miserably, then took her in his arms. "But I will not let you be completely alone. I mean, I will stay near enough that you can call out to me, or I to you, until it's over. Otherwise, I can't let you go. I can't." She stiffened in his arms. He moved away and held up a hand, as if to stop any further objections.

"I know, I said over and over you belong only to yourself, you have the right to decide, but I couldn't live if I let you go off like this and never saw you again. I won't do it. I will be close by, should you need me. I reserve the right to do that much. And if I think something has gone wrong, I will come whether you call me or not. It's the best I can do."

She nodded, her face revealing the misery she felt. It was all she could ask of this man.

That night they didn't make love, but prepared instead for her journey. Because Bone Woman's charms had been lost when Winter Dawn had had her accident in the river, she must prepare her own. She would use the tiny bones of the snake Daniel had found on the creek bank the morning after they made love.

She would need other things for which it would be necessary to search, so they would remain there for a while.

Two days later they rode up a steep animal trail as far as the horses could go, and there Winter Dawn dismounted, kissed him good-bye, and began her climb toward the distant precipice which she had chosen for her fasting.

Bright sunlight blended with crisp mountain air to bring tears to his eyes as he watched her disappear into a crevice.

He should have stopped her. Dammit, he shouldn't have let her go.

Chapter Seventeen

Wading in ankle-deep drifts of snow, Winter Dawn rounded the high promontory as the sun began its decline from the center of the sky. Before her nestled a small lake surrounded by a blaze of wildflowers beside long fingers of brilliant white snow. In the still water, the towering peaks reflected against a brilliant blue sky.

For this most intimate journey she had worn the traditional Tsalagi dress Bone Woman had given her, the one she had worn when she fell into the Platte River. The only possession she had left from that former life.

Within her sang the spirits that urged her toward this destination; drums thundered, blood roared to the rhythm of her heartbeat. Here in this strange and unfamiliar place, she experienced the uncanny lure of the ancient ones, as if she stood on the slopes of the Great Smoky Mountains of her birth. This too was sacred ground, and here she became one with the Tsalagi. The People of creation. The blood of her white father ran silent.

How long she must remain in this blessed place she did not know, but of this she was sure. Being here would save her spirit, unite her forever with her people, and renew the love she would give to Daniel Wolfe.

The ghosts appeared on the morning of the fourth

day of fasting. First came her brothers, slain by the white soldiers when the Cherokee were driven from their homeland. They wished her well, but warned her that she must look deep within herself to find the answers she sought. And they brought with them Henry's spirit. He opened his arms in supplication, for only she could see that the men who had killed him were punished. What she could not give him in life, she could give in death.

Because fasting had made her too weak to stand, she crawled through the sweet grass, knelt beside the water, and stirred her reflection so that it rippled into the images there. As the surface grew still once again, the face of Bone Woman emerged.

"Daughter of my daughter, you have called at last. Do you tire so easily of being white?" The chiding rested lightly on Winter Dawn's shoulders, for she and her grandmother shared the same spirits.

Cupping her hands, she scooped the icy water from the reflection and splashed it over her face, then turned her eyes upward into the glare of the sun. When she looked into the water again she saw herself. She had changed but in such a way that she could not define. There was something of the older woman there, deep within the blue eyes, in the tilt of the lips, in the glow of mature knowledge. Yet when she looked closer the changes all but disappeared. She could finally reclaim her rightful heritage. She had found what she had come here to find.

By telling the truth, she could free Henry's spirit. The men who had killed him would be punished. And she would never again deny her Tsalagi blood.

Resting on her knees beside the lake, she remembered the legend that her mother had told her many times, and chanted it aloud. The Cherokee words hung in the crisp air, mingling with the high-pitched scree of the hawk.

"Once all the people lived together, but they started to quarrel so the Creator decided to separate them. He sent the white ones to their place, the yellow people to their place, the black to theirs and the brown and red people as well. He then gave dreams and legends and stories to guide each of them. They must never be forgotten, or the world would become a place of great turmoil and savage existence."

Winter Dawn raked her fingers through the mud, drew three lines down each cheek, and thumbed color across her forehead. Then she lay back to await Little Deer, for she could not leave this place until he released her.

Far below Daniel heard a high-pitched cry, unlike that of the wolf or bobcat or hawk. He could wait no longer and set off up the mountain, a pack slung over his back and the bowie strapped to his waist. Everything else he left with the two horses, who would be content to crop at the lush green grass and await his return. He followed the print of her moccasins, stopping now and again to check the trail of bent and broken grasses and scuffed rocks.

When he came upon the small mountain meadow there was just enough daylight left for him to find her, sprawled in the grass beside the lake. Dried mud streaked her face. He scooped water and moistened her lips, speaking softly to her. She had been gone five days, and probably had been without food all of that time. He cradled her close, kissed her lips, and fed her water, all the while speaking softly of his love. At last her eyelids fluttered and she gazed up into his face.

From his pack he took jerky, chewed it until it was softened, and placed it between her lips. She ate in silence, watching him. He saw something in her expression that had not been there before. Rather than frightening him, it was quite soothing, for it bespoke a serenity that this young Indian girl had never shown, not since he had met her. She had always been possessed of a wild creature, ready to dart away or fight back.

Because of her weakened condition, Daniel made a camp near the lake rather than try and take her down the mountain. After she ate and drank and fell asleep in the thick grass, he set out to find something more substantial than elk jerky for their evening meal. She had not yet spoken a word, but just gazed serenely at him in a way that made him feel enclosed by tranquility.

He spotted their supper coiled on a rock in the sun. Quietly, he sank to his heels and looked around until he saw a forked stick of just the size he wanted. He tested it for strength, for it wouldn't do to have it break at just the wrong moment. At last satisfied, he rose and walked up on the rattlesnake, raking at the grass until its triangular head lifted and swayed from side to side, tongue tasting air.

With the stick he teased the snake. Muscles beneath the colorful brown-and-gold markings rippled, the coil tightened and the rattles vibrated. Once again he pecked at the moving head. Finally the snake had enough of such flagrant treatment and struck, stretching its length out across the rocky surface. Momentarily helpless to strike again, the deadly reptile was easily caught. He pinned the thing to the ground with the forked stick. Quickly, while the snake thrashed, he reached down and plucked it up, fingers squeezing tightly just behind the fat jaws. The open mouth gleamed scarlet. Fangs extended, the snake hissed. He held it high above his head and the tail whipped at the ground. Truly a giant in the world of belly walkers. With a deftness learned over many years, he slipped his hand down the cool, dry length, grabbed the tail, let go of the head, and popped the great reptile like a whip. A loud crack bit the air, the sound of its neck breaking.

He took his prize back to the bank of the lake to skin and clean it. Then he cut large chunks of the pale, firm meat and threaded them onto an aspen limb Winter Dawn brought to him from the nearby woods. She had also brought blackberries carried in the dried-out shell of a turtle she'd found near the water's edge.

The meat cooked quickly and they ate the sweet chunks with their fingers, jiggling them between their palms to cool. Up until they finished the meal off with the juicy berries, they had spoken only of the beauty of the place, how good the rattlesnake meat tasted, how cold the night might be. They had scarcely touched, and Daniel sensed something in her demeanor that warned him of an unpleasantry yet to come. Whatever it was, she seemed okay with it. He probably wouldn't be.

Wrapped together in a blanket from his pack, they lay beside a large fire. He kissed her tenderly, but they didn't consummate their feelings of desire, just held on tightly to each other, bodies coiled together in a lazy bliss. She fell asleep long before he did, and he watched the sky grow deeply purple after a sickle moon set beyond the snowdrifted peaks. The scattered stars were like peepholes into a brightly lit other world. If only he could peel them away and carry her there, far from what he sensed was coming. Cold air off the snow misted over them, smelling as pure and clean as heaven. He wished oddly that time would stop at this very moment, and they would neither have to go forward nor look backward. He was afraid of what lay ahead, and didn't know why.

The next morning they ate more blackberries, these

wet with sweet dew, and started back down the mountain.

"I'm sorry to go," she said, looking back one last time before they rounded the rocky promontory and began the treacherous descent.

"Well, I suppose we could build a cabin here, settle in. Never leave." His hold on her hand denied that possibility.

"Will Oregon be this beautiful?"

"More so, I've been told." He skidded down over a steep rock and turned to brace her slide. "You no longer want to go to California?"

"My heart is at peace. I do not need what was never meant to be mine."

He stopped and held her there. "But?"

"I do not understand." Looking up at him, her eyes belied the innocence of the question.

"Yes, you do understand. There is a 'but' in your voice when you talk of what we'll do. I'm not sure I like it. Are you going to tell me what happened up there?" He held her arm and looked down into her eyes. "Winter Dawn, we will go anywhere you wish. I want you to be happy."

"I am already happy." She kissed him quickly, then moved off so that her back was to him when again she spoke. "Soon I will tell you everything that happened and what I have decided. You should not worry, though, it is not about us."

"What then? Be careful there, don't slip." He held on to her while they skinned around a particularly narrow turn in the path. Below them lay an avalanche of rock that trailed through the blue-green pines, above them jutted high cliffs of granite iced in snow.

The trail widened out after a few hundred yards, and he again asked the question. "What is it about if not us?"

"Henry Rattlingourd."

"What, I couldn't hear."

"I must go back to the Evans train and tell them what happened to Henry."

"No." The word roared out of him. "Goddammit, no. I won't let you. Just let it be. Leave their business to them, I will take care of ours."

"I must do this thing. I must not be judged harshly in the land of the darkening. Henry is there, waiting for me to do what is right."

"Oh, for God's sake, Winter Dawn."

She stopped and turned to face him. "Do not mock me, Daniel Wolfe."

"Mock you? Where'd you learn such things?"

"Is it that you think stupid savages don't know when a white man mocks them?"

"Stop that." He took her by the shoulders and leaned them both against the high bank away from the drop off. "You are no stupid savage, and I didn't mean to mock you. I only meant that I disagreed with your assessment. We are arguing, Winter Dawn. That's all. I'm not judging you, I only want you to stop and think of the consequences of such action. They might just put you in a stockade, or worse, stand you up before a firing squad. If they think you killed Henry how can you prove otherwise?"

"Perhaps I can't, but I must try. Doaks is a terrible man and he must be made to pay for what he did. That he buys my people as slaves is bad enough, but that he would kill Henry just to get me back, that is . . . is . . ."

"Despicable," Daniel supplied. "Contemptible."

She nodded. "Yes, these words are so like respectable. Your language is very strange, indeed."

Fury overrode Daniel's fear for her. "I should have killed that bastard Doaks when I had a chance. If I'd only known, I would have. I'm sorry, so sorry." He pulled her close and held her there, although she seemed not too happy with him.

The fragrance of her hair touched his nostrils and he closed his eyes to enjoy her proximity. He would not lose her again, but he could sense a stubbornness in her that wouldn't be denied by anything he could do.

"Come away with me. We'll head west on the Overland Trail. Evans is crossing the mountains north of there, they'll never find us, probably never even look. Where did this happen?"

"The wagons were camped in a meadow, they were to cross the mountains then rejoin Evans on the other side. Now, of course, they have probably sent out riders after me. It is a wonder they haven't caught up with us."

"Perhaps they passed by while you were on the mountain. They may already have reached the Evans train and told them. We have to go. We'll head across the mountains here, find a way through somehow. They'll never catch us, Winter Dawn. Not if we hurry."

"Oh, Daniel, we cannot run away. I cannot. Don't you see? I might, except for what has happened. I left my home wanting to be white, and now I know that the Tsalagi holds me forever. I am of them, and the white blood of my father is just a mere small . . . I know there is another word, a better word for it."

"Trivial," he supplied and cupped her chin. "Oh, God, I love you. I never knew there were such feelings, never could have imagined the joy, the supreme glory of it. It's got to be like looking upon the face of God."

"Love is the face of God," she whispered. "To be allowed to love as we have is sacred, and that is why I must do this thing. Do you understand?"

Tears filled her eyes.

He stared down into the blue sparkling pools and thought of his own guilt that she had vanquished. "Oh, yes, I do. But I will not let them hurt you, no matter what you must do. I will die with you before I'll let you die alone."

She pressed against him, arms around his waist, head tucked beneath his chin. This was the man she would love forever, even into the next world and the next after that.

They caught up with the Evans train two days later. The wagons had begun the treacherous climb through the pass of the Medicine Bow Mountains, which had slowed their progress and allowed Daniel and Winter Dawn to catch them on horseback.

For the next few days there was no time for discussions of anything but the tough trail, as the two added their strength to help with the ascent. Wagons were hoisted by only the sheerest of muscle power of man and beast through the meanest of cuts and steep drop-offs. The train by this time had divided itself once again, with yet another group going off in search of faster and easier passage.

Daniel and Winter Dawn helped where they could, and no one asked many questions. He hoped that she would forget her resolution by the time the drudgery of crossing the pass was ended.

Every evening they rubbed each other's sore muscles and existed as they had when alone, accepting nothing from anyone. They did not speak of the matter of Henry's death. Daniel, because he hoped she would forget; she, because it was settled and there was no reason to discuss the matter further.

When grazing and water grew scarce, animals and humans alike suffered. Those who had made it this far were tougher and more determined than ever to see this job through to the end for those who would come after, but also because they didn't want to fail in their quest for gold.

Once they reached the top they were faced with yet another problem. How to keep the wagons from running over the beasts on the downward trail. It became more a contest to see if the animals could move fast enough to stay out of the way of the rolling wagons. No one wanted to discuss anything at the end of each of the harrowing days, and Daniel continued to be spared from witnessing Winter Dawn's confession.

It was with a great deal of relief that the wagons circled up that hot July evening with the Rocky Mountain Pass behind them. Ahead lay miles and miles of sparse grazing and little water as they headed for the Green River.

Here they would spend a few days repairing wagons and resting the animals as well as themselves before they tackled the next stage of the long drive to California. Here too Winter Dawn would at last seek her judgment day from whites and Cherokee alike. She requested a hearing from Captain Lewis Evans first, but Daniel insisted on being present. Evans asked James Vann to sit in as well.

Evans told Winter Dawn, "He is Cherokee, as are you, and if this is as important as your demeanor suggests, I don't want to be put in the position of a white man judging a Cherokee. It may happen that we will have to call together a committee of twelve, but let's decide that after we talk. Vann will record what is said."

There may have been a few who eavesdropped shamelessly on the four who gathered that evening near Evans's tent—it was too hot to sit inside—but no one paid them any mind. Winter Dawn thought that soon enough everyone would know her story anyway, and if Evans did not object, why should she?

Evans took some time lighting a pipe, as did Vann. The tobacco smoke hung sweetly between them on that strangely windless evening. Daniel sat beside Winter Dawn, holding her hand in both of his. Her skin was cold, the palm dry. Small tremors passed within his grip.

As her story about the attack on the seven wagons under Henry's command unfolded, Evans and Vann listened intently. She spoke with nearly flawless English and never used contractions. When she reached the part where Doaks actually tried to drag her from the wagon, she took a deep breath and tightened her fingers in Daniel's grasp. Deep inside he ached for her and what she had gone through. Jasper Doaks did not deserve to live for all the grief he had caused her.

With very little stumbling, she told her story right up to meeting up with Daniel. There she halted and bit at her lip.

Vann and Evans glanced at one another, then at Daniel.

"Had I known," he interjected, "I would have captured the man and brought him to you. He was after us, there was a fight. I think I killed one of the men with him, I did wound Doaks, but left them there to get her away as quickly as possible. I only learned the rest of the story when it was too late to bring them in without endangering her life."

"And you believe this story?" Vann asked.

Though he wondered what good his opinion might do, Daniel answered quietly, firmly. "Yes. Yes, I do."

Evans smirked. "But then, of course you would say so."

"Wait just a moment, sir. She does not lie, nor do

I." Daniel took a step forward, anger overpowering his better judgment.

Vann raised a hand. "Gentlemen, let the girl speak."

Winter Dawn nodded and swallowed noisily. Her heart hammered in her chest until she could scarcely breathe. She spread a trembling hand out in front of her.

"Up on the mountain I spoke with the spirit of Henry Rattlingourd, and with my grandmother Bone Woman. In my vision Little Deer called upon me to avenge the restless spirit of Rattlingourd. And so I am here. Otherwise I would have gone over the mountain and beyond where you could never have touched me. You must punish the man Doaks."

Daniel released her hand and put his arm around her shoulder; she was calm. "That's enough. She has told you everything, now leave her be."

It was over. Done with. A great sense of relief poured through her. Later, perhaps, she would think about what terrible thing they might do to her, but for right now, she could only be relieved that the telling was finished and trust the spirits to protect her.

Evans cleared his throat and shot Daniel a keen look. "Were you there when Rattlingourd was killed?"

"Of course not, sir, or I would have dragged that bastard Doaks here to you on the end of a rope."

Vann held up a hand again, ever the peacemaker. "And you are sure Rattlingourd was dead?"

She nodded her head against Daniel's shoulder. "I heard them shouting that he was, shouting that I had killed him. No one saw me do such a terrible thing, they only supposed so because I was gone and they didn't see or hear Doaks and his men."

"And what will you do now?" Daniel asked.

The two men glanced at each other. "There is no question," Vann said. "We will send someone to find out what happened. Meanwhile, she must remain in custody. The story will eventually have to be heard by the committee of twelve. They will decide what must be done."

Winter Dawn sagged against Daniel, then righted herself. It was what must be. She met the steady gazes of both men.

Evans nodded briskly and stood. "There will be a guard put on the young lady until this is cleared up."

"The hell it will," Daniel said. "You can't treat her like a prisoner."

"I'm afraid I can, sir. She will be confined in the supply wagon, and you, sir, will stay away from her. I'll not have you stealing off with her in the dark of night."

Winter Dawn hadn't bargained on being separated from Daniel, yet she spoke in a clear voice. "It is all right, Daniel. I will go with them." Despite her fear of what was yet to come, she felt cleansed. "Daniel, would you tell Minna I would like to see her, if she does not mind?"

The two women had renewed their friendship during the difficult trek through the pass, and Winter Dawn had been especially compassionate when Minna was forced to unload her precious piano and leave it behind.

He nodded miserably. In the middle of the dark night, he would sneak up on her guard, probably catch him napping, rap him smartly on the head, and ride away with her on their horses, which he would have hidden somewhere saddled and packed with supplies. And if she didn't want to come, he would gag her and tie her up and take her anyway. He would not let anyone punish her for what she had not done, no matter what she thought.

He made the plan as he trudged toward the Von Finster wagons. It was near dusk, with deep shadows around trees and rocks, and he stepped over a long wooden tongue, looking up and across the meadow just in time to see a shadow move suspiciously. Someone was out there. Brush did not leap from one place to another. He hugged back against the wooden sideboards and glared at the spot until his eyes burned. Just as he was about to decide he hadn't seen anything after all, the figure darted from one dark blending into the next. Determined to find out what the hell was going on, he sank down against the wheel to wait and watch.

As stubborn as he, the shadow remained unmoving. Daniel feigned sleep, slumped there against the wheel, forgetting all about his errand to fetch Minna.

At last the sneaky bastard made his move, slipping across the open space between the trees and the supply wagon up ahead. He had vaulted inside where Winter Dawn was being kept before Daniel could stop him.

He saw it was her brother and thought of crying out, alerting the guards and bringing them down on Eagle, but something stayed him. When he reached the supply wagon he heard them talking inside and she didn't sound frightened, just impatient.

Winter Dawn touched her brother's arm and felt the muscles stiff and unyielding. She spoke to him in Cherokee. "What are you doing here, I thought you had gone to Texas?"

"I wanted to make up for what I did. It was not right for me to sell you, I should have found another way to protect all of us. I was afraid of what Doaks would do, and I knew you paid me no attention when I warned you that he was following the train."

Winter Dawn looked thoughtful. "Surely he did not come all this way to recapture a runaway slave."

"No, I told you. He owns a part of a gold mine out in California. They wrote to say they had found much of the gold metal, and so he was going to join them. All of this I heard when they made their plans. He must have seen you with Henry and decided to get you back anyway, since it came handy. If I had known, I could have stopped him, but I was too late. All I could do was trail along and hope for a chance to pick them off, one by one. Then your man came along, and so I have waited for a chance to speak to you before I join Tatsi in Texas."

His words struck her speechless. She stared into the cavernous eyes, only a glimmer in the remote glow from a campfire outside. Did she dare trust him, or should she shout out for help? Since selling her to Doaks, he had actually done more to try to help her than harm her. And perhaps he was sorry. They had loved each other a great deal when they were children. She still felt that love and hoped he did too.

"You must go before anyone catches you here," she told him, touching the scar on his face with the tips of her fingers. "I do not want anything to happen to you."

He covered her hand with long, delicate fingers. "Nor I you, sister. I will take care of this thing, once and for all. I brought Doaks to you, it is my responsibility to stop him."

He moved her palm to his lips. They felt hot and dry against her skin. "There is nothing you can do. Just go, go to Texas and be well," she whispered. "Now, go, before someone hears us."

He nodded and was gone, scarcely making a sound as he bounded to the ground.

"Good-bye, my brother," Winter Dawn whispered. Eagle's spirit had died many years ago, when she was but a child and the white man routed the Cherokee from their homes. She hoped he would find peace at last, but feared he would soon die at the hands of the white man he so despised. The band of renegade Cherokees holed up in Texas would certainly not go silently into oblivion.

Daniel tracked Eagle deep into the woods before accosting him. He knew the young man understood some English, even though he pretended otherwise.

"Where is the white man Doaks?" he asked Eagle.

The Cherokee balanced delicately on the balls of his feet, his eyes measuring distances. Clearly he was calculating whether he should run or attack.

Daniel held out a palm. "I mean you no harm. I need to know about the others."

Eagle shrugged.

Daniel lost his patience and launched himself at the silent man, knocking him to the ground. Like a flash he had the blade of his knife poised across the Indian's throat, his superior weight holding him. He was surprised that Eagle didn't struggle but just glared up at him, lips pulled into a snarl.

"Go ahead, kill me. Lose her."

"I don't want to kill you. I want to know where Doaks and that other fella are. The ones who came after her. I don't want them surprising me. I have to keep her safe. You understand that, don't you?"

Eagle barely nodded, but Daniel knew he got the gist of what was being asked. He pressed harder on the boy's chest. "Then tell me."

"I will take care of Doaks. It is mine to do."

"How will you do that?"

"Do not worry. You see to her if you care for her, I will see to Doaks, I care very much what happens to him." He spat out to one side and the hatred that hardened his eyes sent chills up Daniel's spine.

"What will they do to her?" Eagle asked.

"I won't let them hurt her, but they may want to

put her up before a firing squad if she can't prove she didn't kill Rattlingourd."

Eagle squinted. "She did not, this I know, but they would not listen to me either. You will stop them?"

"If I can. What do you care?"

"Care?"

"Love. Concern. A wish to see she isn't hurt."

"I do not wish her hurt. Let me go and I will bring the man Doaks to you. You can flay his skin until he speaks the truth, if you wish."

Daniel rose, holding the bowie low and pointed upward just in case the Indian decided to jump him. He didn't, but instead regarded Daniel from a crouch for a brief moment before moving from the moonlit clearing into the dark shadows.

Daniel hoped he wouldn't regret letting the man go, but he saw nothing else he could do.

Chapter Eighteen

A perimeter guard showed up around dusk, riding hard and shouting, "It's the Rattlingourd wagons, I see 'em coming. Yonder." He pointed off to the southeast.

Within a few minutes the first rounded white canvas tops came into view. Rachel watched with a thundering heart as the seven wagons drew closer and she could begin to make out men, some driving, others riding. Time had run out.

She moved away from her designated prison area, but the guard assigned to watch her ordered her to stop. Quickly she scanned the crowd gathered to watch the approaching group, but she didn't see Daniel anywhere. Evans had been quite clear that they were to have no contact, but she only wanted to see Daniel's expression and know he was nearby should she need him.

Upon hearing the commotion Daniel had hotfooted it toward the Evans compound, and he lingered near the main tent, where he knew there would soon be a confrontation about Rattlingourd's death. Putting the large trunk of a tree between himself and the clearing, he settled in. He didn't have long to wait.

Two dusty, trail-weary men rode their mounts straight up to Evans's wagon and dismounted in a hurry.

Evans insisted they seat themselves, take off their

hats, and pour cups of coffee before they got down to business.

"Now, I think I know what you men have to tell me, so just get your wind back first. I've sent for Vann since he's privy to the information as well."

One of the two Cherokees, well known for his trading acumen and glib tongue, had obviously been chosen ahead of time to tell the tale of Henry Rattlingourd's murder. Daniel thought his name was Amos, but couldn't be sure. At any rate, Amos did a good job relating what he knew, but his tale ended with the conclusion Daniel dreaded hearing.

"It was that breed, Rachel Keye. Henry took her to his bed and she thanked him by plunging a knife through his heart."

Evans regarded the two serious young men for a long moment. "Kind of a little thing to overpower and kill a man of Rattlingourd's strength, isn't she?"

Vann arrived and stood quietly to the side, busy with the makings of a smoke.

Amos studied his steaming coffee, and when he looked up he appeared to blush, though it was hard to tell with the burnt brown color of his skin. "Sir, if I may say so. There are times when a young lady . . . well, sir . . . has the upper hand, if you know what I mean. We men can't always . . . well, I mean, at the height of . . . you might say, our passion, we are at their mercy, if you understand what I'm saying."

"You are saying, I believe, that she was in bed with the man and stabbed him as he was making love to her?"

"Well, sir. Yes, sir. It's all we can figure out, given that he was rather strong, much bigger than her."

"Did anyone see this?" Vann asked.

"No, but Clark saw her running, just caught a brief glimpse as she darted away from the wagon, then she was gone and he didn't see her again. And he didn't see anyone else, sir. No one at all."

The other Cherokee cleared his throat and spoke for the first time. "She was there and then she was not. Why else would she run if she had not killed the man?"

Evans waved a hand at them. Vann watched him closely and puffed on his pipe. He was clearly not pleased at all. Daniel wondered if perhaps he might be a willing ally for Rachel, should it come to that. He had no time to ponder the possibility before Evans spoke.

"Get cleaned up and settled in. Eat yourselves some supper. We'll call the committee first thing tomorrow and they'll hear both sides of this story. If the girl truly killed Rattlingourd, we may have ourselves an execution on our hands, for by God no one will commit such a dastardly deed under my command. Not man, not woman, Injun, or white."

Daniel didn't wait for the men to react, but slipped away, circling the outer edge of the encampment until he reached the wagons of the Von Finsters. When word of this got back to Rachel, and it would, she would need someone by her side. Evans wasn't about to let that someone be Daniel and he wanted it to be Minna Von Finster, the only person he trusted to take care of Rachel.

The last person he wanted to see was Zoe, but she sat beside the fire, gazing into the flames and sipping at a cup of tea. Minna was not in sight.

Sighing, he took off his hat and approached.

"Miss Zoe, could I speak with your sister a moment?"

Zoe almost dropped her drink, and her eyes flashed briefly before she calmed. "Good heavens, you startled me. I was a million miles away. Daydreaming, I suppose."

Daniel was awed to silence. The woman actually sounded civil, and there was something different about her he couldn't quite put a finger on. He didn't have time to wonder, though, for Minna stepped around the front of the wagon at that moment.

"Ah, Miss Minna."

"Mr. Wolfe, isn't it?"

She knew his name perfectly well, and he smiled wryly. This would not be easy, for they had not parted on good terms. She evidently continued to blame him for Rachel's problems. Maybe she was right, but he wasn't about to argue with her now.

"Yes, Daniel Wolfe. Rachel's husband? She's been arrested."

Minna refused to look at him. "Yes, I heard. Ridiculous that she could have done such a thing."

"Then we could use you on the committee tomorrow."

Minna raised her brows. "So soon?"

"Yes, I just heard. I also heard Evans all but convict her with his own mouth. He's already planning the firing squad."

Minna's eyes flew open and she stared up at him. "That can't be, oh poor child."

"If you are her friend, go to her, please. She has no one, and Evans won't let me near her. She needs your support."

Zoe made a small noise down in her throat.

"Sister, please," Minna said.

"She's a savage, and I'm not surprised at what's happened. Neither should you be, after what she did to me."

Minna glared at Zoe, but didn't reply to her words, instead she spoke to Daniel. "I knew from the very moment I laid eyes on you you were trouble. You have the face of an angel and the soul of the devil. Easy to see why she or any woman would fall for your slick ways. Even tried them out on Zoe here. Why do men like you always . . . always cause so much grief? Damn you all to hell."

Zoe gasped, jumped to her feet, and dropped the fine china cup. It shattered around her feet, but she paid no attention. Her amazed attention flew to her sister. "Sister, I'm shocked that you would speak so! Our dear mother would turn over in her grave."

"She already has, Zoe, witnessing the likes of you and Hiram Tate. He's even worse than this one." She swung an arm toward Daniel.

He knew better than to open his mouth further, so he jammed his hat firmly on his head, murmured a thank you toward Minna and got the hell out of there. Wouldn't do to have both the Von Finster sisters climbing all over him. He had troubles enough already. He knew that Minna would do as he asked, though. She was that kind of woman, and he trusted her to care for Winter Dawn until he could.

He fetched Rhymer from the corral, contemplated leaving the Hawkens so he wouldn't be tempted to shoot that son of a bitch brother of Rachel's, but at the last minute decided to leave it in the scabbard. He rode off without looking back, heading in the direction he'd last seen Eagle.

Minna marched up to the supply wagon, fire in her eye. She addressed Peter Mankins, who was guarding the prisoner. "Young man, I want you to go and tell Captain Evans that Miss Rachel is going to stay with me until the committee meets tomorrow. Will you do that please?"

His eyes snapped in confusion, but he didn't try to stop her when she pushed past him and leaned into the wagon. "Rachel, child. Come out of that dark old place. You're going to stay with me for a couple of days."

Winter Dawn emerged blinking her red-rimmed eyes.

"Mercy, you're a sight. You look like some little pup that's been rolling around in the barn. Well, I can see, it's a bath first, and then we're going to get you something decent to wear. Time Zoe gave you that dress she never replaced. You must have been in those same clothes for weeks now." She whirled on Mankins, who had recovered sufficiently to stand up to her.

"What are you waiting for? I told you to go speak to your captain. If there's a problem, tell him to see me. Now put down that ridiculous gun, you know you're not going to shoot a lady. Git on now, shoo." She flapped her hands at him as if he were a rowdy barnyard rooster.

"Ma'am, it makes me no difference where the little lady stays, but her man charged me with looking out for her and that I intend to do, so I'll just trail along and stand outside your wagon. There'll be no 'ands' or 'ifs' about this, ma'am."

Minna blinked up into the man's serious youthful face. Even her hardest stare couldn't back him down, and so she nodded crisply. "Have it your way, then. What Mr. Wolfe wants, he will surely get."

During the confrontation Winter Dawn stood tall and straight, though inside she was trembling. She could show no less courage than this formidable white woman who had befriended her.

Minna gazed down into her eyes, touched her cheek and pushed a strand of tangled hair back. "Oh, you are so beautiful. No wonder he . . ." She batted moist eyes, put an arm around her new charge, and hustled her away, the bear of a lieutenant right on their heels.

Her sister Zoe sat in a straight-backed chair, an embroidery hoop over her lap. When she caught sight of Minna and Winter Dawn, accompanied by Peter Mankins, her eyes nearly popped from her head. "I heard it but I didn't believe it. You've actually brought her here."

Winter Dawn felt the heat of the skinny white woman's fury but refused to react.

"Hush, now, Zoe. Just hush. I won't have any more nonsense about this girl. I let you talk me into abandoning her once before, you won't do it again. She is staying with us, and if you don't like it, you deal with me and leave her alone. She has enough to worry about."

Only temporarily at a loss for words, Zoe rose. "Where is Papa? We'll see about this."

Minna swung an arm distractedly. "He and the boys are helping with the broken wheels yonder. You just run on and tattle to him if you wish, but it'll do you no good. You get your brittle nature from our poor dead mother, not our dear papa. He will look kindly on this child's needs, and you know it." Without sparing another glance at her sister, Minna began to rummage through a large chest. She finally came up with an armful of rich blue fabric.

Holding the dress over one arm, she spoke to Winter Dawn. "This will do quite nicely. I'll just fetch you some unmentionables, and then we'll go on down to the river, where this gallant young gentleman will keep a distant watch while you bathe. I expect this'll be too long for you, but we can take care of that later."

She eyed Winter Dawn's full breasts, then flushed. "Well, it might be a bit tight too. Zoe and I are flat as flapjacks. Come on, child. Don't dawdle."

Winter Dawn hurried to keep up with the long-legged woman. She could hear Lieutenant Mankins bringing up the rear. He was very nice for a white man, almost as nice as Daniel.

She thought of the beautiful dress Minna had draped so casually over one arm. Scarcely a few months ago she would have given anything for a dress of such beauty. Now all she could think about was what might happen tomorrow when she went before the committee. Everyone thought she had killed poor Henry Rattlingourd. Who among them would believe her? Indian and white alike looked on her as a breed, a woman fit only for drudgery and sexual pleasure.

Minna hauled up just short of the water. "Stay yonder in those trees, young man, and keep your back turned at all times."

Mankins obeyed without question.

The older woman actually blushed when she handed Winter Dawn the soft, creamy "unmentionables."

"After you bathe, put these on and then I'll help you with your dress."

The water was so cold that Winter Dawn spent very little time washing before she waded out shivering. She could hardly wait to get into the clothing Minna held out. What the white woman called unmentionables consisted of a brief sort of pants made of a soft fabric that caressed her freshly washed skin and a long-tailed, sleeveless shirt of the same material that came to her ankles. Over that went what Minna called a petticoat. She had never worn such nice things, but all this before even the dress went on? White women were indeed strange. She slipped into her moccasins and waited shyly for Minna to drop the dress down over her head.

The woman's eyes flickered toward Winter Dawn's firm bosom, then moved elsewhere. The blue fabric floated out around her like clouds and just as Minna had predicted, dragged the ground.

"You'll have to hold up the skirts, dear, but this

evening I'll take a needle and thread to it and fix you right up. You can present yourself tomorrow with dignity that befits a woman of your beauty."

Being reminded of the hearing the next day drew a cloud over Winter Dawn's pleasure. Sharing privacy with a woman friend was quite enjoyable. It was a new experience for her, and she wished it wouldn't end too soon.

Minna finished fastening the hooks down her back and patted her on the shoulder. "Now keep those skirts up out of the dirt and we'll go back and brush that lovely hair. Maybe you'd like me to plait it for you."

"That would be very nice, Minna. Thank you . . . for everything."

"You're entirely welcome. I should have done it sooner. That man of yours is most persuasive. We should all have someone who cares so dearly for us." As they passed Mankins, Minna waved a hand at him. "Come, come, young man, don't dawdle. Keep up." Then she continued her conversation with Winter Dawn. "Especially a woman alone in this country. But then, I'm not alone, so to speak, what with Papa and the boys and of course Zoe. Heaven knows, I sometimes feel so though. What I wouldn't give to have such a handsome lad as your Daniel at my beck and call. Ah, well, perhaps it's for the best. I'm too prickly-natured to keep a good man if I could attract one."

Not nearly so much as your sister, Winter Dawn thought, but didn't say. They walked in silence for a moment, then she did speak. "I am sorry about your sister, but Daniel did not love her, you know."

Minna chuckled. "Of course not, dear. One look at his face when he speaks of you proves that. But poor Zoe, she does so pine for a husband. I'm afraid if she doesn't learn how to smile and be more generous in her judgments, she'll never attract anyone save the likes of Hiram Tate. He's no catch, believe me, but she seems satisfied. We are both so very plain, though she will not admit it and preens for Tate every chance she gets. It's obvious what he's after. Dear Papa has done very well for his family, and we girls might well buy a husband if we were of a mind."

Winter Dawn held back a low-hanging branch. She knew quite well what Tate was after with the unpleasant Zoe, having experienced his pawing on an earlier occasion, and right under Zoe's nose too. "You are not plain, Minna. You are very attractive."

"Oh, my dear, of course I'm plain. But there are plenty of plain men around as well. All men, I'm sorry to say, feel they deserve a beautiful woman as some kind of reward for simply being put on this earth as a male of the species. Some do finally learn though, and it is to be hoped that both Zoe and I will get lucky in that respect."

Winter Dawn listened closely to the way Minna used words. It was very interesting, for she was an educated woman. Perhaps she would practice speaking in the same way, if the committee did not decide she was to be shot. The idea terrified her and dried her mouth so that when she tried to reply to Minna's statement, her tongue stuck to the roof of her mouth.

Her life might well be over before it had really begun.

Daniel tracked the peculiar prints of Eagle's unshod pony until it grew too dark to see them. Purple dusk crept on silent feet from the skirts of the shadowy mountains toward the high plains. Great orange streaks lay along the horizon and kissed the uppermost peaks into a blush. He rode to a high spot in the hopes the Indian would build a fire and he could spot it. He waited a long while, standing beside Rhymer, who grazed languidly. The sound of the horse chewing its cud was broken only by a whip-poorwill calling in the distance. After a while, receiving no reply, the night bird gave up.

He grew weary of standing in one spot gazing into the darkness, and so finally pulled off the horse's saddle and dropped the reins to the ground. Rhymer would stick around. Making a pillow of the saddle, Daniel stretched out for a few hours' rest. He heard the ponies while still deep in sleep and came to his feet almost before he forced his eyes fully open.

Rhymer whinnied before Daniel could stop her, and the moving horses halted abruptly.

It was too damn dark to see his own hand, and he felt as if his eyes were on long stalks as he struggled to see something, anything out there. He didn't have long to wait. A hurtling body hit him low on his body and slammed him to the ground. A naked arm smashed across his throat.

"What do you want, why do you follow me?" The question came on hot breath that washed over his face.

Just above them, a screech owl screamed and the man was momentarily distracted.

Daniel heaved the heavy body off and they rolled around until Rhymer had to dance away.

The man grunted and said something familiar in Cherokee.

"Eagle, dammit, is that you?" Daniel managed the question even with the man's thumb jammed into his throat. "It's me, Daniel Wolfe. Your sister's husband."

For a moment, the thumb kept shoving, then it eased off a bit. "Why are you out here? Is she all right?"

"She soon won't be. Take your damn thumb out of my neck before I break it."

Eagle chuckled. "You are in no such position."

Daniel gagged. He didn't want to hurt her brother, but by God if the man didn't let up, he would. He could take him, of that he was sure, but someone might get badly hurt, and he didn't see the percentage in that. He'd come, after all, to see if the man had had any luck finding Doaks. Killing him would be counterproductive.

"What of my sister, then?" Eagle asked and moved the thumb, but did not take his knee out of Daniel's stomach.

"They will have the hearing in the morning. Have you found Doaks and his partner?"

"I have the one, but not Doaks yet. He has promised to take me to Doaks in return for my promise that I won't skin him alive and use his hide for a water pouch."

"Good God."

Eagle chuckled again.

Daniel thought perhaps he was more bluster than action, though he was afraid to totally believe that. It would put him off guard should Eagle decide he was the enemy.

"Well, then, let me up and let's get moving. We don't have much time. You think he'll talk?" Daniel grunted as he got to his feet and retrieved his smashed hat.

"Who, Doaks?"

Daniel punched the crown back out and screwed on the dusty hat. "Yeah, him."

"There are many things we can do to him that will insure his speech."

"We can't kill him."

"Oh, I have no plan to kill him, only make him wish I would."

"Well, hell. Let's go then. By morning we've got to be on our way back. We have to hope if they do decide to put her before a firing squad, they give her a day or so to ponder it." He shuddered at the thought, but refused to let himself think past the moment when he could lay his hands on Jasper Doaks.

"That would seem the humane thing to do, but then I have not seen many white men be very merciful."

Daniel had no reply for that. Considering Eagle's plans for Doaks and the other prisoner such an argument would go nowhere.

Minna brushed Winter Dawn's hair until it gleamed, then deftly plaited the thick strands into a single braid. The end she tied with the purple thong that had hung loosely in the tangles. The girl was so young, so beautiful, that Minna couldn't bear to wind the braid around her head like some prim old maid's.

Though the woman had taken her into the wagon in which she had slept the night, Winter Dawn had not gone dream-walking. She had been much too frightened to sleep deeply. Not even the prospect of submitting to Jasper Doaks had terrified her as much as the thought of going before the committee of twelve and begging for her life. And there was still no sign of Daniel. She could barely think for the fear that chewed in her stomach like knots of roiling snakes.

"There, child. You look absolutely lovely," Minna said, taking her shoulders and gazing into her eyes. "I have requested that they let me sit beside you, and the captain acquiesced." Seeing the puzzlement on Winter Dawn's face, she added, "He said I could sit with you."

" 'Acquiesced' means you can sit with me?"

Though her lips trembled, Winter Dawn spoke the new word carefully.

"Not exactly. It means that though he might have thought differently, he changed his mind when I asked."

The cords in Winter Dawn's throat felt frozen until she could no longer speak, so she nodded. It was a good word and a good meaning. She filed it away for later use, if there was to be a later for her. A sob choked her and she squeezed her fingers tightly into her palms.

"No, no, child. Don't you break down now. We've got a ways to go, you and I. Quite a ways, and be damned if you let them see you cry." Minna turned and found the hovering Mankins, looking worse for the wear of a nearly sleepless night outside the wagon. "Come help me with her, Lieutenant."

He hurried to obey, taking Winter Dawn's other arm to support her.

Pinching her lips between her teeth, Winter Dawn nodded. Minna was right, she must be brave and not let the white men see her cry. Even though her friend wasn't facing punishment herself, she had taken up the cause.

Where was Daniel? Suppose he didn't arrive in time? How could she die bravely without him? Would they shoot her as soon as they made up their minds, or would they wait awhile? She wanted time to say good-bye to this world and prepare for the next; time to tell Daniel how much she loved him and tell this wonderful friend how she felt. Those were the important things to do before dying. Her love must be left in their care before she journeyed to Twilight Land.

The reality of her own death weakened her knees and she swayed. "Minna, where is Daniel? I'm so scared."

"He'll be here, you'll see. You stand up straight. Look right at me and listen. You must tell them the truth and never look down once. No matter what they say or how they say it, you stare right at them, like this." Minna demonstrated, her eyes hard as creek stones.

Winter Dawn nodded, swallowed past the huge lump that wouldn't go away, and returned the steady gaze.

Mankins spoke in a gruff voice that betrayed his own emotions. "You just let us be strong for you and hang on. I got a feeling your man is on his way back. If not, I'll think of something. Now, we have to go or be late."

Winter Dawn stumbled the first few steps, then moved along with her head held high. On his way back? Where had Daniel gone? And why had he not told her?

Vision blurring, she whispered a silent prayer. If this was to be the final day of her life, she wanted to assure safe passage through the Darkening Land to the other side.

For the committee, Captain Evans and James Vann had chosen six Cherokees and six whites. Martin Schrimsher was the only Cherokee on the committee that she knew by name. She was happy that neither the Christie brothers nor their father had been included. Not because she feared their judgment, but because she liked them and did not want to think of them having to make the decision, for she thought they liked her too.

The six whites were chosen from the hundred fighting men required to go along on this drive to California. She had thought perhaps that some of the more respectable whites of the party would sit in judgment of her, but they did not. No Von Finsters or Claridges or others of their standing. Evans had tried very hard to appoint those who would not be swayed one way or the other by their stations in life or their upbringings.

She was directed to sit in a chair facing the twelve, and true to his word, Evans had provided a second chair for Minna Von Finster. In the third and fourth chair sat two Cherokees she recognized from the train while she had been with Henry. Her heart filled her throat when they stared at her, then she looked back toward the members of the committee.

A tremendous crowd had gathered. It seemed to her that every member of the train except those on duty with the stock had turned out for her hearing. Many people had liked Henry and therefore would want to see her punished.

Evans called the gathering to order and said that he would serve as judge.

"First Amos Corder will speak about the accusations being brought against this defendant," Evans said.

The Cherokee stood, was sworn in, and told his story in a convincing voice. Winter Dawn could tell that the members of the committee believed him, they listened so closely, and looked at him gently, like people do when they want to believe someone. Would they look at her that way when it came her turn to speak?

Corder told of how there had been a great scream that had awakened the camp. And how they had found Henry Rattlingourd with his own bowie knife stuck to the hilt in his chest. How there was blood everywhere and when they searched for "her" she was not to be found.

When Corder began to tell how a man named Clark had seen her run away, Evans hushed him.

"We will call him as a witness. You only tell what you saw and heard."

Corder nodded and didn't say anything else.

"Well?" Evans demanded.

Corder jumped at the authoritative tone.

Rachel looked all around, searching for Daniel. Why didn't he come? Where was he? Didn't he love her anymore? Had he simply ridden away, headed for Oregon all alone?

"That's all I saw or heard. We could not find her and so decided it would be best if we just brought the wagons back here along with Henry's body so he could be buried. That was a fine service you held last night."

That was the first Rachel knew of Henry's funeral. A white funeral, no doubt. And he would be buried out here on the plains forever. She shuddered to think of the hard time his spirit would have struggling through the Darkening Land to the west.

After the witness Clark spoke briefly of seeing Rachel run from the wagon into the herd of horses, Evans called for a recess. When they returned, Rachel Keye would testify, he said. He left and went into his tent. Everyone else hung around, gathering in small groups to talk. There was much attention paid to Corder before Evans returned. Rachel remained seated beside Minna, holding tightly to her hand and not speaking at all. It would soon be her turn and she wanted to save all her words for that.

After what seemed an eternity to Rachel, Evans returned, sat down behind the table, and asked Rachel to stand. She did.

"Now, state your full name," he said.

"My Cherokee or white name?"

"Uh . . . well, I suppose both would be appropriate."

"I am Rachel Keye, daughter of Josiah Keye and Singing Bird. My Cherokee name in the white man's tongue is Winter Dawn."

"You speak 'the white man's tongue' very well, Miss Keye. How were you educated?"

"By my father and my friend Alice Sturdivant. She attends Miss Sawyer's Seminary in Fayetteville. She taught me everything she learned until I . . . until I was sold to Jasper Doaks." She stopped abruptly and glared at the twelve men as if they had been partly responsible. She had not meant to tell them about Doaks, but it had slipped out. Not that it mattered anymore.

Evans waited a moment, then nodded. "Your father is white?" He did not even mention Doaks. Could it be he hadn't heard?

She lifted her chin, fingers brushing the silken smooth fabric of the blue dress. "Yes. But of course that does not make me white."

He cleared his throat. Someone on the committee chuckled and Evans shot a fiery glance in that direction. "Did you want to be white?"

Minna Von Finster bounced out of her chair. "Captain, I fail to see what that has to do with anything. Why don't you just let her tell her story?"

Evans, obviously used to dealing with women like Minna, smiled and inclined his head. He acquiesced, Winter Dawn decided.

"Then tell us what happened with you and Henry Rattlingourd. Start at the beginning and take your time."

"First I will answer your question. I did want to be white. I yearned to be like the white women who wore fine dresses and rode in carriages. But I no longer think that to be desirable, for if what you are doing to me here is an example of what the white man calls justice, I would be ashamed to be a white woman."

A rumble moved over the crowd. Evans struck the

table with the side of his fist and everyone quieted down.

"Tell us what happened."

"Henry loved me and I did not love him. So I did not wish to stay. Also Jasper Doaks thought he owned me because I had been sold to him." She paused and looked around. It was too late to hold back, and there was much more danger here than simply being returned to Doaks as a slave.

"Go on," Evans said.

"I heard a noise in the night. I was going to run away, but before I could they came. I heard them fighting under the wagon and then everything was still. Doaks started to jump into the wagon after me, but I leaped out past him and ran. I already knew the horse I would take to run away with. I had a pack hidden in the woods.

"I did not know they had killed Henry but I knew something was wrong. I was very frightened and I knew what Doaks would do to me, so I ran. I heard the shouts that Henry was dead and I knew Doaks and his friends had done it."

Evans tented his fingers when she stopped talking. All was very quiet. He waited, she licked dry lips and waited too. Minna squeezed her hand.

"Go on," Evans finally said.

"That is all. I ran and ran and they were following me, but Daniel found me first and he . . ." She clamped her lips shut, for Daniel had shot one of the men and had stabbed Doaks. She didn't want to get him in trouble.

"He what?"

"He . . . he saved me, that's all. And then I went up on the mountain and the spirits told me I had to come here and tell the truth, so I did." She took a deep breath and felt herself trembling so hard the chair against which she stood began to shake.

"And where is this Daniel person now? I do not see him. Has he deserted you?"

Tears filled her eyes and rolled down her cheeks, but she said no more.

"Are you finished, then?" Evans asked.

She nodded dumbly and let Minna embrace her.

"Then the committee will consider its options and make recommendations. We are adjourned."

If Peter Mankins hadn't held her up, Winter Dawn would have collapsed in a heap where she stood.

"Take her back to my wagon," Minna said softly, and together they supported her across the clearing. The crowd made way, curiously silent as she passed them by.

Then she heard someone say, "They ought to shoot her dead."

Where was Daniel? He had promised he wouldn't let her die alone, that he would die with her. Of course, she did not want that, but she did want him by her side while she waited for the committee's decision. She didn't think she could stand to be all alone when they told her she would be shot.

Chapter Nineteen

A storm rolled in overnight and Rachel awoke to a damp, uncomfortable day. Thunder rumbled low in the distance and an iron gray bank of clouds obscured the mountains. A fitting day for an execution, she thought dourly.

When the committee hadn't reached a decision by nightfall, Evans announced they would reconvene come morning and reach an agreement by dinnertime or he'd know the reason why.

Rachel stood numbly while Minna fastened up the back of the blue dress, now a little limp and not quite so beautiful. She was unable to eat breakfast, but remained in the wagon while the Von Finster family ate under cover of a square of canvas.

It was spitting rain when Lieutenant Mankins came for her.

Minna went along, and as they approached the Evans encampment she saw that someone had stretched a canvas over the table and chairs to protect those taking part in the hearing. Everyone else would be on their own. Once again a huge crowd had gathered despite the threat of rain.

Members of the committee filed in to be seated as she approached. Seeing their somber expressions, her knees went weak and Mankins was forced to support her. She would die today, in front of all these people.

Dragging in a deep breath she raised her chin and stood straight.

Once again, Daniel was not there. Why had he done this to her? Had everything between them been a lie? Thinking back on it, she could not believe that for an instant. Something terrible had happened to him to keep him away.

Evans hustled from his tent and stood at the table. "I understand you've come to a decision," he said to the committee.

Rachel pushed Mankins away, tottered for a moment, then faced her judges.

Schrimsher had been chosen to speak for the committee members, and he looked right at her as he said, "Yes. We find that Rachel Keye had good reason to kill and so she did. There is no evidence otherwise. It is our judgment that she be put to death by firing squad. No man or woman, white or of The People, can be allowed to commit such an act without consequence."

A great gasp went through the crowd.

Rachel swayed as if she'd been poleaxed and reached blindly for support. It came from both sides. Mankins and Minna. The latter threw her arms around Rachel and broke into sobs. Mankins enclosed them both in a strong embrace.

Evans hit the table hard to silence the babble that arose. "Quiet down. So be it. The firing squad has been chosen and will assemble"—he paused, fished a watch from his vest, and consulted it—"at ten A.M. Lieutenant, guard the prisoner while she is prepared."

Without another word, Evans rose, thanked the committee, and disappeared into his tent.

A great wash of rain swept over the assembly, pattering loudly on the canvas and sending those gathered running toward their wagons and tents.

Lightning split the glowering sky and thunder crashed.

Rachel tried to move when Mankins urged her to accompany him, but her legs felt like wooden stakes, her head drummed until she could barely see.

"Daniel," she cried. "Oh, Daniel, where are you?"

Mankins picked her up, snatching her from the arms of Minna Von Finster and stomped off, clearly very upset.

Rachel clung to him and wished he were Daniel. She would die at ten o'clock. What time was it now? How long did she have?

Mankins deposited her back in the Von Finster wagon, not asking anyone if that was proper. Then he backed up against the canvas, crossed his large arms over his chest, and stood there in the rain, waiting.

Minna climbed up into the wagon and took Rachel in her arms, rocking her and crooning in a soothing voice. Rachel relaxed within the embrace, struggling to make her peace. There they remained until word came that all was ready.

Mankins helped her out, swept her up into his arms, and said, "By God, I'll not have this." With those words, he started out across the meadow, taking great long strides away from the circled wagons.

Minna ran along behind, shouting, "Where are you going? What are you doing?"

A shot rang out, and Rachel buried her head in the man's huge shoulder. There was nowhere to go and she did not want Mankins shot.

"Please, stop. Please," she begged.

"Lieutenant, halt, where you are, or by God I'll shoot you."

Mankins took a great breath, then turned to face Evans, James Vann, Lieutenant Tyner, and several other armed men.

"This just isn't right, sir," Mankins said.

A bolt of lightning jagged from the sky and struck a tree off to their right. It split apart and crashed to the ground.

"It's been decided, Lieutenant. You have nothing to say about it." Evans stopped, squinted his eyes to stare past the man and his captive, swept rain from his face, and looked again. "What in the hell?"

Mankins turned, and Rachel raised her head. Out of the lowering mist and through the pouring rain rode four horsemen, two tied over their saddles. Of the other two, one appeared to be an Indian. The other man rode a piebald mare and wore a big, black hat.

"Daniel," Rachel cried and struggled in Mankins' embrace.

Amazed, the young lieutenant set her on her feet.

She lifted the soaked skirts of her blue dress and took off at a run. Mankins kept pace with her, almost as if, should she falter, he would carry her on to her goal. Oblivious to almost everything but Daniel, she kept running, scrambling through loose rock and almost losing her footing. Rain continued to fall in sheets, but she didn't slow.

Daniel leaped from the mare's back and skidded into her path, taking her into his arms, holding her against himself as if to shield her from harm. His inclination was to toss her on the mare's back, climb on behind, and ride off before anyone figured out what he was doing. Let Evans and the rest make head or tails over the stories Doaks and Rake had to tell them. No one would ever find them in the Oregon wilderness, no matter what they believed.

Winter Dawn leaned back to look up into his face. There was a knot on his forehead, a raw scrape on one cheek and the corner of his mouth was puffy.

She touched her lips to his gently. "You are hurt."

"Nah, not much. These fellas just took a bit of convincing. 'Course your brother there give me a hard time too, for a while. I didn't pound on him too bad, though. Figured you might get irritated at me if I did." He grinned and she thought it the most beautiful sight she'd ever seen. The knots in her stomach unfolded, her heart stopped aching, and she touched his cheek to make sure he was real.

"Oh, I am so glad you are here. I was so afraid you had gone away forever, or were hurt or worse."

Rain poured off the brim of his hat when he lowered his head to gaze into her eyes. "I'll never go away from you, Winter Dawn. It was just that Eagle and I had a bit of business and if I'd a told you, you'd have been . . . well . . . you'd have been worried."

"Worried? Worried? Don't you ever, ever do something like that again. The truth . . . tell me the truth, Daniel Wolfe. Oh, Daniel, they're going to shoot me. They say I killed Henry."

By that time Eagle had slid from his pony's back. "These men will tell them different, sister," he said with a grin. "I . . . we have seen to that."

Rachel turned to her brother. "And why have you not gone to Texas?"

Both men laughed.

"We are here to save you, sister, and you ask why I am not in Texas?"

"Save me?"

"This here is our friend Doaks, in case you didn't recognize him. The other one is Rake. They're going to tell the truth about what happened to Henry Rattlingourd." Daniel reached over and punched at one of the dripping bundles. "Ain't that right, boys?" A grunt sounded.

"Oh, they won't. They'll lie. Besides the committee

has already said I must go before the firing squad. You are too late, Daniel. You have come too late."

She leaned against him, feeling once again the helplessness of the situation.

Evans stepped forward. "What is this, sir? Did I hear you say that these men know something about Rattlingourd's murder?"

Daniel sheltered Winter Dawn as best he could. "That 'un killed Henry, the other one helped. They'll tell you, soon as we get 'em unwound." He glanced at Eagle. "Won't they?"

"They will. Sister, I must go. I wish you well." He took Daniel's arm in strong fingers. "And you will care for her."

Rachel stood between the two men. "I'm glad you two finally became friends."

They looked hard at each other, then burst out laughing.

"What's so funny?"

"Well, we aren't exactly friends."

"We could never be friends."

They both spoke at once, then Daniel touched Eagle's arm. "Ride safe, Eagle."

Her brother bounded onto his pony. "This time I will go to Texas."

As he disappeared into the rain Rachel whispered, "Be well, my brother."

"Let's get us all out of this damned rain and sort things out back at camp," Evans bellowed to be heard above the din of the handful of people who stood out in the rain chattering and arguing about what had occurred.

"We're gonna get struck by lightning if we don't get out of here," Peter Mankins said.

Daniel buried his face in the hollow of Rachel's throat, his breath hot and moist against her skin. She felt the anger in him, throbbing and twisting like a wild thing captured. She feared its escape should things not go well.

The committee had sat to consider the story Doaks had told to see if they could rescind the earlier judgment against Winter Dawn. Daniel was livid that they would even have to think about it, but he and Rachel had retired to await their decision. Peter Mankins again stood guard.

Someone called her name, and for just a moment she pretended she hadn't heard and remained locked in his embrace.

"Miss Keye, Mr. Wolfe. You must come. The committee is ready. Mr. Evans said to bring you back."

A guard moved to either side of them, one took hold of Daniel's arm, the other touched Winter Dawn's shoulder with the tips of his fingers.

She sensed Daniel grow tense, as if he would fight.

"We are coming," she said softly, and with both hands loosened his hold on her.

For a moment she could not stand, her legs trembled so, but then she swayed to her feet, holding her chin high. It was not death she feared, it was leaving this man. He still knelt before her and she lay an open hand on top of his head to gather from him all that he was.

"I love you Daniel Wolfe, with all my heart always." She rose and said with dignity, "I am ready."

Behind her Daniel made a strangled noise, but she didn't look back. Minna caught up, handing her a tin cup of water. She drank it as she walked, then handed back the empty vessel. The liquid slithered down her throat, cold and sweet. She would not die. Not this day. She felt it deep within herself. All that had happened would not have come about only to see her shot down. She knew this with a faith such as she'd never felt.

By the time she and Minna reached the clearing, Daniel was at her side, holding her arm. When she looked up at him, his hungry eyes enveloped her. She smiled tenderly, then turned toward the six Cherokees and six whites who were already seated.

Evans and Vann arrived last and took their seats. Mankins hovered some distance away, near the corraled horses.

"Have you decided?" Evans asked.

The Cherokee named Martin Schrimsher rose. "We have."

Evans nodded.

Schrimsher shifted his steady unreadable gaze toward Winter Dawn. "We believe Miss Keye told the truth, and these men have verified it. Our judgment is that Jasper Doaks and Clete Rake should be transported back to Fort Bridger and tried for the murder of Henry Rattlingourd."

Daniel roared. "Wait. You were ready to shoot her and now you send them back for trial. What is this?"

Evans pounded the table. "Be quiet, sir. That is their decision."

Schrimsher cleared his throat. "May I speak for the committee, sir?"

Evans nodded and gestured at Daniel. "You keep still."

"We all feel," Schrimsher said, indicating the other eleven sitting beside him, "that we almost made a terrible mistake that would have been very hard to live with. We almost had an innocent woman shot, and we would rather not bring that same judgment on these men, even though they have confessed. It is obvious they were forced into confessing by Mr. Wolfe and that Eagle fellow. We would just all feel better if there were a civil trial and someone else made the decision to hang these jugheads."

Nervous laughter tittered through the crowd.

Rachel felt like laughing herself, but the expression on Daniel's face kept her from doing so. He was clearly incensed at the decision. She lay a hand on his arm to soothe him.

Evans rose. "So be it. The committee is dismissed. Lieutenant Tyner, will you choose two other men to accompany you with the prisoners back to Fort Bridger? You can join up with us when it is done.

"Now, let's get in out of this rain. Tomorrow we move on to California."

A great cheer went up from the bedraggled crowd. Everyone scattered toward their shelters.

Rachel and Daniel hugged. Tomorrow they would head out for the Green River and from there on to the Mormon City, and she was free. Free to go with Daniel to Oregon, where they would begin their life together.

She could scarcely contain her joy. When Daniel finally released her, she and Minna hugged and laughed.

Several of the Cherokees came to speak briefly to her, most of them saying simply, "It is good." Each one shook hands solemnly with Daniel. He was the white man who had stood up for her, and they understood what courage that took. Lastly Peter Mankins approached almost shyly. He took her hand and held it to his lips, bowing ceremoniously. When he straightened, his sparkling eyes met hers.

"I'm glad I didn't have to help you escape, it would have gone against the grain, but by God, woman, I . . ." He broke off and shook Daniel's hand.

"Thank you, Mankins. We're beholden to you."

"You're one lucky son of a buck," the young lieutenant said and turned briskly away.

This night Winter Dawn would lie in the arms of the man she loved. She looked up into her friend Minna's eyes and said softly, *"Wado, Selu."*

Minna raised an eyebrow.

"Thank you. Selu is the spirit woman who brought corn to our people. She is the wife of a powerful spirit and valued greatly by the Tsalagi."

Minna's eyes swam. "I am the wife of no one, but I thank you for the honor of such a name."

"One day some man will see your value."

Minna placed her open hand at the side of Winter Dawn's face. "Even if he doesn't, I will be fine. You and Daniel, and your brother Eagle have all shown me the true meaning of love."

Winter Dawn thought how very sad that this wonderful woman had not known the kind of love she and Daniel were blessed with. She glanced at him and squeezed his hand.

Minna stepped away from them. "I will leave you two. You should be alone together. There's a lot of work to do to ready ourselves."

"We can help."

Minna shook her head. "No, please. You need to be together."

Daniel smiled down at Winter Dawn. She felt a shiver of delight course through her. "We are together. What can we do?"

They followed Minna to the Von Finster wagons to begin the arduous preparations for the final lap of their long journey.

Many times during the course of the afternoon, their fingers would touch, their shoulders brush, their breath intermingle. Winter Dawn could not help but think of the coming night. They had no wagon, but the forest would cradle them in its arms, the sky would shelter them. The storm had moved on, leaving the lush, green trees dripping, the sky crystalline.

That evening several men killed a large elk and butchered it out. The mouth-watering aroma of meat cooking filled the encampment. Perhaps as a way of mending the rift caused by the hearing, everyone came together around a central cook fire, each bringing something from his own larder to add to the evening meal. Laughter soon replaced stern glances from those who had fought earlier over the committee's verdict.

For Winter Dawn and Daniel it was a celebration, not only of her victory but for the new life they would soon commence. After the long, hard day of work, he left her at Minna's wagon washing up.

She stripped from Henry's britches and shirt, thick now with sweat and trail dust, and dipped a washcloth into a steaming pan of water carried from the campfire.

Minna talked to her through the curtain hung over the back opening.

"I want you to keep the dress, it's so beautiful on you. Suits your eyes perfectly."

Winter Dawn eyed the drifts of blue fabric hung with care to dry. She had washed the mud from the hem carefully. With trembling fingers she touched the silken cloth, but said nothing. A long time ago Zoe had ruined her dress by spilling ink on it. She had never replaced it. Yet, this was Minna's gift and one had nothing to do with the other. She had learned at an early age that white men always attached strings to their gifts to Indians. But Minna wasn't one of those, of that she was sure.

"Did you hear me?" Minna asked.

She rubbed the cloth over the bar of lye soap and scrubbed a patch of mud off one elbow. "Yes, Minna, I heard you. Are you sure? It's so lovely, so . . . it must have cost very much."

Minna's laughter tinkled like the treble keys of her lost piano. It was a rare thing, that laughter from the staunch woman. Winter Dawn was happy to have been the cause of it.

"Out here, many things come much more dear than a piece of goods. Friendship is surely one of them."

"Yes, of course, you are right. We are friends, are we not?" Winter Dawn shook her head and moved on down her body with the washcloth. Last of all, she set the pan on the floor and immersed first one dirty foot, then the other into the clabbered water. Soap scum floated on the dirt-colored liquid, and she chuckled.

"What is it?"

"I think I am just moving dirt from myself into the water and back to myself again."

"Let me get you fresh . . ." Minna pulled the curtain aside and her eyes widened.

Completely naked, Winter Dawn turned to smile at her friend.

"Oh, dear me. I'm so sorry, I thought you would be covered. Please forgive me." Minna flushed brightly and turned away, hand extended for the washpan.

Winter Dawn decided she would never get used to the modesty of white women. Alice had gone to great lengths to explain this strange phenomenon to her, but she had never grasped it fully. It was truly an amazement.

Daniel prepared himself to eat crow. He knew of no other way to achieve what he had in mind. Hat in hand he found Captain Evans. The man had hung a mirror on the side of his wagon and, bare to the waist with galluses hanging down around his hips, was trimming his beard and shaving the high bones of his cheeks.

Daniel waited until he lifted the wickedly sharp straight razor from his flesh before speaking.

"Ah, Wolfe," Evans remarked smoothly and pulled the skin tight for the blade.

"Yes, sir. I've come to ask you something. In light of what has happened, the hearing and everything, well, I wondered if perhaps I could reconsider having you marry Winter Dawn and me?"

"Said I would originally, but you never chose to take me up on it."

Daniel felt a rush of raw anger and wished he could tell the man how he felt over the way he had agreed, almost calling Winter Dawn a whore. If he did that, though, Evans would probably be so angry himself he wouldn't accommodate him. And he wanted to do this for her.

"Yes, sir. Much has happened since then. And I . . . that is, we would appreciate it very much if you could say the words for us this evening." It was almost more than Daniel could manage, this kowtowing, but for her he could manage, even though each word nearly choked him on its way up his throat and out his mouth.

"Folks'll love it," Evans said. He laid the razor down and splashed his face, then dried it. "How about right after we eat before the dancing commences?"

Daniel screwed his hat down tight on his head and stuck out a hand. Evans's palm was warm and damp from the washing. "I thank you."

As he started to walk away, Evans said his name and he turned. "I just wanted to tell you, Wolfe, how bad we feel about the way things went. We were ready to shoot that little gal, and well, we've talked it over. Rattlingourd put great store by her and well, you've done your share of work, much as I hate to admit it. We want you to have Rattlingourd's outfit. You and your . . . uh, wife. Seeing as how you lost yours a ways back."

The offer left Daniel speechless. These people had never offered him anything and he had no idea how to act. "I don't think I could—"

Evans laughed heartily. "Nonsense, 'course you can. It's only right and proper, considering all we put the both of you through. Think of your bride, sir." Evans stared down at his boot toes for a moment, then said, "Might make up to her a little bit for . . . well, you know, this other thing."

Daniel's hesitation was short-lived. "She'll appreciate it, I'm sure, Captain."

"Wish you'd go on to California with us. Could use a good man. The worst isn't over by far yet. We've got a tough row to hoe. There's not a lot of palatable water down Bitter Creek, and then there's the Humboldt. Hear the dust is shank-deep on oxen."

"I figure to stay with you until we get to Lossom Trail, so I expect we'll be around awhile yet."

"Good, wonderful. Well, you bring that gal around and we'll get you fixed up. She's a beauty, that one is. You're a lucky man."

"Oh, I know," Daniel said softly. "That I well know, sir. And thanks again. I'm obliged." He decided not to bring up that Evans had as much as called Winter Dawn a whore not that long ago. It was best left unsaid. He'd never liked the man and despite what had just happened, he was sure the feeling was mutual.

Now he and Rachel had some things to discuss. With the Rattlingourd wagon they could go on to Oregon and file for a homestead or they could head for California and see what it offered. They would make the decision together.

Chapter Twenty

Daniel went directly to Minna's wagon to fetch his bride. His breath caught when he saw her surrounded by the lavender-and-gold hues of dusk while Minna brushed her long hair with a silver-backed brush. It reminded him of the one that had been lost in the river. He would replace it for her when they reached the Mormon City.

Firelight set Winter Dawn's long tresses aflame and the dress complemented her golden skin and bright blue eyes. Even rather plain Minna seemed to glow in the reflection of Winter Dawn's beauty.

He had worn his best buckskins for the occasion. His hair, damp from a recent washing, was tied at the back of his neck with a leather thong. In deference to the occasion, he'd left his sweaty felt hat behind.

When she caught sight of him, Winter Dawn was filled with such joy that tears poured down her cheeks and she choked back a sob with laughter. He came to her, caught her outstretched hands and kissed them both. His lips were warm, the skin of his cheeks smooth and newly shaven.

He slanted bright gray eyes toward her. "I have a surprise for you."

"Nothing could make me happier than I am right now. What is it?"

The almost childish eagerness of her question brought soft laughter from all three.

Impatient, she grasped his calloused fingers tightly. "Tell me, please."

"God, you're beautiful." He tilted her chin up and placed a feathery kiss on her moist lips.

"Daniel? What is it?" An urge to lie with him nearly overpowered her. She wanted to drag him away, off into the woods, strip out of their clothes and—

"I can't tell you. Just come with me, now. You too, Minna. Get Zoe and your father and your brothers. Get everybody."

"Everyone is already gathered at the supper fire. We are the last. What is happening?"

"First, we'll eat, then I'll tell you." Daniel pulled her along, turning once in a while to walk facing her so he could gaze upon her lovely features.

"That is not fair, Daniel. Not fair at all. I have to wait while we eat? Tell me now, or I'll not be able to eat a bite."

"Ah, no. It will wait. I'm starved, aren't you? You worked as hard as I did all day."

"Well, that is not true. But yes, I am hungry."

They sat together in straight-backed chairs that had been saved just for them. Winter Dawn wondered at the cause of such an honor, but was too caught up in the overall gaiety to consider it overlong.

The delicious meal was no sooner finished than the sweet notes of a fiddle floated in the warm evening breeze. Mankins and Tyner spread a canvas over the grass and trampled it down with the help of some of the others, then Captain Evans strode to its center with a Bible in the crook of one arm. A crowd lined all four sides of the makeshift floor, but left a path to where the couple sat.

Daniel pulled Winter Dawn to her feet and escorted her to stand before Evans. Minna moved forward and presented Winter Dawn with a huge bouquet of wildflowers.

"Daniel, what is this?" Winter Dawn gazed up at him, puzzled.

"Will you marry me?" he asked softly, so that only she could hear.

She couldn't take her eyes off his. Firelight lit his face and she had never seen him look so peaceful, so content. Clutching the fragrant flowers in one hand, she cupped his cheek with the other. He moved his lips into her palm.

"I'll love you forever, Winter Dawn," he said.

"I have loved you forever, Daniel Wolfe," she replied.

They turned to face Captain Evans, who had opened the Bible to read from it.

Winter Dawn and Daniel, already married in the eyes of her people, reaffirmed their love with the white man's words, and the evening breeze kissed them gently.

In spite of the day's hard work, the dance that followed the impromptu wedding went on far into the night. After allowing the bride and groom several dances together, the men had no compunction about requesting Winter Dawn's company for a turn around the floor. She and the other three women were kept busy dancing all evening. Feelings of gaiety ran so high that men danced together and alone, overflowing the canvas and kicking up clods of mud from their shuffling boots.

In crossing the mountains a barrier had been breached, the sense of it was in the air, though there were many miles yet to go.

Young and boisterous Peter Mankins claimed a dance from Winter Dawn. Though Daniel waited impatiently, she circled the floor twice with the nice lieutenant. He noticed and guided her then straight to her husband's arms. He deposited her there with a sparkle in his eyes and a broad, sweeping bow.

"You're one lucky man, Wolfe," he said, "and I thank you, ma'am. Best of luck to both of you in Oregon."

"I want to thank you for your concern and wish you the best of luck in the goldfields, Mankins." Daniel took her in his arms and swept her away. For one spin around the floor he held her properly so that their bodies didn't touch. The bell-shaped blue skirt swung heavily out behind her as they swooped in great circles until she grew dizzy.

Slowly, his right arm snugged her close, the hand that held hers folded against her shoulder. She lay her head close to his heart and matched her steps to the graceful movement of his lithe body. Desire rippled through her on gentle feet and settled deep within her, where it slowly uncoiled into a ravenous beast.

She lay her head against his chest and he lowered his mouth to nibble her neck below one ear. Thigh to thigh, stomach to stomach, breast to chest, they slowed the long, sweeping strides of the dance until they scarcely moved in place, their feet no longer moving along the rough canvas.

His breath shortened, feathering the down along her hairline. "We can't stay here any longer."

Passion exploded within her. She imagined living alone with him in the wilderness with only animals for company. She was free. Free to follow him and love him. Love him forever. It made her shudder to think how close they had come to being parted forever. She would rather have died. In his arms the fervor of the celebration faded, as if the two of them alone glided across the meadow and into the darkening sky among the stars.

She slipped a hand up under the buttery buckskin shirt and he sucked in a quick breath when her flesh touched his. The muscles twitched along his back.

"We have to go now," he said into her ear.

His breath against her flesh sent fresh rivers of passion straight to her loins. Through the voluminous skirt she felt him growing against her. "Agili?"

"Oh, yes. I've missed you so much, and it's been such a very long day. I have to hold you."

"You are holding me, Daniel. And everyone is looking at us. This is not the proper way to dance, not even for a husband and wife, not in this white world." She grinned devilishly.

"Sometimes I wish you hadn't learned so much about behaving in the white world."

"Oh, don't worry, I have decided I much prefer my savage ways."

He laughed against her neck. "Then let's go somewhere where you can show me. I have to be with you with no one looking. And I can't wait any longer." He sighed, lifted his head, and made every effort to compose himself.

She did something she hadn't done in a very long while. She laughed heartily, merrily, then without thought of what anyone might say, she took his hand and dragged him along, breaking through the cluster of men around the dance floor. Shamelessly, she led him across the moonlit meadow and into the shadowy pines. Catcalls and laughter chased them into the darkness.

The ground under their feet rebounded softly, the long, fragrant needles making a thick bed. He turned to look back once before she pulled him to the ground. Light from the great campfire pulsed into the ebony sky, a reddish glow that lent a strange rhythm to the night.

His hands, his mouth, his body consumed her, his

touch kindling fires she had no wish to put out. She had come so close to losing him, losing her own life, that her heart and soul cried out for release. She wanted everything he had to give all at once, yet hoped this night would never end. They must do this slowly, make it last, revel in the joining of their lives forever.

He reached behind her, fumbled at the buttons down the back of the lovely dress, and made an impatient sound. "I can't get the blasted things loose."

"Ssh, my love." She touched his lips with hers. "Be still and listen to our hearts beating. Feel what is within us."

Breath catching, he paused and lowered his cheek to where her heart pounded. She lay a hand on his chest.

"Now, my life is in you as yours is in me. Feel the circle our lives make, one into the other."

She could not see the expression on his face, deep shadows lay there, but sensed that his breathing evened out. He still wanted her in a savage, unbridled way, but he had gone deep into his own soul for that brief moment of time it took to join them truly together forever.

He moved about gently within her, just as she moved within him. In that moment they were complete. Together they rested for a silent moment, the gentle thrumming of their hearts one steady, constant beat.

"Now, my love," she whispered in his ear.

He dragged in a great breath. "Dear God, what was that?"

"Our spirits joining."

For a moment he didn't move, but held her within an embrace that trembled with awe. Then, slowly he began to work the buttons loose down the back of her dress.

Author's Note

History of the Cherokee Trail

Since so little has been written about this trail, readers might like to know more of its history, and so I offer this because what happened then should not be forgotten.

The forty wagons and more than one hundred white and Cherokee men and three white women who left Arkansas in April of 1849 arrived in Woodfords, California in October, 1849, approximately six months after their departure. They had traveled some twenty-two hundred miles along a virgin trail scouted the previous year by Cherokees. It later became known as the Cherokee Trail.

One man was drowned when the party forded the Green River, another died en route, and still another passed on soon after the wagons arrived at their destination. Two spinster ladies, who did walk the entire length of the trip, remained in California, where they made their homes. All of the others returned to Arkansas, many no richer than when they left.

It snowed all day the day of departure, April 15, according to an old newspaper article. Quite an unusual occurrence that far south.

Gold fever among the Cherokees spawned that first trip in April of 1849, and the whites, eager to put some gold in their own pockets, joined the Indians because they felt safer in the company of people who were friends of the Ute and mountain Indians they might meet up with. The route took the party north of the feared and powerful Arapahoe and Cheyenne tribes.

There is no record that any Cherokee women went along, however it is known that after the train pulled out of Fayetteville, Arkansas, many Cherokees joined as it passed through the Indian Territory to the west. It is entirely possible that someone like Rachel Keye (Winter Dawn) was among them. She might even have stowed away. Men like Daniel Wolfe definitely made the trip.

Of the characters in this book, Second Lieutenant Peter Mankins existed in reality, as did First Lieutenant Thomas Tyner, Captain Lewis Evans, and Cherokees James Vann and Martin Matthew Schrimsher. They were all real and helped forge the Cherokee Trail.

Peter Mankins later became a folk hero to natives of Arkansas. He eventually returned from California, it is said with several thousand dollars' worth of gold in his pockets. Some he managed to get rid of when he stopped off in New Orleans for a few days of revelry. He eventually returned to his family's two-story log mansion near New Prospect, Arkansas. There he became known as Squire Mankins, as was his father, who had founded the small town later known as Mankins and eventually as Sulphur City.

During his long life Peter was a cowboy before the term was coined, and more than once accompanied herds of cattle along the Cherokee Trail. He was witnessed killing a bear with only his own two hands, and bragged that he had also killed wildcats in the same way.

Mankins later trafficked in slavery and fought on the side of the Confederacy in the Civil War. When his fifteen-year-old daughter died tragically, he resigned his commission, but it is claimed one had nothing to do with the other. His wife Narcissa was a staunch Yankee and probably was responsible for the resignation. Mankins fathered ten children and died in his eighties. He is buried between his first and second wife in a small, peaceful cemetery on the banks of the Middle Fork of the White River in northwest Arkansas. The elder Peter died at the age of 111, outliving three wives and several children.

Of such stuff were the early pioneers made. Peter Mankins, like our fictional hero Daniel Wolfe, followed his dreams, wrestled with his demons and hewed himself a life from the harshest of circumstances.

Dr. Jack E. Fletcher has researched the trail extensively and has authored a book about it, and also an article in *Overland Trail* (Vol. 13, No. 2). Much of his information came from the family writings of John Rankin Pyeatt, a Washington County native who made the trip and wrote about it. Pyeatt's papers were published in *Flashback*, a quarterly put out by The Washington County Historical Society. Pyeatt is said to have invented a machine which he attached to a wagon wheel and by which he measured the distance between Arkansas and California.

During the cattle roundup days, thousands of head of cattle were driven over the popular Cherokee Trail to northern California. Several wagon trains used it as well. Yet it is all but forgotten in the annals of history, and is never mentioned by most historians.

A museum in Encampment, Wyoming has on display memorabilia from the days of the Cherokee Trail. There folks reverently show visitors the old wagon ruts where the trail crossed the Encampment River. People live there now who are direct descendants of pioneers who traveled west along the Cherokee Trail.

On quiet summer evenings one can sit on the riverbank in Encampment and listen to the muffled rattle of chains and the snort of laboring animals, the creak of wagon wheels, and the distant shouts and laughter, echoing like ghost mist over the cold water.